WHEN THE OLD WORLD WAS NEW

A NOVEL BY

BENJAMIN PRESSLEY WALKER

When The Old World Was New

ISBN 978-0-9666145-8-9

Published in the United States by
Jamin Press
Jacksonville, FL
www.jaminpress.com

Note to the Reader

This is the fourth novel in a series beginning with *Winds of the South*, which is the story of Tony's maternal grandfather, a slave owner before the American Civil War. *When The Old World Was New*, picks up where the third novel, *Return of the Native Son*, left off.

Acknowledgments

Thanks to Bob Bliss, a fellow writer and good friend who has painstakingly reviewed the manuscript and offered many helpful suggestions.

A special thanks goes to George Poe, Professor of French (retired) at the University of the South, Sewanee, Tennessee. This book would have been impossible without his corrections of my rudimentary French.

And last but not least, thanks to Rich Allen, my cover designer for all four of the books in this series. In addition to his creative artwork, he has set up the manuscripts for publication and offered his considerable expertise in technical matters.

FOR

EVERY ANGLOPHONE WHO HAS FALLEN UNDER THE SPELL OF

FRENCH CULTURE

PROLOGUE

Jackie had never been seasick during her two prior Atlantic crossings. Those first two were on steamers that sliced through the waves like a carving knife through tender meat. The prince's yacht, however, though quite large for a private vessel, rode the waves with the abandon of Keystone cops chasing a malefactor; first up one side of a mountainous swell, then down the other until it seemed everyone aboard would surely plunge to their deaths many fathoms beneath the angry sea.

This relentless cycle of disorienting locomotion caused the blood to leave her face, then create a queasiness at the pit of her stomach, and finally sent her to her stateroom where she lay prostrate on the bed, eyes closed and mouth pressed against the pillow as if to smother herself. The nausea, however, subsided after a while but she dared not lift her head for fear of a reprise.

Meanwhile, the prince was at the helm reveling in the salt spray that penetrated his beard and left droplets suspended from its tangle of whiskers. The captain, accustomed to this usurpation of his duties, stood at the binnacle acting as navigator.

Tony, aware of poor Jackie's condition, felt it best not to disturb her in her misery, as there was no remedy in such cases but to lay prone and avoid gazing through a porthole. Instead, he remained on deck, with the prince and the captain. The first mate, like Jackie, had retired below, not because he was seasick, but because there was nothing for him to do topside.

"Glorious! Absolutely glorious!" the prince said. "By Jove, I think there is no other place on earth I'd rather be at this moment. What about you, Tony, my boy?"

Tony was busy hanging on to the railing attached to the hatch forward of the helm. The salt spray stung his face like needles each time the vessel crested a wave. "I can't say as I agree with you, Your Highness, though there is a thrill that runs through one's veins as the bow plunges into the next trough. On the whole, I'd rather be in a studio quietly contemplating a canvas and drinking a hot cup of coffee."

The prince laughed. "Of course you would. You're an artist, my boy, and may you never waver from your calling. But as for me, though others have pre-ordained my calling without consulting me, my first choice would have been that of a sailor."

Tony thought he saw a break in the clouds with the sun lighting up a small patch in the gray mist like the headlight of a locomotive about to emerge from a darkened tunnel. "That's an indication of calmer seas, isn't it?"

"Perhaps," the prince said, apparently disappointed in this observation. "If conditions continue to improve, we can put up the sails."

The weather, in fact, did improve over the next several days, with warm South Atlantic currents encountering colder water to the north.

Jackie was fully recovered by the fifth day, when they crossed the 40th parallel, not far from the Azores. The water was calm, and with the sun warming the deck, the stewards resumed serving lunch in the pavilion aft of the wheelhouse. This pavilion, a colorful affair with a red and yellow striped awning that matched her mother's puffed sleeves, allowed enough light to penetrate the space beneath without exposing the diners to sunburn.

"We shall be at Le Havre in a couple of days," the prince said, donning a white bib which was tied at the back by a steward. "I regret that I will not be able to accompany you all the way to Paris."

"You've done a great deal for us already, Your Highness," Tony said. A waiter filled his glass with champagne. "As if saving my life were not enough."

"Tut, tut, my boy," the prince said. "I could hardly allow those brigands to carry out their nefarious plan to string you up like an unlucky hare at the railroad station. What a ghastly sight that would have been for all the passengers! The mere thought of it gives me indigestion. Besides, I had help from your courageous sheriff as well as Mr. Smalls. I only hope the leader of that gang of ruffians is put away in some dark dungeon with the same accommodations we offer at the Tower."

"I don't suppose you saw the newspaper article when we departed from Savannah," Tony said. "The leader of the gang was let off with a fifty dollar fine."

"What!" the prince exclaimed. "That's a bloody injustice!"

"I agree," Tony said. "But I'm afraid that's the state of affairs in the American South at the moment."

The luncheon party fell silent. Then Lucinda, Jackie's mother and the prince's paramour, spoke:

"We're headed for the New Old World," she said. "Let's not forget that civilized people still exist."

"Tut, tut, Lucy," the prince said, stabbing a prawn with his fork. "America is still young–I have no doubt she'll catch up with us someday. Besides, the three of you are Americans, are you not? I don't feel as if I'm being besieged by savages."

All laughed at this comment and followed the prince's lead in indulging themselves in the dishes of prawns, lobsters, oysters and sea trout set before them.

Jackie wasn't so sure that there was anything 'new' about the Old World. Slavery, after all, was initiated by the Europeans. Or had it always been around, in every country, every culture, since the beginning of the human race? In any case, no one's hands were completely clean.

She gazed at Tony as he cut up a prawn with his knife and fork, while the prince swallowed his whole, tail and all. Here were two men, one the privileged and spoiled scion of a royal family, the other the descendant of African slaves, and it was the latter who exhibited the most refined manners. How even more extraordinary that the two should be friends!

And of course that was due to her mother, who, like Tony, was a kind of outcast. Having a child out of wedlock, she fled to England to escape the scorn and hypocrisy of the South, where she established herself as a theatrical impresario and ultimately mistress of the Prince of Wales. Her mother, her husband…both iconoclasts who have–narrowly, in Tony's case–escaped retribution from the self-appointed guardians of propriety and morality. So where did Jackie fit into this picture? She laughed, which brought curious stares from the other diners.

"I just thought of something funny," she said.

"Well, then, Jackie," Tony said. "Can't you let us in on it?"

Jackie thought for a moment. "It just seems to me that you and the prince make for a rather odd couple."

The prince raised an eyebrow. "What do you mean?"

Jackie, alarmed by the prince's censorious gaze, now wished she hadn't said it. "I only mean that your grandfather would likely turn in his grave to see a member of his family dining with a black man."

The prince frowned, causing Jackie even greater concern that she had overstepped her bounds, but then he smiled in that engaging way he had. "My grandfather was a man of his times, my dear. He assumed the prejudices of his forebears and never questioned the rightness of those prejudices. And you're quite correct—he would indeed turn over in his grave if he were to see me now. In fact, my mother, though she is still very much alive, is spinning herself to distraction as she reads daily press reports about my profligate ways. But I've never understood why one should ape the manners and opinions of one's barbarous ancestors. I think that your Mr. Jefferson said that, actually."

There was a cautious laughter on the part of the other diners, including Tony. He glanced at Jackie, then turned to the prince. "I'm sure that my wife does not presume, Your Highness—"

"Tut, tut, my boy," the prince said, picking up an oyster shell and lifting it to his mouth. "Let's not speak of presumption. Your wife is absolutely charming in her frankness—just like her mother. Why do you think I choose to travel in her company?"

"Lust," Lucinda said.

The prince laughed uproariously and swallowed the oyster. He momentarily choked on it, waved over a steward, and held out his glass for a refill. "By Jove, I can't deny it! But then I do enjoy your irreverent sense of humor, my dear. Else I would drop your acquaintance like a hot coal from Newcastle."

Lucinda turned to Jackie. "You see that I'm obliged to constantly entertain the prince. That is my role—at least until we get back to England."

"Now, Lucy," the prince said. "Let's not speculate about the future. My word—I do believe this lobster is still alive. Steward! Can't you knock him on the head with something? I don't like the way he stares at me with those intense black eyes of his. Bloody malevolent, I'd say."

Jackie was amused by the prince and his irrepressible bonhomie. But his comment about the future of his relationship with her mother concerned her. It was clear that he was 'sowing his oats' as they say, but then he was nearly sixty years old and still sowing. He rarely saw his wife, Alexandra, and made no effort to conceal his numerous affairs. Where was that to leave Lucinda? Well, she had her theatrical company and a small settlement from the estate in South Carolina. She would never starve.

But neither Jackie nor Tony had anything to fall back on unless they prevailed upon her mother. And Tony had never earned a living as an artist. An artist! Would they both starve in some wretched garret in Paris?

Two days later, as they entered the Channel, she found Tony on deck putting the final touches on his portrait of the prince.

"Has he seen it?" she said.

"Not yet," Tony said. "I want it to be a surprise."

The prince suddenly emerged from his cabin. "What, ho! Can't keep away from your work, eh?"

"The game is up," Tony said.

The prince came over to them, kissed Jackie's hand and turned to the portrait. "I say, is that me?"

"Well, Your Highness—what do you think?"

The prince squinted at the painting. "Rather Rabelaisian, no?"

"I can make changes if you wish," Tony said.

The prince continued to assess this image of himself. "No, no...by Jove, it *is* me! I've had others done, but this one is different. It reminds me somewhat of my uncle William—like me, a sailor. Yes, I like it!"

And with this parting gift to the prince, they sailed into the harbor at Le Havre where Jackie and Tony disembarked, bound for Paris.

CHAPTER 1

Tony felt that something was different when he and Jackie stepped on to the platform at Gare Saint-Lazare, but at first he wasn't sure what it was. Then it hit him. No one stared.

Jackie, for her part, seemed not to notice whether anyone stared or not. A remarkable woman, Jackie.

A porter with a trolley approached them and Tony nodded, indicating their luggage on the platform. The porter was an elderly Frenchman, wearing a uniform of sorts and sporting a red beret rather than the traditional porter's cap. Tony addressed him in French, to which the porter responded with, "Mais oui, Monsieur. Tout de suite!"

"What did he say?" Jackie asked.

"He's agreeable. And he says his son has a hansom cab waiting at the entrance for us."

"Oh," Jackie said. "It's so frustrating. I can't understand the simplest French. It's too fast for me."

"It'll come with time."

As they followed the porter to the west entrance, Tony observed the bustle of passengers as they made their way to and from the trains. Again, no one stared as they did in Savannah, or at Le Havre, though he and Jackie, as a mixed-race couple, were of less interest to the denizens of that city, who were accustomed to seeing all manner of humanity entering their port, including immigrants from Africa.

As they emerged from the station into the sunlight, they were presented with a cacophony of the usual sounds of horses' hooves and iron wheels clattering against pavement, but also with the sounds of steel striking cement, hammers pounding iron rivets, and even a distant explosion.

"My goodness!" Jackie said. "What on earth is going on?"

"The Exposition." Tony handed the porter a franc and they climbed into the cab. "They're building an underground railroad system along with exhibition halls in preparation for it. They're trying to outdo the last one, but I doubt they'll succeed."

"Why not?"

"Didn't you see the Eiffel Tower when we emerged from the station? That's a hard act to follow."

Jackie peered out of the window of the cab. "Oh, yes, I see it now. It's kind of...I don't know—awkward, don't you think? It's not the way I always envisioned Paris."

"I suppose you're right."

The horse, seemingly unperturbed by the relentless din of construction, trotted smartly over the cobblestones with its head held high.

"Where are we going?" Jackie said.

"First stop will be our hotel on the Quai Voltaire. It's not fancy, but it's central to everything."

The hotel was a small one facing the Seine and the Louvre, which loomed like an architectural colossus straddling several city blocks. A porter took their luggage up to the third floor and pulled the curtain back, revealing a fine view of both the museum and the river. The room, however, like the hotel itself, was rather small, especially by American standards.

"Lovely," Jackie said, "but where will we put our things? I can hardly fit half my wardrobe into that armoire."

"Just unpack the things you'll need for the next few days," Tony said, standing at the window and staring out at the Louvre. "We'll have to find an apartment."

"That's a nice writing desk. Like one I have at home, but it looks ever so much older."

Tony chuckled. "Who knows? It may have been here for a hundred years. Are you hungry?"

"Famished."

"Then we'll step out for a bite or two. I know a little restaurant on St-Germain not far from here. And then I'll have to leave you to your own devices while I pay a visit to Monsieur Dantec."

"Monsieur Dantec?"

"He owns one of the premiere art galleries in Paris. The prince recommends him highly."

"Oh, yes. And do you have the prince's letter?"

Tony patted his breast pocket. "Next to my letter of credit from the bank. Probably better than a letter of credit."

Jackie smiled and threw her arms round him. "And soon your paintings will be hanging in the Louvre with all the others–Da Vinci, Rembrandt, Delacroix–"

Tony laughed and kissed her on the lips. "I'm afraid 'les Directeurs' may have other ideas. Especially since there's never been a black artist so honored."

"But you said the French are color-blind. I haven't seen any evidence–"

"I meant generally. There are still those–particularly among the traditionalists–who want to keep France white, just as their counterparts do in the States."

Jackie sat down on the bed. "Oh, that's so absurd! I thought we'd escaped all that nonsense the moment we left the harbor in Savannah."

Tony sat beside her. "It's not as bad as that here. You'll see. I just want you to look at Paris with your eyes wide-open." He kissed her hand. "You can already see that no one blinked when we approached the front desk."

She smiled and kissed him on the cheek. "No. No one did. But I promise to keep my eyes open. Because there's so much to see!"

After a meal at a nearby bistro, Tony walked across the Pont Neuf to Monsieur Dantec's gallery on Rue Rivoli, while Jackie went sightseeing and shopping. Unlike the old days in '91 and '92, Paris seemed brimming with activity. Not that there wasn't plenty happening then, but the preparations for the current exposition seemed to generate an atmosphere of excitement and expectation that was more subdued in the years immediately after the Exposition of '89. People were still grumbling about the 'horror' that was the Eiffel Tower. But now the 'Tour' was accepted as a beacon of French culture and people were warming to the idea of a new century. Automobiles, flying machines, electric streetlamps, and above all, Art Nouveau.

He stopped for a moment at the 'prow' of the Île de la Cité to watch a band of acrobats performing for onlookers. With one exception, they were black, eight in all. He supposed the black ones were from Africa, judging from their accents. The white one he would guess was Italian, only because he had never seen a Frenchman roll and tumble with such abandon and ease. After a few minutes of turning somersaults over each other's backs, they formed a pyramid of bodies that culminated in the Italian doing a handstand on the shoulders of one of the others, who straddled the ones below him like a charioteer driving a team of horses. The pyramid looked a little unstable, as if the bodies would come crashing down on one another, the crowd gasped, but the acrobats peeled away from each other one by one and ended in a line facing the onlookers with their hands held aloft. There were cheers and applause and a shower of coins.

Tony dropped a couple of sous into the pail and walked on. He lingered for a moment on the Pont Neuf, leaning on the stone parapet with both elbows, watching the *bateaux* cruise beneath. Only a few years earlier these bateaux carried mostly coal or other cargo, but now they seemed full of sightseers, no doubt in anticipation of the Exposition Universelle. A couple of passengers waved at him and he waved back.

More construction on Rue Rivoli. There was a huge hole in the street which Tony assumed to be for the new underground rail line. Onlookers leaned on the barriers, watching 'les ouvriers' operating mechanical devices for smashing rock. Perhaps a subject for a painting, he thought.

At last he arrived at Galerie Dantec. Nearly in the shadow of the Tour St-Jacques, Galerie Dantec occupied a large space on the ground floor of a building constructed in the time of Napoleon. But the façade had been recently upgraded, with plate glass windows and elaborate cornices and frieze work. A number of prominent artists' works were displayed here, including those of Monet, Manet, Cezanne, and one of Tony's favorites, Pissarro.

He had been deliberately dawdling up until this point. Though he had in his pocket a letter of introduction from the Prince of Wales, he was apprehensive. Regardless of his reassurances to Jackie, he knew that a black man would not be well-received in certain quarters, even in Paris. Monsieur Dantec was one of the most prominent art dealers in France, and though he had never met him, some of his artist friends from the early 90's had, and the reports were not uniformly favorable. Nat, his former roommate, had once approached him and he was summarily dismissed with the advice that he "go back to school—in America, where art is still in a primitive state."

But he couldn't stand outside the gallery forever, admiring the paintings of his heroes. So in he went.

A salesman of sorts, a tall, imposing Frenchman with jet-black hair, a Gallic nose, and his hands behind his back, greeted him with a haughty, "Monsieur? On peut vous aider?"

"J'aimerais voir Monsieur Dantec, s'il vous plaît," Tony responded. "J'ai une lettre pour lui."

"Une lettre? Ah bon, un moment."

The salesman then turned and went to the back of the showroom, where he knocked lightly on a heavy oaken door marked "Privé." It was slightly ajar.

A voice called out 'Entrez,' and the salesman went in.

Tony gazed about the gallery for a few moments, noting that a Cézanne was priced at 15,000 francs. He and Jackie could live on that for a year!

As he continued to peruse the paintings–and the price tags–the salesman returned. "Monsieur Dantec vous verra, maintenant." He indicated the door with a grand sweep of his hand.

Tony went to the door, peered inside, and heard a thundering, "Entrez! Je vous en prie."

He obeyed and entered the sumptuously appointed office. Paintings covered every wall, most by well-known artists like the ones displayed in the window. But there were a few by artists he was unfamiliar with, some with bold colors and abstract, even geometrical, figures. He liked what he saw.

"Asseyez-vous," Monsieur Dantec said, rising from his chair. He indicated an armchair opposite his desk. "I understand you are an American."

"Yes, that's right." Tony sat down. "How did you know?"

"Your accent. I heard you speaking to my clerk." (He pronounced it 'clark.')

"Yes. I suppose that gives me away."

Monsieur Dantec smiled with satisfaction at his astute observation. "I also understand that you have a letter for me. Maurice told me you were too well-dressed to be a mere messenger."

"Well," Tony said, removing the letter from his jacket, "I *am* a messenger of sorts. The prince asked me to give you this."

"The prince?"

Tony laid the letter on Monsieur Dantec's desk. "The Prince of Wales. He tells me the two of you are well-acquainted."

Monsieur Dantec stared at Tony for a moment and picked up the letter. "Yes, that's quite true. Though I haven't seen him in over a year. Well, let's see what he has to say." He nodded his head as he read over the letter, then with a sigh, put it down and looked again at Tony. "The prince speaks highly of you."

"That's gratifying to hear."

"He says that you are a talented artist and a fine young man of good character."

Tony merely nodded in affirmation as he sensed that this was a prelude to bad news.

Monsieur Dantec then abruptly rose from his desk and went to a filing cabinet where he extracted a manila folder, returned to Tony's side of the desk and handed it to him. "If you would be so kind as to read a few of the letters, please. Actually, one will do."

Tony opened the folder and saw a dozen or so letters. He read one. It was almost verbatim the same as the one the prince gave him.

"A good fellow, the prince," said Monsieur Dantec. "He's a very good customer. But he collects young artists the way some men collect bits of string."

Dejected, Tony returned the folder to Monsieur Dantec. "I see."

Monsieur Dantec returned the folder to the filing cabinet. "However, I'm always looking for young artists of talent myself. You obviously are familiar with Paris. Any shows of your work?"

"Yes. In the Rue de la Huchette."

"The name of the gallery?"

"I...I don't remember. It was...something like a bookstore. And art gallery."

Monsieur Dantec sighed. "Can you bring me some samples of your work?"

"Of course. Two, three?"

"Two should be sufficient."

"I'll have to get them out of storage."

"Take your time. I'm here till 18:00 every day."

Tony took his leave and hailed a cab as soon as he was out on the street. He felt humiliated, just as Nat must have felt when M. Dantec suggested he go back to art school a few years earlier. Nevertheless, M. Dantec was at least willing to give him a chance. He only hoped that Nat was still living in the atelier on Rue de Fleurus and that his paintings were still intact. He had written him, advising that he was returning to Paris, but had received no answer. Of course he and Jackie had left Beaufort rather hurriedly, so there may not have been time for a reply to reach him.

He alighted from the cab and saw that the building was in the same dilapidated state as when he left. The atelier was on the fourth floor, and it was a long climb up a dark and decrepit stairway. At the entrance to the building, each apartment was clearly marked with its occupant's name and number. At the top of the list was, 'N° 15 Nathaniel Holmes, Esq.'

Tony opened the heavy door and found the stairway in the same state of disrepair as when he left, with plaster peeling off the walls of the vestibule.

Upon arriving at the fourth floor, he realized that he was not 'en forme,' as he had been a few years earlier. After pausing for a moment or two to catch his breath, he knocked on the door. He heard a muffled word that elicited a 'Oui,' from a feminine voice, followed by the door opening and revealing a corpulent, bearded man of about Tony's age, dressed in a paintbespattered smock.

At first Nat seemed stunned into silence, but after a moment broke into an expansive grin and embraced him. "Tony, old man! I got your letter but somehow I didn't think—well, come in, come in. I'm afraid that the place is in the usual mess, as you can see. Ma Chérie! Je veux te présenter mon ami d'Amérique!

Nat led him to a workman-like table in the center of the room and asked him to sit down while a young woman in a dressing gown came from the kitchen area carrying a bottle of wine and a basket containing two or three baguettes. She was rather petite, brunette and very pretty, with a turned-up nose and lips pursed as if about to suck on a straw. She regarded Tony with a child-like curiosity.

"Tony, this is Marie-Louise," Nat said. "Marie-Louise, ma chérie, je te présente—"

"Enchantée," Marie-Louise said, still regarding Tony with wide-eyed wonder. "Vous venez de New York?"

"South Carolina," Tony said.

Marie-Louise looked at Nat for clarification.

"Du Sud," he said. "Des États-Unis."

"Ah, oui," Marie-Louise said, now enlightened. She put the bread and wine down and went back to the kitchen.

"She's very pretty," Tony said, as they sat down and Nat poured the wine and broke off a piece of the bread.

"Oh, yes. She'd do anything for me. We're very happy here."

"Then...you're married?"

"Married? Heavens, no! My father would never hear of it. He expects me to return to Boston and marry some socialite."

"And do you intend to return?"

"Well, no. Not anytime soon, anyway. And as long as he thinks I'm slaving away at my work, he'll keep the cheques coming. But Tony, old boy, why are you here? I thought you'd given up the artistic life."

"Well, I did for a while. After my father passed away, I took over the bank."

"The bank? Well, that must have been lucrative."

"Well, it was to a degree. But I was drawn back to Paris. So here I am."

Nat seemed agitated. He rose from his chair and began pacing. "So you mean to take up the brush again?"

"Exactly. That's why I'm here. And I've just been to Monsieur Dantec's gallery."

"Dantec? He nearly threw me out a couple of years ago. How did you get in to see him?"

"A long story. But Nat, old pal, I need to get a couple of canvases so he can see a sample of my work." Tony looked around the atelier. "Where are they? I seem to recall–"

Nat cleared his throat, sat down again, and swallowed the remaining wine in his glass. He poured another. "Tony, old man, I didn't think you'd ever come back."

"Well, I wasn't sure, either. But here I am. Where are the paintings?"

Nat filled Tony's glass even though it wasn't even half empty. "I don't know how to tell you this, Tony, old boy, but–"

"But what?" Tony looked around again. "Was there a fire? Did something–".

"No, no. Nothing like that. It's...well, it's like this. I hit a pretty rough stretch last year. My father cut off my allowance in an effort to force me to come home. Eventually, he relented. And for a while I thought I could make it on my own, but...Marie-Louise and I were desperate. On the point of starving, actually. And of course her family has no money. One day, an American gentleman from New Orleans dropped by the Académie and–"

"Yes, go on."

"Well...he had an odd name, sounded German–Gottschott, Gottsch–"

"Gottschalk?"

"That's it. Kind of...dark-complected, like you."

"And?"

Nat took another swallow of wine. "He said he was looking for the works of Negro artists. I couldn't help but think of you."

"You brought him here."

"Yes."

Marie-Louise returned from the kitchen, carrying a tray with an assortment of cheeses on it and set it down on the table. Then, without a word, she went back to the kitchen.

"Then what?" Tony said, ignoring the food on the tray.

"Then?" Nat sliced off some cheese and applied it to the bread. "Well, I showed him your paintings and he liked what he saw."

"'Did he buy one?"

Nat chewed on the bread and cheese, swallowed, and chased it down with some wine. "He bought all of them."

"All? Why–that's splendid! How much did you get?"

"Um...let's see. I think it was about 400...no, 500 francs."

"Five hundred? For let's see–there were about forty paintings–"

"Forty-two. About twelve francs each."

Tony stood. "Well...that's not bad. Not bad at all. But I'll have to paint something quickly to show Monsieur Dantec. I can use the cash. Will you have to go to the bank?"

"That's just it, Tony, old man. I don't have it."

Nat brushed some breadcrumbs from his beard and mouth with the sleeve of his smock.

Tony stared. "Don't have it? You spent it? All of it?"

"I was trying to tell you–my father cut off my allowance."

"But he relented, you said."

"Yes, but I went into a tremendous amount of debt during the interim... and my allowance barely covers the rent."

Tony sighed. "Now I have no money and no paintings."

"But you said you made a fortune with the bank."

"I didn't say that. I sold my shares, which was enough for the passage and to put down a deposit on an apartment. And Jackie–"

"Jackie?"

"My wife."

"Oh...congratulations, old man."

"Thank you. Though Jackie, like you, comes from a wealthy family, unlike you, she doesn't get an allowance. She'll have to work at–something."

"In a bit of a pickle, then aren't we? I mean all of us. But something will turn up. And when it does, I'll pay you back. I promise."

"I know you will, Nat. Or at least I know you'll try. But in the meantime... Well, I'd better be going." Tony rose to leave.

"Wait a bit, Tony, old boy."

"Sorry, Nat, but Jackie is expecting me–"

"I was just thinking."

"Yes?"

"We could both save a good deal of money if you and Jackie moved in here.'

"Here? There's hardly room for–"

"I know it'll be a bit tight. But there're two bedrooms upstairs, as you know, and the studio is quite large enough for the two of us to work here. As we did before."

"Well, I don't know. Jackie is used to–"

"We could try it for a while, at any rate."

Tony sat down again. "I suppose if it doesn't work out, we'd at least save some money."

"Of course we would. Come on, I'll show you your room. I've made a few alterations, but it's essentially as you left it. And you know, there's that access to the attic space–*grenier aménagé*, the French call it–and Jackie could use that for–Mon Dieu! I just remembered!"

"Remembered what?"

"I put a few of your paintings in that *grenier* and forgot all about them. Monsieur Gottschalk didn't get those."

Tony's eyes widened. "Which ones?"

"I can't remember. Come on–let's take a look."

There were six paintings in all in the loft. Tony picked out two that he thought were the best, tucked them under his arm and carried them downstairs.

At the door to the studio, Nat held up two of his fingers, the index crossed over the middle. "Bonne chance, mon ami!"

Tony smiled and started again for Monsieur Dantec's gallery. Rather than carrying the paintings through the streets and risking damage to them, he hailed a cab and was on his way.

At the gallery, Monsieur Dantec was unimpressed. He leaned the paintings against his desk, resting on the floor. One was an impressionistic scene in the Luxembourg Gardens. The other was a Cézanne-like portrait of a Negro boy hawking newspapers on a busy Parisian street.

"Not bad in terms of technique," Monsieur Dantec said. "But rather conventional. I see a lot of this these days." Then he turned to Tony, who looked downcast. "You do have talent, however. I'll take them on consignment, but I can't promise you anything."

Tony could think of little to say. Now he wished he had chosen one or two of the other paintings in the loft that he thought were more original. "I have others."

"I'm sure you do, "M. Dantec said. "But let's see if these sell, and then I'll take a look at the rest of your *oeuvre*. Asseyez-vous."

Tony sat. "How much will you be asking?"

M. Dantec took his seat and rolled his eyes to the ceiling. "Alors, as you are an unknown artist, I would be surprised if the garden scene brings more than fifty francs. Perhaps the American tourists will like it. The one of the Negro boy, on the other hand, may be of more interest, especially to our European buyers. Perhaps 100 francs."

"I see. Well, where do I sign?"

CHAPTER 2

When Tony returned to the hotel on the Quai Voltaire he found Jackie in an excited state. She greeted him at the door with a hug and a kiss and led him to the little writing table between two ladder-back chairs. She picked up a copy of *Le Figaro* that was folded to the back pages with an ad circled in red lipstick.

"An audition?" Tony said.

"For *Fédora*—by Sardou."

"What's it about?"

"A Russian princess who plots to get her revenge against the man who killed her husband but then falls in love with him."

"With the killer?" Tony laughed. "Sounds like a melodrama."

"It is. But a very successful one. Sarah Bernhardt played the title role in the première in '82."

"So it's a revival."

"Yes."

Tony put the paper down on the table. "But it's in French. You don't speak the language well enough to—"

Jackie smiled and put her arms around him. "I don't have to. I know the role by heart. I played it in a production at school when I was seventeen."

"At school? In Charleston?"

"Of course. Where else?"

Tony picked up the paper again. "L'Odéon. That's one of the national theatres of France. The competition will be fierce."

She smiled coquettishly and kissed him. "I have certain advantages."

Tony smiled. "You certainly do. But your accent—"

"What's wrong with my accent?"

"It's...well, it's obviously American. Even I stand out like a sore thumb the minute I open my mouth. Monsieur Dantec—"

"Oh, yes. Monsieur Dantec. How did it go?"

Tony sighed and disengaged himself. He sat down at the table. "He took a couple of my paintings on consignment."

"Oh, Tony! That's wonderful!"

"Not really. He's doubtful that he can sell them. Too conventional, he says."

"Well...you have others."

"Yes, but he's not interested in seeing the others. And I only have, actually, four others."

"Four? I thought you had forty or fifty."

"That was before Nat sold all but six of them."

"Well, all the better. How much did he get for them?"

"Five hundred francs."

"Is...is that a lot?"

"Fair enough for what I had. That's the good news. The bad news is that he's already spent the money."

"Spent it!"

"Oh, he's not a bad sort, Nat. But he was desperate. He says he'll pay me back. In the meantime, we've got to be careful about how we spend our money."

"I should say so. But if I get this part—"

"It's a long shot, Jackie. They'll spot you as an American as soon as you walk in the door."

She sat down in the chair beside him. "Oh, these chairs are as hard as rocks. Can't we find a better hotel?"

"A better hotel? I just told you that we're nearly destitute."

"Destitute? Don't exaggerate. You still have money from the sale of the bank stock, and I have some money Edwina gave me as a wedding gift. We'll make do until—"

"You're a star at the Odéon? And I sell my paintings at Monsieur Dantec's gallery for thousands of francs? No, Jackie—we've got to tighten our belts now."

"Well...how?"

Tony rose and began pacing the room. "Nat's offered to put us up for a while. Actually, to share the rent."

"Share? How big is this atelier? I thought it was just a studio with a loft."

"Well...it is that. But the loft is really two rooms. And the studio itself is quite large. Nat and I can paint without getting in each other's way."

"Well...I suppose if it's just the three of us—"

"Four, actually."

"Four?"

"Nat's girlfriend. And model. Marie-Louise."

Jackie lowered her eyes to the floor. "I guess my expectations were a little too high. We can't expect to live like royalty, can we?"

"No. It'll be a little rough for a while."

"What will you do for income until Monsieur Dantec sells your paintings? *If* he sells them?"

Tony stopped pacing, shoved his hands into his pockets, and stared out the window over the Seine. "I've been thinking of that...I can set up an easel across from the Île de la Cité. Across from Notre-Dame. Sketches, maybe. That'll be quicker."

"Notre-Dame? You mean for the tourists?"

"Exactly."

The next day Tony and Jackie checked out of their hotel and took a cab to the atelier on Rue de Fleurus.

Jackie looked up at the façade of the building. "It looks like it's falling down."

"It's perfectly sturdy," Tony said. "Just needs a little maintenance."

Jackie looked to the building to her left. "Well, someone's doing more than a little maintenance next door. It's rather noisy."

"The studio's on the fourth floor–fifth by our standards–so we won't hear the noise."

"Fifth floor? Is there an elevator?"

Tony chuckled. "Not yet. That's probably one of the new conveniences being installed next door."

"Oh, Tony! I don't know if I can–"

"Of course you can. You're young and fit. You'll just get more fit."

Jackie looked at their luggage sitting on the sidewalk. There were two valises, a portmanteau, and a steamer trunk. "How are we going to get all of this upstairs?"

At this point Nat appeared at the front entrance. "Bonjour! I saw you from the window upstairs. I'll give you a hand. And this lovely lady is–"

"Jacqueline," Tony said. "Jackie, this is Nat."

Nat made an exaggerated bow and kissed Jackie's hand. "Je suis ravi de faire votre connaissance, Madame!"

"Enchantée, Monsieur," Jackie said, pleased at the opportunity to show off her limited French.

"Well," Nat said to Tony, "Let's get this luggage upstairs. It'll be covered with cement dust if we leave it here much longer."

They moved the luggage into the foyer of the building and Nat and Tony picked up the steamer trunk and lugged it up the stairs. Jackie followed, carrying the two valises. When they arrived at the landing, Marie-Louise was waiting for them, dressed in her robe de chambre. She smiled and spoke to Jackie in French, who stared blankly at her, barely understanding a word.

Nat seemed to notice Jackie's incomprehension. "She says that you are very pretty. And perhaps you would like to model for us."

"Model?" Jackie said. "You mean in the nude?"

Nat laughed. "Not necessarily. It's up to you."

"Jackie's an actress," Tony said. "She's been on the stage in London, where her mother is an impresario."

"London?" Nat said. "You don't say. Anything recently?"

"*The Second Mrs. Tanqueray*," Jackie said. "By Pinero. But that was a couple of years ago."

"Oh, yes," Nat said. "I've heard of it." He turned to Marie-Louise and explained this in French. Marie-Louise seemed impressed.

"She'll be auditioning for a new play here in Paris," Tony said.

"A revival," Jackie said. "Of *Fédora*."

"In any case," Tony said, "she'll be too busy to model for us. And besides, I'll be setting up my easel at Notre-Dame tomorrow."

"Notre-Dame?" Nat said. "For the tourists?"

Tony looked slightly embarrassed. "Just to get some money coming in. A stop-gap measure."

"Of course," Nat said. "I've done it myself. It's good for a few sous, at least."

Tony was anxious to change the subject. "I'll go downstairs and fetch the portmanteau."

"And I'll show Jackie upstairs to her room," Nat said.

After Jackie was settled in the room–which was only slightly larger than their hotel room on the Quai Voltaire–she went downstairs and perused Nat's paintings, which covered the walls nearly all the way to the ceiling. She did not consider herself a connoisseur, but nevertheless had her opinions. Some of the paintings seemed amateurish, as if a first-year art student had painted them as exercises in perspective and draughtsmanship. Others were rather outlandish, with bold strokes of the brush depicting outdoor scenes, several of matadors taunting ferocious-looking bulls. But the vast majority were of nude women, some of which resembled Marie-Louise. She wondered at their relationship.

She learned at dinner that night–a modest affair at the all-purpose table in the middle of the studio–that Marie-Louise was from Marseille, in the south of France. When Nat discovered her on the Boulevard St-Michel, he brought her to his studio and used her as his principal model. From what Jackie could gather, he did this not so much out of the goodness of his heart, but because she was cheap. In exchange for room and board–and other considerations–she would model for him for as long as he would have her.

This situation made her uncomfortable. She said as much to Tony that night as they lay in bed with a thin wall between their room and Nat's. The sounds coming from the other room were unmistakable.

"Tony?" she said in the half-darkness. A sliver of moonlight streamed in through a transom that opened to the roof.

"Hmm?"

"I don't think I can live here."

"What? Why not?"

"You...you know. The sounds."

"The sounds? Oh, that?" Tony placed his hands behind his head and sighed. "Well, they'll have to put up with us, too. You'll get used to it."

"I don't know if I can."

Tony turned to her and stroked her hair. "This is not the South, Jackie. Or Victorian England. The French are used to living in close quarters. And sex is as natural to them as cleaning their teeth."

She nestled her head against his shoulder. "Well, I don't clean my teeth in the presence of strangers, and I don't expect them to clean theirs in mine."

Tony laughed. "I seem to remember you giving your mother–I mean Edwina–a lecture on tolerance."

"Well...I did. But that was a completely different kind of tolerance."

"About race?"

"Yes. And other things."

"Listen."

"What?"

"They're quiet now."

Her ears perked up. "Yes. Thank goodness."

Tony kissed her on the lips. "It's our turn now."

She pushed him away and said with a whisper, "I can't do it this way. We're going to take turns annoying each other with sounds of lovemaking?"

Tony sighed and returned his hands to the back of his head. "We can always go to bed at different times."

She rose on one elbow and kissed him on the cheek. "I'd like that. And maybe we could get up earlier, too."

"That'll be easy enough. Nat usually sleeps till ten o'clock or so."

"I've always been an early riser."

"Me, too. But Jackie–"

"What?"

"It occurs to me that we've never made love."

"Of course we have. What are you saying?"

"I mean we haven't had time. After the wedding we went directly to the prince's yacht. And our stateroom connected directly to his. It would be unseemly, you said–"

"To make noise and disturb them. But we made love anyway."

Tony laughed. "We kissed and...fondled a bit. But...you're still a virgin."

Jackie remained silent for a few moments. "Oh, my God! I'm so stupid!"

Tony put his arm around her again. "You're hardly stupid. Just... inexperienced."

"I suppose I am, aren't I? What can we do about it?"

Tony kissed her again. "We'll have to start somewhere. Why not Paris?"

She smiled and kissed him back, but with a tremor of her lips. "Yes–why not Paris?"

CHAPTER 3

When Jackie returned from her audition for *Fédora* the next afternoon, she found Nat and Marie-Louise in a heated argument.

"Putain!" Nat shouted at Marie-Louise.

"Je te dis merde!" Marie-Louise retorted.

Nat had just raised his hand as if to strike her when Jackie appeared at the door. When he saw her, he lowered his hand, looked somewhat sheepish and muttered, "Salope!"

Marie-Louise, who was stark naked during this argument and protecting herself only by keeping the table between them, retreated to a divan where she had been posing and wrapped her familiar robe de chambre around her torso. She pulled the sash tight, sat down on the divan, and crossed her arms over her chest.

"I'm afraid I've barged in at the wrong time," Jackie said.

Nat sat at the table. "No, no, it's all right. Marie-Louise and I were just having a little spat." He forced a laugh. "It's nothing really."

"Well...it must be something. Are Tony and I—"

"No, no. It has nothing to do with you and Tony. It's...it's that Spanish bastard downstairs."

"Spanish?"

"A kid. Thinks he's a painter like me and Tony. I think he's an imposter on the make."

Jackie looked at Marie-Louise, who continued to pout. "What's he done?"

Nat went to the sideboard and poured himself a glass of wine. "He's asked Marie-Louise to pose for him."

Jackie set a sack of fruit and vegetables on the table. "Well...there's nothing wrong with that, is there? I mean if he pays her—"

"That's just it— he's offered her ten francs a day. Ten! He wants something more than just a model."

"Surveillant d'esclaves!" shouted Marie-Louise.

"What did she say?"

"Sale garce!" Nat shouted back at Marie-Louise. Then to Jackie: "She said I'm a slave driver." He sat down again at the table and swallowed some wine. "Now, do I appear to you to be a slave driver? I pay the rent, buy her clothes, not to mention the food and wine, and she claims—do you see a mark on her? She claims I abuse her in every way. Well, maybe I've slapped her a couple of times, but she tries my patience sometimes. And now this! This greasy Spaniard, Pablo something—"

"Ruiz!" Marie-Louise ejaculated. "C'est un gentil gars!"

"Merde!" Nat shouted back. "Il est vicieux!"

"Please!" Jackie said. "Can't we calm down? Surely Marie-Louise's intentions are—"

At that moment, Tony appeared at the door. "What's going on here?"

Nat looked up. "Nothing. I was just telling Jacqueline that Marie-Louise and I were having a little disagreement about—about her employment."

"Employment?" Tony, who was carrying an easel under his arm and a paint box in his right hand, put both down just inside the door. "She's looking for a job?"

"No, no. At least she wasn't looking...until this greaseball downstairs offered her one."

"Greaseball? What greaseball?"

"Pardon my language," Nat said. "I shouldn't disparage all Spaniards. It's just this one. Says he's a painter. But it's clear what he's looking for."

"How do you know what he's looking for?"

"Like I said. It's clear. He's offered her ten francs a day to pose for him."

"Ten francs? A day?"

"That's what I said. Where he gets that kind of money, I don't know. He's just a kid."

"Why don't you lend Marie-Louise out for a couple of hours a day—say, from 10 to 12—and see how it goes? Don't you trust her?"

Nat looked out of the corner of his eye at Marie-Louise, who looked back in contempt. "Well...I suppose I could check in on them from time to time...as a fellow painter interested in his technique."

"There you go," Tony said. "An easy solution. What's for dinner?"

As passions seemed to simmer between Nat and Marie-Louise, Jackie followed Tony upstairs to their room. He pulled a few francs out of his pocket.

"Is that all?" Jackie said. "For a full day's work?"

Tony sighed. "Six francs. Less than this Spanish fellow offered Marie-

Louise to pose for him. I'll do better tomorrow. It was overcast today. A sunny day makes people feel more generous."

Jackie sank onto the bed, which was little more than a down-filled mattress resting on a low platform. "What will we do? We can't live on six francs a day, even sharing expenses with Nat and Marie-Louise."

Tony sat beside her. "No, but–how did the audition go?"

"Quite well, Jackie said. "For the other girls. They chatted merrily with each other, and with the director, while I pretended to understand. When it came to my turn, I delivered Fédora's little speech at the end and everyone melted into tears."

He put his arm around her. "Why, that's wonderful! What did the director say about it?"

"I don't know. It was all in French."

Tony laughed. "Well, did he say anything in English?"

"Yes. When he realized that the only French I knew had been memorized for the part, he broke into English. He speaks it quite well."

"And?"

"And...like you said, there was a little problem with the accent."

"A little problem?"

"Yes. He said that can be fixed. But he didn't have time to coach me. He suggested that I go to the Sorbonne and sign up for lessons."

Tony remained silent for a moment. "In the meantime another actress will be awarded the role."

"He said I might be suitable for a non-speaking role. Oh, Tony! This will never work. I've got to go to London."

Tony leaned back on his pillow. "So you think that would be easy pickings?"

She leaned back beside him. "Not easy. But my chances are much greater there. Mother knows everybody."

"I notice that you've stopped calling her 'Aunt Lucinda.'"

"Well, of course she is my mother. But she's always introduced me to her friends in London as her niece. I suppose I'll have to get used to calling her 'Aunt Lucinda' again when I go back."

"A strange woman, your mother."

"She is. But I know she loves me and wants what's best for me. She'll do whatever she can to advance my career."

"But Jackie, darling–he leaned over and kissed her–I don't know if I can do without you for a whole–what? A month? Six months?"

"If I land a role quickly, there would be four weeks of rehearsals, then a break. I could come see you. Or, better yet–you could come with me. We discussed that before the wedding, remember?"

Tony shook his head. "It was just a suggestion then. I hadn't thought of how close at hand I'd have to be to Monsieur Dantec, who by the way wants me to attend a party at the gallery for young artists. He says the fact that I'm African American will appeal to his clientele. It could result in some sales."

"Then he wants to display you as a curiosity."

Tony sighed. "I suppose so. But what does that matter? One sale in his gallery could sustain us for six months. We could even get our own apartment, one with good light and perhaps even a garden."

"A garden. Oh, how I would love to have a garden to stroll in every morning. Did you know that Mother has one of the best gardens in London?"

"No, I didn't know that. And I'm getting a little tired of hearing about your mother. If she can offer you the way of life that I can't, why don't you go live with her permanently?"

Jackie was silent.

Tony stroked her hair and kissed it. "I'm sorry. I didn't mean that. I'm just a little frustrated at the moment. But Jackie–I don't want you to go to London. Not now."

Jackie rose from the bed and arranged her hair in the mirror while avoiding Tony's gaze. "I'd better go downstairs and help Marie-Louise prepare dinner."

Tony remained on the bed, brooding over the first significant argument of their marriage. He wondered if he had been wise in marrying a well-heeled white woman in the first place. Jackie had fascinated him from their first meeting on the outskirts of Beaufort in '93, when he came upon her carriage with a broken wheel. There seemed to be an instant chemistry between them. Both had just come from a sojourn in Europe, both were involved in the arts, and both had grown up in the un-Reconstructed South. But Jackie's family had been slave-owners, while his family–or at least his father–had been the son of a slave. Could this marriage work?

Dinner was a very solemn affair. After an interminable silence, Jackie began talking to Nat in English and Tony began talking to Marie-Louise in French. The poor girl was lonely, Tony thought. A runaway with little education and few skills. She was totally dependent on Nat, who treated her like a domestic employee, if not a slave. A slave? He wondered at Marie-Louise's dark complexion–not as dark as his–and suspected that her family probably came from Algeria. An Arab, or at least part

Arab. Discriminated against and despised by the French, just as white Southerners in the States discriminated against and despised Negroes. For a moment he thought this would be a better match.

But he ran out of things to talk about with Marie-Louise. She seemed ignorant of the most basic history, even of her own country. She knew nothing of Algeria, though she confirmed that her grandparents came from there. In fact, she asked Tony if *he* were an Arab. He politely explained that he was an American, the son of a white mother and a mixed-race father. She seemed puzzled by this revelation and asked if white people in America still owned slaves. He said no, all the slaves had been emancipated after the war. What war? She asked. The Civil War, he said. Oh, she said, like the French Revolution. Not exactly, he replied, but there were similarities.

Somewhat frustrated with this conversation, he turned his attention to the one between Jackie and Nat. They seemed to be getting along famously.

"And that was the last time I was invited to a debutante party. Newport was scandalized!" Nat laughed and refilled his wine glass.

Jackie seemed to find this story very amusing as well. "But you were soaking wet. Did you have a change of clothes with you?"

"Well, yes," Nat said. "As it turned out I was one of the bachelors invited to stay at the girl's mansion, so I simply marched into the house, dripping water all over the oriental carpets and for the *pièce de résistance*, a goldfish fell out of my pocket as I mounted the stairs." He laughed uproariously at this, and poured more wine into Jackie's glass, as well as Tony's and Marie-Louise's, the latter thoroughly puzzled as to what could be so funny.

Tony managed a chuckle, but no more, since he had heard Nat tell this story at least a dozen times.

"And the poor girl who fell into the fountain with you," Jackie said. "What did she do?"

"Ah," Nat said. "Matilda. She was mortified. She had on this, this chiffon or taffeta–I don't know much about ladies' fabrics even though my father is a textile manufacturer–that was paper-thin and the soaking exposed her, well, you know–she was exposed."

"Oh, my goodness!" Jackie said.

"Yes, that's what she said. Needless to say, the engagement–engineered by my father–was off."

Jackie laughed and Tony could see that she was getting a bit tipsy. "So that's when you dropped out of Harvard and came to Paris?"

"Shortly thereafter. And that's when I met Tony. On the boat, actually."

"You didn't know each other at Harvard?"

"We traveled in different circles," Tony said. "But we discovered during the crossing that we had similar goals."

"And Father was only too glad to see me go," Nat said. He downed the remaining wine in his glass and poured himself another. Then he turned to Marie-Louise and grabbed her by the waist. "And coming home from the Louvre one day I met Marie-Louise. N'est-ce pas, ma chérie?"

It was clear that Nat was drunk and was feeling amorous so Tony announced that he and Jackie would do the cleaning up. Marie-Louise seemed to have forgotten all about her differences with Nat earlier and laughed as he picked her up in his arms and staggered up the stairs to their bedroom.

"Looks like Nat and Marie-Louise have made up," Tony said, as he dried a plate over the sink.

"Yes, she seems to have a short memory." She placed a dish on a shelf above the sink. "What were you and she talking about?"

"Her, mostly. It seems unlikely that she can do anything but model and cook."

"I noticed you staring into her robe de chambre."

"I could hardly help it. She allows it to flop open and seems unconcerned about who's looking."

"She is a pretty girl."

"I think Nat noticed that when they first met."

They remained silent until the dishes were dried and put away.

"Tony–"

"Yes?"

"I'm going to London."

Tony sighed. "I can't stop you."

"This situation is impossible. I hate to even go to bed at night no matter how tired I am."

"I understand."

"Do you?"

Tony put his hands on her shoulders. "Jackie, I told you when we got married that I wouldn't stand in the way of your career. You can go to London with my blessings."

Jackie stared into his eyes. "Do you mean that? Even now?"

"Yes. I'll look for another place. Nat's carousing is a distraction. I don't think he's completed a painting in the last six months. With a place of my own I could get some work done. And when you come back–"

"Oh, Tony–" She put her arms around him. "I do love you. You're so talented and I know you'll succeed here. It might be better for me to be out of your way for a while."

Tony gave her a kiss. "You could never be in my way. With a place to ourselves we could both thrive."

"Then why don't we find a place now? It can't be that expensive."

"You said you wanted a garden."

"Well, of course that can wait. And we do have some money."

"Not enough to last more than a few weeks. Go on to London. That'll give us both time to earn enough to get that apartment with a garden and a separate studio."

"Oh, that would be lovely."

She kissed him, lingeringly, and he took her by the hand and led her upstairs.

"What's that noise?" she said.

"Nat. He's snoring."

CHAPTER 4

On the platform at the Gare du Nord, Tony waved as Jackie got settled in her seat. He had the sinking feeling that he might never see her again. Nonsense! London was only a day's journey and he could pop over to see her at any time. There were in fact crowds of Americans and Englishmen who crossed the channel in the ferries daily, even in the most inclement weather.

He was still thinking of Jackie as he stood awkwardly in a corner of M. Dantec's gallery that same afternoon when a very handsome woman of about thirty-five entered. After a short conversation with M. Dantec, who she seemed to know, she began walking around the gallery, stopping briefly at each painting and occasionally speaking to other patrons, who she also seemed to know.

This was a tightly knit community, Tony thought, of very wealthy people who shopped for paintings like other people shop for shoes or handbags. They no doubt competed with one another for the latest objets d'art and bragged about their acquisitions at cocktail parties.

As this woman stopped to chat with one of the artists, a Dutchman who Tony did not know, he examined her more closely. She had black hair swept back into a bun beneath her hat, which was of felt and broad-brimmed with a band of some kind of animal fur around the crown–mink?–and several peacock feathers tucked inside of it. She carried a parasol that she used almost as a weapon, poking at labels beneath the paintings as if contesting their veracity. She was very slim in the waist and buxom at the chest. She had a straight, narrow nose and a wide mouth with full, sensual lips. Her almond eyes seemed to smile all on their own.

She dallied with the Dutchman only for a few moments and, swinging her parasol like a truncheon, approached Tony. At first she nodded towards him as if acknowledging the presence of a doorman or waiter, and quickly looked away at one of the paintings. Then after a moment of scrutiny, passed on to the next one, which happened to be Tony's portrait of the

Negro boy hawking newspapers. Her expression changed as she examined this one, to one of somber reflection. After perhaps a minute or two, she turned to Tony.

"Are you the creator of this sad little creature?"

"Sad? I haven't thought of him as being particularly sad," Tony replied.

"Then it is yours."

"Yes."

"Autobiographical?"

Tony laughed. "I never sold a newspaper in my life."

"But he resembles you."

Tony moved to her side so he could get a more direct view of the painting. "Do you think so?"

"Most definitely. The sad eyes, the slightly upturned nose, the earnest, almost arrogant curl of his lips—as if he knows he is superior to those who buy his newspapers."

Tony chuckled. "He was a street urchin. I was thinking only of him and his desperate situation when I painted his portrait. I wondered how he got to Paris, who his parents were, and where he slept at night. Personally, I have never known poverty or neglect."

"Haven't you?" She seemed amazed at this revelation. "You are an American."

"True."

"With a hint of the South, I perceive by your accent."

"Also true."

She extended her hand, bent delicately at the wrist. "Amelia Goldman. Of San Francisco."

Tony kissed her hand. "Enchanté. Tony Jones. Of Beaufort, South Carolina."

She seemed to restrain herself from laughing. "Beaufort? You pronounce it 'Bew-fort'? I thought it was 'Bo'-for'."

"I suppose it was originally. Certainly French. But it filtered down from the English over the centuries. I never heard it any other way when I was growing up."

"I see." She looked again at the painting. "You are a very talented man, Monsieur Jones. How much is this one? 500 francs? I'll take it—but I'd like to see more."

Tony pointed out that the price was only one hundred francs.

"One hundred?" She took a pair of opera glasses from her purse and examined the price tag. "Why Monsieur Dantec is shamelessly underestimating your talent. How much is the other one–the one with the toy boats?"

"Fifty francs."

"I'll take both. And I'll have a word with Monsieur Dantec, who is an old friend of mine. Would five hundred francs for the two of them suit you?"

"That would be more than generous."

"Generosity has nothing to do with it. I'm paying what they are worth. Excuse me for a moment."

And she went off to find Monsieur Dantec.

Tony remained rooted to the spot, wondering whether Miss–Mrs?– Goldman was going to return or simply ask to have the paintings sent to her and leave the gallery. While he was waiting a waiter came over to him and offered him a glass of champagne. He took the glass and then saw that Miss Goldman was in fact returning to speak to him. The waiter stopped to offer her a glass. She took it and approached him.

"I believe this event calls for a toast, don't you?" she said.

"I'm always looking for an excuse to drink champagne," Tony said.

"Actually," she said, "I don't need an excuse at all. I enjoy a glass at breakfast. And it can be nice during a bath as well."

Tony's imagination was set off by this statement, evoking an image of Miss Goldman soaking in a tub with gold-plated fixtures and soap bubbles popping one by one, revealing her delicate shoulders down to the tops of her ample breasts.

"I'm curious as to how you came to be in Paris," she said, after a sip of her champagne. "Do you have a sponsor?"

"A sponsor?"

"Yes. As distinct from a mere patron. A sponsor, as I understand it, underwrites an artist's career. At least until he's off and running."

"Well, Miss–"

"Call me Amelia."

"Of course. Well, Amelia, I have no 'sponsor,' as you put it. I'm simply winging it on my own."

She laughed. "'Winging it'? Like a bird returning to his nest?"

"Something like that."

"But a bird may encounter strong winds and be dashed to the ground."

"I understand the metaphor, Miss–Amelia–but I don't think it's an apt one. I don't intend to be dashed to the ground, in any case."

"Of course you don't. But the winds of the art world–to continue the metaphor–are every bit as treacherous as those of nature, if not more so. You have funds to sustain you? For six months, a year?"

"Well...your purchase helps considerably."

"Five hundred francs doesn't go far in this town, Monsieur Jones–"

"Tony."

"Of course. Tony. I would like to see more of your work. Perhaps we could come to an agreement."

It was becoming increasingly apparent to Tony what Amelia Goldman had in mind. "I must tell you, Amelia, that I am married."

"You misunderstand me, Tony. I, too, am married. But my husband is in San Francisco and I am here, where I intend to remain for some time. And where, may I ask, is your wife?"

"She's...actually in London."

"London? Then you see little of each other."

"I saw her off this morning. But, yes, she will be away for a while."

Amelia planted the point of her parasol in the floor in front of her and spread her feet as if digging in for an assault. "Let us understand one another, Tony. I am not a lonely dowager desperate for male companionship. I am a collector. And I am looking for young artists who I think have talent and promise. In short, I intend to be a force in the arts. Do you understand?"

"I think I do. And forgive me if I implied that–"

"No need to apologize. I'm used to men misunderstanding my intentions. And underestimating my abilities. Now, when can I see other examples of your work?"

Tony now felt somewhat more at ease. "Any time. But I must confess that I have only four paintings left."

"You've sold the others?"

"My roommate did. While I was in America. What's left are my more experimental works. Nothing like the ones you have purchased today."

"Experimental? I am all the more intrigued. I have an engagement this evening. How about two o'clock tomorrow afternoon?"

"That's fine."

"The address?"

Tony extracted a calling card from his pocket that he used when he managed his father's bank. He wrote the address on the back of it.

Amelia examined the card, then turned it over. "Beaufort National Bank. Antonio Jones, Jr., President.' Ah! You are indeed a man of many talents, Tony. May I call you Antonio? It has ever so much more panache to it. I think you should sign all your work that way."

Tony chuckled. "Jackie says the same thing."

"Jackie?"

"My wife."

"Oh–of course. But she has merely suggested it. I will insist upon it. I know something about marketing, you know."

"Indeed. I think you do."

"Well, then." She deposited her empty glass on the tray of a passing waiter. "À demain."

Tony kissed her hand. "À demain."

He watched as Amelia sauntered to the door, stopping only to exchange a few words with Monsieur Dantec. When she was gone M. Dantec came over to speak to him.

"You are a fortunate young man," he said. "Madame Goldman is one of my wealthiest clients. And she has taken a liking to your work."

"Yes," Tony said. "I'm pleased that she has. But what do you know of her? She says she is a serious collector."

"And she is. Not a connoisseur, but she is very determined once she sets her mind on something."

"I can see that. But why isn't her husband here with her?"

"Ah, Mr. Goldman. He is a mining executive in San Francisco. They are somewhat estranged, I understand."

"Why?"

M. Dantec opened his palms to the air. "Who knows? He is said to be a very jealous man. Perhaps they see marriage differently. We French have a very efficacious solution to marital discord."

"And what is that?"

"We men take mistresses. And our wives take lovers. It seems to be a mutually agreeable arrangement."

Tony was not unaware of this sort of 'arrangement' in France, but as a young newlywed in love with his bride, he felt that such an 'arrangement' would never apply to him or Jackie. Such practices, he felt, were for middle-aged couples who, after a number of years, discover they have little in common aside from their children. He and Jackie, on the other hand, had much in common to sustain their relationship–their interest in the arts, for example. And progressive ideas in regard to race. Jackie's marriage to him was proof of that. "And has Madame Goldman taken a lover?"

M. Dantec laughed. "I have no idea, mon cher ami. But I am sure there is no lack of candidates." He put his hand on Tony's shoulder. "Let's step into my office for a moment. I need to write you a cheque."

Tony was only too glad to follow M. Dantec into his office for this purpose. He thought of Jackie and how pleased she would be when he told her he had sold two of his paintings before she had even reached Calais. And for five hundred francs!

He resolved to write her a letter that evening.

CHAPTER 5

The next day at precisely two p.m. there was a knock on the door of the atelier. When Tony opened the door he encountered Mme Goldman breathing heavily and leaning for support on her parasol.

"Fourth floor? And no elevator?" she said.

"Désolé," Tony said. "The times have not quite caught up with Rue de Fleurus."

"But I see that next door one is being installed."

"Is there? Well, we shall have to petition the landlord. Entrez, je vous en prie."

Mme Goldman stepped inside. "Merci. Oh! This is quite a large space. I would not have thought–"

"The studio is spacious enough. The upstairs quarters are a bit cramped, however."

Mme Goldman put her parasol in the umbrella stand next to the door and began looking around. "Are these your paintings?"

"Most of them are Nat's. He's at the Louvre this afternoon copying Old Masters."

"Hmm. And where are yours? The experimental ones?"

"Over here. I've retrieved them from the attic and dusted them off." He led her to the far wall, where he had propped them up, four in a row.

She studied them for a few moments. "Cubism."

"Well, I wouldn't describe them that way myself."

"How would you describe them?"

"I would say there is a cubist influence–I very much admire Monsieur Cézanne's technique–but I am more interested in the play of light and its ability to bring out color in various hues. The cubist aspect is merely to present different perspectives simultaneously."

"Hmm. Yes, I can see that you are still rooted in Impressionism. Pissarro? Monet?"

"Both."

"I like them, Tony. Can you bear to part with all four?"

"I've promised Monsieur Dantec two."

"Which two?"

"Any two. He hasn't seen them."

"Then I have my pick. This one and...that one. It's of the Pont Neuf, is it not?"

"It could be any bridge. I was interested in the effects of artificial light in the fog."

"Yes, I see. Very original. How much do you want for the pair?"

Tony shrugged his shoulders. "I don't know. A hundred francs?"

"You persist in underestimating your worth. I would say 300 francs. Each."

"Each?"

She laughed. "Let's not quibble. I'll write you a cheque and my man will pick them up later." Her eyes scanned the walls covered with Nat's paintings. "I see your roommate is preoccupied with bullfighting. And nude women in various attitudes of submission. Is he such a brute?"

Tony laughed. "Nat is actually a very gentle person. Except when he's drunk."

"Ah! A not uncommon condition. Especially for men of common talents."

A noise emitted from the loft that resembled that of a cat being pulled by her tail.

"That's Marie-Louise," Tony said. "Nat's girlfriend. This is about the time she usually gets up."

Mme Goldman looked at her watch. "At 2:30 in the afternoon? And I thought I was a late riser."

There was suddenly a muffled sound like that of an underground explosion, followed by a feminine cry: "Merde!"

"That's the toilet," Tony said. "It backs up occasionally."

"Tch, tch. Tony, you must find more suitable accommodations. I don't see how you can work in this environment."

"Well, it is...distracting at times. And I am looking for another space."

"Any luck?"

"Nothing affordable. Even with these sales—"

"I have plenty of room."

Tony's suspicions as to Mme Goldman's intentions were again aroused. "I don't see how—"

"'It's quite a large house. And at present there are only myself and five servants living there. Three of them live in the carriage house. There is a large space above the carriage house with plenty of morning light. And a garden of considerable size."

"I appreciate the offer, Amelia, but I can't just–"

"Of course you can. There is nothing untoward about it. I would require that you pay rent. But far less than you would pay for a comparable space anywhere else in Saint-Germain-des-Prés."

Tony considered this for a moment. "My wife will be returning from London in a few weeks."

"That would be lovely. There's plenty of room for both of you. In the meantime, you would have a very private place to work, three meals a day, and I would have a house full of 'joie de vivre,' and 'créativité.' At present I feel that I am living in a museum–I have some beautiful artwork–but there is no 'animation.' What do you say?"

"I don't know, Amelia. I'd have to think about it. Where is your house?"

"Rue de Furstemberg. Here is the address." She produced a calling card from her purse. "Come anytime. Actually, ten o'clock is best. That's when the light shows to best advantage."

At that moment Marie-Louise appeared at the top of the stairs clad only in her robe de chambre, which was not secured around her waist. In other words, she was exposed in her nudity with the robe serving only to keep her shoulders warm. She yawned and started down the steps when she spotted Amelia.

"Bonjour," she said.

"Bonjour, Mademoiselle," Amelia said, somewhat aghast.

"Je te présente Madame Goldman," Tony said.

"Enchantée," Marie-Louise said. She reached the bottom of the stairs and went straight to the kitchen.

"The girl in your friend's paintings," Amelia said.

"The same," Tony said.

"Well...you must have an interesting ménage-à-trois."

Tony chuckled. "Not at all. I've gotten used to Marie-Louise walking around half-naked. Even my wife became accustomed to it."

"I must admit that, though I am a *passionnée* of the arts, I am not used to the Bohemian life myself. Oh!" She reached into her purse. "Let me write you that cheque."

She pulled her cheque book out of her purse, set it on the table, and wrote the cheque. "Remember, any time after ten. À demain!"

"À demain, Amelia."

She stopped at the door and looked back at Marie-Louise, who had by now removed her robe entirely and was standing stark-naked in the kitchen preparing some *pain perdu*. "Déjeuner nu, no?"

Tony laughed "I try to keep my mind on my work."

"You are remarkably disciplined. Adieu!"

After Amelia had gone, Tony looked at the cheque. Six hundred francs! Now a total of eleven hundred. More than enough to secure a nice apartment...but for how long? He had no more paintings to sell. Well, there were these two promised to M. Dantec. But who knows how long it would take to sell them?

By this time Marie-Louise had finished preparing her *pain perdu* and was sitting at the table in the middle of the studio. Still stark naked. She looked up from her meal as Tony walked by on his way upstairs. "Il fait chaud," she said.

Tony started to brush past her, but she grabbed his hand and looked up into his eyes. "Tu ne m'aimes pas?"

He said in French that he liked her very much, but that he was married to Jackie.

"Mais, Jacqueline n'est pas là."

Tony sighed and withdrew his hand. "Et tu n'aimes pas Nat?"

"Oui, mais Nat n'est pas là non plus."

"Il vient bientôt," he said, and continued up the stairs, where he sat down at the little bureau and wrote the second letter in as many days to Jackie.

CHAPTER 6

Jackie was greeted at Victoria Station by her mother, who was now ensconced in a townhouse facing Eaton Square, only a few blocks away. She had a hansom cab waiting for them just outside the station.

Once settled in the house, Jackie collapsed in an armchair in the drawing room with a sigh of relief.

"Was the journey that arduous?" Lucinda said, as she sat on a sofa opposite her daughter. A servant arrived with a tray of tea and crumpets.

"Oh, it wasn't so bad as that," Jackie said. "Except for the crossing. I was green at the gills for much of it."

"Motion sickness? I think it runs in the family."

"Yes. Edwina absolutely refused to venture out on the *Southern Pride* with father because of it–except that one time when she wanted to escape when I broke off my engagement to Rav Coleman."

Lucinda took a sip of her tea after blowing off the steam. "Yes, I wonder if that old reprobate succeeded in winning the election."

"I believe he did. And now he's married to a woman even younger than I am. But let's not talk about him. Are there any new plays in London?"

"There're always new plays in London. I'm currently engaged with Mr. Shaw in an effort to produce his latest offering."

"Mr. Shaw? George Bernard Shaw?"

"Of course. He was hardly known when you were last here. But now his plays are much in demand and it's difficult to get his attention."

"And what is his latest offering?"

"This one is called *Caesar and Cleopatra*."

"Really?" Jackie took a bite of a honey-soaked crumpet. "How interesting."

"I haven't read it yet, but no need to. Anything GBS writes will be successful. The difficulty may be finding an ingénue to play Cleopatra."

Jackie brightened. "Aren't I an ingénue?"

"My dear, Cleopatra was seventeen at the time You are now–"

"Thirty-two. But don't you think I could pass for–"

"Possibly. It would be up to Mr. Shaw. And there's no guarantee that he will accept my offer. He has this scandalous relationship with Mrs. Pat and–"

"Mrs. Pat?"

"Mrs Patrick Campbell. I thought you were aware that she was a star of the stage here."

"Yes, I met her once. But she was known as Beatrice Campbell then, I believe."

"Right you are. But everybody calls her Mrs. Pat now, even though her husband is off in Australia or South Africa or some other God-forsaken place."

"And Mr. Shaw is considering her for the part? She must be nearing forty."

"Actually, she's closer to your age."

"My age? I always thought she was older."

"She looks it. Perhaps that's why she's seeking to become an impresario. She certainly can't count on support from her husband."

Jackie scanned the walls of the drawing room, which contained more photographs than paintings, mostly of theatrical performers, but several of handsome men, including Mr. Shaw. "And your relationship with Mr. Shaw is–"

Lucinda laughed. "Purely platonic, I assure you. I think it may even be platonic between him and Mrs. Pat. I'm told he fires off love letters to all the actresses who appear in his plays, but there is no evidence of concupiscence."

"Concupiscence?"

"Lust. Or maybe I should say consummation. The point is, there is no sex between them."

"How do you know?"

"I don't. But my sources are generally reliable."

Jackie wondered at her mother's intrigues. "And you–have you a...a lover these days?"

Lucinda laughed and rolled her eyes to the ceiling. "My dear, I always have a lover even though I'm approaching my dotage. But they have a way of disappearing once they discover that I have no intention of supporting them."

Jackie smiled. "You're still a quite handsome woman, Mother."

"Handsome, yes. Beautiful, no. And it remains to be seen when 'handsome' will metamorphize into 'formidable,' or 'redoubtable,' like Windsor Castle.

But tell me, Jackie, how does it go with your husband? It seems that you have abandoned him."

"Abandoned him? I thought I told you in my letter that Tony's former roommate sold all of his paintings and spent the money."

"Yes, yes. I remember that part. But couldn't you stick it out together in Paris? Until Tony comes up with some new work?"

Jackie felt this was a reproach, which indeed it was. "There's no telling when he might sell enough of his paintings even though he does work quickly. Fashions have changed since he was last there, and—"

"There's no guarantee that you can land a role here that will pay, my dear. I'll do what I can to introduce you to the right people, but as in Paris, things have changed since you were last here."

Jackie had no rejoinder for this observation, which was the reality she had refused to acknowledge. Yes, things have changed, as they always do, especially in large cities. Perhaps she had been too faint-hearted in the face of trivial difficulties. What was the vow they had taken at the wedding? 'For better, for worse, for richer, for poorer, in sickness and in health, to love and to cherish till death do us part...' She had abandoned her husband at the first sign of adversity! Perhaps she should turn around and run, not walk, to Victoria Station. She could be back in Paris by noon tomorrow. She could—

A servant interrupted this sense of panic and announced: "Mr. Forbes-Robertson to see you, ma'am."

"Show him in, Alastair. I'd like for him to meet my niece."

"Yes, ma'am."

When Alastair had gone, Jackie leaned over to Lucinda and whispered, "Mother! Do we have to keep up this charade that you are my aunt?"

"Well, not if you don't want to. But I must protect my reputation, you know. Besides, I always introduced you as my niece when you were here before. It would be terribly confusing to suddenly start calling you 'daughter.'"

Jackie sighed and leaned back in her chair. "I suppose you're right. I even refer to you as 'Aunt Lucinda' when I'm talking to Tony, and he knows all about it."

"There! You see—habit is a hard thing to break. Let sleeping dogs—"

"Lucy!"

Lucinda rose to greet Mr. Forbes-Robertson and extended her hand. "Johnny! So good to see you. To what do I owe this unexpected visit?"

He kissed her hand. "Dash it! You know—Oh, I'm sorry. I didn't realize you had company."

"Johnny–I'd like you to meet my niece, Jaqueline Jones."

Jackie rose and extended her hand.

Forbes-Robertson kissed it. "Jacqueline Jones? I say, that's rather alliterative, isn't it? Delighted to meet you, Miss Jones."

"It's *Mrs.* Jones," Lucinda said.

"Oh–drat! Hard luck. I mean to say–"

"She knows what you mean to say," Lucinda said. "But she is, unfortunately for you, unavailable. Her husband is currently in Paris pursuing an artistic career."

"Is he? Well, jolly good for him!"

"Sit down, Johnny," Lucinda said. "What was it you wanted to speak to me about?"

Forbes-Robertson took a seat. "It's Mrs. Pat–she wants to try Shaw's new play out in Newcastle-upon-Tyne."

"Newcastle? Whatever for? It's miles out of the way–"

"She seems to think that the play still needs work. It will be a staged reading."

"A reading?" Lucinda looked at Jackie, then back at Johnny. "Then the roles aren't settled? Anyone may try out?"

Johnny glanced at Jackie. "Well, I wouldn't say anyone. Of course Shaw wrote the part of Caesar for me, and Mrs. Pat is interested in the part of Cleopatra, but–"

"Are you aware that my niece is an accomplished actress, Johnny? And though she is an American, she has performed to the highest accolades in Mr. Pinero's plays, both here and in America."

Johnny stared at Jackie for a moment, who blushed and lowered her eyes. "Has she? Well, I'll be dashed! She's about the right age, I should say. And Mrs. Pat is a bit past her prime–"

"When is the reading to take place?"

Suddenly it seemed that Johnny couldn't take his eyes off Jackie. "Not till March, but an audition is set for next week. Are you adept in the English way of speaking, Mrs. Jones?"

Jackie responded in her best Oxonian English. "I think so, Mr. Robertson. I played Rosalind in *As You Like It* at the Shakespeare Festival in Stratford only three years ago."

"To rave reviews," Lucinda said. "And no one suspected that she was an American."

"Oh, jolly good. Well, then, I'll call on Mrs. Pat straightaway and inform

her that you'll be at the audition. There will be others, of course, vying
for the role of Cleopatra." He rose from his chair. "Well, I'll be off now.
Delighted to make your acquaintance, Mrs. Jones. And Lucy–dash it! I've
forgotten what I came to ask you about."

"Perhaps it was Mrs. Pat's garden party."

"Right you are! You will attend?"

Lucinda smiled coquettishly. "Will I have an escort?"

"Of course you'll have an escort. Namely, me. Shall we say two-ish? And
of course I can speak for Mrs. Pat when I say that your charming niece is
invited, too."

"That's very kind of you, Mr. Robertson," Jackie said. "I'd be delighted
to attend."

"Then it's settled. I'll come round in the motorcar on Saturday at two."

After Forbes-Robertson left Jackie leaned forward and said, "He has a
motorcar?"

"Men must have their toys, you know," Lucinda said. "It's a noisy thing,
and breaks down constantly, but it draws admiring stares. Just what an
actor needs to buoy his confidence."

After tea, Jackie retreated to her room, which was spacious and furnished
with Regency chairs and a four-poster bed. The walls were covered with
prints and posters from many of Lucinda's productions. She sat in one
of the chairs upholstered in a moiré silk fabric and stared at a bust of
David Garrick, the great 18th century actor. She luxuriated in this rarefied
environment and couldn't help comparing it to the tiny room in the loft
in Paris with the paper-thin walls and creaky floors that she felt might
collapse at any moment. But was that so hard to endure? And it would only
be temporary.

She resolved to write Tony a letter and went to the Queen Anne secretary
against the wall opposite her bed to do so. And what an extraordinary
man he was! Strong, handsome, intelligent, immensely talented...faithful?
Of course he was...even with Marie-Louise walking around the atelier
half-naked, he...how different the French and the English were! Could he
resist all the temptations that Paris presented to him every day? Perhaps he
needed some encouragement, some reassurance...

She began to write the letter: "Mon cher mari..."

CHAPTER 7

Rue de Furstemberg is a charming little street between Rue de l'Abbaye and Rue Jacob not far from Boulevard St-Germain. It is really no more than a very private drive serving several apartment buildings, with an island green set in the middle.

Tony stood before Mme Goldman's door, whose entry was tucked into a corner where two of the buildings met at right angles. It was almost hidden from the passersby, some of whom stopped to peer into a flower shop next door, or a jewelry concern directly across the street.

It was a blustery fall day, cloudy but sunny. He stepped up to the door and pressed the bell. He looked at his pocket watch. Eleven o'clock. After a delay of some three or four minutes, he heard footsteps descending a stone stairway. The door opened and there stood a swarthy young man of short stature, dressed in a cutaway jacket of green velour with white piping and gold buttons.

"Monsieur Jones?" he said.

"Oui."

The young man–barely out of his teens–opened the door wide and indicated the stone staircase with a broad sweep of his arm. "Entrez, s'il vous plaît. Madame Goldman vous attend."

At the top of the stairs, Tony was ushered into a large drawing room with red brocaded silk wall coverings above black walnut wainscoting. There were few chairs, but two sofas and a coffee table between them. Numerous paintings were hung from floor to ceiling, which was twelve to fourteen feet high. Delacroix, Rembrandt, Rubens, but also more contemporary painters like Sisley, Renoir and Manet. As he perused the artwork, Mme Goldman entered the room and extended her hand.

"Tony! You have come."

Tony kissed her hand. "Did you think I wouldn't?"

"Well, I couldn't be sure. You seemed reluctant."

"A little, to be honest. But, you know, I must have morning light."

"I'll show you the studio."

Amelia led him through two more rooms, also filled with artwork, and stepped down to an outdoor landing that led to both the carriage house and to the garden below. The young man who had admitted him seemed to magically appear and opened the door to the carriage house. They then passed through a narrow passageway, which emerged into a large room with a very high ceiling and an enormous Palladian window overlooking the garden. In addition, there was a skylight above the window. Sunlight poured in.

"This is magnificent!" Tony said. "It seems to have been made for an artist."

"Actually," Amelia said, "it is just a carriage house with a loft for storage of fodder for the animals. I had it made into a studio with the idea that I would use it myself."

"And have you?"

"Used it myself? Yes, for a while. But you see, I have no talent. It took me only a few weeks to discover that. But I can't bear to have it go to waste."

Tony walked around the room. It was almost too perfect. The sun, in winter, would rise from the southeast, shining directly into the garden, but also through the skylight. In the afternoon, the light would be from the southwest, streaming through the huge window. The buildings on the far side of the garden were low, no more than three stories. A high wall ensured privacy.

"Would you like to see the bedrooms?" Amelia said.

"The bedrooms?" Tony was still mesmerized by the view through the window.

"Yes. Your accommodations, should you decide to take me up on my offer."

"Oh. Of course."

By this time, the little doorman had disappeared and Amelia led the way up the stairs and into the house. On the second floor they emerged into a long hallway adorned, like the drawing room, with a number of paintings, only these were considerably more recent, ranging from Impressionist to what was already being called post-impressionist in some circles. Cézanne, Van Gogh, Seurat and others Tony was not familiar with.

Amelia opened one of the doors and entered. Tony followed.

This was another large room, appointed with Louis XVI furniture, an Aubusson rug nearly covering the entire floor, a canopied bed, and a gilt mirror over a chest of drawers with a marble top and ormolu fittings. A few portraits adorned the walls, apparently by the same hand, but Tony could not identify the artist.

"Very nice portraiture," he said. "Who did them?"

"Oh–those are mine–except the one of Monterey Bay. That was done by a friend of mine in San Francisco."

"Yours? And you said you have no talent. I think they're very well done. Who is this?" He pointed to a boy with tousled blond hair wearing a blue suit reminiscent of Gainsborough's *Blue Boy.*

"That's my son," she said. "Unfortunately he died of consumption shortly after that."

"Oh. I'm sorry. And this gentleman?"

"My husband."

"Quite a handsome fellow."

"Yes. He is. A bit younger at the time."

Tony moved to the bed, tested the mattress and went to the window. He looked down at the street below, which was partially obscured by plane trees in the central island. A woman sat on a bench holding a leash attached at the other end to a small white dog.

"Would you like to see the other rooms?" she said.

"What? Oh, yes. The other rooms. I was just admiring the view."

Mme Goldman led him through three other bedrooms, all in line with adjoining doors and facing Rue de Furstemberg. They were similar in size, though with different styles and decor.

"And there are two more upstairs," she said, "but they are hardly ever occupied. Would you care to see them?"

"Not now, thank you. Perhaps later. Do you have many guests?"

"Oh, yes. From time to time. Mostly friends from America. Would you care for some tea?"

"That would be delightful."

They descended a staircase that opened into the drawing room, where they sat on one of the sofas side by side. Mme Goldman pulled on a cord adjacent to the sofa and in seconds a young woman appeared dressed in the traditional maid's uniform of black dress and white lace apron.

"Sabine, du thé, s'il te plaît."

"Oui, Madame."

While they were waiting for the tea, Mme Goldman turned to Tony. "Well? Do you think you could be comfortable here?"

Tony chuckled. "There's no doubt of that. Anyone would be. But you mentioned the rent earlier. How much is it?"

"Oh, well, I was thinking of ten francs a week."

"Ten francs? That's less than my share of the rent at Rue de Fleurus. This is like a luxury hotel!"

"If you would prefer to pay more, I won't object. But you don't know how long it will take to sell your paintings. And you have to start again from scratch."

Tony considered this uncomfortable truth. "Well...what if we tie the rent to my sales? Should my paintings begin to sell, and perhaps even increase in price, you could raise the rent accordingly."

"As a percentage, then?"

"Yes."

Mme Goldman pursed her lips and gazed at a self-portrait of Raphael over the mantlepiece. "What if we dispense with the rent altogether and I take a ten percent commission on all of your sales the first year? You sell nothing, you pay nothing. However, if you should establish yourself as an artist to be reckoned with–as I expect you will–then I will be more than compensated for your room and board. And, of course, it would give me an incentive to promote your work."

Tony gazed at that same Raphael over the mantlepiece. "A year...and when my wife returns? She will be an additional burden on your staff."

Mme Goldman laughed. "Hardly a burden. Sabine, Jean-Pierre, and the cook, Eugénie, have served parties of twenty or more. And Hasan and Fatima in the carriage house can always be called upon to assist for larger parties."

"Then you have dinner parties on a regular basis?"

"Perhaps once or twice a month. You, of course, will always be welcome to join us, but you may choose to remain in your studio to work, or retire to your bedroom."

Tony thought that this arrangement was too good to be true. He looked at Mme Goldman for a moment from a different point of view. She was no less attractive than when he first met her at Monsieur Dantec's gallery. She wore a velour dress, the same color as her doorman's uniform, with the bodice cut low, her breasts rising and falling with each breath. A cameo attached to a black ribbon around her neck, also of velour, drew attention to her eyes, which were nearly as black as the ribbon. "Would I have any other duties? Perhaps I could help with the horses, or–"

Mme Goldman laughed. "I think Hasan can take care of the horses. That's all he's ever known. And he's a good mechanic, too. No, I think you should focus all of your efforts on your painting. Remember, I will have an investment in your work. Are we agreed?"

Tony looked at her, the carpet—a design of stylized birds, flowers, and scarabs—and finally the window that overlooked the garden. "For one year?"

"For one year. Let's put it in writing. I'll have my *avocat* draw it up and we can sign it in his office. Rue Scribe near the Opera House."

Tony took his leave after finishing his tea and walked back to Rue de Fleurus. Along the way, he wondered about Mme Goldman and her interest in young artists. Was it purely aesthetic? A business venture? And what about her husband? The portrait was of a large man, with sideburns extending to his jaw line, and piercing blue eyes. He wielded a cane like a royal scepter. Obviously a man of strength and authority. What broke them apart? Perhaps the death of the child. In any case, she seemed to have no expectation of a reconciliation. She was ready to commit herself to a year of patronage to him, Antonio Jones, Jr., and no other! What if Monsieur Goldman decided to come and join his wife in Paris? Or perhaps to forcibly drag her back to San Francisco? And Jackie—what was she to think about their 'arrangement' when she returned from London?

These many unanswerable questions plagued him until he turned into Rue de Fleurus and saw someone flinging clothes, followed by a suitcase, out of the window of the atelier.

"Putain! Salope! Sors d'ici!"

It was Nat, shouting at the top of his lungs. These execrations were followed by the sound of Marie-Louise's voice. "Assassin! Vieux vicieux!"

Suddenly Tony's reservations concerning Mme Goldman's offer evaporated.

CHAPTER 8

Jackie thought the audition went well. Mr. Shaw, as well as Mr. Forbes-Robertson and Mrs. Pat, encouraged and politely applauded her portrayal of Cleopatra. However, when Mrs. Pat auditioned for the part herself, Jackie noticed that Johnny was unusually attentive, even mesmerized, by her performance. Shaw also seemed enthralled. Afterwards, both men hovered around her, heaping praise upon her as if she had just succeeded to the throne of England.

Jackie decided that she was unlikely to get the part.

"You can't tell by that," Lucinda said. She was clipping roses from their stems in her garden behind the house. "Both men are shameless flatterers. And neither has any intention of carrying on a *real* love affair with Mrs. Pat."

Jackie walked slowly behind her mother holding a basket for the clippings. "How can you be so sure?"

"Because I know the English. And I know these two men. They relish the newspaper reports of their flirtations–didn't you notice that man in the back row from *The Times*?–and carry on their affairs by letters. Can you imagine? One touch by a beautiful woman and they quiver like jelly."

Jackie couldn't help but laugh at her mother's characterization of English men. "But they do marry–don't they?"

"Oh, yes. And any progeny that results seems to be by immaculate conception. The letter-writing, of course, continues."

"What about your affair with the prince?"

"That's a different sort of Englishman entirely. The aristocracy are like the underclass in that respect. They're both secure in their social positions and therefore care nothing about what people think."

Jackie sighed. "But mother, what am I to do? Poor Tony is nearly starving in Paris, and I promised I would send money."

Lucinda clicked her tongue. "I'm sure Tony is far from the brink of starvation. He's a very talented and resourceful young man. But if it comes to that, I will be glad to help in any way I can. Isn't this a beautiful Lady Mary Fitzwilliam'–?"

Jackie peered over her mother's shoulder at the rose in question. It was a fully opened, blush pink flower with gently-curved petals. "I'm afraid I don't know the names of flowers, Mother. Not the different varieties, anyway."

"Well, you should. They may be your only solace in later years, you know. Men are so fickle, and so easily distracted."

Jackie smiled. "I don't think Tony's easily distracted. He's the most focused man I know."

"I hope you're right. That's enough for the parlor, don't you think? Why don't we take them inside and have some tea while Alastair finds some water for them? And Jackie–do stop calling me 'Mother.' It makes me feel absolutely decrepit. Besides, it's confusing to the servants, not to mention our guests. A short, crisp, 'Lucy' will do."

After tea, the mail came and Lucinda sorted the letters at her writing desk. "This one's for you, dear. From Paris."

"Oh, it must be Tony!" Jackie took the letter and retired to the sofa, where she slit the envelope open with her fingernail. She read every word carefully, relieved that it was not in French. "He says he's already sold two of his paintings in Monsieur Dantec's gallery!"

"There–you see? I told you he was resourceful. And–Oh. Here's another one for you."

Jackie leapt up from the sofa and examined the second letter, also from Paris. She slit the envelope open, this time with the letter opener, and extracted a short note accompanied by a cheque. "Five hundred francs! And he says that the same collector has purchased the other four."

"My goodness! He'll be getting rich at this rate. But...the other four? He has only six paintings altogether?"

"Well, yes. Remember? His roommate sold all the rest."

"In that case, he'll have to get busy if he expects to support the two of you. Oh, Jackie, I'm afraid that as industrious and talented as Tony is, the life of an artist is too precarious. Perhaps you could convince him to come here. There's a vibrant art community here and you could both live under my roof indefinitely and we could–"

"He's too proud for that, Mother."

"Lucy."

"Lucy. Besides, he believes his fortune lies in Paris. It's the center of the art world, he says."

"Well, Mr. Turner and Mr. Sargent haven't done so badly in London. But I suppose there's no dissuading a man who's set his sights on conquering a city, is there?"

Jackie collected the two letters and kissed them as if they were Tony's lips. "No…and conquer it he will."

CHAPTER 9

$\mathcal{A}$rtist in Residence. That's the way Tony thought of his arrangement with Mme Goldman. Once settled in the first bedroom he was shown, he went to the studio, unpacked his paints and brushes and sat before the large easel in front of the window that looked onto the garden. With brush in hand he stared. And stared.

It was always hard to get started. Poplar and spruce trees were scattered about, the larger ones encircled by boxwoods with benches round the trunks. There were islands of roses and camellias accessible by a network of walkways paved with tiny white pebbles. Ivy climbed the trellises attached to both the walls of the main house and the carriage house. This idyllic scene of peace and tranquility in the midst of a bustling city, mesmerized him for several minutes, though he couldn't have said for how long.

"The cherry trees bloom in April."

He turned from the window to see Mme Goldman at the door of the studio.

"It's a lovely sight," she said. "The pomegranates, however, are in bloom now. A symbol of fertility to both the Greeks and the Jews. Biblical scholars in fact believe it was the forbidden fruit of the Garden of Eden." She came over to the easel and looked at the blank canvas. "Trouble getting started?"

Tony looked out the window. "There's so much to see here. Ordinarily, I'm not a landscape painter. I tend to gravitate to the human form."

"Well," she said, folding her hands in front of her. She was wearing a green silk dress patterned with stylized birds, flowers, and forest animals. The bodice, as with all of the dresses Tony had seen thus far, was cut low. (He tried to keep his eyes off of her cleavage, and focused on her dark, hooded eyes). "You need a model, then, don't you? I would volunteer, but I don't have the patience to sit motionless for hours at a time."

Tony laughed. "It's not necessary to sit for hours at a time. A half-hour, an hour. I would only need enough time to sketch the figure and then work it into a painting."

"Really? Well, would you require me to pose in the nude?"

"Not necessarily. Clothing sometimes can convey an aura of mystery, of restrained eroticism."

"'Restrained eroticism'? That seems to me to be a contradiction in terms."

Tony was beginning to be uncomfortable with this conversation. "Perhaps…'suggested' is what I meant to say." He turned back to the window. "At any rate, I think I'll experiment with what I can see from this window. The petals, the leaves, the texture and color of tree bark."

She looked out the window. "Yes, it would be a shame to let all this beauty go to waste–from an artist's point of view, I mean. Well, I'll leave you to get started." She went to the door and stopped for a moment. "Oh, Tony–I'm having a dinner party tonight. Of course you're welcome to join us."

"Dressy?"

"Only for the Philistines. Artists may dress any way they like." There was a twinkle in her eye as if to say, 'We are of the same mold, you and I.'

Once she was gone, Tony considered her offer to pose for him in the nude. What did that mean? That she was willing to do anything to serve his artistic needs, or…to satisfy her own needs? And if the latter, just what were those needs?

But to work. It seemed silly to sit inside a comfortable studio, sheltered from the wind and the cold–it was November now–and paint a natural scene viewed through a window. He resolved to move outside.

He sat on a bench that encircled one of the plane trees and opened his sketchbook. After surveying the garden, which in many ways was like any other garden, his eyes kept returning to the carriage house. The entrance, on the ground floor, was accessed by a double door hardly tall enough for a man to walk through, much less a horse. He supposed the horses were led in from the other side of the building, facing another street. Above the door was an entablature with a dozen or so figures in relief, depicting Greeks at a banquet. And above the entablature was the floor-to-ceiling window, its panes divided by muntins painted white. A spruce tree on the left nearly touched a wall of fieldstone, and ivy climbed a trellis on the right, next to the stairway to the studio.

He began sketching.

The sketch took fifteen minutes. Then he went back to the studio–it was getting a bit chilly in the late afternoon–and sat down at the easel in front of the window. Green, green, green everywhere, only a touch of red from the hardier variety of roses. Rather boring. He noticed that the sun was now low in the sky, just peeking over the buildings to the southwest. Orange, red, even purple. This called for some adjustments.

In another hour, it was done. He stood back from the easel to assess his work. Now what was this? Not Impressionism, not Neo-Impressionism, not Classical, not Cubist, not post-anything in particular. Just light and color and the suggestion of a carriage house. He was a good draftsman, but there was nothing representational here. Color. Just color.

He was considering whether to frame it or trash it when there was a knock at the door.

"Entrez," he said.

Mme Goldman sailed in, almost literally as her dress billowed behind her. This was a silk affair, almost gossamer, like the flowing gowns of the women depicted in the entablature over the carriage door. A gold necklace with a pendant featuring a large emerald was suspended beneath it.

"Tony!" she said. "It's six o'clock. My guests are already arriving. Are you—oh, my goodness!" She stopped and stared at the painting. "It's...it's—"

"Strange?" Tony said with an ironic smile. "Bizarre? Nothing like a carriage house with a dying sun splashing indirect light on its façade?"

Mme Goldman stared a moment longer. "It's magnificent! And you did it in two hours!"

"An hour and a half, actually. Do you really like it?"

"Oh, yes!" She approached the painting to examine it more closely. Then she backed away several paces. "It's strange, though—in a good way. Up close it's just a jumble of color. Like someone knocked over buckets and mixed the paints all together. But from ten feet, it's lovely and somehow... inspiring."

"Inspiring? Well, that's high praise indeed. I only meant for the color to give a rather conventional garden scene a dash of verve, some *joie de vivre*."

"Oh, it does that. I think I'll ask my guests to come and look at it. You are coming to dinner, aren't you?"

"I don't suppose I can refuse. Can I come like this?" Tony looked down at his smock which was splattered with paint. "I mean without the smock. The shirt underneath is decent enough."

Mme Goldman came over to him and lifted the smock. "I suppose it's all right. But you need a cravate. They're several in the cupboard in your room."

"I'll need to wash up first."

She went to the door. "And Tony—we need to do something about your name."

"My name? What's wrong with my name?"

"Nothing really. But as I mentioned before, an up-and-coming artist needs something more distinctive."

"Like…Antonio?"

"Yes. It has panache, brio!"

"Well…all right. In tribute to my father."

"I'm sure he'd be pleased." She left the room.

Tony chuckled as he thought about this upgrade to his name. He approached the painting, examined it once more, picked up a brush that had been dipped in black paint earlier, and with a sweeping gesture signed the painting, 'Antonio.'

CHAPTER 10

Over the next six weeks, Tony did some of his most productive work. He created more than twenty paintings, nearly all of which went to Monsieur Dantec's gallery, and half were already sold. He continued to send Jackie money, gathering from her letters that she was struggling with her career in London. Despite her connections through her mother, she was often deemed too old or too young, or too American, to land the plum roles.

Why did she stick it out? It wasn't necessary. And Christmas was almost upon them. He fully expected to be with her for Christmas, but they couldn't agree on which city. London or Paris? Tony finally agreed that he would come to London. Part of this was because it was easier for a man to travel than for a woman, with all of her dresses and portmanteaus and steamer trunks, and partly because of Tony's ambivalence about Jackie's reaction to his 'arrangement' with Mme Goldman. There were, in fact, times when he felt Mme Goldman's hints and overtures and allusions to sex were more than simply banter or teasing. She did, however, have a retinue of 'escorts' who accompanied her to dinner parties, or the opera, or grand openings of exhibitions. But her escorts never stayed overnight, except for once when a dinner guest fell on the stairs to the garden and broke his arm. A doctor came the next day, set his arm, and the gentleman left, never to be seen again.

Tony arrived at Victoria Station on a snowy afternoon a few days before Christmas. Jackie waited on the platform for him along with Johnston Forbes-Robertson, who had offered his services as a chauffeur. Tony had no idea who this man was or why he was in the company of his wife. Jackie simply introduced him as a friend of her mother's without further explanation.

As they exited the station, Forbes-Robertson took his valise–Tony's only piece of luggage–and trundled it into his motorcar. This was the first time Tony had ever ridden in one of the new contraptions.

Though it was only a short trip to Lucinda's house on Eaton Place, Tony was a bit apprehensive. There were numerous other automobiles in the streets, competing for space with each other, as well as with horse-driven trams and carriages. Forbes-Robertson seemed to delight in squeezing the rubber bulb mounted next to the windscreen, emitting a loud honk that startled the horses as well as their drivers.

Lucinda greeted them at the door and ushered them into the drawing room, leaving Alastair to carry Tony's valise upstairs to Jackie's bedroom.

They all sat down to tea.

"It's so good to see you again, Tony," Lucinda said. "I understand your paintings are taking Paris by storm."

Tony chuckled. "Hardly by storm, Lucinda. But they are selling well, it seems."

"I say, Tony, old man—I may call you Tony, I presume."

"Of course."

"I read in the *Herald* that you are the most promising young talent among Negro artists in Paris."

Tony frowned. "I'm not really acquainted with other Negro artists, Mr. Forbes-Robertson. Sad to say, there aren't many of us."

Forbes-Robertson suddenly seemed to realize that he had made a blunder and reddened. "I don't mean to imply that your achievements are in any way diminished by the lack of competition in your, ah…"

"Tony is only one-sixteenth Negro, Johnny." Lucinda said. "Though, unfortunately, people tend to judge him by the shading of his skin. Would you want to be praised as the best actor in England above six feet in height?"

Forbes-Robertson blushed an even deeper red. "Of course not." He turned to Tony. "I apologize, Mr. Jones, if I expressed myself in an awkward fashion. Certainly race is of no account in the field of art. I have dabbled in painting myself and one particularly contemptible critic offered that my work in that area was very fine—for an actor."

Even Tony laughed at this remark, and he was much more inclined to reserve judgement on Forbes-Robertson's views on race.

Later that night, after a light supper, Lucinda and Jackie entertained Tony with piano duets and songs from Gilbert and Sullivan, concluding with "Silent Night." Lucinda announced that actors from her latest production, Dickens' 'A Christmas Carol,' would be joining them for punch and eggnog on Christmas Eve.

Tony and Jackie retired to the bedroom.

"I've missed you," Jackie said, while in Tony's embrace.

"I've missed you, too." Tony looked into her eyes, which were moist with tears. He wasn't sure whether they were tears of joy or regret. "You seem to have adapted quite well to Lucinda's very busy social life."

"Adapted? I don't know that I have. Her social and business life are indistinguishable. Actors come and go, stage designers, costume designers, theatrical critics–it never stops."

"Well, at least it keeps her busy. And you? It seems that with your mother's connections…"

"Oh, she can't guarantee me any roles–not good ones, at least. I'll be playing a small part in this Christmas production of hers, but the plum roles are going to people like Mrs. Pat–"

"Mrs. Pat?"

"Mrs. Patrick Campbell."

"Oh, I've heard of her."

"Of course you have. Everybody has. Between her and Ellen Terry, they dominate the English stage. Mrs. Terry, like Sarah Bernhardt, is getting a bit on in years, but still plays younger women and no one seems to notice–or care. I'm relegated to the serving girls and the evil stepsister."

Tony laughed.

"Tony–"

"I don't mean to laugh–it's just that I can't see you as the evil stepsister. Though it might be an interesting challenge."

"Then you can come see me in *Cinderella* next week. It's another one of Lucinda's productions."

Jackie sat down on the bed, looking forlorn.

Tony sat down beside her and put his arm around her. "Jackie–come back to Paris with me. In spite of your mother's influence here, as you say, she can't guarantee you good roles. Besides, my paintings are selling. We can live quite comfortably on my income alone. Mme Goldman has provided me with a beautiful studio and a–"

"Mme Goldman? Who is she?"

"I didn't tell you in my letters? I thought I did."

Jackie turned towards him, so that his arm slipped from her shoulder. "No. You didn't. Who is Madame Goldman?"

"Well…she's my patron…sort of."

"She's married?"

"Um…no. Well, she is, but her husband's in California."

"And she provides you with a studio? She pays your rent?"

"No, I pay her rent. It's a carriage house converted into a studio–overlooking a garden. Now don't jump to conclusions."

Jackie folded her arms over her chest. "And you still live with Nat?"

"No...I live in the house."

"What house?"

"Madam Goldman's. The rent includes a bedroom in the house. Quite a large house. And Mme Goldman knows all about you. She's asked me to bring you back to Paris so that we can be together."

Jackie sighed. "How old is this Madame Goldman?"

"I don't know. About 35 or 40, I suppose."

"Not that much older than we are. Is she attractive?"

Now it was Tony's turn to sigh. "Attractive? I guess you could say that. But she has friends–gentlemen friends. And she seems most interested in promoting young artists like me."

"So are there other 'young artists' living there as well?"

"Not yet. But I'm sure that–"

Jackie jumped up from the bed. "Tony, can't you see? She wants to be your lover!"

Tony rose from the bed. "Now you're jumping to conclusions again. If she wants to be my lover, why would she encourage me to encourage you to come live with us?"

"Us. 'Us,' you say. A *ménage à trois*. That's the French for you. They see nothing improper about two women sharing the same man."

Tony began loosening his cravate. "She's not French. And you're blowing this all out of proportion. There will be no ménage à trois. She's not interested in me in that way, and if she was, I don't think she'd care for a ménage à trois any more than you would."

Jackie stared at the cravate that Tony had just flung onto the bed. "Is that a new tie? I've never seen it before."

Tony looked at the cravate. "No, Well, yes. I found it in the–"

"She gave it to you, didn't she!"

Tony grasped her by the shoulders. "Calm down, Jackie. I've never seen you like this. It must be the stress and frustration of not landing the roles you–"

Jackie burst into tears. "It's not stress! And I don't care about these silly acting roles. It's you I care about, and now you–"

He put his arms around her and pulled her gently to his chest. "Jackie–it's *you* I care about. I have a business relationship with Madam Goldman, nothing more. And this tie–it was one of a dozen in the room she assigned to me."

Jackie sat in silence for a moment or two. "What would I do if I came to live with you and Mme Goldman? Watch you paint? Help plan her dinner parties?"

"You could do as you like. I still think that if you improve your French–"

"My French is schoolgirl French and it's likely to remain so. I can't say anything beyond 'Bonjour,' and 'Comment allez-vous.' And when the French respond, it's too fast for me."

"It's just a matter of time. And practice. I had the same problems at first."

She pouted like a child as another tear rolled down her cheek. "You're smarter than I am. I always knew that. You learn quickly. You do everything fast. I don't know if I can keep up."

He put his hand on her cheek and brushed away the tear. "You don't have to keep up with me. We're not in a race, you know. I just want you to be with me."

She sniffled and looked at him intently. "Do you mean that?"

"Of course I do."

"I can't leave England for a while. I've committed to a tour in February. It doesn't pay much, but–"

"'February? That's two months from now. How long is the tour?"

"Six weeks."

"Then...it will be spring before you come to Paris. Can't you get out of it? After all, you said you'll be playing bit roles–"

"No. I'll be playing Desdemona in *Othello*. It's the one good role that I've been offered. I can't turn it down."

Tony sighed in resignation. "Then I guess we'll have to carry on our marriage through the post."

She managed a smile. "But you're here now..."

"And you can come to visit me in January–if your busy schedule permits."

She leaned forward and kissed him gently on the lips. "Yes. My schedule will permit."

CHAPTER 11

Tony remained in London over the holidays until shortly after New Year's Day. It was the last year of the century and everyone seemed ambivalent about the next. On the one hand, new technologies were emerging, like the telephone, electric lights, motorcars, and aircraft. On the other hand, war drums were being heard in South Africa, metaphorically speaking, since it was white Dutch farmers who were resisting British rule, not black Africans.

In France, the cause célèbre was the Dreyfus affair. Émile Zola's letter to the newspaper *L'Aurore*, accusing the French military of a cover-up, had been published in '98 and public clamor for a new trial of Dreyfus was demanded.

The Dreyfus Affair made Tony think of Mme Goldman. France was increasingly very divided into 'Dreyfusards' and 'anti-Dreyfusards.' In other words, pro-republican, anti-clerical Frenchmen and pro-Army, pro-Catholic anti-Semites. There had already been violent demonstrations in the streets of Marseille, Lyon, and Paris.

On the train to Paris, he read several articles about the 'Affaire,' and brought himself up to date regarding the shameless–and blatant–scapegoating of Dreyfus. It was clear that justice had miscarried, and it reminded him of the Jim Crow South. He had been lucky–an almost comical band of Klu Klux Klansmen attempted to string him up at a railroad station but had been thwarted by a posse sent out to rescue him. Dreyfus, on the other hand, had spent the past five years on Devil's Island, somewhere off the coast of South America. He could only speculate about what tortures he endured there.

Madame Goldman was, no doubt, Jewish. But she had made no references to the fact, nor did she seem to observe the Sabbath or other Jewish rituals. In fact, he knew little about her even after living for six weeks in her house. A child had died, her husband was a wealthy industrialist; she had fled

San Francisco, a city barely fifty years old and built on gold mining and banking. Perhaps she simply came for the same reason he and so many other Americans did—the 1,000-year-old culture, the vibrant arts scene, the *élégance*, the *joie de vivre* and—to escape.

These were the thoughts that he turned over in his mind as the train pulled into the Gare du Nord. As in London, the pavements were covered in snow. Paris had a wedding-cake appearance in this condition, in sharp contrast to London, where snow made the massive neo-classical buildings appear to be frozen mausoleums, a constant reminder of one's own mortality.

He thought first of going to Rue de Fleurus to see if Nat might pay him some of the money he owed him. On second thought, however, he considered this to be unlikely, and besides, he was through with refereeing the fights between him and Marie-Louise. It occurred to him that they actually enjoyed these battles, that there was something erotic about it, and that they would become bored with one another without them.

Instead, he directed the cabman to Rue de Furstemberg, where he encountered a half a dozen boys—around ten or twelve—throwing eggs against the windows of Mme Goldman's house.

"Dreyfusard! Juive!" They shouted, as they hurled their missiles.

Tony could see through one of the lighted windows—it was already growing dark—Jean-Pierre peering out and drawing back every time a volley came his way.

He got out of the cab and paid the cabman, who was apparently eager to turn his cab around and make his escape.

"Allez donc!" Tony shouted.

"Trouble-fête!"The boys shouted. "Nègre marron!" Nevertheless, they scattered.

He went to the door and knocked. Shortly thereafter, Jean-Pierre opened the door and, looking a bit shaken, admitted him. Tony asked about the whereabouts of Mme Goldman.

"Elle est en haut," Jean-Pierre said.

Tony followed the diminutive servant—he had become accustomed to calling him 'Le Petit J-P'—up the stone steps where he was met by Mme Goldman. She had been wringing her hands, but when she saw Tony, she threw her arms around him.

"Oh, Tony! I'm so glad you've come. I've felt absolutely under siege for the past week."

Tony patted her on the shoulder and disengaged himself. "What's caused all this? Dreyfus?"

"Of course. Won't you sit down? Jean-Pierre will take your valise upstairs. Goodness! You certainly travel light. Are you hungry?"

"Not particularly. But a glass of wine would be nice."

Eugénie appeared, and Mme Goldman asked her to bring some wine and hors d'oeuvres. She sat down on the sofa next to Tony.

"I don't blame the children," she said. "They only sit at their parents' table and listen to their anti-Semitic ravings without understanding."

"It's the same with white children in the South," Tony said. "And once the idea of racial superiority is planted in their minds, it's difficult to dislodge it."

"Exactly. My husband grew up in Alabama and though his best friend was a black boy, he can't be dissuaded from the notion that black people are an inferior species and must be kept in their place."

"Alabama? How did he make his way to San Francisco?"

"The gold rush. But he gave up mining for gold after a few weeks when he realized that there was more money to be made in selling supplies to miners than digging for gold himself."

Tony chuckled. "A smart man. And so he built a business of it?"

"Quite a successful business. At first, just mining equipment and comestibles. Later, he purchased gold fields from others that were deemed to be mined out. They weren't. Only better digging equipment was needed, which he had a patent on. Finally, he moved to San Francisco and founded a bank."

Eugénie arrived with the hors d'oeuvres and poured some wine into their glasses.

Tony felt that he had at last opened one of the doors to Mme Goldman's past life. But the next question was the hardest to get out of his mouth. "Why did you leave San Francisco?"

Mme Goldman ignored her wine and looked out the window into the snowy night. "When Willy died, Bill blamed me. He said I had neglected the child, which wasn't true. We had a nanny, but I took Willy with me to art galleries, the opera, even horse races. Bill was the one who was always absent."

"He simply shifted the blame because he couldn't accept his own sense of guilt."

"Exactly. But it was more than that. He frequented bordellos in San Francisco. I told him I would no longer put up with it and he struck me. That was the last straw."

Tony took a sip of his wine and put the glass down on the coffee table.

"So you left."

"Indeed I did. In the middle of the night while he was sleeping. I brought the clothes on my back and nothing else."

"Nothing else?"

She smiled. "Well...my check book. I wasn't stupid. I had convinced him earlier to put the bank stock in my name in order to protect him from lawsuits, of which there were many. He was constantly getting into fights with creditors and debtors alike. He could be quite violent."

"So then...you control the bank?"

"I am Chairman of the Board. Bill still owns the gold fields and the mining equipment company, but he has no position at the bank. In fact, he is in debt to the bank. My lawyers are in the process now of recovering the money that he owes."

Tony looked at Mme Goldman as if she were a formidable engine of capitalism. Which indeed she was. "Is Mr. Goldman also Jewish?"

She laughed. "Of course he is. With a name like that, how could he not be? But he's Southern Jewish–an altogether different kind of animal. And incidentally, I'm not Jewish. Except by marriage. My parents were Lutherans from Minnesota. But, Tony, dear, now that I've revealed all of my family secrets, you must tell me about yours. First of all, how did you become so well educated?"

Tony had been asked this question before and generally considered it to be racist and condescending. But he knew that Mme Goldman intended it to be neither. "My mother was a teacher and the daughter of a newspaper editor from Connecticut. My father was an army officer and the son of an escaped slave, but his mother was much more than that. She made her way to New York City and became a famous actress. She also helped other slaves escape the South via the Underground Railroad. I was very lucky–I got a rigorous education at my mother's school and was one of the first blacks to be admitted to Harvard University. Unfortunately, Harvard did not suit me and I dropped out my junior year to pursue my first love–painting."

Mme Goldman seemed to look at him in a new way. "My, you have a much more interesting background than I imagined." She picked up her wine glass and took a sip. "The Underground Railroad? I've heard of it. Is it actually a railroad?"

Tony laughed. "Only metaphorically. It was a system of handing off escaped slaves from one 'station' to another until the slaves reached freedom. Only occasionally did it involve actual railroad cars. It was too dangerous."

"And your parents? Are they...?"

"My father died in the hurricane of '93 that devastated Beaufort. But my mother is still alive and well, thank you. And your parents?"

"My father was a sea captain."

"In Minnesota?"

She laughed. "No, no. He left the farm in Minnesota when he was fifteen to see the world. And he did–first as a cabin boy, then a first mate, then a captain. I only saw him about twice a year."

"And your mother? How did she cope with you and–"

"My siblings? Well, it was difficult. She worked at the Customs House in San Francisco for many years and later for an insurance company. She was very clever with numbers and eventually became the chief financial officer of the company. That led to the purchase of the *Pacific Wanderer*, my father's ship."

"She became your father's employer?"

"Indirectly. But I assure you that my father wore the pants in the family."

Tony was amused by this story. And he was beginning to feel very comfortable with this woman, who he felt an increasing bond to. "And you–did you go to work for the family business?"

"I did. Like my mother, I was clever with numbers. I eventually took over her job. But when my father was lost at sea, she became very despondent and lost all interest in the business. She and her co-owner sold it, and about that time, I met Bill."

"And one thing led to another."

"Yes. Doesn't it always happen that way?" She took another sip of her wine and put the glass down on the table. "Well, now that we've put each other's history under the microscope, I should bring you up to date on your current prospects."

"Prospects?"

"Prospects. A member of the Arts Committee for the Exposition Universelle was snooping around Monsieur Dantec's gallery last week and asked whether you might be interested in submitting a few of your paintings to the Committee."

Tony's eyebrows arched high. "Would I be interested? Are you teasing me?"

"Not in the least. He was very impressed with your work."

"Well, then...of course I'm interested. Where do I sign?"

Mme Goldman laughed. "You don't have to sign anything. They'll give you a receipt for the paintings when they pick them up." She rose from the sofa. "Dinner will be ready at seven, as usual."

Tony rose as well. "Any other guests?"

"Only Baron de Rothstein and his wife."

"De Rothstein? *Baron* de Rothstein?"

"The same. You'll find him quite charming–and an enthusiastic aficionado of the arts. As a matter of fact, he was in Monsieur Dantec's gallery recently and bought one of your paintings. And, oh! I must remind Jean-Pierre to clean that mess off the windows before they arrive. Excuse me."

She dashed off to the kitchen.

Tony retired to his room, where he observed egg yolks dripping down the windowpanes. He wondered if J-P had access to a ladder so he could clean them. Well, he could simply open the windows from the inside.

He felt a bit tired and lay down on the bed. Mme Goldman was a fascinating woman. Beautiful, brilliant, and apparently unflappable. A sea captain's daughter. A violent husband. A dead child. She had endured much, despite her wealth.

He thought of Jackie, who had known nothing but wealth and ease all her life. Material hardship was as foreign to her as Chateaubriand to a cat. She had her own kind of strength, however. A certain moral rectitude. He wondered at the kind of women he was attracted to. Strong, beautiful and white. Why not black? He remembered Violet back in Beaufort. She was black, and like him, educated at the Penn School and went on to college. A bright girl. And pretty, if not beautiful. But if he had married Violet, he probably never would have left South Carolina. They probably both would have become teachers, though not at a white school. Their lives would have been insular, their opportunities limited...No–Jackie was his proper mate, his kindred spirit. They both had early experience abroad, both interested in the arts. And he was on the verge of being able to support her in the manner to which she had become accustomed. But was that a condition of their marriage? She seemed unwilling to join him in Paris until he had established himself.

He fell asleep for he knew not how long but was awakened by a squeaking sound. He looked up to see the smiling face of J-P, perched at the top of a ladder, cleaning the eggs off the windows.

CHAPTER 12

The Exposition Universelle would not open until April of 1900. In the meantime, architects, contractors, decorators, brick layers, carpenters, stone masons, engineers, and excavators were working furiously to meet deadlines. As were artists, sculptors and vendors of everything from automobiles to stereoscopes who planned to exhibit their wares in the structures being prepared for them.

Four of Tony's paintings were accepted by the Committee. He had hoped for all six that he had submitted, but the last two–both garden scenes–were rejected as being 'redundant.' By which Tony supposed the Committee meant they were too much like other garden scenes in his 'oeuvre.' He pointed out that these scenes were a series of studies that experimented with the effects of light on Mme Goldman's garden at different times and different seasons, much like Monet's series of haystacks. The representative of the Committee that was in charge of the packing had abruptly told him, "Monsieur, vous n'êtes pas Monet."

Ok, so he wasn't Monet, who was sixty now and the leader of the Impressionist movement. But Impressionism was getting a little tired, and there were new ideas about painting, new ways to paint, new ways of seeing.

It was still January, and Paris was laboring under a heavy mantle of snow. Tony stopped one afternoon on his way back from Monsieur Dantec's gallery and watched the workers digging the trench that would become the first metro line to open in time for the Exposition. They were bundled up in wool jackets and leather caps that did nothing to protect them from falling rock. Their faces were begrimed with soot and grease and dust so that they looked like coal miners–or black people. He was grateful that he was not one of them. The noise from steam-driven hammers was deafening. Subject for a painting? Possibly, but how long could he stand in the cold at his easel and would his paints freeze? And would he be arrested for obstructing traffic?

Approaching the door of the house, he noticed a crumpled figure squatting in the alcove of the entrance, wrapped in a tattered overcoat and a wool muffler. The man's face was barely visible but somehow looked familiar. As he paused for a moment to decide whether to shoo the man away or prepare for a struggle, the figure stood and brushed off the snow that had settled on his shoulders. "Tony!"

It was Nat. His nose was red, not from the cold but from drinking. "I've been waiting in this damn cold for an hour. The footman said he mustn't let anyone in the house without permission of Madame Goldfarb, or whatever her name is, and she wasn't in. But no matter–this is nothing compared to a New England winter."

"I'll knock and bring J-P down to let us in."

"You don't have a key?"

"No. Madame Goldman is very careful about security. But J-P is always here." He raised the iron knocker.

"No, no! I don't want to see that little bugger again. He's rather snooty. But Tony, old man, I need to ask you a favor and I'll be on my way."

"A favor? What kind of favor?"

"Well...I'm a little hard up. Can you lend me five hundred francs?"

"Five hundred francs? You still haven't paid me the five hundred you owe me from the sale of my paintings."

"I know, old man, but things have changed. Marie-Louise has left me and I can't seem to find any buyers for my work. Oh, I've sold a couple of sketches to the tourists at Notre-Dame. But it's not enough."

"Well...what happens when the five hundred runs out?"

"I'll have a cheque from the old man by then. A big one. He wants me to come home."

"He's wanted you to come home for the last two years."

"True. But this time he's including the money for the passage. I can pay you out of that."

"The passage? You won't have enough left for the passage."

"Well...actually, I won't be going home. I can't face the old man, going to work for him, enduring the condescending looks and the sniggers from the other employees behind my back. They all think I'm the prodigal son."

Tony sighed and pulled out his wallet. "Here's the five hundred, Nat. But this has to stop somewhere. Why don't you submit a painting or two to Monsieur Dantec?"

Nat tucked the money into his coat pocket. "Dantec? He insulted me the last time I talked to him. And I won't be insulted!"

"Then you need to approach some other dealers. Or go back to the Julian—it's a good place to make contacts."

"Good idea. I haven't been there for a while." Nat looked up at the facade of the house. "Speaking of contacts, you've got a pretty good one here. This Madame Goldfarb—"

"Goldman."

"Goldman. What's her angle? Do you have to bang her once a week for the—"

"She's a very distinguished patron of the arts, Nat. She happened to take a liking to my work and offered to promote it."

Nat raised an eyebrow. "Did she? And she wants nothing in return?"

"A percentage. She's my manager."

Nat whistled shrilly. "That's a tidy arrangement, old man. But you'd better look to your manhood."

"My manhood?"

"She wants to make you her pet. Like that footman who answered the door. Before you know it, she'll be dressing you like him, too." He chuckled and looked Tony up and down. "A nice little uniform—velvet waistcoat and gold buttons. Like a monkey—"

"You'd better leave, Nat."

"Oh, I didn't mean it that way. I meant a monkey in a general sense, like—"

"Goodbye, Nat."

"Um, okay. Goodbye, old man. And don't worry—I'll pay you back in spades...I mean extra—"

"I know what you mean."

"Right. Goodbye."

Tony watched Nat trudge through the snow towards St-Germain, pulling the wad of francs out of his coat pocket to count them as he did so. He wondered what was to become of him.

J-P came to the door and let him in.

"Bonsoir J-P. Où est Madame Goldman?"

"Elle est en haut," J-P said. "Elle vous attend."

"She's waiting for me?" Tony knew that J-P understood English but was reluctant to speak it, like so many Frenchmen who feared that they would be ridiculed for their accent.

Tony followed him up the stairs and found Mme Goldman sitting in a familiar place on the sofa.

"How did it go?" She said.

"The paintings? They took four, rejected the other two."

"It's bitter cold outside." She patted the cushion beside her. "Come and sit down. Who was that man waiting for you?"

Tony handed his coat to J-P and sat down. "That was Nat, my former roommate."

"What did he want?"

"Money."

"And did you give it to him?"

"Of course. He's hard up."

She smiled. "You're a soft touch."

"Maybe I am. But he's desperate and I'm doing all right."

"You're doing quite well, I'd say. Did I tell you that the baron would like to employ your services?"

"You said he was thinking of putting some artwork on his wine bottles."

"Well, he's thought about it, and now he's decided he wants you to design the label for the '99 vintage."

"Does he? What does he have in mind?"

"He'll leave that to you."

Tony leaned back against the backrest and closed his eyes for a moment.

"Tired?"

"A little." He opened his eyes and looked at her. She had leaned her head against the backrest only inches from his and smiled at him the way Jackie did sometimes in the morning after lovemaking.

"You don't have to accept the baron's offer, you know. It will be a small commission and it's a little bit out of your line. But it could be terrific for 'la publicité.'"

"I suppose so. He must sell thousands of bottles all over France."

"All over the world, actually. Can I tell him you'll accept?"

"By all means. But Amelia, I'd like to get back to my real work."

"Of course. Your garden scenes have created a sensation—"

"But it's winter now and I've just about exhausted the possible variations. I need to get back to human subjects."

"Female nudes?"

"Yes, and male, too. I'm not biased, you know."

She laughed. "No, I'd say you're the least biased person I know. Should I hire models?"

"I don't know that you need to hire them. But of course they'd have to be paid. What about Eugénie? Or Sabine?"

Amelia frowned. "I don't think they'd be suitable. For one thing, they're both very shy, and they would be mortified if I were to walk into your studio to see them—either of them—in the nude. No. I think you need to look elsewhere."

"All right. Where?"

Her frown turned into an enigmatic smile.

Tony cleared his throat. "Well, you've offered before, but I didn't think that you were serious."

"I'm very serious. And I'm vain enough to think I would be a good subject."

"Of course you'd be a good subject. A beautiful subject. But you might not find my method of dealing with your figure very flattering."

"You mean you might break it up into cubes?"

"Possibly. Or I might present you as a kind of voluptuous vampire."

She laughed. "I think I'd like that better. But Tony, dear, I want you to do whatever you want. It doesn't matter to me how you render this frail vessel. It's up to you. And I would never object to being portrayed as a shrieking Harpy flying off into a Walpurgis night."

Tony found this proposal to be intriguing. Indeed, he could see Mme Goldman as either a Harpy or an angel soaring into the heavens. Or just an ordinary, beautiful, sensuous woman of fine sensibilities and intellect. "All right. When do we get started?"

"Tomorrow."

"Tomorrow? What about the baron's wine labels?"

"The baron can wait. He doesn't even start bottling until the spring."

"Well then—nine o'clock? The light will be at its best then."

It was the first time Tony had seen Mme Goldman blush.

CHAPTER 13

Jackie was a bit intimidated by Johnston Forbes-Robertson. After all, he was widely considered the best actor of his generation. He had mesmerized audiences with his Hamlet, and more lately, with his Caesar, that is, Shaw's Caesar. And now he was cast as Othello to Jackie's Desdemona.

During rehearsals, Jackie paid more attention to what Forbes-Robertson was doing than to her own role. He had a gaunt, expressive face that seemed endlessly mobile. His slender figure stormed across the stage as he gave orders to his soldiers or made love to Desdemona. His black-face makeup seemed as if it had been stenciled into his skin with sharp needles that gave him the aura of a tormented animal.

Though she was never afraid of Tony, and had initially considered Forbes-Robertson a mild-mannered, even timid Englishman, she found herself terrified at his rages to the point that she feared he might indeed strangle her at the end of the play.

"That's typical of English actors," Lucinda said, after Jackie expressed her concerns. "They live for the characters they inhabit, and offstage they are merely a shell of themselves. But Johnny is a man, after all, and he's constantly on the prowl for a suitable mate. Unfortunately, he has apparently decided that I am unsuitable—too old. But you, my dear, are squarely in his sights."

"Me?" Jackie put down her teacup with a clatter. "But I'm married."

"It matters little to him. Mrs. Pat is married. And your husband, like Mrs. Pat's, is living abroad. He sees a clear path for himself."

"Oh! What am I to do?"

Lucinda laughed. "Absolutely nothing, my dear. So long as you don't encourage him, he will soon lose interest and pursue another. He will not engage in violence like Othello, I assure you."

Jackie considered this assessment of the male of the species and trusted in her mother's judgment. After all, Lucinda had had many men in her life, including married ones, and she always emerged with her dignity–and her fortune–intact. "Whatever happened to the prince?"

"Bertie? Nothing, actually. He's still the playboy he always was, waiting for his mother to kick the bucket so he can assume the throne."

"'Kick the bucket.' Really, Mother, he can't be so callous as to hope she dies."

"He can too be so callous. Do you know he's the longest tenured Prince of Wales in the history of the monarchy? His mother has reigned now for more than sixty years and he's grown tired of being regarded as an errant child. Though he is that in many respects."

Jackie suppressed a giggle at this remark. "Do you still see him?"

"Oh, Jacqueline–how naïve you are about men. He grew tired of me even before we landed at Cowes and has had a string of mistresses since. I did encounter him last year at the Court Theatre–a Sheridan play I think it was–and he was cordial enough, but I do believe he had forgotten my name."

"How sad."

"Not really. I enjoyed my time with him and don't regret a moment of it. Speaking of the Royals, I'm invited to Lady Gregory's for tea. Would you care to come along?"

"Lady Gregory? Who's she?"

"Well, she's not really royalty, at least not English royalty. She's Irish. But she has something of a literary reputation and founded a theatre company in Dublin. GBS speaks highly of her. She could be an important person to know."

"Important? Mother, I have no desire to go to Dublin."

"I do wish you would break that execrable habit of calling me 'Mother.'"

"'Sorry. Lucy."

"That's better. Now, regardless of your prejudices against the Irish–"

"I have no feelings about the Irish one way or the other."

"Nonsense. Everyone is prejudiced against the Irish. Even GBS, who is himself Irish, is prejudiced against the Irish."

"Why?"

"Because they are a savage people. However, there are exceptions, like GBS and Lady Gregory. And I suspect there are others."

"Mother–I mean Lucy–you've become more English than the English."

"I take that as a compliment. After all, I've spent much of my adult life here. Now, do you wish to accompany me to Lady Gregory's?"

"I suppose it would be amusing. Will Mr. Shaw be there?"

"I expect so."

"Then I will go."

CHAPTER 14

At precisely nine o'clock Paris time, Mme Goldman presented herself at the door of the studio wearing a blue and gold kimono. Tony had just laid out his brushes and was adjusting the level of his easel. She was striking in the pose, her black hair piled on top of her head and held in place by a pair of long needles with coral tips. She smiled almost as a young girl would, somewhat shy and embarrassed.

"Bonjour, Tony," she said.

"Bonjour, Amelia. You look absolutely lovely this morning. And the light is perfect. Let's get to work."

Amelia walked slowly and deliberately towards a divan that was positioned near the window and three or four meters from the easel. She untied the sash to her kimono and began to slip it from her shoulders.

"No, no," Tony said. "Keep the kimono on for now. I like the way the light plays off the gold embroidery. And remain standing."

Amelia looked surprised and relieved at the same time. "Standing? How long must I stand?"

"Until you get tired. And then you can sit."

"Well...all right."

Tony knew what she was going through. He had had many models, and they were often novices who needed to feel comfortable with him before removing their clothes. And Tony himself felt like a novice in this instance because Mme G was both his subject and his benefactress.

The key, he felt, to putting both of them at their ease was to talk.

"Tell me, Amelia," Tony said, as he began to sketch in charcoal, "how you came to land in Paris."

"Do you want me to just stand like this?"

"Just like that. No. Your left hand on your hip. Like that. Now, did you come directly to Paris?"

"No. First I went to Rome. I wanted to see the Uffizi—Michelangelo, especially. I thought I wanted to be a sculptor."

"Did you?" Tony sketched quickly, as usual, using a minimum of line, shading in place of detail. "My grandmother went to Rome with the same idea."

"Your grandmother? The escaped slave?"

"Yes, that one. Actually, she didn't really escape. Her father, also her owner, gave her a sum of money and let her go."

"Why would he do that?"

"It's a long story and I'm not sure of the details. According to my father, Cora–my grandmother–had been raped by her half-brother and her father had to let one of them go. And, of course, that had to be Cora since Randolph was his heir and Cora was merely a slave."

Amelia seemed to contemplate this and lose all sense that she was posing. Which was exactly what Tony intended.

"So how long did you stay in Rome?" he said.

"Rome? Oh–not long. I couldn't stand the dust and noise of the sculptor's workshop where I had apprenticed. Not to mention he was a tyrant to put my husband to shame. So I came to Paris."

"And you began to paint here?"

"Yes. As in Rome, I found an artist who was willing to take me on–for a price, of course."

"And what happened?"

"He encouraged me, actually. And I won a prize at a minor exhibition, but I could see that I would never be an artist of genius. What was the point, I thought, of pursuing mediocrity? And that was about the time I saw your paintings at Monsieur Dantec's."

Tony paused and stepped back to examine his sketch. "And you saw genius in my work?"

"Yes. Oh, Tony, can't you see it yourself? Monsieur Dantec sees it, the baron sees it–everyone but you sees it. Rembrandt, Monet, Renoir–they all knew they were geniuses from the start."

"I'm not so sure they did. I'm not sure anyone knows what genius is, and I'm not about to confer that honor on myself."

"Then why do you paint?"

Tony thought for a moment. "Because I must. You can relax now."

She dropped her arm from her hip and the sash loosened, thus exposing her left breast. But she seemed not to notice and came over to examine the sketch. "It hardly looks like me.'"

"It's a sketch. A model to work from. The finished product may not look like you, either. But it will be a thing of beauty. Do you have other kimonos?"

"Of course. A half a dozen."

"Then wear them all. A different one each day. I want to do them from every angle."

"You seem to be more interested in my clothing than me."

Tony looked at her and grinned. "Don't worry. It will be you who triumphs. Not the kimonos."

She looked at him in wonder for a moment, then broke into a tentative smile. "I trust you."

After the short break, Mme Goldman returned to her position in front of the window and again placed her left hand on her hip. She moved to tighten the sash.

"No. Leave it like that," Tony said. "If you are comfortable with it."

Mme Goldman dropped the sash.

Tony continued to paint. But now there was little conversation.

At noon, there was a knock at the door. Mme Goldman tightened the sash. "Entrez, s'il vous plaît."

It was Sabine. "Le déjeuner est prêt, Madame."

"Très bien, Sabine. Apporte-le."

"Là?"

"Oui."

"I'm not really hungry," Tony said.

"Nor I," Mme Goldman said.

"Well? Why are we stopping?"

"Sabine will bring our lunch and set it down. We can eat when we feel like it."

"You're not tired?"

"Not in the least."

Mme G went back to her pose and the sash fell away. Tony continued to paint.

There was again a knock at the door.

"Entrez."

Sabine entered with a tray of cheeses, fruit and grilled lamb kabobs. Also a carafe of wine with two glasses. She hesitated when she saw Mme G in her state of *déshabillé*, but then proceeded as if she had only spotted a mouse scampering across the floor and into a hole.

Tony noted a smile on Mme G's face that seemed to say, "It's my house and I'll dress any way I please."

Though both sitter and painter were intent on continuing their work, the aroma of the grilled lamb filled their nostrils and stimulated their appetites.

"We'd better not let it get cold," Tony said.

"No. That would be a pity."

He put his brush down and went to the table in front of the divan where Sabine had set the tray down. He removed the meat from its skewer and took a bite. "Excellent! Eugénie is a master chef."

Mme G tightened her sash and sat down on the divan, where she poured them both a glass of the baron's wine. "She's from Provence. I prefer their style of cooking."

Tony sat down beside her. "Tired?"

"I told you, not at all."

"Most models start complaining about now. 'Je suis fatiguée, Monsieur Jones. J'ai mal à la tête, au dos, au bras.'"

She laughed. "Then they weren't paying attention. I love to watch you work."

After their meal, accompanied by one glass of wine each, Mme G resumed her position in front of the window and Tony his at the easel.

"I think..." he said. "I think you should drop the kimono to your waist."

Mme G looked a little surprised. "Are my breasts so important?"

"Well, they're certainly important to you, and they're important to the viewer as well. But if you'd prefer not to—"

"No, no, of course. You're the artist. Whatever you say." She looked around. "Perhaps I should sit on the divan."

"Good idea. It'll give you some rest as well."

Tony worked for another two hours, intent upon his subject, oblivious to the time until he noticed the winter light fading.

He put his brushes down. "Well, I think that's enough for today, the light's gone. Are you exhausted?"

Receiving no answer, he looked to the divan. Mme G had fallen asleep. He went over to her and saw that her head was leaning on the backrest, her kimono settled around her hips, her mouth slightly open but no sound came from her lips.

She was a truly beautiful woman. Her breasts were full but not overly large, well-shaped with rose-colored nipples the size of silver dollars. Her neck was slender and swan-like, with a gentle curve that receded into her bobbed hair like a sinuous drainpipe. Drainpipe? A neck like a drainpipe? Well, there were some beautifully sculpted drainpipes in Paris, especially the new ones in the Art Nouveau style. Good Lord! What an unruly imagination he had. A neck like a drainpipe indeed!

"Oh…" her eyes opened. "I must have fallen asleep. I'm sorry."

"Don't be. I'm done for the day. You've been a perfect model."

She looked around for a moment as if she had fallen asleep in a stranger's house. Then she looked down at her bare torso and pulled the kimono up and covered her breasts. "May I see?"

"Of course."

She sat up, tightened the sash and rose from the divan.

Tony watched as she approached the painting.

"'It's…it's lovely. But is it me?"

"I told you you might not recognize yourself. Are you disappointed?"

"No, not at all. Do…do my breasts look like that to you? So large and …irregular."

"Symmetry is not one of my primary concerns. We live in an asymmetrical universe."

"Do we? So I should have asymmetrical breasts?"

Tony laughed. "You already do have asymmetrical breasts. Have you ever tried to measure them?"

"No, but now you've made me curious. Does a man have asymmetrical testicles?"

"Absolutely."

She stared at him skeptically for a moment, then burst out laughing. "Honestly, Tony, you are turning my world upside down."

"Glad to be of service."

She shook her head. Then she looked at the painting again. "I love the colors. I love the brushstrokes. But I don't know if I love *me*."

"I'm sorry to hear that. But if you're still game, I'll try again tomorrow."

She stepped away from the painting but continued to stare at it. "I'm game. You say I should wear a different kimono tomorrow?"

"The most colorful one you have."

"All right. Will you be accompanying me to the baron's soirée Friday night?

"His soirée? Am I invited?"

"Of course. Your name is on the invitation. He wants to show off the painting he purchased from you to his guests."

"Well, then, I suppose I'll have to attend. Where does he live?"

She laughed. "Where does he *not* live? He has a house here in Paris just off the Place de la Concorde. But this particular event will be at his château in la Forêt de Ferrières. About 25 kilometres east of the city."

"Will it be dressy?"

"Very. Do you have a cutaway with a waistcoat and white tie?"

"I've never had the occasion to wear one."

"No matter. I'll have the baron send his tailor to you. I'm sure with his influence the process can be expedited. Medals?"

"Medals? Well, I won one in an exhibition a few years ago."

"Wear it. All the men wear medals–even if they purchased them in a pawn shop."

"It's not a very big medal."

"At least it will be genuine. Now, I think I'll retire to my room and soak in the tub. You needn't be dressy for dinner tonight."

"That's a relief."

She smiled as if he had made a witty remark and left the room, her kimono trailing behind her, rustling along the highly polished wood floor.

CHAPTER 15

The tailor arrived the next day and took the appropriate measurements while Tony stood stock still, only moving his arms as instructed. Mme Goldman supervised the process, suggesting a tightening here, a loosening there, and finally a shortening of the trousers.

"À revers," she said of the trousers. "It's the fashion now."

The suit and its accessories were delivered the morning of the soirée and after a morning session in the studio, Tony and Mme Goldman dressed in their respective bedrooms and met in the drawing room.

"Lovely," Tony said, as Mme Goldman turned slowly to show off her *vêtements habillés.* She wore a Barège gown, saffron in color, with a deep *décolleté* and her hair twisted into a chignon at the nape of her neck. A single rose was pinned to the chignon, with what appeared to be glistening dew drops at the tips of the leaves, while a necklace of graduated pearls adorned her neck. A bit of powder concealed a strawberry birthmark that Tony had noticed–and painted–during their modeling sessions.

"Why cover it up?" he said.

"What?" She looked down at her left breast. "Oh–that. I've always thought it was rather ugly."

"Not at all." He approached her and raised his thumb to the mark. "I think it's charming. May I?"

She looked at him quizzically for a moment. "All right, if you think it's so charming."

"I do," he said, and removed the powder with a swipe of his thumb as if it were a dab of paint on a canvas. He stepped back to admire the entire tableau.

She laughed. "Do you ever stop painting?"

"In my mind–no."

After she complimented him on the fit of his new clothes, they went to the carriage house and descended the steps to the garden, which provided a

path to the ground floor. Tony had never been in this part of the building
and had only heard an occasional murmuring of voices and neighing of
horses. It turned out to be a combination stable and apartment containing
two bedrooms—one for the groom, Hasan, and his wife, Fatima. Tony
wasn't surprised to discover that these servants in charge of the horses were
North Africans, but he was surprised that J-P was their son, who occupied
the second bedroom. He often wondered where J-P disappeared to after
dinner, and now he knew. Eugénie had her own room on the ground floor,
and Sabine occupied one of the bedrooms adjacent to Mme Goldman. A
tidy and efficient household.

Hasan was about fifty by Tony's estimate, though he could have been
older. He was much taller than his son, with gray at the temples and a
piercing stare. Fatima was short and rotund, about the same height as her
son. J-P assisted with the harnesses, then climbed onto the driver's perch.
The carriage was a barouche with seating for up to four passengers. There
was a retractable hood to protect the two rear-most passengers in inclement
weather, and as it was snowing outside, the hood was up.

Hasan opened the doors of the carriage house, J-P cracked his whip,
and the two bay horses suddenly came to life, vapor from their nostrils
suspended in the air. They turned into an alley that debouched onto Rue
Jacob and then to Boulevard St-Germain. It was still light outside, though
everything seemed shrouded in a blue haze.

"How long does it take to get to the château?" Tony asked, shouting over
the din of hooves striking pavement.

"About two hours. Are you warm enough?"

"I'm quite comfortable. And you?"

"Likewise. It's beautiful out, is it not?"

"Yes. The light is particularly fascinating. I should take my easel up to
the roof sometime and paint there."

"The paints would freeze."

"Perhaps a new technique would be required. 'Peintre à glace.'"

In forty minutes they were in the country and the sun had gone down.
The road was well-paved for a few miles but when they turned off to the
chateau, it became a mixture of mud and snow. J-P stopped at one point
to light the lamps, though there were other carriages traveling in the same
direction that lit the way ahead of them.

Two gate houses flanked the gravel drive to the main house. These were
Baroque structures of brick and limestone with balustraded upper stories
surmounted by snow-covered cupolas. They looked as if they each could

house a small family.

The uniformed gatekeepers waved them through and onto the gravel drive that led to the château. Couchant marble lions flanked the drive about halfway to the house, and oak trees, denuded of their leaves, mingled with spruce along the outer perimeter of the estate.

J-P pulled the carriage in line with the others as they approached the entrance, which was ablaze with torches outside and electric lights within.

"This is his country house?" Tony said, peering out at the façade, which rose three stories and was flanked by two towers that added an additional story to each corner.

"One of them," Mme Goldman said. "Another in Bordeaux, one in Switzerland, and still another on the Côte d'Azur. You have to understand that his family has been in the banking business for nearly two hundred years."

"Yes. I suppose two hundred years is ample time to accumulate property. Maybe I should go back into the business in Beaufort."

She laughed. "Compound interest is a marvelous thing. But it does take time."

At last they were next in line.

"How many guests were invited?" Tony said, as they waited for the ladies in the carriage in front of them to disembark.

"About one hundred and fifty, I think. Some from abroad."

A liveried footman opened their door and extended a hand to Mme G. She stepped down and Tony followed. They were sheltered from the weather–it was beginning to snow again–by the portico, and ascended a few steps to the front door, where the baron awaited them.

"Ah!" the baron said. "Ma petite Amélie!–you are stunning tonight. My word! You'll put the other ladies to shame!" The baron spoke flawless English. He kissed Mme G on both cheeks, then turned to Tony. "And Antonio!" He shook his hand vigorously. "The genius of Beaufort!" He pronounced 'Beaufort' as the French would, 'Bo-four.'

"Hardly a genius, sir," Tony said. "At least not in the world's estimation."

"Well, then," the baron said, "the world will just have to catch up." And he indicated the grand stairway, divided into two sweeping wings, that led to the first floor. A massive chandelier with pendants of cut glass illuminated by electric bulbs dominated the space between the stairways. Tony studied the frescoes in the ceiling, which seemed to be in imitation of Michelangelo or Da Vinci–imitations, perhaps, but exquisitely done.

He had visited Versailles once, but the baron's house, though huge, seemed to be on a more human scale and with a view to living with art rather than looking at it in passing, as in a museum.

At the top of the stairs were the requisite busts of Roman orators and more current luminaries such as Voltaire, and the curious placement of streetlamps that one might encounter on any Parisian boulevard.

The mezzanine opened onto a grand ballroom where most of the guests had assembled. Waiters circulated through the crowd, offering champagne and canapés.

"Do you know any of these people?" Tony asked Mme G.

"A few. You know, I'm really new to Paris, though I've met quite a number of people through Monsieur Dantec. When word got out that I was a collector, suddenly I was included on guest lists."

"Speaking of Monsieur Dantec, I don't see him anywhere."

"Apparently, he didn't make the cut. The baron only invites the rich and the talented to his parties."

"Is that Loïe Fuller over there? Surrounded by admirers?"

Mme G squinted at the young woman, who was wearing a pale green diaphanous gown with little underneath. "I don't know. Who is Loïe Fuller?"

"She's a dancer. Created a sensation not long ago at the Folies Bergère. She does something called the Serpentine Dance. Hailed as the leading spirit of Art Nouveau by the pundits and critics."

"Fuller? Is she French?"

"She's American. But the French seemed to have adopted her."

A waiter approached and they each took a glass of champagne. They moved cautiously through the crowd as if they might be bitten by a poisonous snake if they were not vigilant. At last Mme G encountered an acquaintance from the gallery. She introduced Tony, who was met with a stony reception.

They moved on.

"Who was that? I've already forgotten their names," Tony said.

"Vicomte and Vicomtesse de Koenigsbourg. He is a colonial administrator of some sort, French Guinea, I think. A strange man, but very rich and an avid collector."

"I get the feeling he doesn't care for black people."

"Quite possibly. Or he simply doesn't approve of the social intermingling of the races. I'm afraid he's not alone in that opinion."

"No. And I'm prepared for it, of course. But the baron seems to be oblivious to any such prejudices."

"He's a Jew. He knows what it's like to be snubbed, even by shopkeepers."

Tony chuckled. "I suppose he does."

As if conjured up by their conversation, the baron suddenly appeared at the double doors leading to another room. He announced that dinner would be served shortly and that the guests could seat themselves according to place names, which were arranged alphabetically rather than by rank. This created a minor stir among some of the guests, who seemed to think it highly improper. Nevertheless, they all began to file into the dining room, where tables had been set up in a U-shape, with the baron at the head. White linen covered the tables and candelabra were positioned every meter or so. Silver platters of delicacies like lobster and quail eggs were placed between the candelabra, and after they were seated, waiters filled the goblets with both red and white wine.

Tony scanned the diners on the other side of the 'U.' "My little exhibition medal seems puny compared to the silver crosses and gold medallions and red sashes of some of these gentlemen."

Mme G laughed. "Most of them never came within one hundred kilometres of the front lines during the last war. Medals were passed out to aristocrats and bankers like the baron for simply writing cheques. At least you earned yours."

Musicians seated in a gallery above the dining room played through the meal, mostly concertos by Mozart and Chopin. At the end of the meal, the baron clinked his glass with a spoon, again welcomed his guests, and apologized for the inclement weather that may have inconvenienced them. But to Tony's surprise–and embarrassment–he introduced Tony as a particularly talented young American artist who was bound someday to become a Chevalier de la Légion d'honneur. Tony stood and gave a little bow to polite applause. The baron then invited all to view a few of Tony's paintings in the adjacent gallery before moving on to the ballroom.

The dancing began with a traditional quadrille, which Tony was unfamiliar with. Mme G tried to show him the steps, but the sequence was complicated and he invariably found himself outside of the foursome to which they had been assigned, as if he had been an asteroid spun off from a larger, spinning planet. After a few turns around the floor, however, he seemed to get the hang of it.

Next came a waltz number, with which he was more familiar. But just as the orchestra was striking up the tune and he had taken Mme G by the waist, Vicomte de Koenigsbourg appeared and put his hand on his shoulder.

"I cannot allow this," the vicomte said, in English.

Tony paused and looked at him quizzically. "Allow what?"

"The dance is indecent enough, Monsieur, but to see a *nègre* put his hands on a white woman is intolerable."

As Tony stared at the vicomte in disbelief, another hand landed on his shoulder.

"Tony, old boy! How good to see you! I'm afraid I was delayed at la Gare du Nord due to the storm, but here I am. And who is this charming lady?"

"Your Grace," Tony said. He looked at Mme G. "May I present my good friend, Madame Amelia Goldman, of San Francisco. Amelia, His Royal Highness, the Prince of Wales."

"Enchanté," the prince said, raising Mme G's hand to his lips and kissing it. "By Jove, I regret that my itinerary in America did not include San Francisco. You must tell me about it."

By this time, the vicomte seemed to have been reduced in height by four or five inches and was looking for an exit but the prince would have none of it. He turned to him and said, "Monsieur, I am afraid I have not had the pleasure of making your acquaintance."

The vicomte bowed his head slightly. "Your Highness. I am Vicomte Jean-Louis Raynouard de Koenigsbourg."

"Koenigsbourg? I believe my great-great-grandfather vanquished your great-great-grandfather on the fields before the duke's castle." The prince laughed uproariously. "No, hard feelings, eh? The Bas-Rhin is no worse for it. Though your title has been diminished, I see." He turned to Mme G, who seemed amused. "I say, Tony old chap, would you permit me to have a turn with Madame Goldman? My wife is around here somewhere, but the last I saw of her, she was dancing with the baron."

Tony graciously assented, though he had no claim to Mme G, and she and the prince went twirling off among the other dancers. Tony and the vicomte were left standing awkwardly together, trying to avoid each other's gaze.

"Um, yes," the vicomte said. "I must be off."

The dancing continued until three in the morning, with only two breaks for refreshments. By four, most of the guests from abroad, like the prince, retired to their bedrooms while the locals mounted their carriages and returned to Paris or its environs.

The weather had cleared, and the stars were like bright jewels suspended against a felt cloth.

"How did you come to know the prince?" Mme G asked Tony.

"Well, it's a long story, but to make it short, when the prince visited America back in '96, he came to Beaufort along with his mistress at the time, my wife's mother."

"Your wife's mother? How strange. Is she English?"

"No, but at the time she was a resident of London. I told you it was a long story."

"Go on."

"It turned out that the prince was a keen hunter and he became a guest of the LeRoux at their estate near Beaufort."

"The LeRoux?"

"Jackie's adoptive parents."

"Oh."

"While there, and just as Jackie and I were about to get married, I was kidnapped by the local chapter of the Ku Klux Klan."

"My goodness! What did they do to you?"

"Well, aside from hogtying me and hustling me off to a railroad station in order to lynch me, very little. Thanks to the prince and the local sheriff, who happened to be black."

"What did the prince do?"

"He saved my life, actually." Tony chuckled. "One of the great ironies of my life. The heir apparent to the throne of the world's most powerful monarchy dedicated to the premise of white supremacy rescued me from certain death at the hands of a band of illiterate bigots. It helped that he was a crack shot."

Mme G laughed, tentatively, as she considered Tony's narrow escape. "How extraordinary! And he saved you again tonight."

"Yes, but under far less threatening circumstances. I hardly think the vicomte would have physically attacked me, and it would have been beneath his dignity to challenge a black man to a duel."

"No, but still, the prince punctured his balloon."

"And his sense of pride. That's enough revenge for me."

She leaned against his shoulder. "You're a good man, Tony."

"Let's not jump to conclusions. It's easier to make great art than it is to be a good man."

"I disagree. Men are born good, though they may stray from the narrow path later in life. But greatness in art is a mighty struggle."

Tony had no answer for this, because he had never thought about it. Was it possible to be a great artist and a *bad* man? Certainly it was possible to be a good man and a failed artist. Examples were legion. Was talent amoral?

Mme G fell asleep against his shoulder while he was contemplating this question. He was wide awake and anxious to see the dawn as they approached Paris.

CHAPTER 16

On the morning of the day that Jackie was to accompany her mother to Lady Gregory's tea, she fell violently ill. Headache, vomiting, and a general sense of weakness. She spent nearly an hour in the loo, and when she returned to her bed, her mother was at her side.

"What's the matter, Jacqueline?" Lucinda said. "A touch of the grippe?"

Jackie opened her eyes for a moment, tried to focus on her mother's face, and closed them again. "I don't know. Something I ate, I suppose."

"Poached salmon never made anyone sick. And the vegetables last night were fresh from Spain." She put her hand to Jackie's forehead. "No fever... Oh, my goodness! You're pregnant!"

"Pregnant? How could that be?"

"Have you had your period since Tony was here?"

"Well...no. I thought it was just one of those times that it was delayed or skipped altogether."

"Possibly. But I doubt it. I'll call Dr. Thurloe to verify. Meanwhile, you need some nourishment. Betty will bring you some soup."

"I don't feel like eating anything, Mother."

"You can be forgiven for calling me 'Mother' when you're sick. But please observe our agreement in front of the servants."

"All right." And she turned over to try to sleep.

Later that morning, Dr. Thurloe came and examined Jackie. He confirmed that she was pregnant.

By this time, however, she was feeling better and sat up in bed. "What am I to do?"

"Do?" Lucinda said. "Why, what all young mothers do–care for the child and ensure that it will be healthy."

"Of course. I will do everything I can for the child. But what about Tony? And what about Desdemona?"

"You must notify Tony at once. But Desdemona can wait. I can rotate another play into the repertory and save *Othello* for last. You can continue to rehearse in the meantime if you like, or if you don't feel up to it, I'll find another Desdemona."

"Perhaps you'd better do the latter. I don't see how Desdemona can waddle about the stage great with child."

Lucinda pursed her lips in deep thought. "Actually, it may add a bit of sympathy to the character. Othello strangles both mother and child. The monster! The audience would lap it up."

Jackie stared at her for a moment. "Honestly, Lucy, I think you'd better start looking for another Desdemona."

Lucinda sighed. "Let's not worry about that now. The first priority is Tony. He must know as soon as possible. A telegram is the quickest way."

"No. A telegram is too cryptic, too impersonal. It may even sound like an ultimatum. I'll write him a letter."

"All right. I'll leave it to you."

After luncheon, which consisted of another bowl of soup and some biscuits, Jackie asked Betty to bring her a lap desk with stationery, pen, and ink.

She sat with her back against a pillow, dipped the nib of the pen into the inkwell and began to write:

Dear Tony,
~~*I have the most wonderful news*~~
~~*I miss you terribly darling*~~
~~*Guess what?*~~

Dr. Thurloe, Mother's personal physician, has just informed me that I am pregnant.

I hope and pray that you will find this welcome news. I know that you are terribly busy and that you are preparing for the Exposition. But could you not visit me before then? The doctor says it's best for me not to travel or I would come to you. I believe my acting career is over.

Dear Tony, I so much want you to be with me. Please, let's arrange for your visit. The baby will not be due till late August or September, but I cannot wait til then to have you in my arms.

Could you not come in the spring? The weather will be fine then, and travel will not be difficult.

Your loving wife,
Jackie

She sealed the envelope, affixed the stamp and called for Betty to take it downstairs. When Betty was gone, she gazed out the window onto the bleak landscape against the background of a nearly white sky. Dead leaves swirled about in the wind and settled on the thin blanket of snow on the ground, which seemed to be melting. How was it in Paris?

She thought of Tony's 'arrangement' with Mme G. How was that working out? Tony said she was 'attractive.' What did that mean? A matronly woman of middle-age and dimpled cheeks? Or a real beauty, sloe-eyed and irresistible to men? She had no reason to suspect that Tony had ever been–or would ever be–unfaithful to her.

Her mother, however, had a more cynical view of men. In her eyes, men were vain creatures constantly on the prowl for sexual conquests. The prince, she said, with whom she had a torrid romance, even forgot her name after a few months!

But no, Tony was not like the prince. Nor was he like Mr. Forbes-Robertson or GBS, who pursued their objects of desire through letters. Letters! How queer. Tony was somehow between the two types–virile, but restrained and principled where women were concerned.

Wasn't he?

CHAPTER 17

Tony was churning out a painting a day at Mme G's studio. There were now five paintings of Mme G in various poses with the kimonos. By the sixth session, he decided that the kimono, colorful as it was, needed to take on a lesser role. It would be a backdrop to Mme G's curvaceous figure rather than the focus of interest.

Mme G did not seem to object to this total disrobing. She lay on the divan like Manet's *Olympia*, the only concession to modesty being the placement of her left hand over her pubic region. Tony decided that he didn't want a mere imitation of Manet's famous painting but thought some elements of it combined with elements of Goya's *La Maja desnuda* would produce a charming–and provocative–effect.

As he prepared his paints, he made his usual attempts to put Mme G at her ease, chatting about the weather and news of the day.

"I wonder, Amelia," Tony said, "Why you don't dispense with the bother and expense of keeping a carriage and horses and simply purchase an automobile."

"An automobile?" Mme G let her hand slip away to her thigh. "What on earth would I do with an automobile? They're noisy, unreliable, and always belching smoke and oil. Didn't you notice that one of the baron's friends stood in the freezing cold as we departed the soirée, cranking the motor over and over until he was positively drenched in perspiration? I've heard that men have had their arms broken exerting far less effort."

Tony laughed. "I've heard those stories, too. Perhaps we should wait until they invent a mechanism that starts the engine automatically."

"That won't be in our lifetimes. Where should I put my hands?"

Tony looked at the way she had positioned herself. Reclining on the divan, which was upholstered in a figured damask fabric, she had now shifted both hands to her pudendum. Her head rested against two or three pillows, which were of satin. She had the look of a Dutch housewife who had rebelled against the constraints of her bourgeois life but could not yet bring herself to abandon the modesty that had been bred into her since birth.

"Perhaps we should ask Sabine to bring us a carafe of wine," he said.

"Wine? Well, all right." She sat up and put her arms into the sleeves of her kimono and pressed the button on the wall that was wired to a bell in the pantry. "Now–can I see?"

"I have nothing to show you yet. I wonder if Sabine might like to pose with you."

"Sabine? With me? What do you mean?"

"I mean that she might add interest to the tableau if she were to present you with, say, a basket of flowers, or perfumes."

Mme G seemed to consider this. "Would she have to be naked like me?"

Tony laughed. "No. I hardly think we could convince her to do that. Besides, she's a servant, and would be posing as a servant. Would you be uncomfortable with her in the picture?"

"Well, no...after all, she dresses me and pours my bath in the evenings."

At that point, there was a knock on the door.

"Entrez," Mme G said.

Sabine appeared. "Vous m'avez appelée, Madame?"

"Oui," Mme G said. "Une carafe de vin rouge, s'il te plaît, et un panier."

"Un panier?"

"Oui. Un panier rempli de fleurs. Et des flacons de parfum."

"Parfum? Quel genre de parfum?"

"N'importe quel genre."

"Oui, Madame."

When Sabine was gone, Mme G turned to Tony. "Sometimes I think the girl has no sense. What kind of perfume, indeed!"

Tony laughed. "She has no idea of what we're up to."

"For that matter I don't either. What do you want her to do–sprinkle me with flower petals and spray my body with perfume?"

"No. She will simply offer them to you from her basket."

"Oh...Well, I think I *could* do with a glass of wine before we start."

Sabine brought the wine and the basket of flowers and perfume. She started to leave.

"Reste-là," Mme G said.

"Comment, Madame?"

"Monsieur Jones voudrait te peindre."

"Moi?"

"Oui."

Sabine looked more puzzled than ever, but was finally made to understand that she simply needed to pose with the basket at Mme G's side. She was invited to join them in a glass of wine but declined.

Mme G disrobed again and reclined on the divan. Tony gently positioned them both so as to achieve the desired effect. He went back to his easel.

As usual, he worked quickly. Sabine, a pretty girl, at first threatened to detract from Mme G's central role as a beautiful concubine in a seraglio, but he flattened her features somewhat with his palette knife. In fact, he liked this effect so much that he put down his brush and began using the palette knife exclusively.

To Tony, it was about color and exotica, not sex. He continued to work until Sabine asked for a break, not because she was tired, but because she felt she was falling behind in her household duties.

"Ça ira, Sabine," Tony said. "Merci pour votre aide. Allez-y."
Sabine put down her basket and left the room.

"The girl has little stamina," Mme G said.

"Oh, I think she's just conscientious. You would have scolded her if she hadn't finished her chores by the end of the day."

"Well...perhaps. Are you nearly finished?"

"Nearly."

Tony continued to work for another hour. Then he put his palette knife down and began to clean some brushes. "Would you care to take a look?"

Mme G rose from the divan and put her kimono on, though she didn't bother to tighten the sash. She had become accustomed to being naked in the presence of Tony and walked over to the easel with her silk *pantoufles* sliding along the polished floor. She folded her arms over her chest and examined the painting. "I like it."

"Really? You're not just patronizing me?"

She laughed. "Well, I am your patron, I suppose, but I do like it. Of course, it doesn't really look like me, which means it can be displayed in any salon without people speculating about our relationship."

Tony thought about this word, 'relationship.' He felt increasingly close to Mme G, and in spite of his professional detachment while working, now felt excited by the proximity of her nearly naked body. She put her arm around his waist, almost unconsciously it seemed, as if he were a child and she were intent upon encouraging him. "You have a flair for line and color. It seems to come effortlessly to you."

"It's not without effort, I assure you. It's a matter of letting go of my natural inhibitions and self-doubt."

She turned her eyes up to his. "I feel the same, in a way." She rose slightly on her toes and kissed him.

Tony was surprised at first but responded almost reflexively. He reached inside of her kimono and caressed her right breast, causing the nipple to become erect. Then he pulled his hand away. "I think we should maintain our professional relationship."

"So do I," she said. "But I don't see why...there can't be a parallel relationship. Work is work and play..."

Tony closed up his box of paints. "Yes. Work is work and I'd like to be able to continue in that vein. As for play...I must remind you that I am married."

"And so am I. But my husband is in San Francisco, and your wife is in London. And neither seems interested in coming to Paris. Are we to be celibate in this city of love?"

"I don't know, Amelia. I know nothing of your husband or his intentions, nor of your feelings about him. But I do know I love Jackie and she loves me."

"Then why doesn't she come to you? I would follow you to Timbuktu if you decided to go there, yet she won't cross the Channel to be with you that same afternoon. I suspect that her Southern upbringing has caught up with her."

"What do you mean?"

"That she has certain inbred prejudices that she once rebelled against but now that she finds herself in an environment that confirms those prejudices, and a highly sophisticated environment at that, she has second thoughts."

"That's enough, Amelia. You don't even know her."

Mme G closed the kimono around her waist and tightened the sash. "No, I don't know her. And I apologize for speculating about a person I know little about. But she's there and I'm here." She rose again onto her toes and kissed him.

He watched as she crossed the room and passed through the door to the landing. Then he looked again at the painting. It was true that no one would recognize her due to his liberal use of the palette knife. Broad swaths, or blocks, of paint. Her features were suggested more than defined. He liked this style of painting. It was an escape from reality but forced the viewer to think. But...think about what? Personality, character, the mystery of existence? Perhaps all three.

Amelia's intentions were clear. And as she said, she is here, while Jackie was in London and showed no sign of wanting to come to Paris. She really didn't like Paris. He really didn't like London. Could these two affinities be reconciled?

He looked at his watch. Two p.m. He would go out to a brasserie, have lunch, and perhaps buy a newspaper.

CHAPTER 18

The snow was melting on the sidewalks and the crisp, cool air was invigorating. The farmer's almanacs were predicting an early spring.

Tony stopped at a kiosk and purchased a copy of the *Paris Herald*. He liked to read the English language newspapers now and then, as they often had stories about life in the States that were ignored or overlooked by the French papers.

He decided to treat himself to a hot meal at an ancient watering hole patronized by the likes of Voltaire, Jefferson and Franklin. Seated at a white linen covered table, he unfolded the newspaper and read the headline:

McKinley to Run for Reelection

It seemed that McKinley favored Theodore Roosevelt as his vice-presidential running mate to fill the position left vacant by the death of Garret Hobart in '99. On the Democratic side, William Jennings Bryan intended to make another run with Admiral Dewey as his running mate. Tony tended to favor the Republican Party, the party of Lincoln, but McKinley's failure to enforce the 15th Amendment troubled him. He seemed to pay lip service to equal rights for blacks but looked the other way when the Klan went on its murderous rampages throughout the South. But he considered McKinley preferable to Bryan, who advocated for the little man—as long as he was white.

As his waiter arrived with a glass of wine, Tony turned to an inside page and noticed a short article entitled:

American Actress Scandalizes London

Mrs. Jacqueline Jones, née LeRoux, a native of Beaufort, South Carolina, has scandalized London with her offstage romance with her co-star, Johnston Forbes-Robertson, in a new production of Othello. The irony is that Mrs. Jones is married to a real Negro while pretending to make love on stage to an ersatz Negro, namely Mr. Forbes-Robertson. To add fuel to this potential conflagration, it is rumored that Mrs. Jones is with child...

Tony sat stunned, not having touched his wine.

"Monsieur?"

He looked up to see the waiter with a silver tray poised above his shoulder.

"Pardon." Tony folded the paper and set it aside. His *plat* was a steak with steamed carrots and potatoes on the side. At the moment, however, he had little appetite. He unfolded the paper and read the article again.

Could this be true? *The Paris Herald* was a relatively new paper published by the *New York Herald*, directed primarily at American expatriates. Known for sensationalism at home, there was no reason the editors weren't following the same policies in Europe. Still, the article got most of the details right, even Jackie's maiden name...but could she be pregnant? Why wouldn't she have told him—unless it was not his child?

He set the paper aside and consumed his meal without savoring its delicate flavors. He swallowed the remaining wine in his glass, paid the bill and left the restaurant.

During the short walk home, he tried to reconstruct the sequence of events that led to Jackie's departure from Paris and his subsequent visit to her in London. They had made love shortly before she left in early December, and again over the holidays in London. Let's see...four, no six weeks...plenty of time to discover that she was pregnant...how many weeks since he was in London? Two, three...if Forbes-Robertson was the father, could that be enough time for her to know for sure?

He turned into Rue de Furstemberg and let himself into the house with the key that Mme G had recently given him. He was beginning to regard her home as his, though he obviously had no legal right to it. J-P met him at the top of the stairs and took his coat. Even J-P was beginning to regard him as the man of the house, asking him whether he should order more coal for the furnace or wood for the fireplaces.

J-P also handed him a letter that had just arrived. It was postmarked 'London.' Tony recognized the handwriting.

According to J-P, Mme G was out shopping. Tony took the letter upstairs, closed the door to his room, and went to the writing desk. He slit opened the envelope and read the letter.

So she admits to being pregnant and wants him to be at her side. But not until the spring? Why not now? The weather, she says, as if a little snow would prevent him from traveling. Will she try to pass off the child as his? Maybe even she doesn't know who the child's father is.

Tony crumpled the letter into a ball and threw it into the trash. He thought of Mme G's comment that Jackie had been brought up in a very conservative, slave-owning family that refused to acknowledge that the South had lost the war. And that she, like many young white Southerners, rebelled against her parents' values, but as an adult was succumbing to the powerful opinions and prejudices that were inculcated in her since childhood. And now she was in England which had supported the Confederacy until it became clear that it would lose the war. London, the new citadel of white supremacy!

He was now so agitated and angry that he paced around the room like a caged animal, kicking the furniture. At last, finding this in no way productive or cathartic, he descended the stairs to the first floor, passed through the dining room where Sabine was setting the table without offering his usual cheery greeting, and went into the studio. Once, there, with the last rays of the sun streaming through the window creating an eerie, gothic atmosphere, he examined the series of paintings he had made of Mme G from the first of her standing with the gold kimono wrapped tightly around her waist, to the middle portraits with her sitting on the divan with the kimonos more loosely draped about her shoulders, to the last one in which she was completely naked, wearing only a seductive smile.

The woman knows what she wants, he thought. And almost always gets it. But is she honest? The classic question posed by Hamlet. Is she honest? Is Jackie honest? Is any woman honest where men are concerned?

He sat down before the easel, which now contained a blank canvas. He had intended to paint one last portrait of Mme G with her back to the viewer, peering over her shoulder. Now he wondered whether he shouldn't take a different approach. Or perhaps he should paint one of Jackie. He had only painted one portrait of Jackie, which now hung over the mantel of the salon on her father's yacht, *The Southern Pride*. Southern Pride? 'The Southern Whore' would be more appropriate.

He slipped his smock on and opened his paint box. Then he took out the palette knife and began applying, almost flinging, paint at the canvas. He had no idea what his subject was to be.

After an hour of painting, during which time he calmed down considerably, Tony stood away from the canvas to assess his efforts. There was the discernable figure of a woman, though with distorted features such as one enormous breast juxtaposed to a much smaller, almost disease-ridden one, along with eyes that looked like those of a feral animal, like those of a panther. The background, in fact, was jungle-like, with spiky palm fronds much like the ones that proliferated in the Lowcountry of South Carolina, and enormous philodendrons, like the ones he and his childhood friends called 'elephant ears.'

"My goodness! What on earth is that you're working on?" It was Mme G, who had silently entered the room, carrying a small box tied together with a red ribbon.

He didn't turn to look at her but continued staring at the canvas. "I'm not sure. Something abstract, fragmented, primitive. It just burst out of me."

She cautiously approached, as if Tony were one of those jungle animals about to leap off the canvas. "Yes, I would say it's very primitive. And very unlike your other work. Are you well?"

Tony turned to look at her. "Quite well, thank you. I just needed to release some pent-up energy. I think I need to get outside more."

"Yes, the winter has been particularly severe this year. But things are beginning to thaw. I must have walked ten kilometres this afternoon and it was invigorating."

"Ten kilometres? Where did you walk? And what's that in your hand?"

She smiled coyly. "I went shopping, mostly along the Champs-Élysées. There are scores of new shops that have opened recently, all in anticipation of the Exposition. And this is for you."

Tony looked at the little box tied with its neat, red ribbon. "For me? What's the occasion?"

"Well, we didn't exchange Christmas gifts—you were in London and I had no one to celebrate with but the servants, to whom I gave cash gifts. I saw this in a shop window." She extended the box to him.

"Well, now I feel guilty that I have nothing for you."

"It's not necessary. Think of it not as a Christmas gift but a gift of appreciation."

"Appreciation for what?"

"For making *me* feel appreciated again. Open it."

Tony looked at her for a moment, then took the box and slipped the ribbon off. "A wristwatch?"

"It's the latest thing," Mme G said.

"But Amelia, I thought wristwatches were for ladies. In fact, my mother has one."

"This one is made for men. You can see that it's larger than your mother's, and bold in design. A lady would never wear this one."

"No, I suppose not. It *is* quite handsome. Gold is it not?"

"Eighteen carats, with precious jewels inside. Do you like it.?"

Tony looked at Mme G for a moment, and then the watch. "I love it. Thank you."

She gave him a kiss. He responded, a little more enthusiastically than he intended.

"Put it on," she said.

"All right. But what am I to do with my pocket watch?"

"Wear it for special occasions. Like dinner parties. Pocket watches are for letting your host know it's time for you to leave."

Tony laughed. "Yes, it is useful in that way. Speaking of dinner parties, do you have any plans for tonight?"

"Yes, of course. Dinner for two–in the dining room."

"What time?"

The usual–seven. It will be very casual. And be sure to wear your new watch."

"I'll never take it off."

She smiled, gave him another kiss, and left the room.

Tony stared at the painting for a few moments, then picked up his palette knife and dragged it across the canvas, obscuring the image he had created earlier. "Insanity," he said. "A case for Dr. Freud."

He laughed rather self-consciously, put the palette knife down, and closed the lid of his paint box.

CHAPTER 19

Jackie was furious. She waved a copy of the *Daily Mail* in front of Forbes-Robertson as he was rubbing off his make-up in front of his dressing room mirror. She had burst into his room without knocking.

"Did you see this?"

Forbes-Robertson looked at her reflection in the mirror. "See what?"

"This...this pack of lies! What did you tell them?"

He turned around on his stool, wiping the make-up from his face. A single gold earring dangled from his left ear. "My dear–you are upset. I haven't told anyone anything."

"Well, *somebody* told the newspapers that you and I are having an affair!" She shoved the paper into his hands.

He unfolded it and read the brief article. "I say, this is outrageous. Not a bit of truth in it...except...are you great with child?"

Jackie folded her arms across her chest and blew a strand of hair out of her face that had fallen forward as she stormed into the room. "Yes, I am 'great with child.' Great with my husband's child. Who can say otherwise?"

Forbes-Robertson tossed the paper aside and sighed. "My dear, the newspapers in this country can say anything they please–unless the injured party can prove libel. And that's very difficult to do. And very costly. They know that."

Jackie sat down in a chair and put her head in her hands. "Oh, what am I to do? If Tony sees this, he'll divorce me!"

Forbes-Robertson patted her on the shoulder. "There, there, Jacqueline. He probably hasn't seen this trash. He's in Paris. Unless, of course, he's in the habit of reading the English newspapers there."

"Oh, he's a voracious reader. He reads everything. How is he going to believe me when the whole world is convinced that I've been unfaithful to him?"

"The whole world? Tsk, tsk. British readers take this kind of malicious gossip with a grain of salt. And I'm afraid you'll have to get used to it as long as you are in the theatre here. We all do."

Jackie stood up abruptly from her chair. "I don't want to get used to it! I don't care a fig for the theatre! I want to be with my husband."

"Well...I had no idea. But can't you wait till the play is over? We'll be in Brighton next week and then it will be–"

"No! I'm going to Paris tomorrow."

"Tomorrow? Dear, dear, Jacqueline–you'll disrupt the whole company. Your aunt has sunk a small fortune into this production. And you're on your way to a brilliant career! Don't be so rash."

Jackie sat down again and burst into tears.

Forbes-Robertson again patted her on the shoulder but she pushed him away.

"Oh, you're no help. You've encouraged this notion of our having an...a relationship."

"Me? I've done no such thing. I've merely tried to be agreeable to you and your aunt. And of course I like you both. But speaking of gossip, Jacqueline, haven't you heard that I'm engaged?"

She looked up and wiped away her tears. "Engaged? To whom?"

"To Gertie."

"Gertie?"

"Actually, her name is Gertrude. Gertrude Elliot. She's an American actress like yourself. She recently returned from a tour in Australia. I regret that I haven't had the occasion to introduce you."

"Gertrude Elliot. Yes, I've heard of her. You're really getting married?"

"If all goes well. In the meantime, she's joining my company."

"Your company?"

"Yes. As soon as I've fulfilled my commitment to your aunt, I intend to embark on a tour throughout the Isles. Shakespeare, mostly, but Shaw and Ibsen, too."

"Oh...well. I'm sorry if I've–"

"No need to apologize. I understand your frustration with these Fleet Street chaps. But if there's anything I can do–"

"You could make a public announcement."

"Announcement? What kind of announcement?"

"That your relationship with me has been purely Platonic."

Forbes-Robertson rubbed his chin. "Platonic...well, yes of course it has. But you know, such an announcement may simply invite more scurrilous speculations. What if I write a letter to the *Mail* denying the accusations and announcing my engagement to Gertie? We had wanted to keep it quiet, you know, but—"

"Oh, would you, Johnny!" Jackie jumped up from her chair and clasped Forbes-Robertson's hands. "And perhaps you could write a letter to my husband, too."

"Your husband? Well, if you think it would do any good. On the other hand, it may only provoke him. Better to leave it to one letter. If your husband is the voracious reader you say he is, he'll see it in the *Herald,* no doubt."

"The *Herald?*"

"The Paris edition of the *New York Herald.* A gossip rag like the others, they scour the British press for just such sensational stuff as this."

"Well...maybe that will suffice. In the meantime, I'll write Tony myself. Oh, thank you, Johnny." She gave him a hug and a kiss on the cheek just as a prop man stepped into the door of the dressing room.

They both saw him as he abruptly stepped back and disappeared down the corridor.

"Uh, oh," Jackie said. "What can we do about him?"

Forbes-Robertson laughed. "Well, we can't shoot him, so we'll just have to hope he doesn't report directly to the *Mail.*"

CHAPTER 20

After Mme G finished her bath, she donned her gold-embroidered kimono and gave orders to J-P to remove several leaves from the dining room table. The remaining ends were pushed together so as to reduce the table to a more intimate size for two. J-P also built a fire, though the coal furnace in the basement supplied enough heat to warm every room in the house.

Tony descended the stairs and entered the dining room just as Mme G was lighting the candles, though a chandelier above the center of the table was electrically lighted.

"Are the candles necessary?" Tony said. "The electric lights are bright enough, it seems."

Mme G said nothing but went to the wall and depressed a lever. The electric lights, both in the chandelier and the wall sconces, dimmed.

"How did you do that?"

"It's called a rheostat. I recently purchased one for each room. Clever, don't you think?"

"Very."

"The merchant said that they will be used extensively during the Exposition."

"And you are ahead of the exhibitors. You seem to be up to date in everything."

"Why not? A new century is upon us. A new world. Good riddance to the old."

J-P entered the room carrying a silver tray with a bucket of champagne on it, along with two glasses. He set the glasses down on the table and placed the bucket on a stand near the wall. Then he took the bottle out of the bucket, placed a towel around the neck, and popped the cork without spilling a drop.

"Shall we sit?" Mme G said.

"Yes." Tony went to her chair and slid it beneath her, then went to the opposite end of the table and seated himself.

J-P filled their glasses and left the room.

Mme G raised her glass. "Here's to the new century and all that it may bring."

"Be careful of what you wish for," Tony said, as he raised his glass. "All of this new technology may be used for good or ill."

"That's the cynic in you. Perhaps necessary for a serious artist. By the way, I like your shirt. Where did you get it?"

"My mother gave it to me. As a going-away gift."

"It's like a smock–only silk."

"It *is* a smock, actually. My mother bought it from a local store in Beaufort that stocks exotic items from abroad. In fact, it was made in Paris."

"Your mother has good taste. I'd like to meet her someday."

Tony chuckled. "Not likely–unless she comes to Paris."

"We should invite her. I'm sure she would like to see your paintings displayed at the Exposition."

"Yes. She would be proud. But it's a difficult trip. I'm not sure her health is up to it."

At this point, Sabine entered with a tray of hors d'oeuvres.

"What are these things that look like black caviar but aren't?"

Mme G laughed. "Truffles. Haven't you ever had them before?"

Tony sniffed at the black spores. "They don't have much of an aroma."

"Try one. Or better yet, crush it and mix it with the pâté."

Tony did so, spread it on a cracker, and popped it into his mouth. "Not bad. Is it expensive?"

"These cost about one hundred francs per kilo."

"I can think of better ways to spend a hundred francs."

"Don't worry. As my guest, there's no charge."

The meal continued in this fashion, with Tony being presented with a new delicacy at each course. The caviar he had sampled at the baron's soirée was fine, but Mme G's seemed tastier. The same with the braised medallions of venison and the sautéed scallops. Only the wine matched the baron's, for it was the very same wine that came from his cellars in Bordeaux.

Tony patted his lips with his napkin. "You've apparently found a gem in Eugénie. Where did you find her?"

"Eugénie, as I think I told you earlier, is from Provence. She studied under a great chef there, and after receiving her certificate, came to Paris and offered her services, but no one would hire her because she was a woman. At least not as head chef—she was a sous-chef at a new and rather pretentious restaurant called Maxim's. I ate there when I first arrived in Paris and when I asked the waiter who the chef was who cooked this fabulous meal, he confided in me that it was actually the sous-chef who prepared it. I negotiated with the owner, who had just spent a great deal of money renovating the premises, and we came to an agreement. Alors, la voilà!"

Tony laughed. "You are truly a woman of business."

"Yes, I'm afraid that is my only talent. But if I could choose, I would be an artist, like you. How nice it would be to paint side by side!"

"'Well, you can do that if you wish. It's your studio."

J-P. returned and filled their glasses. The desserts were still to come.

"I'm afraid I would only hinder your work. I will have to be content with knowing that I am providing the best possible environment for a very talented artist to grow and develop."

"Yes. Well, I hope I won't disappoint you."

"I'm a businesswoman, remember? I don't invest in losing enterprises."

Sabine arrived with the dessert, *profiteroles au chocolat*. J-P followed her with a bottle of sweet wine, Château d'Yquem.

Tony pushed his chair back from the table. "I have to say, that was the best meal I've ever had."

"I'm glad you liked it. Are you quite full?"

"Quite."

"Then perhaps we should go for a stroll in the garden. The snow has melted and Hasan has even managed to coax a few rose buds into bloom."

"Won't you be a bit chilly in just your kimono?"

She smiled. "Not if you stay close to me and keep me warm."

"I'll do my best."

Mme G tightened the sash on her kimono and slipped on a pair of pantoufles that she normally wore only around the house. Tony noticed this.

"Your feet will freeze," he said.

"I'll have Sabine bring me some socks. The Japanese wear them, you know, in all kinds of weather."

Sabine brought the socks and Mme G sat in her chair while the girl knelt before her and put them on her mistress, unrolling the white silk fabric to Mme G's knees as the kimono fell open to her thighs. Tony watched this process with keen interest.

"Alors!" Mme G said, dropping the folds of the kimono again to her ankles. "On y va!"

They proceeded to the garden, descending the stairway to the gravel path. It was a bit wet from the melting snow, so to avoid a puddle, Tony picked her up and stepped over it. Mme G put her arms around his shoulders.

"You could have been an athlete," she said. "Such strong shoulders!"

Tony laughed. "I was never much of an athlete. I played baseball my freshman year at Harvard but struck out nineteen consecutive times at bat. The coach suggested I take up rowing."

"And did you?"

"I did. We won the boat race against Yale that year. Fortunately for me, rowing does not involve a moving ball." He put her down on drier ground.

Mme G laughed. "That accounts for the strong shoulders. Well, you see? These buds are already struggling to burst out in all their glory."

Tony took a rosebud in his hand and examined it. "My grandfather died while cultivating roses like this."

"Did he? How sad."

"Not really. He loved his roses more than anything after his wife and children. Dying between rows of roses that he had bred for all seasons, some of which were named for him, must have been gratifying."

"I suppose so."

They walked on, until they came to the center of the garden, where a statue stood on its pedestal.

"I've seen this from the studio but have never looked at it up close. Who did it?"

"You don't recognize it? It was originally called *Francesca da Rimini*, but French critics call it '*The Kiss.*'"

"Rodin?"

"Of course it's not the original, which is in the Musée du Luxembourg. This is a smaller copy in bronze, probably executed by his assistants. But you see he signed it at the base."

Tony looked down at the signature. "It must have been very expensive. How many copies are there?"

"I don't know. And don't care. It's beautiful, don't you think?"

"Very. It has a certain tenderness that you don't see in Greek sculpture. Or even in the Italians."

"I agree." She squeezed his arm. "Let's go into the studio. I want to see what you've been working on. Did you finish that...that strange painting of a diseased woman?"

"Yes. It's finished and ready for the trash heap."

"What? Oh, no. You mustn't destroy any of your work. I'll buy it."

"I wouldn't want to wish it on you. It's not for sale. Let's go back into the house."

"No. I want to see it one last time before you destroy it."

Tony sighed. "All right. If you insist."

They ascended the stairs to the studio and Tony switched on the lights.

Mme G approached the painting in question. "Oh–what have you done to it? It's completely obscured."

"I told you–I didn't like it. It was done in a fit of anger."

"Anger? What were you angry about?"

Tony sighed and sat down on the divan. She sat down beside him.

"A newspaper article. In the *Paris Herald*. About my wife."

"Your wife? What did it say?"

"That she was pregnant–by another man."

"Oh...but it may not be true. The *Herald* is hardly a reliable newspaper. Gossip, sensational stories…"

"It *is* true. I received a letter from Jackie afterwards admitting she was pregnant."

"Did she say the father was this...other man?"

"No. But she didn't deny it, either."

They sat in silence for a few moments

"Are you going to London?" Mme G said.

"No. At least not until the spring. And maybe not then."

Mme G caressed his shoulder. "She's not worthy of you, Tony. Not worthy…"

Tony said nothing for a few moments, staring into the darkened window. Then he turned his head towards Mme G. She was still caressing his shoulders, now his neck, now the side of his face. She was neither smiling nor frowning but stared piercingly into his eyes like a Madonna into the eyes of the Christ child. This painterly image, of course, had nothing to do with religiosity, but only with his peculiar type of imagination. He saw everything from an artistic perspective, every scene as a potential painting.

"Take off your kimono," he said.

She looked surprised, but then loosened the sash from the kimono and let it drop around her shoulders. "Like this?"

"All the way. And lie on your side. Your left side."

She complied and Tony rose from the divan and went to the easel where the ill-fated painting of the diseased woman was resting. He took this canvas down, set it aside, and put a blank one in its place.

"You want to paint me now?" she said.

"Yes. Prop yourself up a bit on your left elbow. And think of your son."

"My son? Willy? Oh, Tony–I don't want to think of Willy. I want to forget."

"Then think of having another child."

A smile came slowly to her lips. "I have thought of having another child."

"Good. Keep thinking of that child."

He went about opening his paint box and arranging his brushes.

As usual, he worked quickly. By ten o'clock he felt that it was finished and put his brushes down.

"You're finished?" she said.

"Yes."

"Let me see." She rose from the divan without donning her kimono again and approached the painting.

What she saw was a beautiful woman with a serene, enigmatic smile on her face, her eyes slightly hooded, looking down at a child. A child as naked as his mother, its face barely discernible, looking up and reaching for her breast. Though painted in a realistic vein, the divan and the wall behind it, with its panoply of paintings, were merely suggested with broad brush strokes.

"Oh–it's beautiful! Better than all the others."

"You think so?"

"Yes. Absolutely. Tony–" She put her arms around him and brought her face close to his. "I want you so much. Please don't tease me any longer."

Tony said nothing but picked her up in his arms and carried her to the divan. He put her down gently and took off his shirt, which had been ruined now by splotches of paint. He tossed it aside, bent over and kissed her. She ran her hands over his back and shoulders, then pulled at his trousers. He took them off and lay beside her, both of them naked now. He thought of the Rodin sculpture in the garden. Was she Francesca? To his...

"You're teasing me again, Tony," she said. "I want you inside of me."

He looked at her, her eyes imploring, her mouth half-open, her lips ripe as succulent fruit. He hesitated, the image of Jackie before his eyes.

"What is it?" she said.

"Nothing," he said. "Nothing at all."

CHAPTER 21

Lucinda's production of *Othello* wrapped up its final performance in Brighton the following week. The reviews were favorable for the most part but there were snipes by the London papers at both Forbes-Robertson and Jackie. Forbes-Robertson was said to be 'too English' to be convincing as the Moor. Jackie, on the other hand, let slip a few colloquial pronunciations of her native South Carolina, and was said to be 'too American.' The local audiences, however, seemed to overlook these finer points, and the production was generally a success.

Jackie, earlier in the week, sat down at her writing desk to write to Tony, explaining that the press reports of her romantic liaison with Forbes-Robertson were completely false. But as she looked over what she had written, she hesitated, reasoning that she was only adding fuel to the fire. How did she know that Tony had read of this malicious gossip in the Paris papers? He generally ignored the 'yellow' press, devouring all the national and international news in *Le Figaro* and *Le Matin*. In fact, she couldn't recall ever seeing him read the *Paris Herald*.

Why put herself in the position of defending herself against the indefensible? Forbes-Robertson was right—any such defense would create the suspicion that 'she doth protest too much.'

So she tore her preliminary attempts—which consumed four sheets of stationery—to bits and then burned them in the fireplace.

She was beginning to show a bit. It wasn't obvious, but at least one member of the audience at Brighton, an elderly man in the front row with hoary whiskers and a mischievous glint in his eye, muttered to his wife, "Desdemona will be in need of a pram afore long."

The next afternoon she and Lucinda took tea at a cafe on the town square, watching the procession of theatre goers and vacationers that visited Brighton all year round.

"Johnny will be taking his new company to the provinces in the spring," Lucinda said, "and I don't wish to compete with him. I've been talking to

Elizabeth Robbins recently, and she's been thinking of a revival of Ibsen's *Hedda Gabler*. It caused a scandal in '91, and as such was very successful. She has just come back from New York and wants to do it here again but is wary of the role. The lead character, Hedda, is thought to be pregnant as she engineers the destruction of her lover. It's a wonderful role. Would you consider auditioning for it?"

Jackie contemplated this proposal. "I'm familiar with the play, but I didn't know Hedda was pregnant while she went about her scheme. I should be showing more in the next few weeks."

"No matter. It may add some urgency to Hedda's character. Should I tell Elizabeth you're interested?"

"I was thinking of going to Paris to see Tony."

"Jackie, dear, this could be the opportunity of a lifetime. Tony has shown little interest in your present condition. Don't sacrifice your future in order to subjugate yourself to a man's whims."

"But the child?"

"The child will be cared for regardless of whether Tony comes to fulfill his responsibilities as a father. I'll see to that. We both will."

Jackie felt that Tony was drifting farther and farther away from her. She had come to Europe to be with him, to support him in his career, not to pursue her own career in the theatre. Still, as her mother said, he has not answered her letters and seems content with his 'arrangement' in Paris with this, this Madame Goldman. Why should she go to him? Wasn't it the duty of a husband to come to his wife's side, especially when she was about to give birth to their first child?

"All right, Mother," she said. "I'll try out for the part."

"Splendid!" Lucinda said. "But do remember to—"

"Call you 'Lucinda.' But there are no servants present, and I would think you would like to hear your only child call you, 'Mother,' once in a while."

Lucinda looked absolutely hurt. "Quite right, Jacqueline. Quite right."

CHAPTER 22

Snow returned to Paris in late February and early March, though intermittently. The Exposition was scheduled to open on April 14, and almanacs predicted sunny weather and moderate temperatures.

Tony decided to replace one of four paintings accepted for the exhibit with a portrait of Mme G, the one in which she looks over her bare shoulder at the viewer with the kimono seeming about to fall to her waist. He had originally wanted to submit the last portrait, the one in which she posed completely naked, looking down at a Christ-like infant, but the representative from the Exposition declared it to be both scandalous and sacrilegious so he settled for his second choice.

For Tony it was a kind of homage to Sargent's 'Madame X,' which scandalized the Paris Salon of 1884. 'Madame G,' was far more provocative, but Tony reasoned that both the public and the judges had come a long way in the last sixteen years. Though there were numerous paintings and sculptures of nudes submitted to both the earlier salon and the present Exposition, the scandal of 1884 erupted because it depicted a high-society matron in a daring black evening dress held up by straps that were nearly invisible. Mme G, on the other hand, was also a rich socialite, but a relative newcomer to Paris, an American. In short, she was immune to scandal.

In the meantime, he was at a loss as to what to paint next. This had not been a problem before and he wasn't sure why it was now. He stood in the studio one morning and simply stared at the blank canvas. He'd heard of writer's block, but never painter's block.

"What are you thinking of?" It was Mme G, who had just entered the studio and was dressed in business attire.

"Nothing. Absolutely nothing," Tony said. He didn't turn around but continued to stare at the blank canvas.

"Surely you must be thinking of something." She came up behind him and kissed him on the cheek. "An image. Something from memory."

"No. Nothing."

"Have you ever thought of painting from a photograph? I have books–"

"No. I have to see the subject with my own eyes."

"How about horses?"

"Horses?"

"Yes. I've just come from a meeting with the baron. Banking matters. At the end of the meeting he asked if you and I would like to attend the first major race at Longchamp. He has two of his thoroughbreds entered."

"Does he? I suppose that could be interesting. Should I bring my easel?"

She laughed. "I think that would be rather cumbersome. But perhaps you could bring your sketchbook."

"I suppose it's worth a try. And it could be amusing."

"Very amusing. Have you ever been to a horse race?"

"Of course. But not at a track. Just the scions of rich alumni racing around Harvard Yard on a bet and terrorizing everyone in the process. I couldn't afford a horse at the time or I probably would have joined them."

She laughed and brushed at his beard, a goatee, which he was just beginning to cultivate. "Then you've never been to a real horse race. It's quite a spectacle. And the baron has invited us to join him in his private box."

"Well, then, I suppose we can't refuse. When is the big day?"

"Sunday."

Three days later, during which Tony made several attempts at the easel with unsatisfactory results, J-P prepared the barouche and brought it around to the front door. Tony stood in the parlor in a morning suit purchased for him by Mme G, which consisted of a tailcoat, black and gray striped trousers, a paisley double-breasted waistcoat, winged collar, gray kid gloves, a cane, and a silk top hat.

Mme G circled around him, straightening his tailcoat and cravate. "Not a bad fit for off-the-shelf. Of course there was no time for the tailor."

Tony tugged at the tight collar. "It doesn't seem designed for a sporting event. Can I take off the coat while I'm sketching?"

"Certainly. But you want to make a favorable first impression. And the waistcoat will help you stand out from the others."

"I think the color of my skin will make me stand out enough."

"Clothes make the man. No one will care about your skin color, which is very nice in any case."

"Will the vicomte be there?"

"Possibly. But I think the prince put him in his place at the baron's soirée. He won't want another dressing down like that."

Tony noted Mme G's outfit, which was of the latest fashion, with a pigeon bodice, high neckline with lace collar, and an enormous hat adorned with wax fruit and stuffed hummingbirds. The hemline was a bit higher than customary, only to the ankles, which were covered with lace-up leather boots. "Careful that your hat doesn't fly away."

"I assure you, the hummingbirds are quite domesticated."

Even J-P was dressed for the occasion, in a mouse gray top hat, frock coat, and ruffled shirt with bow tie. He led the way downstairs, opened the door to the carriage, and his passengers being settled, climbed onto his perch. The weather was sunny and cool, with a few cumulus clouds drifting overhead in a light breeze.

A Sunday excursion to Longchamp was meant to be more of a 'promenade' than a means of getting from one place to another efficiently. Thus, J-P turned the barouche up Boulevard St-Germain, past the church of the same name, past the literary cafés, past the myriad of small boutiques, and past the Palais Bourbon until they reached the Pont de la Concorde, where they crossed the Seine and arrived at the premier showcase of elite strollers, the Champs-Élysées.

"People are staring," Tony said.

"Of course they are. That's the point. Otherwise, we could have taken the tram and already be there."

"Perhaps they think I'm an African prince."

Mme G laughed. "No doubt they do. Let's not disillusion them."

They rounded the Place de la Concorde, where there was still construction underway to complete the first metro line. Mme G instructed J-P to stop and put up the hood to protect them from the swirling dust, which caused even the horses to cough. But soon they were on their way again, the clouds of dust behind them and the wide Avenue des Champs-Élysées before them. On the left, however, was more construction, though it was nearly finished–the Grand Palais of the Exposition. This was an enormous building of daring design, built of iron, steel, and reinforced concrete. The most outstanding feature, though, was its great glass barrel-vaulted roof over two hundred meters long that would house exhibitions of locomotives, automobiles, and even hot air balloons. On the river side, the new Pont Alexandre III was nearing completion.

They continued the length of the Champs-Élysées until they reached the Arc de Triomphe, circled the great monument, and with the horses now head high and breathing in fresh air, trotted down the Avenue Victor-Hugo towards the Bois de Boulogne.

The Bois was a welcome contrast to the noise and bustle along the Champs-Élysées. But it was no less crowded. Aside from the carriages jockeying for favorable ingress to the track, thousands of pedestrians, many carrying picnic baskets or pushing prams, streamed into wooded paths to Longchamp.

The path they chose opened suddenly onto a wide expanse of greensward dotted with colorful tents set up on both sides of the track, which was demarcated by white picket fences.

"How do we find the baron?" Tony asked.

"It will be one of the larger tents inside the paddock," Mme G said. "Red and yellow stripes, with a little flag on top, he said, displaying the de Rothstein coat of arms...there!"

They entered the paddock area and were directed to a parking space adjacent to several motorcars.

After J-P assisted them from the carriage, he went over to examine one of the cars more closely while Mme G and Tony proceeded to the baron's tent. As at the château at la Ferrières, the baron stood at the entrance, greeting his guests.

"Ah," he said, "Madame Goldman et le peintre, Antonio! Bienvenue, mes amis!"

After exchanging a few pleasantries with the baron, they entered the tent. This was nearly as elaborate as the drawing room of his château. Chandeliers hung from ropes strung between the poles, though they were lighted by candles rather than incandescent bulbs. Oriental carpets concealed the grass beneath and long tables laden with all manner of fruits, meat, seafood, and desserts were set up parallel to the side panels, which were unfurled to about three feet to allow light and air to enter. As at the château, liveried servants served the guests and waiters circulated, pouring champagne. Armchairs and canapés were scattered about for those who wished to sit.

As luck would have it, among the first guests they encountered were the vicomte and his wife. The vicomte regarded Tony with an icy stare, then turned away to speak to his wife. Then they moved off to another area of the tent.

"I gather that the vicomte is uncomfortable with my presence," Tony said.

"Ignore him," Mme G said. "Even the baron dislikes him. The only reason he invites him to his parties is that the vicomte owes him 100,000 francs and he wants to keep an eye on him."

"A hundred thousand francs? What for?"

"Gambling. The vicomte is a compulsive gambler who invariably loses at the tables. The baron owns a private casino in Baden-Baden, mostly for the amusement of his friends. The vicomte derives most of his income from mining and shipping concerns, which provides a constant stream of income, so he eventually pays his debts. At one point, he owed the baron over a million francs."

"How did he come to own the mining and shipping companies?"

"The old-fashioned way–he inherited them."

"I suppose everyone here has inherited their wealth."

"Mostly. But at least the baron works."

After circulating among the guests, which included many of those who attended the baron's soirée, a trumpet was heard announcing the first race. The guests filed out of the tent and entered a series of box seats set up adjacent to the track. The master of ceremonies introduced the baron and other sporting dignitaries, followed by the roster of 'poulains,' or colts, entered in the race.

"Are we betting on any of these horses?" Tony asked.

"'Indeed we are," Mme G said. "One hundred francs on 'Le Prince du Soleil' and two hundred on 'Boxcar.'"

"Boxcar?"

"The baron owns a railway company. He noticed that this particular colt is powerfully built, like a boxcar."

"Why two hundred on Boxcar?"

"I like the way he looks. Sturdy legs and a tawny coat. Like you."

Tony looked askance at her. "Tawny coat? Me?"

She laughed. "Almost an exact match. You'll see."

Tony was about to object to this method of choosing a horse, but before he could get the words out, the trumpet blared again. The horses lined up at the starting line with considerable jostling of equine bodies, a flag fell, and with some minor collisions, they were off.

"Which one is Boxcar?"

"Number seven."

"He's running last."

"He carries more weight. But once he sets going–*attention!*"

They watched the horses round the first turn and then disappear from sight. Boxcar was still dead last.

"Now what?" Tony said.

"We'll have to wait until they come round again. Did you check your watch?"

"Oh, um..." He looked at his watch and saw the tiny second hand running its circular course and concluded it was useless for this sort of event. But he didn't wish to offend Mme G. He looked up at the chronograph on a post next to the master of ceremonies' tower. "Exactly eighteen seconds to the first turn."

"Oh!" Mme G said. "That's fast. He's already catching up."

By the second turn, the MC announced the order of the contestants: Le Prince du Soleil was in first place, Boxcar second, and Plume d'Argent third. By the third and final turn, Tony and Mme G were on their feet with all the others cheering on their favorites. Mme G peered through her opera glasses to identify the front runners.

"Allez, allez!" she shouted.

"Where is he?" Tony said.

"In front, of course. I told you–"

The MC confirmed Mme G's observation. "Boxcar, suivi de Plume d'Argent, et Le Prince du Soleil..."

But fifty meters from the finish line, Boxcar, clearly in sight now, fell behind a half a length.

"Oh, no!" Mme G said.

"What's the matter with him?" Tony said.

"I don't know. He's pulled up a bit–as if he's hurt."

"Le vainqueur," shouted the MC, "Plume d'Argent! Le Prince du Soleil, deuxième, Boxcar, troisième."

"Third!" Mme G said. "Merde!"

This was the first time that Tony had heard Mme G utter an expletive, either in English or French. It amused him, though he was careful not to laugh, as Mme G was visibly upset that her horse had not won.

"They're other races," Tony said.

"But poor Boxcar is through. There must have been foul play."

"Couldn't he have just stumbled, or struck a stone?"

"Not likely. The track is impeccably groomed. The weather is perfect. He was clearly ahead. I hope the baron lodges a complaint."

"Well, let's go back to the tent. Perhaps we'll learn what happened there."

As they made their way to the tent, they saw the baron in a heated exchange with the MC, who shook his head as if to say there was nothing he could do. The baron stalked off and met them just as they were about to enter.

"What happened?" Mme G said.

"The jockey riding Plume d'Argent struck Boxcar on his rear leg with his whip. I saw it through my binoculars."

"I knew it!" Mme G exclaimed. "What did the MC have to say?"

"He says it cannot be proven. No one else saw it."

"Can't they examine Boxcar to see if he's been injured?"

"They're doing that now. But it's doubtful that the whip left a mark."

"Perhaps if you went to the owner of Plume d'Argent—"

"I intend to. The owner is none other than our friend the vicomte."

"The vicomte?" Mme G said.

"Mais oui!" The baron said. "He made a wager of 90,000 francs on Plume d'Argent. At three to one odds, he's made more than enough to pay off his gambling debt."

"The scoundrel!" Mme G said.

"Je suis d'accord," the baron said. "But of course, we must have proof."

CHAPTER 23

Jackie won the role of Hedda, in part due to the enthusiastic endorsement of William Archer, Elizabeth Robbin's partner in a new theatre project to promote Ibsen's work.

She revealed to both Robbins and Archer that she was pregnant, but neither objected. The play was expected to run for only six weeks, to be followed by other Ibsen plays.

Her morning sickness returned. As annoying and discomforting as this was, it was intermittent and usually over by late afternoon, so she never missed a rehearsal or a performance.

The reviews were favorable, but not exceptional, as the critics could not refrain from comparing Jackie's performance with that of Miss Robbin's several years earlier. Some even hinted that Miss Robbins intentionally cast Jackie in the part with this purpose in mind. The fact was that Miss Robbins was simply desirous of moving in a new direction, namely as a manager/director.

Now sixteen weeks into her pregnancy, Jackie was beginning to feel a tightening in her pelvic area. A sort of knot just below her stomach. Dr. Thurloe said that this meant it would be a boy.

"When I had you," Lucinda said one afternoon while they strolled along the new pier at Brighton, "no one had a clue whether it would be a boy or a girl. As soon as I noticed the bump, I did everything to cover it up. When I could conceal it no longer, Dr. Fischer came in and declared that I had a malignant tumor. Imagine! I didn't know whether he was ignorant or trying to save me from scandal and exile."

"But you *were* sent into exile," Jackie said.

"Yes–in a manner of speaking. Well...you know the story. But I'm not sure Dr. Thurloe knows any more than Dr. Fischer. Who can predict the sex of a child? Especially at this early stage."

"Mother–sorry, Lucinda–what am I to do when the baby comes? People will look around and there will be no father to be found."

"At least they know you are married. I didn't have that advantage."

"But Tony doesn't answer my letters. I think he somehow got hold of the article in the *Mail*. That's the only explanation. He thinks Johnny is the father."

"Oh, look!" Lucinda said. "There's a vendor selling ices. Just the thing in this warm weather."

"Warm? You call this 'warm'? Well, they do look delicious."

"Of course they do. I think I'll have vanilla."

"And I'll have the raspberry."

"Tha' un's boysenberry, Miss," the vendor said. She was a stout, elderly woman who looked as if she had worked in a blacking factory all her life. She squinted as if the sunlight were too much to bear.

"How much?" Lucinda said.

"Thruppence, m'lady. Each."

"Each? Highway robbery," Lucinda said. "Nevertheless, we're on holiday." She paid the woman and they walked on. "You were saying that Tony thinks that Johnny is the father?"

"I don't know that. But Tony may think that he is."

"I don't suppose he would accept Johnny's denial, would he?"

"Probably not."

"Then you'll have to go to him. He knows you are incapable of lying, as I do. Go to Paris and take that outrageous article with you. It's the only way."

"But what about the play?"

"'It'll be done soon and you'll only be into your eighteenth week or so. Lots of women travel right up until they're about to deliver."

"But what if...what if I miscarry?"

"Then the problem is solved."

"Mother!"

"Oh, I'm just joking. And can't you train yourself to exclaim, 'Auntie!' whenever you're surprised?"

Jackie frowned. "I'll try."

"Good. And speaking of trains, the ones that travel between London and Paris these days are quite comfortable and efficient. Far more so than the cabs that rattle your teeth over the city pavement."

Jackie sighed. "Well...I suppose there's little chance of miscarrying. And I miss Tony so much."

"He'll be delighted to see you. And when he realizes you've traveled all that way to see him, this mad theory that you're carrying another man's child will completely evaporate."

"I hope you're right."

"Of course I'm right. I'm your mother. Now eat your ice before it melts all over your dress."

"Yes, Mother."

"Jacqueline, I thought we had agreed–"

"You just uttered the dreaded word yourself."

"Yes...quite true. And you're right–it's nice to hear it once in a while."

CHAPTER 24

After a thorough investigation by the race committee, it turned out that two of the jockeys saw Plume d'Argent's rider strike the left knee of Boxcar with his whip on the home stretch. The rider was summoned and confessed, explaining that his employer, the vicomte, instructed him to do so, adding that he would receive a bonus if Plume d'Argent won.

Then the vicomte was summoned, but denied the charge, even striking his jockey across the face and calling him a liar.

The Committee voted unanimously to disqualify Plume d'Argent, awarding Le Prince du Soleil first place and Boxcar second. They also barred the vicomte from entering horses in the race for three years, at the end of which time he could apply to the Committee for reinstatement. The harsher penalty, however, was levied at the instigation of the baron, who, as President of the Jockey Club, recommended that the vicomte be expelled for life.

"And not only that," Mme G said, as she removed her white gloves when they returned to Rue de Furstemberg," but he still owes the baron 100,000 francs. Not to mention the fine and the wager he lost on Plume d'Argent."

Tony was relieved to be able to remove his tie and collar. "The vicomte seems to be a vindictive sort. Do you suppose he'll retaliate against the baron?"

Mme G sat down in an armchair, exhausted. She removed her boots. "I don't know how he can—the baron is a very powerful man. And he surrounds himself with bodyguards and retainers. Sabine! Mes pantoufles, s'il te plaît."

"A glass of wine might be nice, too," Tony said.

"Et du vin rouge!" Mme G said. She turned again to Tony. "Well, it's been a long day. Did you complete any sketches?"

"As a matter of fact, I did. J-P's taken my sketchbook to the studio. I'll take a look at them tomorrow."

Sabine entered the room carrying Mme G's slippers and a bottle of wine. Mme G slipped them on as Sabine poured the wine.

"Ah! Mme G said. "That feels so much better. New boots want a certain amount of breaking in."

Sabine left the room.

Tony's eyes followed her. He took a sip of his wine. "I've been thinking about Sabine."

Mme G, who had just raised her glass to her lips, paused. "Have you? What about her?"

"She's a pretty girl."

"Yes, she is. What of it?"

"Does she have any suitors? She seems to live like a nun, committed to service–but to you, not the church."

Mme G laughed. "She's hardly a nun. She and J-P tryst secretly–or so they think–at every opportunity."

"Do they? And where do they meet?"

"I'm not sure. But I often hear Sabine's door squeaking on its hinges late at night and then closing. I suppose they consider his coming up to her room is too risky as it's adjacent to mine, so she must go to the carriage house. But I hardly think his parents would approve, so perhaps they–of course! J-P has a key to the studio."

Tony chuckled. "Lovers will find a way."

"Yes, they will." She raised her glass. "Here's to young lovers–everywhere."

Tony raised his glass. "To lovers, young, and not so young."

Deep furrows suddenly appeared on Mme G's forehead. "What do you mean by that?"

Tony, alarmed at his faux pas, tried to recover. "I simply mean that lovers come in all ages and sizes. Speaking for myself, I'm not the young buck I once was."

"So what does that make me? I'm six years older than you are."

Tony sighed with exasperation. He hadn't intended to insult her. "You're still a beautiful woman, Amelia. Your age makes no difference to me."

"My age!" She stood up from her chair so abruptly that she spilled half the contents of her wine. "I'll soon be forty, if you'd like to know. Then I suppose you'll turn your attention to Sabine or some 'dancer' like Loïe Fuller. Don't think I didn't notice your obsession with her performance at the baron's soirée!"

"Obsession? Come now, Amelia. I was only admiring her artistry. Better have Sabine come and clean up that wine before it–"

"Call her yourself! Perhaps you can persuade her to linger for a while and join you on the divan. Va te faire foutre!"

She stormed out of the room.

Tony sat for a few moments on the divan, staring at the wine stain on the carpet. "Sabine! Venez ici, s'il vous plaît."

Sabine entered the room and Tony pointed to the stain. "Madame a renversé du vin. Nettoyez-le, s'il vous plaît."

"Oui, Monsieur." Sabine returned to the kitchen and brought back a sponge and a bottle of vinegar.

Tony watched as she got down on her hands and knees and began scouring the carpet. Though her skirt extended to the floor, it pulled tightly around her posterior, which swayed back and forth in rhythm with her scouring motion. He suddenly found it amusing that Mme G was the cause of this spectacle. It was far more arousing than Mademoiselle Fuller's dance of the veils.

He sighed. Why were women so sensitive about their age? Mme G, as long as she continued to take care of herself, would still be beautiful decades from now. Well, one or two more decades, anyway.

Meanwhile, Sabine was putting her nose almost to the floor in her quest to eradicate every vestige of the stain. Her bottom consequently rose higher, as did her skirt. Just as Tony was beginning to feel guilty about enjoying this show, J-P appeared in the doorway to the kitchen. He looked at Sabine's undulating posterior, then at Tony.

"Sabine! Arête ça!"

Sabine looked up, realized that her rear end was the object of Tony's attention, and made an effort to gather in her skirt. "Ça suffit, Monsieur?"

Tony, who affected to be preoccupied with a painting on the wall, turned slowly to her and said, "Oui, Sabine. Ça suffit. Merci."

Sabine quickly rose to her feet and hurried past J-P, who gave her a stern look as she passed by him. Then he followed her into the kitchen, where Tony heard some very heated whispering between them.

Tony remained on the sofa for a few minutes and finished his wine. He wondered whether he should go up to Mme G's room and try to make amends. No, he could only make things worse. Better to give her time to cool off.

He rose from the sofa and paced the room for a few minutes. Then he decided to do what he always did when he was idle or agitated: he went to the studio.

He picked up his sketchbook and leafed through the pages. There were six of them. Three were of the horses, one of Prince du Soleil in the paddock before the race, one of Boxcar in the lead on the final stretch, and one of all the horses as they lined up at the starting line. The other three were of people: Mme G peering through her opera glasses at the finish, one of a jockey whispering to his horse prior to the race, and one of a groom–a boy of twelve or thirteen–rubbing down a horse in the paddock after the race.

To get a better view of all six at once, he tore the pages out of the sketchbook and pasted them to the wall. After surveying these very different sketches for several minutes, he decided that the one of the jockey whispering to his horse was the most intriguing. What was he whispering? What was the relationship between the jockey and the horse? Between man and beast?

He took that sketch down and attached it to the top of his easel. There was still light streaming in through the great window, though it was fading in the late afternoon sky, casting long shadows across the studio floor. Better to start the next morning...but no, the shadows created an eerie, mysterious aura that emphasized the mystery of the horse whisperer.

He opened his paint box and at once started to paint with broad strokes: a darkened sky with threatening clouds, though the sky had been sunny and cloudless at the time of the race; gray and black. Shafts of light, tempered by dust particles, illuminating the horse's and jockey's head; orange and red. Then there was the dark blue of the horse's blanket, with the white of its number: 13.

He worked for an hour until the sun set and put his brush down. He would start again in the morning–the almanac predicted rain.

He returned to the house, passing through the kitchen, where Eugénie asked him what he would like for supper. Mme G, she said, would not join him.

"Pourquoi pas?" he said.

"Parce qu'elle est fatiguée et n'a pas faim."

Tony sighed. This was not a good sign. But after all, they had had their fill at the baron's tent before the race, and he wasn't very hungry, either.

"Je prendrai du pain et du fromage–dans ma chambre."

"Dans votre chambre? Avec du vin rouge?"

"Oui, s'il vous plaît."

"Bien sûr, Monsieur."

He went up to his room and removed his clothes, lying on the bed briefly before deciding to take a bath. The dust from the construction on the Champs-Elysées, along with the dirt and grime of the racetrack, had found its way into the crevices of both his clothes and his body.

He was in the tub for no more than five minutes when there was a knock at the bathroom door. This surprised him. For the servants never entered his room without knocking at the hall door first. Naked, he wondered what he should do. There was a second knock. His curiosity overwhelmed his modesty and he simply called out, "Entrez."

The door to the bath swung open and there was Mme G in her gold kimono. She smiled, approached the tub, loosened the sash, and let the kimono drop to the floor.

"May I join you?" she said.

Tony, a bit unnerved, but aroused by the sight of her curvaceous body, could only answer: "J'en serais ravi!"

"De même, Monsieur."

And she slipped noiselessly into the tub.

CHAPTER 25

The six sketches that Tony made at Longchamp were turned into colorful and dynamic paintings that sold very quickly in Monsieur Dantec's gallery. "Horses are always popular," Monsieur Dantec said. "You should do more like this."

But Tony did not want to become a 'genre' painter and said only that he would think about it. He was still preoccupied with the human figure–especially Mme G's figure–and he wanted to explore the possibilities of expressing the whole range of human experience in this way.

'The range of human experience.' What did that mean? Sadness, joy, pain, anger–all of that to be sure, but were there human experiences of which he knew nothing about? He himself had faced bigotry in the South, and even death, but what of women like Mme G and Jackie? Or the coal miners of Anzin that Monsieur Zola had written about? Some of those coal miners were women.

The opening day of the Exposition was approaching. He and Mme G were both looking forward to it. But Mme G had become rather unpredictable lately, beginning with her emotional outburst the afternoon of the races. That night she had surprised him in his bath and acted as if nothing had happened. A couple of days later, she remained in bed all day and refused to talk to him. But the following morning, she was up early and full of energy, insisting that they take a ride in the country.

Today she was at another meeting with the baron. Tony, meanwhile, was thinking of doing another portrait of her, but fully clothed, perhaps in one of her business suits. After all, that's what she was–a businesswoman. What did she think about all day when she wasn't thinking of business? What did any of us think about when we weren't thinking of work? Sex. Even banking had some subterranean sexual impulse beneath its stodgy image, devoted to piling up limitless amounts of wealth. But unlike material wealth, which wore out and had to be replaced with something else, sexual pleasure was an endlessly renewable commodity. Or so it seemed. Perhaps

Mme G feared that this particular commodity had, in fact, a limited shelf-life, and was determined to make the most of it while she still could.

Despite the coming of spring with its warmer temperatures and blooming flowers and longer days filled with sunshine, Tony was not particularly inspired with the miraculous 'renewal' that he was witnessing just outside the studio window. His desultory strokes with the brush were unproductive and even unintelligible. Not that a painting had to be intelligible, but it should at least have some verve, some 'brio.'

As he was contemplating this latest effort, J-P arrived holding an envelope aloft. "Un télégramme, Monsieur."

"Un télégramme? Pour moi?"

"Oui, Monsieur." He left.

Tony removed the telegram from its envelope.

London SW   9 April am 10:33

Mr. Antonio Jones
6 Rue de Furstemberg, Paris

Tony darling STOP Must see you STOP Will arrive at Gare du Nord
Tuesday 5:15pm STOP Will return to London next day if you wish it STOP

All my love
Jackie

Tony folded the telegram and put it back in the envelope as if it were to be a souvenir. What can be her purpose in coming all the way to Paris on such short notice? No doubt she was getting along in her pregnancy–four, five months? Is it safe for a woman to travel in that condition? And what of her paramour, Johnston Forbes-Robertson? Has he abandoned her?

He stared at the blurred image on the canvas, an image as inchoate as his mind at the moment.

He looked at the wristwatch that Mme G had given him. Nearly noon. He still wasn't used to the effeminate motion of his wrist necessary to view the dial. But it was very practical. As he never wore a waistcoat when he was painting, there was no place to put a pocket watch.

And Mme G–what was she to think? Even though she had approved–even urged–him to invite Jackie to come live with them, that was months ago. Things had changed. Mme G had changed. Fits of jealously alternating with a blasé, even Bohemian attitude towards sex.

He felt a rumbling in his stomach. When he was in the midst of a painting he was passionate about he forgot all about eating. This was not one of those times.

He put down his brushes and headed for the house.

Tuesday? That's today. He supposed he would have to meet Jackie at the station. She would have luggage whether she stayed one night or a week. A cab would be sufficient—no sense in bringing out the barouche and making a big production out of it. Perhaps he could even put her up at Nat's place.

He turned these thoughts over in his mind as he entered the kitchen and asked Eugénie if Mme G had returned from her appointment with the baron.

"Oh, Monsieur, Madame est de retour, mais elle a mal à la tête."

"Mal à la tête?"

"Oui. Elle est dans sa chambre."

A headache. Mme G seemed to be plagued these days with either a headache or an upset stomach. He decided that he had better go upstairs and see about her.

He knocked on her door.

"Entrez."

He stepped inside and saw Mme G lying on her back, fully clothed, her forearm across her forehead, her eyes closed.

"Amelia?"

She opened her eyes, then closed them again. "Tony—I'm so sorry to be such a pill. But this headache has got me down."

He went to her bedside and pulled up a chair. "When did it start?"

"Shortly after I left the baron. It was the noise and dust of the construction around the Place de la Concorde, I think. Or—something else."

Tony put his hand on her forehead. "No fever."

"No."

He moved his hand from her forehead and gently grasped her right hand. "I'll send for the doctor."

"No. It'll pass. But I'm so glad you're here. You're a great comfort."

Tony sat in silence for a few moments. "Amelia—"

"Yes?"

"I received a telegram today. From Jackie."

"Oh? What did she have to say?"

"She's coming to visit me. Today."

Mme G opened her eyes and looked at him. "Today?"

"Yes. She's arriving at the Gare du Nord at five p.m."

Mme G closed her eyes again. "Then you'll have to pick her up at the station. Take the barouche. And be sure to put the hood up so she won't be covered with cement dust by the time she gets here."'

"You don't mind if she stays here?"

"Mind? Of course not. I'm anxious to meet her. My headache will be gone by then and we'll have a delightful dinner together."

Tony collected his thoughts. "You know that she's pregnant."

"Yes. You told me. How far along is she?"

"I don't know exactly. Sixteen, eighteen weeks."

"Then she's hardly showing. And she's coming to visit you. Maybe you're the father after all."

"Possibly. Then you have no objection to her staying for a few days?"

"Not at all. She can stay as long as she likes."

"That's very kind of you, Amelia."

"Just ordinary civility. I want to sleep now, Tony. I'll be as good as new by the time you return from the station."'

He leaned over and kissed her on the forehead. Then he quietly left the room.

CHAPTER 26

J-P took the shortest route to the Gare du Nord, which was across the Île de la Cité and up Boulevard de Sébastopol. The construction that Mme G had complained about was confined to the area around the Théâtre du Châtelet where one of the new metro stations was almost completed.

As they proceeded up the boulevard, Tony became preoccupied with the coming meeting with Jackie. Was he the father of the child, or was it Forbes-Robertson? He had met Forbes-Robertson only briefly in London and knew little about him other than the fact that he was an actor. Was Jackie so easily seduced? Perhaps Mme G was right–the article in the *Herald* was nothing more than malicious gossip meant to sell newspapers. And if he, Tony, were the father, then he would owe Jackie an apology. And perhaps a confession. A confession of his own infidelity.

J-P parked the carriage in front of the station and Tony, after being informed that the train was on time, proceeded to the platform. Great clouds of steam filled the cavernous station, whistles blew, and the hissing of air brakes dissipated like a collective sigh as the train finally came to a halt.

Tony scanned the crowd of passengers as they emerged from the cars and soon spotted her, a woman taller than most, wearing a straw boater hat and a white blouse tucked into a navy-blue skirt. She saw him, smiled broadly, and made her way to him. At first she seemed about to embrace him, then hesitated. But he embraced her warmly and lifted her off the ground.

"You're not angry with me?" she said.

"Why should I be angry? Of course I'm delighted to see you."

"But those rumors?"

"I haven't heard any rumors. Just what I read in the papers."

"Then you saw the article."

"Yes."

"It's not true."

Tony looked into her eyes and saw the innocence and lack of guile that he saw the first time they met on the road to Beaufort. "I believe you."

Jackie said nothing in reply, but only stared at him as if he were her father who suspected her of being naughty but was willing to give her the benefit of the doubt.

"Madame?"

She turned to the sound of the porter's voice. "Ah, oui. C'est mon mari."

"Bonjour, Monsieur." The porter doffed his cap, then replaced it. "Est-ce que vous voudriez un fiacre?"

"Non," Tony said. "Nous avons une voiture. Suivez-nous."

The porter complied, pushing his cart with Jackie's luggage behind them.

Tony pointed out the progress that had been made on the metro line since she was last there along with the pavilions that had been set up along the Seine for the Exposition. They crossed the Île de la Cité and trotted down Boulevard St-Germain, where Jackie showed a keen interest in the boutiques where ladies of fashion stopped to window shop.

Tony glanced down at her belly, which was protruding slightly from the voluminous folds of her skirt. "When's the baby due?"

"Oh," Jackie said, turning her head from the shops. "August, I think."

"Another five months. I think we should find you some maternity clothes."

"I hadn't really thought much about that. Oh, it's so nice to be in Paris again. Now I realize how much I miss it."

Tony chuckled. "I seem to remember that you found it absolutely squalid when you were here before."

"Well, that atelier on Rue de Fleurus *was* rather squalid. Speaking of which, how is Nathaniel? And Marie-Louise?"

"I haven't seen Nat for a while. But the last time I saw him, he told me that Marie-Louise had left him."

"That's too bad."

"He also borrowed some more money from me. I'm afraid Nat is more interested in avoiding his father than he is in painting."

"Speaking of painting, are you getting any work done at Madame Goldstein's?"

"Goldman. As a matter of fact, I am. Monsieur Dantec can hardly keep my paintings in stock."

"That's wonderful! Then this...this arrangement with Madame Goldman is working out?"

"Yes...it's working out."

J-P pulled into Rue de Furstemberg.

"What a lovely street," Jackie said. "It must be very peaceful here."

"Yes, it is. Wait till you see the garden out back."

J-P turned into the alley behind the house and drove through the open doors of the carriage house. He assisted Jackie as she stepped down and then tended to the horses. Tony escorted her through the main door that led to the garden.

"Oh, my goodness!"she said. "It's a garden of Eden! And where is your studio?"

"On the first floor of the carriage house. I'll show it to you, but first I think I'd better introduce you to Madame Goldman."

Tony led her up the stairway to the main house. When they arrived in the drawing room, Mme G was standing in the center of the room, dressed in a blue velvet dress, almost a robe de chambre, but with a bodice embroidered with white lace.

"Your headache's gone?" Tony said.

"Completely," Mme G said. "A long nap is usually the best cure."

"Amelia, allow me to present my wife, Jacqueline LeRoux."

"Enchantée," Mme G said, extending her hand.

"Enchantée, Madame Goldman," Jackie said, extending hers.

"Please call me Amelia," Mme G said. "We need not be so formal as the French. After all, we are Americans."

"Oh," Jackie said. "I thought you were French."

"Only by adoption. Paris is my home now."

There was an awkward silence.

"Well, "Mme G said, "would you like a tour of the house?"

"Oh, yes," Jackie said. "It's beautiful. And I suspect very old."

"Quite old. It is said that Delacroix lived here for a time. It was in disrepair when I bought it and I've restored it to its original condition. But before the tour, I'm sure you'd like to get settled. You'll be staying in Tony's room, of course."

Tony and Jackie looked at each other.

"Of course," Tony said.

J-P appeared at the dining room door with Jackie's portmanteau, awaiting instructions.

"Montrez la voie, J-P," Tony said. Jackie followed, and the three of them ascended the stairs.

After J-P had made a second trip to retrieve the rest of the luggage, including a hat box, Jackie stared out of the window overlooking the square while Tony sat on the bed.

"It is lovely," she said. "I can see why you don't want to leave."

"Oh, I don't intend to stay here forever," Tony said. "The studio's the main thing–but should you decide to return to Paris, we could rent a nice apartment near here."

She turned away from the window. "Do you want me to?"

Tony looked at her in silence for a moment. "You're sure the child is mine?"

"You said at the station that you believed me."

"Yes, but–how can you be sure?"

"Because Tony, I've never even kissed another man!"

"What about Rav Coleman?"

"Rav Coleman? Well, I did allow him to kiss me, but after all, we were engaged."

"Well, that's old news. But Forbes-Robertson–"

She took a newspaper article from her purse, unfolded it, and thrust it into his hands.

"What's this?"

"A letter to the *Times*. From Mr. Forbes-Robertson. Read it, if you please."

Tony read the short letter. "All right. He says he's engaged to marry someone called Gertrude Elliot. And he denies the rumors about the two of you."

"Well?"

"I don't need this, Jackie. Like I said at the station, I believe you." He handed the article back to her. "I just wanted to be sure that *you* were sure."

"Well, I *am* sure. One doesn't get pregnant from kissing."

Tony laughed. "No."

"Then it's settled," Jackie said. "But you still haven't answered my question: do you want me to return to Paris?"

"Yes."

"You don't seem to be very enthusiastic about the idea."

He stood and embraced her. "Of course I want you to be here with me. I'm just thinking of the child. Do you want it to be born in Paris?"

She put her head against his breast. "I don't care where it's born so long as we can all be together."

"What about your career in London?"

"I don't care about that. It's not much of a career, anyway."

"Well, then, I suppose I'll have to start looking for an apartment."

After Tony helped Jackie unpack, they descended to the drawing room where Mme G was again waiting. She led the tour, pointing out the paintings that she had collected over the years. Finally, they made their way to the studio. Along the way it suddenly occurred to Tony that Jackie would be presented with a half a dozen paintings of Mme G in various stages of undress. But it was too late to change course.

"It is said," Mme G said, as they entered the studio, "that Delacroix did some of his finest work here."

Jackie looked around at the paintings, some of which were by famous artists of the past, but there was one wall devoted exclusively to Tony's work. She moved closer to these. "'Antonio'," she said, reading the signatures. "Who was he?"

Mme G and Tony exchanged amused glances.

"Don't you recognize the style?" Mme G said.

Jackie looked at Tony, then the paintings, then again at Tony. "You? You are Antonio?"

"That's my name," Tony said.

"Well, of course that's your name," Jackie said. "But I'm used to–" she turned back to one of the paintings of Mme G, the one of her as the Madonna looking down at her child. "This is so touching. It's wonderful, Tony. I'm so proud of you."

Tony and Mme G again exchanged glances. It was clear that Jackie did not recognize Mme G in the portraits. Whether this was due to the broad brush strokes, or simply to Jackie's inability to imagine this elegant maven of the arts *déshabillé*, it apparently did not dawn on her that Mme G was the model in the paintings.

At the end of the tour, they returned to the drawing room, where Mme G asked Jackie about her experience in the theatre. Jackie dismissed her 'career' as simply a vocation that she fell into because of her mother's activities in this area, and that she didn't take seriously.

"But you have striking features and a statuesque figure. I would think that all eyes would be upon you every moment you are on the stage."

"Thank you, Madame Goldman, but–"

"Please–'Amelia'."

"Of course. I was about to say that there's more to acting than simply having a striking appearance. Acting is an emotionally draining experience. I had rather channel my efforts into being a good mother and a good wife."

"Of course it's a fine thing," Mme G said, "to be a good mother. Perhaps women need no other occupation. But there are some women–"

"Dinner is served," Sabine announced from the dining room.

"Sabine," Mme G said with surprise, "you speak English?"

"A leetle, Madame. Jean-Pierre has been, uh, to teach me."

"Very good! Mais pour ce soir, on va parler français, d'accord?"

"Oui, Madame. D'accord."

Mme G turned to Jackie and said with a smile, "Sabine thinks you're English. I don't suppose you came all the way to Paris to speak only English. "Que la conversation en français commence!"

CHAPTER 27

Over the next few days a curious ménage à trois was established at Rue de Furstemberg. This was not the traditional French notion of the term, of which the three members of the household are thought to be living in a continuous orgy of sexual gratification and sybaritic pleasure. Rather, it was oddly celibate for all three parties–at least at first.

Jackie, for her part, put aside her earlier suspicions that Tony and Mme G were involved in a romantic relationship. She accepted Tony's suggestion– never explicit–that his relationship to Mme G was as student to teacher, or artist to patron. After all, she had a similar relationship to her mother in London. Besides, she grew not only to like Mme G, but to greatly admire her for her multiple qualities, including business acumen, knowledge of art, and social finesse.

Tony, on the other hand, lived in constant fear that Jackie would somehow discover the truth. Though he had told himself that he would have to enlighten her at some point, he could never find just the right moment. At times he felt that he needed to take her aside, almost as a lawyer would a client, and inform her of the situation. But this seemed too cold, too impersonal. At other times, usually in the intimacy of their bedroom, he felt that it would destroy the bond between them that had deep roots in their upbringing and familial relationships. For in spite of his growing dependence on Mme G both emotionally and financially, he didn't want to lose Jackie. And now that he accepted the fact that she had always been faithful to him, he was wracked with guilt that he had not been faithful to her.

For Mme G's part, it was difficult to tell how she viewed the situation. On the surface of it, she seemed to encourage Jackie and Tony to spend as much time as possible with each other, as if she were a matronly matchmaker determined to patch up the recent misunderstanding between them. She also genuinely seemed to like Jackie, and the two of them often went shopping together.

Tony welcomed Mme G's acceptance of this new arrangement and began to think that he might never have to make his confession to Jackie. After all, he reasoned, what purpose would it serve? Things were going well, he was as productive as ever, and soon the Exposition would open. Still, a little demon inside him continued to gnaw at his conscience.

Mme G's headaches and stomach upsets seemed to have evaporated. No more mood swings, no more outbursts of jealousy, even though she knew—or suspected–that Tony and Jackie were enjoying their conjugal rights as she slept alone.

But Mme G was wrong in this instance–Tony refrained from initiating sexual intercourse with Jackie, partly out of his own ignorance of a woman's desires during pregnancy, and partly because of his conventional notion that having sex with a woman in an advanced state of pregnancy was somehow unseemly. Nor did Jackie's growing belly arouse the passions in him that her once slender figure did.

So the celibate ménage à trois continued.

Things began to change, however, when the big day that everyone in Paris had been waiting for finally arrived: the grand opening of the Exposition.

J-P readied the horses and brought the barouche out front. Mme G and Jackie spent an extra hour in their respective boudoirs dressing–or being dressed, in the case of Mme G–and applying the appropriate accessories. Tony, now himself a man of fashion, adjusted his cravate and his waistcoat which he still found suitable for chain and pocket watch in spite of his new dependence on the wristwatch that Mme G had given him. Thinking of this wristwatch, he recalled that when Jackie asked him about it, he told her his first lie: that he had bought it for himself when M. Dantec had sold his first painting.

After a substantial breakfast in anticipation of a great deal of walking, the three of them mounted the barouche and J-P took the familiar route to the Place de la Concorde. Crossing the bridge, the Porte Monumentale loomed ahead like the entrance to the palace of an oriental potentate. A grand and sinuous arch surmounted by a statue of 'La Parisienne' dressed more like Mme G than a Greek or Roman goddess, was flanked by two towers that resembled minarets. Directly below the arch was a sculpture that suggested the prow of a boat, presumably one that might navigate the Seine. The towers and arch were decorated with thousands of variegated ceramic tiles.

J-P parked the barouche beneath a poplar tree, one of six that flanked the approach to the ticket booths. Tony reached into his vest pocket and produced the price of admission for the three of them.

"Well," said Mme G, "we'll see if the expenditure of 100 million francs is justified." She opened her parasol to shade her eyes from the sun and Jackie followed suit.

"We can't see it all in one day," Tony said. "But I suppose we can hit the highlights this morning. I want to see the *Cinéorama* I've heard so much about."

"What about your paintings?" Jackie said. She was beginning to waddle a bit with the extra weight but was still steady on her feet. "Where are they?"

"In the Petit Palais, just up the road. But we have plenty of time for that." He took her by the hand. "Are you sure you have the stamina for all this walking?"

"Quite sure," Jackie pulled her hand away. "Don't treat me like an invalid."

"There's a moving sidewalk from Les Invalides to the Champ de Mars," Mme G said. "We can do that after the Petit Palais."

"On y va!" Tony said.

After consulting a map, Tony discovered that most of the scientific and technology exhibits, including the Cinéorama, were located across the river along the Champs de Mars, in the shadow of the Eiffel Tower. So it was decided that they would visit the Petit Palais first.

This 'Petit' Palais was only 'petit' compared to the Grand Palais across the street. It was more like the summer château of a Renaissance prince. Nevertheless, it was designed to exhibit art and the central courtyard afforded an idyllic resting place for visitors.

After wandering the galleries for an hour or so, and admiring the work of Rembrandt, Rubens, Poussin, Ingres, and Delacroix, as well as contemporary painters like Monet, Pissarro, and Cézanne, Jackie stopped for a moment to rest on an upholstered bench. Tony and Mme G sat down on either side of her.

"Tired?" Tony said.

"Only a little. But Tony—where are your paintings?"

Tony looked around the gallery. "I'm a newcomer. Perhaps they put my stuff in the basement with the other rubbish."

"Don't you dare denigrate yourself like that," Mme G said. "Even as a joke. People will hear and start to believe it. I'll ask that attendant over there." She got up and walked over to a uniformed attendant who was about to nod off. He seemed startled, then engaged in a brief conversation with Mme G that neither Tony nor Jackie could hear.

She returned. "He says that the work of the young artists is in the national pavilions. On the other side of the river."

"The national pavilions?" Tony said. "Which one?"

"He didn't say. There're only two possibilities, however–the French and the American."

Tony stood. "Well, then, we'll have to visit both. I should have consulted Monsieur Dantec before we came."

"They probably think you are French," Mme G said. "That would be my first guess."

Tony looked at Jackie. "Rested?"

"A minute longer," Jackie said. "How far are these pavilions?"

"Just across the new bridge," Mme G said. "And from there we can take the moving sidewalk to the Champ de Mars."

So off they went, stopping briefly to look at the fish in the Aquarium.

After reviewing the paintings in the French Pavilion, where they saw the unmistakable figure of Toulouse-Lautrec entertaining his admirers, and not having seen one of Tony's paintings, they moved on to the American Pavilion. Here they discovered an area called the Exhibit of American Negroes, which was primarily devoted to the achievements of African Americans since the Civil War. There was a statue of Frederick Douglass as a centerpiece, a tribute to Booker T. Washington, and numerous photographs of black men and women standing proudly before churches, homes, and businesses. And off in one corner there were a dozen or so paintings, some by Henry O. Tanner–whom Tony had met once during his first sojourn in Paris–and four by 'Antonio.'

This placement of his paintings seemed a pyrrhic victory to Tony. He was an *American* painter, not a Negro painter. On the other hand, seeing his work next to Mr. Tanner's, as if he were the latter's equal, instilled in him a sense of pride, for he greatly admired Tanner's work.

One of his paintings particularly interested Jackie. It was the one of Mme G, her back to the viewer, looking over her shoulder. Tony had dared to call it 'Mme G,' but it was not labeled as such on the painting itself, but in the catalogue. There were several other people looking at it as well.

"This is of the same model as the ones in the studio, isn't it?" Jackie said.

Tony glanced at Mme G, who simply continued to stare at the painting. "Yes. A different look, though."

"I think it's exquisite," Jackie said. "More realistic than the others, more detail."

"The judges, I'm told," Tony said, "favor more traditional paintings than the newer, more adventurous ones. I wish I had—"

"Oh," Jackie said. "I prefer this one to all the others. She has such an impish smile, like a child slightly embarrassed at being surprised, but flirtatious all the same."

Tony cleared his throat. "That's a good assessment. Still, a bit conventional. Let's move on. I'm anxious to see the scientific exhibits on the Champ de Mars."

He walked off, hoping that Jackie would follow, but she continued to stare at the painting. Instead, Mme G followed him.

When they all emerged from the pavilion, Jackie briefly regarded Mme G with a curious stare.

"I will ask Monsieur Dantec," Mme G said, opening her parasol, "if he can't arrange to move your paintings to the Petit Palais. I think they deserve a better venue. On y va! I'm as curious about this moving sidewalk, Tony, as you are about the Cinéorama. And it will provide a restful conveyance for Jacqueline."

"Yes, I'm sure," Jackie said.

CHAPTER 28

While Jackie was willing to sit in a basket the size of Mme G's garden with two hundred other people beneath a hot air balloon at the Cinéorama, she drew the line at the Grande Roue de Chicago. This was a giant Ferris wheel modeled after the one that debuted at the 1893 Columbian Exposition and carried up to twelve hundred passengers in forty cars to a height of 110 meters above the Champ de Mars.

At least the Cinéorama was stationary. The passengers sat motionless while ten synchronized cameras projected the entire panorama of Paris onto a circular screen as the basket 'ascended.' This was an interesting and visually exciting experience, but the Grande Roue, in Jackie's opinion, was suicidal.

"One hundred and ten meters?" she said, as they exited the Cinéorama. "That's over three hundred feet up in the air! What if something breaks–a cable, or a pulley for instance–and the car crashes to the ground?"

Tony chuckled. "I see your point. It's unlikely, though."

"Well, unlikely doesn't sound like very good odds to me. And I'm not going to risk Tony, Jr.'s life as well as my own on such a contraption." Jackie instinctively grasped her belly. "You and Amelia go. I think I'll take a look at the Palace of Optics. Can you lend me five francs? I have only pounds sterling."

Tony gave her the five francs and he and Mme G headed for the Grande Roue. Jackie walked on until she arrived at the Palace of Optics, which was hard to miss due to the colored lights that radiated inside a shell-like arch.

As Tony and Mme G ascended in the Grande Roue, they discussed Jackie's condition.

"Do you think I should have left her on her own?" Tony said.

"Oh, you're like all first-time fathers," Mme G said with a twinkle in her eye. "Overly protective. She'll be fine."

"I suppose you should know."

"Of course I do. All mothers do." She looked away wistfully as the wheel lifted them to greater heights.

"The view is spectacular," Tony said.

"It is indeed. Look—we're nearly as high as the Tour Eiffel. And you can see the Arc de Triomphe."

Tony looked to the northeast. "Napoleon's monument to his own vanity. And to war. The South is littered with statues and monuments glorifying the Confederacy. Not as impressive but driven by the same impulse."

Mme G patted him on the knee. "You take these things too seriously. The thousands of people who admire the Arc de Triomphe everyday are hardly thinking of war. Rather the beauty of its architecture and its sculpted reliefs. What if you were commissioned to paint it?"

"I'd show a pile of mangled bodies beneath it."

Mme G laughed. "Goodness! Are you a pacifist?"

"No, but most wars are just like Napoleon's—adventures in vanity."

"And who is it that starts wars? And fights them?"

Tony smiled. "Men."

"Correct. Napoleon was simply doing what all men do—only he was more successful at it."

Tony laughed. "Sometimes I think you are absolutely perverse, Amelia. Here you are making a case for perpetual war."

"I'm doing nothing of the kind. I'm just teasing you. Oh, the wheel has stopped."

Tony looked down at the base of the great wheel where the operator seemed to be frantically manipulating the levers. "Perhaps there's a short circuit of some kind."

Mme G folded her hands in her lap. "Well, we'll just have to wait. Let's hope Jackie's fears aren't realized."

They sat in silence for several moments along with the other passengers. In fact, the air at this altitude seemed unusually calm and quiet.

"Tony…" Mme G finally said tentatively, "I have something to tell you."

Tony looked at her, a bit surprised by her suddenly solemn tone. "What?"

"This is not easy for me."

"What is it, Amelia?"

"I think I'm pregnant."

Tony stared at her for several seconds without a word. Suddenly the wheel began to turn again, and several of the passengers began to clap. The car slowly descended. "Are you sure?"

"No. But it's highly likely. I'll go to the doctor tomorrow and see what he says. Are you angry with me?"

"How can I be angry with you? It's not as if you did it intentionally. I thought you were past...well, that it would no longer be a problem."

"Because I'm over the hill?"

"I didn't say that. I ...I just don't know that much about women, I guess."

"No, you don't. Some women bear children into their late forties. But that's beside the point. The point is that we are going to have to tell Jackie. She's going to find out anyway."

"Not if I send her back to London." Tony laughed, rather nervously.

"Even if you send her to China. She's going to find out. I think we should all sit down together and discuss it."

Tony looked at her incredulously. "Now who's the one who doesn't understand women? Are you mad?"

"No, I'm not mad. And though it will be hard, it will not be as hard as trying to conceal it from her and compounding the problem over a period of weeks or even months. Better to lay our cards on the table. Ah, here we are."

When they approached the Palace of Optics, Jackie was standing outside waiting for them.

"Are you all right?" she said. "I saw the wheel stop."

"Only a temporary malfunction," Tony said. "No harm was done."

"Well, I'm glad I didn't go with you. I would have been terrified."

"Why don't we check out the Globe Céleste?" Tony said. "That should be safe enough. And we'll simply sit and watch."

"Watch what?"

"The stars. It's a planetarium."

"I think I've had enough for one day. The light show was marvelous. Like being inside a kaleidoscope. I don't think the planetarium can match that."

"Then let's get back on the moving sidewalk," Tony said. "J-P must be getting bored."

So back to the moving sidewalk they went, and when they arrived at the Porte Monumentale on the right bank, they found J-P in the carriage– asleep.

CHAPTER 29

The next morning Mme G was out of the house before Tony and Jackie awakened.

At breakfast they discussed the previous day's events at the Exposition and the possibility of Tony's paintings being moved to the Petit Palais.

"My paintings have been selling well," Tony said, "But I'm still a relative unknown."

"Well," Jackie said, "if your work is exhibited at the Petit Palais, maybe you'll become a known."

Tony smiled as he buttered a croissant. "As I said, I will speak to Monsieur Dantec. But there's only so much he can do."

"You say Madame G is your patron and manager. Surely she must have some influence."

"She does. But the Committee prides itself on being incorruptible and above the fray. Trying to influence them in any way can backfire. They do listen to dealers, however."

Jackie struggled to dislodge a wedge of grapefruit with a tiny silver spoon designed for that purpose. "Speaking of Madame G–where is she?"

"She said yesterday that she had an appointment of some kind. Probably business–she seems to be working out some sort of deal with the baron."

"The baron?" Finally she succeeded in extracting the wedge from the rind of the grapefruit and popped it into her mouth.

"Baron Alphonse de Rothstein. They're both bankers. I suppose they're negotiating to buy the Eiffel Tower."

Jackie looked up from her grapefruit in astonishment. "The Eiffel Tower?"

Tony laughed. "I'm joking. But I have no doubt that between the two of them they could manage it."

They continued to eat in silence for a few minutes. When they finished, Sabine appeared and removed their plates.

"Chocolat, Madame?" Sabine said.

"That would be delicious," Jackie said. "S'il vous plaît."

When Sabine left to retrieve the chocolate, Jackie turned to Tony.
"Tony–"

"Yes?"

"Madame G is the model in that painting at the Exposition, isn't she?"

Tony had just picked up a copy of *Le Figaro* that J-P brought in for him
every morning and was reading the front page. He affected to be absorbed
in the paper. "Hmm? Madame G? Uh, yes–she was the model."

"So she models for you in between these huge business deals she's involved
in?"

"Well...she volunteered. And it so happens that she was the just the sort
of model I was looking for."

"Just the sort you were looking for–beautiful, sexy and rich?"

Tony put down the paper. "What are you getting at, Jackie? Madame G
is all business. As my manager she wants to see me succeed. And she'll do
anything to see that that happens."

"Anything?"

Sabine returned with the chocolate on a dish, which she first offered to
Jackie, who took a *fourrée à la fraise*, and then to Tony, who waved her
away.

"Not anything," Tony said. "But she is like the French–nudity is not
something she considers to be 'dirty' or necessarily salacious."

"Mmm," Jackie said, savoring the chocolate. "Salacious–like this
absolutely divine strawberry cream chocolate. A good word, 'salacious.' In
its proper place, of course."

Tony felt that she was tormenting him and could stand it no longer. "All
right! We were going to tell you, anyway. Yes, Madame G and I have had
a...'relationship,' while you were in London. I thought that you had been
unfaithful to me and that you were going to have another man's child. I
thought it was over between us. And Madame G was here."

"And very available, apparently."

"You could say that."

Jackie finished her *fourrée à la fraise* while Tony picked up his newspaper
again and tried to focus on an article. She pushed the plate aside and leaned
back in her chair.

"What are we to do?"

Tony looked at her. "What do you want to do?"

"Well, I can't stay here, obviously."

"Why not?"

"To be part of your harem? Number Two wife?"

"Jackie—you'll never be Number Two to me. You're my wife. I love you and I want you to have the child—here, in Paris."

Jackie looked down at her belly, then looked up again. "If you really love me—you'll leave Madame G and come with me to London. I'll have the child there."

"Jackie—my work is here. My career is about to take off. If I go to London, I'll have to start all over again."

Jackie looked around the dining room, which was filled with the work of Old Masters. "Your work. Your career. I was always willing to subordinate my career to yours, but only if—"

"If what?"

"If you were faithful to me."

Tony put the paper down again and laced his fingers together with his elbows resting on the arms of his chair. "I told you why I was...why I was unfaithful. It was a mistake. I'm sorry. I truly am. Can't you forgive me?"

Jackie looked at him so sternly that he turned away. "I don't know. I'll have to think about it."

After breakfast, Jackie retired to their room and Tony went to the studio, where he embarked upon a new painting. This was inspired by the Porte Monumentale. It seemed to Tony the most exotic of all of the architecture of the Exposition. Certainly oriental in design, it was actually a romanticized version of some Middle Eastern country, with a sensuously curved archway decorated with brilliantly colored ceramic tiles and statues of eunuchs guarding the forbidden delights within. Or at least that was the illusion. But he would give it his own perspective—that of a Negro boy in rags looking up in wonder at the splendor of the Orient...a splendor that would forever be out of reach.

Shortly before noon, Mme G returned from her appointment with the doctor. Finding no one in the drawing room or the dining room, she went to the studio, where she discovered Tony intently at work. She entered without his noticing her and stood several feet behind him for a few moments studying the canvas.

"An interesting departure from your usual subject matter," she said. "Are you now an architectural painter?"

Tony didn't respond at first, almost as if he expected her to be there. "I don't care for categories, as you must know. But the Exposition offers so many visual delights, I can't resist taking advantage of them." He turned around and looked at her, brush in hand. "What did the doctor have to say?"

"He confirmed my own diagnosis."

Tony put the brush down and used a rag to wipe his hands. "Then we are in a fix."

"Fix? There's no fix. We only have to sit down with Jacqueline—"

"She already knows about us. I told her this morning."

"Good. What did she say?"

"She said she would make a decision soon as to whether to stay and have the baby here or go back to London."

"'And did you tell her I was pregnant, too?"

"I didn't know whether you were or not until now."

"So, we still need to sit down with her."

"Not necessarily. If she goes to London she need not know."

Mme G sat down on the divan. "Oh, Tony—she's going to find out. Better to tell her now."

Tony stared out the window "Why? If we tell her and she goes to London to have the child, it's over between us. She might as well file for divorce at the same time."

"Divorce is not so easy to get. Why do you think I left California without one? I'm still legally married. If anything, a French or British divorce is even more difficult to obtain."

Tony sighed and turned to look at her. "Then we're in the same boat. Adulterers."

Mme G laughed. "That's your Puritan upbringing. European couples have been maintaining separate households for centuries."

Tony sat down beside her. "I must say I never thought of myself as a Puritan. But it doesn't seem right to me."

She patted him on the knee. "You'll get used to it. And I think Jacqueline will, too. We only have to tell her."

"You don't know her like I do. She's even more of a Puritan than I am. No, it's impossible. At least for now. Let's wait to see whether she decides to go or stay."

"And if she decides to stay?"

"She won't. But if she does, we'll have to tell her. In which case, *then* she'll leave."

Mme G rose from the divan. "You underestimate the power of a woman's love, Tony. Jacqueline is deeply in love with you. I can see it in her eyes whenever you're in her presence. Why do you think I'm willing to share you with her?"

Tony stared at her uncomprehendingly. "You would accept such a situation? A ménage à trois?"

"Yes. It's better than nothing. I'll go get her."

Tony leaped up from the divan and grabbed her by the arm. "No! It's impossible. At least wait for her decision."

"Let go of my arm–you're hurting me!"

Tony released his grip. "Sorry. But we can't tell her. Listen to me this once, Amelia."

Mme G stared at him for a moment. "All right. She's your wife. But how long will we have to wait? I don't like this kind of skulking about."

"There's no need for 'skulking.' Just give her some time to digest the initial shock of my confession that we've been having an affair."

"An affair? Is that what we've been having? It sounds like a stroll in the park. If that's all our relationship means to you, I'll throw you both out!"

"Amelia–don't get excited. Until now you've–"

"I have my limits, Tony. Every woman does. I've made you an offer–a very generous one, I'd say. I'll share you with another woman on the condition that we are both on an equal footing. I won't be your concubine."

Tony sighed and fell back onto the divan. "Concubine? Now you're sounding like Jackie, who says she won't be my Number Two wife." He put his elbows on his knees and looked at the floor. "All right. Go get her. We'll lay all our cards on the table as you suggest. But I know what the result will be. And then you won't have to share me with anyone. Isn't that your strategy in the first place?"

Mme G suppressed a smile. "We'll wait until tomorrow morning."

She left the room and Tony went back to his easel.

CHAPTER 30

The next morning Tony rose early while Jackie remained in bed. She appeared to be asleep. So Tony dressed and came downstairs to the little breakfast room adjacent to the dining room. It had a nice view of the garden.

Mme G came down a few minutes later as Tony was reading *Le Figaro*. He rose to greet her.

"Sleep well?" he said.

"Quite well, thank you. Where's Jacqueline?"

"Still asleep."

"Any discussion last night?"

"Just the usual pleasantries. You'd think she was visiting a distant relative."

Mme G smiled as she sat down and rang her little dinner bell. Sabine appeared.

"Bonjour, Sabine," she said.

"Bonjour, Madame."

"J'aimerais bien des crêpes, un peu de crème, des fraises et un jus d'orange, s'il te plaît."

"Oui, Madame. Et Monsieur?"

"La même chose," Tony said. "Oh–et du café, s'il vous plaît."

"Oui, Monsieur."

After Sabine had retreated to the kitchen, Tony went back to his paper.

"You needn't be so formal with Sabine, you know," Mme G said.

Tony looked up. "You'd rather I be more familiar?"

Mme G frowned. "You know what I mean. You're part of the family here now."

Tony stared at her for a moment, then went back to his paper.

While waiting for their breakfast, they heard someone descending the stairs. They both looked up to see Jackie appear dressed in the same skirt, blouse and broad-brimmed straw hat that she had arrived in.

Tony rose from his chair. "Good morning."

"Good morning," Jackie said, somewhat uncertainly. She clung tightly to her purse, which rested on her growing belly. "I've made my decision."

"And…" Tony said.

"I'm returning to London."

Tony exhaled slowly with a sigh of resignation, then pulled out a chair next to him. "You know what's best, I suppose. But let's discuss it a little more while we have breakfast. It's not too late to–"

"No," Jackie said, still standing rigidly at the foot of the stairs. "I'm not hungry at the moment. I'll get something on the train."

"When does the train leave?" Tony said. "I'll have J-P bring the carriage around and–"

"J-P's already arranged for a cab."

Tony let go of the back of the chair. "Jackie, the least I can do is–"

"You've done all you can do. I don't blame you for what happened. It was inevitable, I suppose, once we separated. I should have remained here in Paris with you. It's as much my fault as yours." She turned to Mme G. "Amelia, I can't thank you enough for your hospitality and your friendship. You've been very kind. And just as I don't blame Tony for the present state of affairs, I don't blame you, either."

J-P appeared at the door.

"Well," Jackie said. "The cab man is here. J-P has already taken my luggage down. Goodbye."

Tony went to her and attempted to give her a kiss, but she gently pushed him away.

"No, Tony," she said. "No false displays of affection, please. I can't bear it."

"False?" Tony said. "Jackie, I can never be–"

"False? You already have. Please Tony–I'm trying to make it as easy for all of us as I can. Goodbye."

And she hurried out, tears in her eyes, followed by J-P.

Tony and Mme G were left staring first at the empty door frame, then at each other.

Tony sat down. "What have I done?"

"You gave her a choice," Mme G said. "That was your first mistake. You should have insisted that she stay here."

"How could I do that? She's not my slave. She's a free woman, just as you are."

"Women don't always want so much freedom."

Tony laughed. "That's rich, coming from you. You left your husband because you wanted to be free."

"He was a brute. I never loved him. But Jacqueline loves you. If you had put your foot down, she would have gladly complied."

"Gladly? I doubt it."

Sabine arrived with their breakfast plates and set them down.

"Sabine," Mme G said, "que J-P prèpare la voiture á son retour. Monsieur et moi allons faire un tour ce matin."

"A ride?" Tony said. "To where?"

"The Bois de Vincennes. The Luxembourg. Anywhere. The weather's beautiful. It'll do us good."

The weather was in fact beautiful and J-P drove them at a leisurely pace as they had no particular place to go.

"When are you due?" Tony said as they passed by the ancient church of St-Germain.

"December. It will be just in time for Christmas."

"Jackie is due in August. My God! What will I do with two children, one in London and one in Paris?"

Mme G smiled. "You'll love them both. And they'll be well-cared for. Of that you may be assured."

They rode on for a half-mile or so, noting the literati sitting out on the pavement of their favorite cafés, drinking their coffee and in deep heated discussions.

"I'm going to have to go to London for the child's birth," Tony said. "Whether I'm invited or not."

"I think you should," Mme G said. "After all, it's your child. Jacqueline can't bar you from her door. As her husband, you have certain rights."

"Rights? Well, I don't know about that. There's no more natural right than a mother's right to her child. And even if the law would allow it, I wouldn't want to separate them."

"Perhaps you could, by that time, convince her to return to Paris."

"Perhaps."

"À la gauche!" Mme G suddenly barked out to J-P.

"What's to the left?" Tony said.

"The Luxembourg. It must be lovely this time of year."

They proceeded to the Square Boucicault, a pretty little park at the intersection of Rue de Sèvres and Boulevard Raspail and turned towards the gardens on Tony's former street, Rue de Fleurus.

"I wonder if Nat is still living there," he said, looking up at the fifth-floor atelier as they passed by.

"Nat? Oh, your former roommate. I thought you said he went back to America."

"Not that I know of. In any case, he still owes me money. I don't suppose I'll ever get it."

"Let's not think of such things today. Ah, here we are."

J-P drove through the spiked-iron gates of the gardens and among the plane trees that flanked the drive.

"Oh, look!" Mme G said. "A puppet theatre!"

Tony gazed past the trees to a clearing where his eyes came to rest on a miniature proscenium with wooden heads of marionettes bobbing up and down. "I've had my fill of Punch and Judy shows. They seem primarily designed to teach kids the Golden Rule: Might makes right."

She gave him a playful slap on the arm. "Oh, you're taking an innocent pastime too seriously. J-P! Arrête-toi!"

Tony sighed. "Okay. But let's not spend a great deal of time here. I want to see some of the statuary around the central basin. Have you seen them? They're all of notable women."

"No, I haven't. But we can do that later. Look! There's Louis XVI and Marie Antoinette. How life-like they are!" Mme G practically dragged Tony along the path to the theatre, where they found a seat among the folding chairs set up in front of the little theatre. The marionettes were indeed quite life-like, carefully and expertly carved, with period dress and powdered wigs. At this moment, Marie-Antoinette was upbraiding the king for having an alleged affair with one of his courtesans.

Perhaps it was appropriate that few children were present, as the subject of the little drama was a bit risqué and no doubt quite boring to the younger set. But the adults seemed mesmerized by the performance.

After this harangue on Marie-Antoinette's part, to much laughter on the part of the audience, the two marionettes took a deep bow and the curtain closed rather abruptly. But more clapping and cries of 'Bis! Bis!' resulted in the curtain opening again, and this time the queen chased the king around the little stage with a rolling pin. There were howls of laughter and the curtains closed again.

When the clapping died down, Tony turned to Mme G. "Just goes to show that adults are children, too."

Mme G laughed. "And laugh at the same things. Look–the puppeteers are coming out for a bow."

Tony turned back to the little theatre and saw a man and a woman bowing deeply to applause.

"Good Lord!" he said.

"What's the matter?"

"It's Nat."

"Your painter friend? Are you sure?"

"Of course I'm sure. I lived with the man for three years."

"Well...what's he doing manipulating puppets?"

"I haven't the faintest idea. And that woman—I've never seen her before. I wonder what's happened to Marie-Louise?"

"Well, let's go and see. You've never introduced me."

They rose from their chairs and approached the little theatre.

Nat, who was packing up the marionettes, looked up from a wooden box made for this purpose. "Tony! You've come to see my new handiwork, have you?"

Tony extended his hand. "It was just by chance. We were out for a drive. Oh—Nat, this is my friend Amelia Goldman. Amelia, Nat Holmes."

"Enchanté," Nat said with a little bow.

"Enchantée," Mme G said.

Nat turned to the young woman next to him, a pretty brunette with spit curls pasted against her forehead and large hoop earrings. She was wearing a colorful calico dress. "Et je te présente ma femme, Carlotta."

"Ta femme?" Tony said. "You're married?"

"That's right, old man," Nat said, grinning. "Going on two months now."

Tony extended his hand to Carlotta. "Enchanté, Madame."

Carlotta smiled and gave a little curtsy. "Enchantée, Monsieur Tony."

Then the ladies exchanged greetings.

"Well, ah, Nat," Tony said. "My congratulations, of course. But this is all rather sudden. Are you still painting?"

"Oh, I dabble at it a bit. But Carlotta's introduced me to a whole new world. You should come out to our camp and I'll show you how the freest people in the world live!"

"Your camp?"

"A gypsy camp. It's in the Bois de Boulogne." Nat laughed. "At least until the gendarmes run us off. But then we'll find another spot."

"'I see. Well, perhaps—"

"By the way, Tony old boy—I can pay you five hundred francs of the money I owe you now. The old man kicked the bucket a few weeks ago and my brother sent me a small amount of cash while the estate is being settled. When that's done, he'll have to send me my half and we'll be square."

"Well, of course, Nat," Tony said. "There's no hurry. Where, uh, where exactly is this camp in the Bois?"

"In the Parc de Bagatelle. Into the Porte de Passy, round the Hippodrome, and up the Allée de la Reine Marguerite. You can't miss it. Or rather, you can, so you have to plunge into the trees and look for the tents. To keep the authorities guessing, you know."

"Yes...well, I'll make a point of it. Good to see you, Nat. We must be off."

"Au revoir!"

Tony and Mme G walked back to the carriage and continued their exploration of the gardens.

"A gypsy," Mme G said. "Your friend is quite adventurous."

"'Impulsive,' I think is the better word. I didn't even know gypsies married."

"Oh, yes. It's quite an elaborate ritual, I'm told. But do you think it's safe to go to their camp?"

"Safe? I don't know why it wouldn't be. Ah! Here's the basin. This is where I painted that scene of the boys sailing their toy boats."

"Mon Dieu! Mme G said. "They're still here!"

Tony laughed as J-P drove the carriage around the basin, which was flanked by statuary on either side.

As they passed by these statues, they seemed to form a gauntlet, each with the face of Jackie gazing down at him with sadness and reproach.

CHAPTER 31

Jackie's trip back to London was anything but pleasant. She felt nauseous just before Abbeville and had to spend a half hour in the loo. And on the ferry to Dover it was even worse. By the time she reached Victoria Station, she felt spent and emaciated, but managed, with help from a porter, to make it to the entrance where she took a cab to Eaton Square.

"Goodness!" Lucinda said, as Alastair escorted Jackie into the drawing room. "You're as pale as a ghost. What's happened?"

Jackie collapsed into an armchair. "Nothing's happened. At least not on the train. I just couldn't keep anything down."

"You poor thing–do you feel like eating?"

"Perhaps some soup."

Lucinda ordered the cook to prepare some soup and then sat down opposite her daughter. "How did it go in Paris? Did Tony believe you?"

"Yes, he believed me."

"And?"

"And he's staying in Paris."

"Staying? Then he's not going to be here for the birth of his child?"

"I don't think so. He prefers the company of Madame Goldman."

"Who is Madame Goldman?"

"His landlady. And patron. And lover."

Lucinda seemed not to be the least shocked by this news. "Frenchman take lovers as casually as cats take milk."

"But Tony's not a Frenchman."

"He's becoming one, apparently."

Jackie sighed. "I'd rather not discuss it right now, Mother."

Alastair brought a bowl of soup with biscuits on a tray and set it down. Lucinda looked up at him. "Do you have a mistress, Alastair?"

"Madam?"

"A mistress, a lover. We needn't pretend that you have no personal life, do we, Alastair? After all, you and the other servants are privy to every intimate detail of my life, isn't that so?"

Alastair cleared his throat. "I must say, Madam, that we are used to your, ah, shall I say, 'casual' American ways, but–"

"Out with it, Alastair. This is nothing really personal–it's a sort of survey to make a point. Do you have a mistress?"

"I am married, Madam."

"I know that. I also know that your wife works for Lady Carstairs and that you rarely see each other. What do you do for companionship?"

"Well...I do have a female friend who occasionally accompanies me to the opera. But it is entirely innocent, I assure you."

"Of course it is. I apologize if I've made you uncomfortable, Alastair. As I said, it was to make a point to my niece. Men will seek out female companionship whatever their marital status, isn't that so?"

"I would not venture to contradict you, Madam."

"Thank you, Alastair. That will be all."

Alastair made a little bow and left the room.

"Mother! Why do you torment your own servants?"

"It's a game we play. They pretend not to notice my lovers' coming and going and I pretend that they have no carnal appetite whatsoever. And speaking of appetite, you haven't touched your soup. You must eat something."

Jackie picked up her spoon. "Then I assume that you think that I should simply ignore Tony's philandering?"

"I wouldn't say 'ignore.' I would say put it away until such time that the knowledge may become useful."

Jackie tested the soup. "My mother, who 'set the murderous Machiavel to school.'"

Lucinda emitted her peculiar breathy laugh. "I see you know your Shakespeare, Jackie. I think you would make a fine Lady Anne to Johnny's Richard III."

Later that night Jackie lay in bed wondering at the events of the past couple of weeks in Paris. She rested against a pillow in a half-sitting position, a book in one hand, her belly beneath the other. She could feel the fetus moving from time to time, though there were no violent kicks. Perhaps it would be a girl. Her mother's blasé attitude towards Tony's infidelity disturbed her. Granted, her mother was always a rebel against convention, a Bohemian by both nature and choice, but she couldn't believe that she would take her own husband's–if she had one–infidelity so lightly. Looking around the bedroom, which was so carefully appointed with fine furniture and exquisite fabrics, she felt that Lucinda was really a *grande bourgeoise* at heart. She had established herself in London as a maven of the theatre, ran an efficient household of which a noblewoman would be proud, and was discreet in her amorous adventures.

What would she do if Tony returned and brought Mme G with him? Would she be so blasé then?

In any case, Tony was not her problem. He was her own. Oh, why can't people keep their promises? What was more sacred than the bonds of holy matrimony?...Perhaps her mother was right. She was too old-fashioned. Old fashioned! She laughed. The irony of it. Her mother was born before the Civil War! She, Jacqueline, was supposed to be of the 'liberal' generation, the generation of suffragists and trousers for women and smoking in dining cars. But somehow she didn't feel so 'liberated.' Absolute freedom, someone said, led to absolute tyranny–and, she might add–chaos.

She laid the book down–a copy of Emily Dickinson's poems–and carefully turned on her side as she had been instructed to do by Dr. Thurloe so as not to put too much pressure on her pelvic area. She wondered what the child would be like. After all, Tony, though only 1/16th African, was assumed to be black by all who met him. Light-skinned, but still 'black.' The child would be only 1/32nd African, but the world–especially in the American South–would consider him to be black. Oh, that ridiculous 'one-drop' rule! If he does appear to be black, perhaps they should remain in Europe. Or if Tony decided to continue to live with his paramour, and the child appears to be white, perhaps she should return to South Carolina. Or perhaps remain in London with her mother and send the child to Eaton and Oxford!

She laughed at this notion and began to doze off until she felt some movement in her belly. It was a kick! Very definitely a kick. But then silence and stillness.

She fell asleep quickly, her hand on her warm belly.

CHAPTER 32

As spring became summer, Paris burst open into a *fête champêtre* with flowers that seemed to sprout from every window, every balcony, even the cracks in the sidewalks. One could hardly walk along the Champs-Elysées without being accosted by a peddler of peonies, poppies, or primroses that had no doubt been snatched from their stalks in the Tuileries or the Luxembourg.

Tony was uncertain as to what to paint during this vernal effulgence. There was color everywhere. But he had exhausted the potential subject matter in the garden beneath the studio window and though he returned to the Luxembourg several times since encountering Nat there, he had grown tired of this kind of painting. M. Dantec, however, found his efforts in this regard charming, and had sold more than a dozen of his canvases.

He wondered whether he might venture out to the Bois and collect his money. But knowing Nat, he was doubtful whether he would really get it, since Nat was prone to offering all manner of excuses at the last moment. Still, he was curious as to what this gypsy camp was like. And perhaps it would offer new subject matter.

So he announced to Mme G that he was going to the Bois for this purpose.

"It could be dangerous," she said, as they finished their breakfast.

"Why?"

"Gypsies are notorious thieves. They've even been known to murder people."

"I hardly think even Nat would be so foolish as to live among a band of murderers. A lot of that talk is just that–talk. It reminds me of the prejudice against blacks in the South. Sure, there are Negroes who rob and murder, just as there are whites who do so. But the numbers are greatly exaggerated."

Mme G eyed him skeptically and buttered her croissant. "Will you be taking the carriage?"

"I don't think so. Just one of the horses. I'd take the metro, which originates at the northeastern end of the Bois, but I don't believe it's open yet."

"Then take Araby. He's spirited but very calm in the midst of noise and chaos."

Tony laughed. "Chaos? I hardly think it will be chaotic. Nat likes peace and quiet for his painting, like I do. He'd leave the camp in a second if there was the slightest disturbance."

"Just the same–I think you might be wise to take a pistol. I have one upstairs, in the library."

Tony pushed his chair away from the table and wiped his beard with his napkin. "Now you're really being ridiculous. Firearms only get one into trouble."

"But they can get one out as well. It's up to you, however. I have an appointment with the baron this morning."

"The baron? It seems that you and the baron have a close relationship. Can this business deal you're working on be so complex as to need a dozen meetings or more?"

"Jealous? I assure you it is all business. And the meetings *are* necessary. The baron wants to expand his banking empire into California, and he feels that my bank would be a perfect fit. We're very close to an agreement, but the authorities in California have to sign off on it."

Tony sighed. "Well, it's all beyond me, even though I have some banking experience myself." He chuckled. "Beaufort is a bit out of the way, you know."

"I'm sure you were a wonderful bank manager," Mme G said with a twinkle in her eye. "And a handsome one, too."

"That wasn't a requirement."

She laughed. "For your female customers, I'm sure it was. Well, I'm off." She stood from the table. "And do take a weapon of some sort with you to the Bois. I'm still not convinced that it's entirely safe."

Once Mme G had departed, Tony stuck his head into the kitchen, where J-P was eating his breakfast with Sabine, and ordered him to get Araby ready for his excursion. Then he went upstairs to his room to put on his riding boots when he thought of Mme G's warning. Perhaps she's right, he thought. It couldn't hurt to be prepared in case something did happen.

So he went down the hall to the library, which was situated between his bedroom and Mme G's, and rummaged through a set of drawers beneath a bookshelf. Ah, there it was. A Colt Navy revolver much like the one his father carried during the war. There was a box of cartridges next to it. He picked it up and was a bit surprised at the weight of it. It also had a long barrel—rather cumbersome and not so easy to conceal. He thought of his discussion with Mme G and decided that he was right: firearms were more likely to lead to trouble than to protect oneself. He put the revolver back into the drawer and closed it.

He went back to his room and put on a light wool jacket—it was a bit cool for April—as well as a wool cap. There was no sense in wearing a silk top hat to visit gypsies. Doubtful that he could blend in in any case, but at least he could dispense with the trappings of wealth.

He descended to the carriage house and found J-P brushing down Araby. It was a magnificent horse, aptly named. He thought of poor Leto, his father's wartime mount in Beaufort. Leto was in good health when he left South Carolina, but she would be nearly forty now if she were still alive. In any case, she was not as impressive as Araby, and in spite of carrying his father through the war, was no match for a thoroughbred.

Out on the street, Araby seemed liberated now that he was free of his double harness. Head held high, disdainful of the other horses, who seemed to be mere drudges by comparison, it was all Tony could do to restrain him from breaking into a gallop.

He decided to follow the new metro line rather than take Nat's advice and enter the Bois via Passy. The streets were convoluted and crowded that way, and besides, the Champs-Elysées was a straight shot to Porte Maillot.

Araby trotted smartly across the Pont de la Concorde and from there Tony could see that several more pavilions had been set up along the south bank of the Seine. They turned left at the Porte Monumentale and Araby now seemed to want to take advantage of the broad expanse of greensward before him and break into a full run. Tony allowed him to do so for a quarter mile, but then restrained him as they were getting dirty looks from pedestrians on either side of the boulevard. He noticed, however, that his steed was not the only one to indulge in this kind of exercise.

At Porte Maillot he turned into the Bois and followed the Allée de Longchamp to the Parc de Bagatelle. Araby seemed to think he was in the country again and would have run off into the trees if Tony had let him. Though there were a few carriages and other riders, there was no more traffic than if they had been in, say, the barons' country estate at la Ferrières.

They came upon elaborate gardens that were maintained with hundreds of brilliantly colored roses and a pond where Araby stopped to drink. A little further up the path there appeared a Chinese pagoda that looked oddly out of place, and beyond that a small but charming chateau with an inscription above the entry that read, 'Parvus sed Apta,' which Tony remembered from his Latin meaning something like 'Small but sufficient.'

This did not seem like a place for gypsies.

Suddenly someone called out his name in what sounded like a stage whisper. "Tony!"

Tony looked to his left and saw nothing but a line of trees at first, then a man waving him over. He walked Araby to the tree line.

"Nat?"

"Through here, old boy. What a magnificent stallion! But hurry, the gendarmes are patrolling the area."

Tony obeyed and he and Araby slipped between the trees as Nat took the reins and led them to a little clearing. There were perhaps a dozen tents set up here, with a fire pit in the center and a couple of small boys playing mumblety-peg while others watched. A number of adults milled about, some watching the children, others going about daily tasks such as cooking and washing clothes in the nearby pond.

Tony dismounted and took the reins from Nat. "Quite a little community you have here, Nat. But can you keep out of the way of the gendarmes for long?"

"Sure. They only patrol the area twice a day—once in the morning and once when the sun goes down. And they stick to the beaten paths for the most part."

"Well..."

By this time several men had gathered round them, admiring Araby. Nat introduced a couple of them, using words that Tony was unfamiliar with.

"Romish?" Tony said.

"Right. I've picked up a few words and phrases since I married Carlotta. Some of the men speak French, some Spanish. They're a jolly lot. Come on—I want to show you Carlotta's wedding dress."

"Her wedding dress?"

"It cost me a pretty penny, I'll tell you that. But the gypsies go in for elaborate costumes at weddings. Wait till you see it."

Nat led him to a large tent nearly the size of one of the pavilions at the Exposition. He lifted the flap that served as a door and Tony ducked his head. In the center of the tent there was a huge white dress on a headless mannequin with its skirt spread out over a carpet. It must have been ten feet in diameter.

"There are more than 10,000 rhinestones sewn into the dress," Nat said.

"The whole thing weighs over forty pounds."

"Good grief," Tony said, truly astonished. "And the dress itself–what is it made of?"

"Silk tulle and fox skin."

"Fox skin?"

"Right." Nat picked up the hem of the dress. "See? The folds at the perimeter are a soft, suede-like fox skin. The collar, too, only with fur."

"You say it cost you a pretty penny. How much?"

"Five thousand francs. A couturier in Paris. Only the best for my Carlotta."

Tony was tempted to ask Nat for his five hundred francs now but decided it would be in poor taste. "Well…where is the lucky bride? And is the dress going to simply remain on display here, or will she ever wear it again?"

"She's at the pond washing clothes with the other women. There was a big party last night. Sorry you missed it. To answer your question, though–no, she'll never wear it again. She'll save it for her daughter's wedding."

Tony was about to ask whether he and Carlotta expected to live in a tent the rest of their lives when they heard a gunshot. This was followed by the thunder of horses' hooves.

"Uh, oh," Nat said. "The gendarmerie! They must have gotten complaints about the party last night."

"What can we do?" Tony said.

"Well, we could run, as I suspect some of the men are already doing. But I can't leave Carlotta. I'd better see about her." He rushed outside of the tent and Tony followed.

Once outside, Tony saw people running as uniformed gendarmerie on horses trampled down the smaller tents and dispersed the ashes in the fire pit, causing them to cloud the air and add to the confusion. One of the gendarmes, who wore gold stripes on his sleeves, waved a pistol in the air, fired it and shouted, "Halte! Vous êtes en état d'arrestation!"

Nat ran to the pond, where the women, like the men, scattered, but he managed to scoop up Carlotta and they disappeared into the woods.

Tony stood rather stupidly in front of the tent, thinking that there was no reason for him to run since he was only a guest. But the gendarme with the pistol had other ideas. He pulled up his horse just inches from Tony and leveled his revolver at his head.

"Vous êtes qui?" he said.

"Un ami," Tony said.

The gendarme laughed. "Un ami de qui?"

"De la famille."

The gendarme thought this was even funnier. "Quelle famille? Il n'y a pas de famille ici, seulement des rats. Vous êtes en état d'arrestation!"

And with that pronouncement, the gendarme dismounted and placed the barrel of his pistol against Tony's temple. "Chien!" Then he waved over another gendarme and ordered him to take Tony into custody.

Tony's first thought at this point was the whereabouts of Araby. "Mon cheval!"

"Quel cheval?" The gendarme said. "Celui-là que vous avez volé? Il est aussi en état d'arrestation!"

This statement was followed by another burst of laughter louder than the first, as it was joined in by the other gendarmes.

Tony was roughly escorted to a van that was parked at the edge of the tree line and conveyed along with six others to the Préfecture de Police on the Île de la Cité. At the préfecture, he was examined by a desk sergeant who seemed at a loss as to how to classify him.

"Vous êtes gitan?"

"Non."

"Marocain?"

"Non."

"Sud-Africain?"

"Non."

The sergeant threw up his hands, overturning an ink well in the process. "Alors! Vous êtes quoi, donc?"

"Américain."

The sergeant rubbed his chin. "Américain?"

"Oui."

Suddenly a light bulb seemed to go off in his head. "Ah, bon! Un nègre marron."

"Plus ou moins."

"Quartier D." He stamped the admission form with conviction. "Le suivant!"

Though summarily dismissed, Tony lingered as he noticed a telephone on the wall behind the sergeant's desk. The gendarme who was escorting him grabbed him by the arm.

"Allez-y!"

"Un moment," Tony said. "Puis-je utiliser le téléphone?"

The desk sergeant looked over his shoulder at the phone. "Pourquoi?"

"Ma femme," Tony said.

The sergeant sighed and nodded to the gendarme.

Mme G had installed a telephone in the house only a week before. Few residences on the Left Bank had one, but she was wealthy and saw the advantage, particularly for business.

Tony had not used it, but he remembered the simple four-digit number.

"Vous êtes bien chez Goldman," Mme G said into the mouthpiece.

"Amelia!"

"Tony?"

"I'm at the Préfecture de Police."

"What! What happened?"

"The gendarmes raided Nat's camp."

A sigh came over the earpiece. "I'm not surprised. Where's Nat?"

"He escaped somehow. With Carlotta. They think I'm a gypsy."

Mme G chuckled. "Why wouldn't they? I'll be right there."

She sent J-P out into the street to hail a cab as she didn't want to waste time. While waiting, however, she called the baron.

"Ah, the préfet," the baron said. "I'll call him directly."

When she descended the stairs to the street, she was surprised to find an 'auto taxi' waiting for her.

"C'est plus vite," J-P said.

She climbed into the taxi and noticed that there was a meter next to the driver. "La Préfecture de Police–dépêche-toi!"

They were off and soon clipping along Boulevard St-Germain at 15 kilometres per hour.

At the Préfecture, she approached the sergeant's desk while he was on the telephone.

"Oui, Monsieur le Préfet…Oui, tout de suite." He replaced the receiver on its hook and looked up. "Madame?"

"Je suis Madame Goldman. Je viens chercher Monsieur Jones."

"Ah, oui." He instructed a guard to fetch Tony then turned back to Mme G. "Asseyez-vous, Madame."

Mme G sat on a very hard chair for about five minutes until she heard a jangle of keys, followed by a heavy iron door opening. Tony appeared, with the guard behind him.

She stood.

"S'il vous plaît, Madame," the desk sergeant said. He pushed a piece of paper towards her and offered her a pen. "Signez ici."

Mme G signed the form and Tony followed her to the door. The taxi was waiting.

"Where did you find this contraption?" Tony said.

"J-P found it. Just a bit of luck. There's scarcely a dozen in the whole city."

"I expect that number will double in the coming months."

They climbed into the taxi and headed to Rue de Furstemberg.

"What have you done with Araby?" she said, as they bumped over the cobble stones.

"I haven't done anything with him. I suppose he's enjoying the fodder in the Bois. Or perhaps he's been appropriated by the gypsies."

"What about Nat? Couldn't he retrieve him for us?"

"I hope he does. But I have no idea where he is. Maybe the police caught up with him, too."

"The baron could track him down. He hires private detectives from time to time. You owe him a favor, by the way."

"A favor?"

"How do you think you were released so quickly? And without paying a fine—or a bribe?"

"I see. I'll have to think of some way to repay him."

"You could paint his portrait."

"An excellent idea. But will he have time to sit for me?"

"I'll make sure he does."

They turned into the heavy traffic on Boulevard St-Michel where the driver cleared the way with his horn.

To their astonishment, when the taxi pulled into Rue de Furstemberg, Araby was waiting for them. Or rather he was enjoying himself while munching on the low-lying leaves of a plane tree in the tiny square.

While Mme G paid the driver, Tony went over to the horse and patted him on the neck. There were rivulets of sweat streaming down his withers, suggesting that he had been running.

Just as Mme G entered the house to find J-P, a policeman on horseback entered the street, soon to be followed by another.

"C'est votre animal?" the first policeman said as he pulled up to the square.

"Oui," Tony said.

"Il a terrifié la ville!"

"La ville entière? Comment?"

"Il faisait la course à côté des pavillons et des marchés, à travers la circulation!"

Araby seemed unperturbed by these charges and continued eating the leaves.

"Et maintenant, il mange la propriété de l'État!"

By this time, J-P arrived and took charge of Araby, who, apparently having had his fill, allowed himself to be led around to the alley behind the carriage house.

"Quel sont les dégâts matériels?" Tony said.

The policeman rubbed his chin. "Je ne sais pas. Mais j'ai besoin de faire un rapport."

Tony gave him his name and Mme G's address, along with her telephone number. The policeman asked him to sign the report and apparently satisfied that he had done his duty, mounted his horse again and left, followed by his partner, who seemed rather bored with the whole affair.

CHAPTER 33

Over the next few weeks, Tony made several trips to the baron's townhouse at the northeast corner of the Place de la Concorde. The baron was a gracious and patient sitter, and seemed to take an interest in Tony's personal life.

"Were you a slave in America?" he asked at the second sitting.

Tony tried not to show his amusement at this question. "No, but my grandmother was. I was born shortly after the war."

"Ah, yes. I apologize for my ignorance. Of course you were too young. But what was your grandmother's experience? Was she treated very badly?"

Tony continued to paint in broad, quick strokes. "Actually, she was the favorite of my great-grandfather. In fact, he freed her. But she did suffer at the hands of her half-brother, I'm told."

The baron shook his head. "Such an atrocity. A stain on the great American experiment. Is it all reconciled now? I mean to say, do the former slaves and their masters get on together?"

"It varies. It's really the poor whites who can't accept the situation–they feel threatened by blacks and often attack them without provocation."

"Like anti-Dreyfusards."

"Something like that. Could you please turn your head a little to the right, Baron?"

These sessions usually only lasted for forty-five minutes to an hour as the baron was a very busy man.

When he returned to Rue de Furstemberg, he found Mme G still in bed. She was about six weeks on now and often had morning sickness. When she felt better and arrived for breakfast, she consumed vast quantities of bananas.

"You'll turn into a monkey," Tony said one morning as he witnessed this gorging.

"You're already a monkey," she said with an impish smile.

"Not funny. Don't you realize that's a racial slur?"

"Race has nothing to do with it. I was referring to your agility in bed."

"In bed? We haven't been in bed together since you became pregnant." Tony was getting annoyed with her and made a show of ruffling his copy of *Le Matin* which, unlike *Le Figaro*, supported Dreyfus.

"My door is always open," she said.

Tony was not inclined to visit Mme G in the middle of the night and he wasn't sure why. He thought often of Jackie and wondered if she ever intended to reconcile their differences. He was doubtful of this. He hadn't received a letter from her since she left Paris. On the other hand, Mme G, though experiencing the usual hormonal changes of the first few weeks of pregnancy, was still attractive and alluring to him. Perhaps he *would* visit her in the middle of the night.

At the moment, however, he was preoccupied with the baron and his portrait. He had never had such a distinguished sitter. Dignified but affable, the baron had almost single-handedly rescued the French government from financial collapse after the Franco-Prussian War of 1870-71. He had been awarded the Légion d'honneur for his efforts then and elevated to the Grand-Croix recently. Thus, he wore the gilded medal on his left breast and the red sash over his right shoulder during the sittings. Tony couldn't recall seeing him display these resplendent honors at any other time, including at the soirée he and Mme G attended over the winter at his château in La Forêt de Ferrières.

He retired to the studio and worked on the portrait till noon. He was aided by a photograph he had taken of the baron at the first sitting with a camera borrowed from M. Dantec. M. Dantec was always up on the latest technology and even owned a motorcar—a Renault with tufted leather seats and a retractable roof.

It was said that photography would be the end of painting. Tony did not believe this. It seemed to him that rather than being the death knell of painting, it was both an aide and a liberator. No longer would painting be confined to strictly representational forms with slavish adherence to realistic detail. The human eye was often deceived, and a photograph could only represent the surface of things. On the other hand, having a virtual image of the subject to refer to was helpful in recalling details of dress and eye color and anatomical peculiarities that could lead to a more expressive representation of deeper qualities.

Just as Tony was about to put his brushes down and seek out Eugénie to find out what was for lunch, J-P appeared at the door of the studio. Unlike his usual custom of knocking whether the door was open or not, J-P simply stood at the door looking rather tentative.

"Oui?" Tony said.

"Monsieur Tony—pourrais-je vous parler de quelque chose?"

Tony was a little nonplussed at this request. J-P was a highly efficient and discreet servant who never invoked personal matters into his duties. "Bien sûr, J-P."

J-P came cautiously into the room, head down, and stood about ten feet away while Tony finished cleaning his brushes. He stood staring at the floor for a few moments, his hands clasped behind his back, and said nothing.

"Asseyez-vous," Tony said, indicating that he should sit down on the divan. J-P looked around, seemed reluctant, but finally sat down.

Tony came over and sat down beside him. "Est-ce que vous êtes malade?"

"Non, Monsieur."

After a few more attempts to elicit his concerns, J-P finally burst into tears and put his head into his hands.

"Qu'est-ce qui'l y a, J-P?" Tony said, putting his arm around his shoulder.

J-P finally blurted it out. "J'ai mis Sabine enceinte!"

So that was it—he had gotten Sabine pregnant. He went on to say that he truly loved Sabine and was willing to marry her, but he was afraid that both of them would lose their jobs.

Tony reassured him that Mm G was quite understanding about such matters and that he and Sabine had nothing to worry about, but that he would speak to her and put in a good word for them. But even as he said this, he wondered whether Mme G would take the news so lightly and allow things to continue as before. After all, she was pregnant herself and subject to extreme swings in mood.

"Ne vous inquiètez pas," Tony said, again patting him on the shoulder. "Je lui parlerai pour vous."

J-P stood abruptly and kissed Tony's hand. "Oh, merci, Monsieur Tony! Merci beaucoup!"

Once he had gone, Tony stroked his chin. Now what? Two pregnant women in the house and one in London. And...oh, no! Mme G is going to think that *he* got Sabine pregnant! This put a new wrinkle into the mix. How was he going to convince her otherwise? He hadn't been to her bed in weeks, and surely she would be suspicious that he had been sneaking down the hall to Sabine's room in the middle of the night. Perhaps he should postpone the news...but no, she's going to find out soon enough and besides, J-P would feel that he had betrayed him.

Well...a fine kettle of fish.

At lunch, Mme G came downstairs yawning. "I hardly slept at all last night." She looked at Tony, who was wearing the denim shirt that he usually wore under his smock while painting. "That shirt is nearly threadbare. Can't you wear one of the silk ones I bought for you? The ones with your monogram on them."

"I'm afraid I'll get paint on them. Were you up much last night?"

Still wearing her gold kimono, she sat down at the dining room table and looked around as if in a foreign environment. "Yes. Three times. Oh, I'm ready for this stage of the pregnancy to be over! It's such a nuisance."

Tony sat down opposite her. "Can you eat anything?"

"I'm as hungry as a horse. What's Eugénie prepared for us?"

"Lamb chops."

"Good. I'll have three." She rang her little bell and Sabine entered. "Bonjour, Sabine. J'aimerais bien du thé, s'il te plaît."

"Oui, Madame. Et Monsieur?"

"Un verre de vin rouge, s'il vous plaît"

Sabine went back to the kitchen.

"You do need to start using 'tu' with the servants, Tony. It makes me feel like Lady McBeth by comparison."

"It just seems that I should show them a little respect."

Mme G picked up her napkin and unfolded it. "Yes, well, that's very noble of you, but there should be some distance between masters and servants, otherwise—"

"They don't respect you."

She looked up at him. "Are you mocking me?"

Tony sighed. "No, Amelia. It's just that I've heard that before. Not only from you but from my wife's aunt back in South Carolina. The fact that you're paying them and they're rendering a service in return is enough for them to understand their place in the order of things."

Mme G laid the napkin across her lap. "My, aren't you the *philosophe social* this morning. The fact is they respect me and there's no question of their 'place in the order of things.' It all worked quite nicely before you came along."

"You're having second thoughts about my being here?"

A flush of anger reddened Mme G 's face. Then she composed herself. "Of course I want you to be here. But I wish—"

Sabine entered with the tea and wine. She seemed to sense the tension in the air and quickly removed herself from the room.

"You were saying that you wish–"

"I wish you would come and visit me in my room some time."

Tony took a sip of his wine. "I'm sorry if I've neglected you, Amelia. I'll make a point of it tonight."

Mme G smiled. "Why wait till tonight? Surprise me."

Tony was beginning to think this was not a good time to inform her that Sabine was pregnant. "I'll bring you something."

"That's not the kind of surprise I meant."

"Yes, well...I'll see what I can do."

"'I know you will. You're very resourceful."

Sabine returned with their meals and Tony watched as Amelia consumed the three lamb chops, along with a pile of new potatoes, diced carrots, and a whole tomato cut into six slices. This was topped off with a plate of several varieties of cheese.

Tony ate about half as much and felt full. He finished off his glass of wine and rose from the table. "Well, I'd better get back to work."

Mme G wiped her lips with her napkin. "How's it going?"

"Quite well, I think. Perhaps you'd better go back to bed and rest."

"Oh, I'm not tired now. Can I come and watch you paint?"

"'Um...sure. Why not? But I'm afraid I won't be very good company."

"I just want to watch."

Tony excused himself and returned to the studio, while Mme G remained and asked Sabine for some ice cream.

When Sabine returned to the kitchen, she encountered J-P, who was sitting on a stool having a cup of coffee. Eugénie, her work being done, retired to her quarters on the ground floor.

"Qu est-ce qui se passe?" he said. "Lui a-t-il dit?"

"Je ne sais pas. Je crois que non."

J-P slammed his fist down on the table. "Merde! Quand est-ce qu'il va le faire?"

Sabine began to cry and J-P continued to remonstrate against 'Monsieur Tony.' Finally, he put his coffee cup down with a loud rattle and left the kitchen.

Sabine remained and wiped the tears from her eyes. She sat on the stool vacated by J-P and contemplated her condition. She wasn't even sure she loved J-P though she found him to be sexually attractive and amusing. He was, after all, an Arab and a Muslim. If they married, would it be a Muslim or a Christian wedding? Her parents in Montpellier would be appalled if she were to marry a 'béni-oui-oui', much less convert to Islam.

Her father was a former army noncom who served in Algeria and detested North Africans as being an untrustworthy and inferior race. Her mother, a seamstress, was passive and accepted her husband's prejudices as to be expected of men.

However, Sabine had had little contact with her parents since she ran away from Montpellier only three years earlier. She occasionally exchanged letters with her sister, who kept her informed of the family's struggles, especially her father's periodic brushes with the law, as he was a heavy drinker and had a tendency to engage in street brawls.

The problem, though, was what to do if Mme G dismissed her. She couldn't go home without being subjected to the rages of her father, nor stay in Paris unless she could find another employer immediately. And who would hire a pregnant girl from the South with little education and no skills other than domestic ones that would be hampered by her condition?

Even if she married J-P, what employment opportunities would be available to him if Mme G dismissed him as well?

Her only hope, as she saw it, was to throw herself on the mercy of Mme G. Perhaps she should go to her directly and confess rather than wait for Monsieur Tony to act.

Yes—she would go to Mme G…if only she had the courage!

J-P entered the carriage house and discovered his father repairing a harness. "Rends-toi utile!" his father said. "Nettoie à fond les stalles."

This was probably J-P's least favorite task, but he obeyed his father and began shoveling manure and straw from Araby's stall. And as it was spring, he carried the manure out to the garden where he spread it among the flower beds. When he started back to the carriage house, he noticed that Mme G was hurrying along the landing that connected the main house to the studio. She was clad only in her kimono, which he knew from Sabine's confidences was *sans sous-vêtements* underneath. He also learned from Sabine that Mme G often used 'modeling' as an excuse to engage in sexual intercourse with M. Tony.

He re-entered the carriage house and finished the job of cleaning out the stalls in record time. His father congratulated him for his industry, but before he could think of another task for him, J-P was out the door and climbing the stairs to the studio.

The studio was accessed by a short hallway, such that if one were to peer through the keyhole of the door, one would have only a partial view of the enormous room. J-P found this narrow view sufficient for his purposes, for the only piece of furniture in the room was the divan, which was directly in his line of sight. The divan itself, however, was directed away from the door so that he could not see the tufted cushion at the head of it. No matter, he could see well enough.

At the moment, however, nothing much seemed to be going on. Mme G was sitting on the edge of the divan, looking towards the window. He could not see either M. Tony or the easel.

After a few minutes, she seemed to call to him. He then came into view, stood beside her for a moment as she caressed his leg, and returned to his easel. Mme G remained perfectly still.

This happened twice more over a period of twenty minutes or so. J-P was about to give it up when M. Tony appeared a fourth time, bent down and kissed her. Again she caressed his leg, but he started away and she pulled him back. Then she stood and almost simultaneously dropped her kimono to the floor.

Ah, now this was more like it!

Monsieur Tony seemed reluctant, but Mme G seemed intent on removing his trousers. At last he threw off his smock, unbuttoned his shirt and stepped out of his trousers. Mme G leaned back on the divan, her head of jet-black hair in a chignon draped over the bolster. M. Tony mounted her like Araby on a mare in heat. But unfortunately, J-P could only see his head and chest moving rhythmically up and down and Mme G's legs wrapped around his waist and locked behind his back.

J-P looked down at his own trousers and noticed a stain on them. Yes, this was thrilling but more importantly, how could he use this information?

The show being over, J-P noiselessly retreated to the staircase and returned to the carriage house. His father was waiting with a new task—repair the bridle that Araby managed to break on his wild ride along the Champs-Elysées.

At the end of the day, Mme. G returned to the main house with a smile of satisfaction on her face and thinking of Tony. She passed through the pantry and found Sabine polishing some silver.

"Madame?" Sabine said.

"Oui, Sabine?"

"J'aimerais un moment avec vous, si vous me le permettez."

Mme G paused for a moment. "Qu'est-ce que c'est?"

Sabine put her polishing cloth aside, folded her hands in front of her, and stared at the floor.

"Dis-moi, Sabine," Mme G said. "Qu'est-ce qu'il y a?"

Sabine trembled, as if suddenly seized by a fever. Finally, she looked up at Mme G. "Je suis tombée enceinte."

Mme G stared at her for a moment, her face flushed, and suddenly she lashed out at Sabine with a hard slap across the face. "Putain!"

Sabine tried to rub away the sting on her cheek and began crying. "Je suis desolée, Madame!"

"Tu es désolée? Je suis desolée! Sors d'ici!"

Sabine was now drowning in tears and used her apron to wipe them away. "Oh, Madame! Tant pis pour moi, mais veuillez ne pas punir Jean-Pierre!"

"Jean-Pierre? Pourquoi Jean...Oh, la la! Jean-Pierre t'a mise enceinte?"

Sabine lowered her eyes. "Oui, Madame."

Mme G's entire demeanor changed in an instant. She put her arm around Sabine's shoulder. "Et Jean-Pierre–il t'aime?"

"Oui, Madame."

"Je suis désolée, Sabine. Je n'ai pas compris. Et Jean-Pierre–il veut t'épouser?"

"Je ne sais pas."

"Je lui parlerai."

Sabine then took Mme G's hands in hers and kissed them profusely. "Merci beaucoup, Madame. Vous êtes très gentille!" She then went back to polishing the silver with renewed vigor as Mme G took the back stairs to her room.

CHAPTER 34

As the Summer Olympics (a component of the Exposition) got underway, Mme G, who took a keen interest in women's sports, convinced Tony to accompany her to the various events in which women were allowed to participate. The first venue was the Jeu de Paume in the Tuileries Gardens, where the fencing competition was held. Tony thought this spectacle was rather bizarre, with women wielding swords and attacking one another with a ferocity he had never seen in the female sex. He much preferred the tennis events that took place in Puteaux, just north of the Bois de Boulogne.

As it turned out, this event was dominated by an English woman, Charlotte Cooper, who thrashed all opponents easily, including the French champion, Yvonne Prévost, on the way to the championship.

Just as they were leaving the stadium after witnessing one of Miss Cooper's triumphs, a man tugged at Tony's sleeve.

"Tony!" It was Nat. "I heard the gendarmes caught up with you. Sorry I wasn't much help old man, but it was every man for himself. Carlotta and I hid in the woods all night and when we returned to the camp, her wedding dress was gone! I had a devil of a time convincing the gendarmes that it was a family heirloom that belonged to my mother. Anglo-American property rights carry more weight, you know."

Carlotta stood by and smiled complacently while Nat explained all of this. It wasn't clear whether she understood English.

"Again, sorry old man," Nat said.

"Where are you living now?" Tony said.

"Rue de Fleurus. It's safer. Carlotta and I are back in the puppet business."

He glanced at Mme G's belly, which revealed a modest bump at this stage. "A little one on the way, eh?"

"There's no denying it," Tony said.

Mme G merely smiled.

"Well," Nat said, "Carlotta and I had better be off. I thought we would take in a little of the tennis, especially since Carlotta had never seen a match before. If you'll remember, I was the singles champion at Harvard."

"I remember, Nat. You were quite impressive."

"Ah, well–those days are gone. On sort d'ici!"

When Nat and Carlotta were gone, Tony said to Mme G: "Notice that he didn't say anything about the money he owes me."

Mme G put her arm into Tony's and laughed. "I think it's time you forgot about Nat altogether. He's a rather fair-weather friend, it seems."

"But resourceful. Beats me how he managed to convince the gendarmes to return his wife's wedding dress. It's worth a small fortune."

"I wonder what happened to his other gypsy friends?"

"Banished to the banlieues, no doubt. Or maybe even deported."

They made their way through the crowd to the parking area where J-P was waiting with the carriage.

"I forgot to tell you," Mme G said. "J-P and Sabine are getting married."

"Married?"

"Sabine is pregnant."

"Oh–I see."

"Actually, there will be two ceremonies–first a Christian one, then a Muslim one. Both will take place in the garden."

"A compromise, then."

"Yes. Hasan threatened to quit and return to Marseille if it were to be a Christian wedding. And of course he would have taken J-P with him."

"What does Sabine think of this arrangement?"

"She doesn't care, really. But she wants to be able to tell her parents that her marriage has been consecrated by the Catholic Church."

"Well...which one will be legal in France?"

"Both. I consulted a avocat. He says as long as the Muslim contract doesn't conflict with French law, it's valid. Sabine will even have more rights under Islamic law than she does under French. For example, she can keep whatever property she acquires during the marriage should they divorce."

"She's not likely to acquire much property."

"No, but I'm setting up a trust for her."

"A trust?"

"It will be a sort of pension, assuming she outlives J-P."

"That's very generous of you."

Mme G winked at Tony as they approached the carriage. "It ensures that

Sabine will be loyal to me. I can revoke the trust at any time. Here we are–Chez moi, J-P!"

CHAPTER 35

One day in August, Tony was sitting at his desk in his bedroom reading a letter from Jackie when Mme G burst into his room without knocking, contrary to her custom.

Tony looked up. "What is it, Amelia?"

"Someone tried to kill the baron."

"Kill him? Is he hurt?"

"No. Fortunately he wasn't at home, and a servant sent the parcel to his office, where his secretary opened it. It exploded and the secretary was seriously injured. The baron is at the hospital now."

"Why would anyone want to kill the baron?"

Mme G sat down on the bed. "Who do you think?"

"I have no idea."

"The vicomte, of course."

"The vicomte? Because of the money he owed the baron?"

"That and the fact that he was kicked out of the Jockey Club."

Tony folded the letter and replaced it in its envelope. "I wouldn't think that getting kicked out of a sporting club would be sufficient motive to kill someone."

"You don't know the vicomte. He's very thin-skinned. It must have been humiliating for him. Who's the letter from?"

Tony slipped the letter into a drawer. "Jackie. She wants me to come to London."

"She's about to deliver?"

"Yes."

Mme G, who was herself beginning to show, folded her hands and looked out the window onto the square. It was an unusually warm day and she was sweating. "Can't you open the window? This heat is intolerable."

Tony rose and went to the window. It was already cracked open, but he raised it all the way. "That better?"

"A little. Are you going?"

"To London? I suppose I must. It's my child, after all."

Mme G continued to stare out the window. "I've been bleeding... excessively."

Tony came and sat down beside her. "Excessively? What does it mean?"

"That I may be having a miscarriage."

"Good lord! We'd better get you to the hospital."

"No, not yet. It could be simply...well, the body doesn't respond normally to a pregnancy when a woman is my age."

Tony felt completely out of his depth, which in fact, he was. "Then what can we do?"

"Nothing at the moment. If it continues, I'll go to Dr. Pignaud." Suddenly she burst into tears and threw her arms around him. "Oh, Tony! This is my last chance. I so want to have the child!"

Tony patted her on the back. "Well...I want you to, too. Are you sure you don't want to go to the hospital? I'll get J-P to–"

"No. It's not imminent. But I don't want you to leave me now."

"We'll wait a few days. Jackie isn't due till the end of the month."

She dried her tears. "I think you should go. If it's a false alarm, there's no reason for you not to. If it isn't, then...it won't matter."

"Well...of course it will matter. I can't leave you if...if something goes wrong."

She put her head against his chest. "Whatever happens, I don't want to come between you and Jackie. If you could convince her to come back to Paris–"

"Let's not get ahead of ourselves. I have a feeling that there will be two children and...somehow we'll work it out."

She lifted her head. "You're a good man, Tony. Any other man would have abandoned me by now."

Tony kissed her lightly on the lips. "I won't abandon you, Amelia–I promise." Was he likely to abandon a beautiful woman who provided him with not only room and board, but a spacious studio overlooking an idyllic garden? What artist could abandon such a woman? But he did, in fact, love her. He no longer believed, as poets immemorial have claimed, that a man could love only one woman.

Mme G rose from the bed. "I think I need to rest now. Could you ask Sabine to bring me some tea?"

"Of course."

She went back to her room and left Tony in a contemplative mood. He stared out the window for a while, then returned to his desk where he took Jackie's letter from the drawer and reread it. What does she really want? It wasn't clear that she wanted anything but to have the baby and to be able to claim that it was legitimate because of his presence. Mme G, on the other hand, was clear as to what she wanted: a child before it was no longer possible. And unlike Jackie, she wanted *him* no matter whether they were married or not, even if she had to share him with another woman.

So what if he didn't go to London? The child would grow up without a father, that's all. Millions of children grew up without fathers and did perfectly well in life. Or did they? Was it always a stigma? Always a sense of loss? Or simply a question of respectability? Did Jackie care so much about respectability when she married him? A black man?

He would go to London.

CHAPTER 36

It turned out that there was no proof that the vicomte was responsible for the bombing.

Although the parcel had been mailed from Neuilly-sur-Seine, the suburb where the vicomte lived, no one at the post office could recall seeing the vicomte or anyone in his employ there on the day of the postmark. Police detectives obtained fingerprints on the remnants of the parcel, but there was only a very limited number of prints in the files, and they almost all belonged to career criminals well-known to the police.

The baron, highly suspicious of the vicomte, demanded that all the vicomte's servants be fingerprinted, but the vicomte objected on the grounds that it was an unwarranted invasion of privacy. The préfet de police, though a friend of the baron's, agreed with the vicomte. He could only do this if there was some other, more concrete evidence pointing to the vicomte's household.

Mme G did indeed go to Dr. Pignaud, who told her what she suspected and hoped for: it was a false alarm. However, he warned that the danger had not passed, and recommended she ingest large amounts of iodine in foods such as seaweed, tomato, and fish. Thus, Mme G had Eugénie shop in the open-air markets for these items and when Tony left for London, Mme G was sitting up in bed with a tray across her lap, eating a huge salad composed of these foods.

"I hope it's a boy," she said.

"Which one?"

"Jackie's. Of course, I'd like a boy, too, but at this point I'd be delighted with a healthy child of either sex."

Tony kissed her on the forehead. "I'll send you a telegram as soon as we know."

"Do. Je t'aime."

"Moi aussi, ma chérie."

Tony sat by a window on the train, alternately reading a copy of
Madame Bovary and staring out the window at the passing scenery
without really seeing any of it. Mme G had recommended the book to
him, saying that it would give him new insight into the feminine psyche.
So far, though, it only seemed to offer an insight into the rather dull and
commonplace mind of a country doctor.

Had any man found himself in such a dilemma as he now found
himself? Surely it's happened many times. But not to anyone he knew.
Who to turn to for advice? Mme G was wonderfully helpful and
understanding, but then she was a woman. And a sort of rich Bohemian.
But in regard to women's liberation, there was hardly a suffragist in
America or England who could match her for energy and drive.

He wished his father were still alive. He was wise in so many ways.
And he certainly was no stranger to Bohemian life–his mother became
a Broadway actress after escaping bondage in the South. She never
married, and neither did he. Hah! Tony was a bastard, as was his father.
But what did it matter? Jackie was a bastard as well. Strange to think
of it–a well-bred Southern woman with impeccable manners and the
highest moral standards. A bastard! Well, it just goes to show that social
norms are arbitrary and capricious. It's the family that counts, however it's
composed.

As the scenery between Amiens and Abbeville was rather monotonous,
he turned back to *Madame Bovary*. After a few pages, however, he fell
asleep. The next thing he knew someone was shaking him by the arm.

"Monsieur! C'est le terminus."

He looked around and saw that the car was nearly empty. "Calais?"

"Oui. Il faut prendre le ferry pour Londres."

He grabbed his valise from the overhead rack. "Merci, Monsieur."

At Victoria Station he hailed a horseless cab that seemed to move
miraculously on its own without noise or the usual clouds of smoke. The
driver informed him that electric taxis were the latest innovation and were
more economical and reliable than their gasoline-powered counterparts.

When he arrived at Lucinda's house on Eaton Square, Alastair greeted
him, took his valise, and ushered him into the drawing room, where he
was informed by the maid, Sybil, that 'Miss Jackie' had been rushed to
the hospital that morning and her 'Aunt Lucinda' was with her. Tony, in a
near panic, asked which hospital.

"The Grosvenor Hospital for Women," Sybil said. "Dr. Thurloe said
there were complications."

"Complications? Where's the hospital?"

"I don't know exactly, Mr. Jones. Somewhere near Westminster."

"Number 37 Vincent Square," Alastair said. "But I'm sure Miss Jacqueline is in good hands, sir. There's no need to–"

Tony didn't wait for Alastair to finish his sentence and rushed out into the street where he hailed another cab, the old-fashioned kind drawn by horses. "To Grosvenor Hospital–hurry!"

"I'll try, Guv'nor–the old nag ain't a racehorse, you know."

Nevertheless, traffic was light for the time of day and they arrived at the hospital within ten minutes. Tony sprinted up the steps and banged on the door, failing to note that it was unlocked.

"Am I to understand that I'm to wait for the missus to give birth, Guv'nor?" the cabbie called from the street. "Otherwise, we need to settle."

Tony ran back down the steps and paid the driver–in francs.

"'Francs? Ain't no good to me, Guv'nor. A half crown will set us right."

Tony ran his hands through his pockets, though he had no English money. "Wait here." He ran back up the steps where the door had opened and there was a uniformed nurse waiting. She reluctantly reached into her pocket and produced a half crown. Tony promised to pay her back before he left and rushed again to pay the cabbie.

"Good luck, Guv'nor! I've got six little ones m'self. You quit rushing to the 'ospital with your trousers on fire after the second one." He snapped his whip and drove off.

Tony rushed past the nurse into a high-ceilinged corridor before realizing that he had no idea where to go. He walked rather sheepishly back to the nurse. "Ah, what room is she in?"

"'Who?"

"Mrs. Jacqueline Jones."

"Oh. Third floor."

"Thank you." He rushed off again.

"Mr. Jones?"

He stopped. "What is it?"

"The baby came an hour ago."

"He?"

"Yes."

Now Tony felt a little ridiculous. He could stop running. But as he approached the stairs, he suddenly felt compelled to take them two at a time.

"Mr. Jones," the nurse said. "There's an elevator."

But Tony either ignored this last statement or didn't hear it. He continued leaping up the stairs until he arrived at the third floor completely out of breath.

A second nurse took him by the arm. "Are you all right?"

"I think so. Where is Mrs. Jones' room?"

"I'll take you there." She escorted him down a long hallway until they came to an open door where Dr. Thurloe was just emerging.

"Mr. Jones," Dr. Thurloe said with a big smile. "You're here after all."

"Yes. I came all the way from Paris. Is she all right?"

"Oh, there was a minor scare, so I thought it prudent to admit her to the hospital. But she and the baby are fine now. See for yourself." Dr. Thurloe stood aside and indicated a bed where Jackie lay, with a bundle of swaddling clothes in her arms. Lucinda stood next to her.

Tony cautiously approached as if he might not be welcome.

"You've come!" Jackie said.

"Yes–of course. Sorry I didn't make it in time to–"

"Come say hello to your son."

Tony came nearer, and as he did so, Jackie pulled the cloth down and exposed the child as it suckled at her breast. He stared in wonder. The child's skin was fair, like his mother's. His hair was also like his mother's– blond. He kissed Jackie on the cheek, then the baby, and sat down in a chair next to the bed. "What's his name?"

Jackie laughed. "What do you think? Antonio Jones III."

"Antonio? How will people be able to tell us apart?"

Jackie smiled and glanced at Lucinda.

"That shouldn't be a problem," Lucinda said.

Tony looked at the baby with its fair skin. "No, I don't suppose it will. But in conversation we'll refer to him as…'Trey.'"

"Trey?" Jackie said.

"Well, 'Trois' doesn't sound right. Besides, if he grows up in France, it will be confusing."

Jackie laughed. "Trey it is. I like it–Trey Jones."

After a visit of an hour or so, Jackie grew tired, and the nurse took the baby from her. Dr. Thurloe said that he would like to keep both of them under observation for another day or two, but then they would be able to return home.

Tony asked if he could spend the night there, but Dr. Thurloe said it was against the rules. So he and Lucinda left the hospital, climbed into

Lucinda's waiting carriage, and returned to Eaton Square.

CHAPTER 37

Tony was back at the hospital the next morning and was allowed to hold the baby and walk about the room for several minutes at a time. It would have been hard to say which parent was the more delighted at this new addition to the family. Tony rubbed its nose and repeated the name 'Trey' over and over until the baby seemed to think that 'Trey' was some kind of treat.

After a mid-morning feeding, Dr. Thurloe said that mother and child were ready to go home.

Several nurses accompanied them to Lucinda's carriage, laughing and hovering over the child as if he were their own. When they arrived at the house, they discovered that Lucinda had assembled a welcoming party of her theatrical friends: Forbes-Robertson, his fiancée Gertie, Mrs. Pat Campbell, Ellen Terry and George Bernard Shaw. The women brought gifts, while the men seemed not to know what to do with their hands. Should they hold the baby or not?

"I say," Johnny said, "he looks to be the spitting image of his mother."

"Don't be so crude, Johnny," Gertie said. "'Spit' is hardly a complimentary term."

"Simply an expression, dearest. I think it means—what the devil does it mean, Bernard?"

"Gertie's quite right," Shaw said, with a twinkle in his eye. "It's an Anglo-Saxon reference to the father expectorating at the sight of his first-born."

"Really?" Forbes-Robertson said. "How ghastly. I sincerely apologize for my faux pas, Miss Jones."

"But the idea," Shaw said, "is actually complimentary. It means that the child looks so like the father that he could have spit out his own image to create it."

"Then I am redeemed!" Forbes-Robertson said.

After some more of this banter, the well-wishers took their leave and

Jackie went upstairs with Trey, followed by Lucinda. After a few minutes, Lucinda returned.

"Out like a snuffed candle," she said. "Mother and child are fast asleep. You look like you could stand some rest, too, Tony."

"I'm not really tired. I can't get over it—a son!"

Lucinda laughed. "You're like all first-time fathers—a miracle has occurred and it's a unique event in the annals of mankind. But you need to start thinking of how you will raise the child."

"How do you mean?"

"Well, I mean, or I should say, *where* are you going to raise the child? I can see that you will be a doting father. But you can't 'dote' if you live in Paris and Jackie lives here."

Tony sat down on the sofa and rested his forearms on his knees. "Jackie must come and live with me in Paris. I'm her husband."

"That's rather old-fashioned, isn't it?" Lucinda sat down beside him. "The idea that a wife must follow her husband wherever he goes."

"It may be old-fashioned, but it's an unwritten law of nature. Besides, my career, my life, is in Paris. Jackie isn't even interested in pursuing an acting career anymore."

"Are you so sure? Once the child is old enough not to need constant attention, what will she do? She has too much energy, too much talent, and too much pride to be merely a housewife."

Tony was getting visibly annoyed. "'Merely' a housewife? You're assuming that your own values apply to Jackie, Lucinda. She's more of a traditional type of woman than you are. Home and hearth appeal to her—acting is something that she simply fell into and can just as easily fall out of."

Lucinda pursed her lips for a moment, as if to restrain herself from saying something she might regret. "Acting is not a frivolous profession, Tony, anymore than painting pictures is. It's in Jackie's blood and she'll only give it up for a time."

"Then she'll have plenty of opportunities in Paris. As for her French, she'll improve considerably over the next few years while she's tending to Trey. We could even hire a nanny if need be."

"A nanny? Yes, that's certainly a possibility." She stood. "Well, it's not my decision to make. Would you like something to eat?"

Tony said he would and Sybil served them lunch on the terrace overlooking the garden. Afterwards Tony went upstairs and found Jackie awake while Trey slept. He sat down beside the bed. Jackie was smiling from ear to ear.

"He's a beautiful child," he said.

"Of course he is. Did you expect anything less?"

"No...but I was a bit surprised at how...how white he is."

Jackie laughed. "I have to say I was, too. But what does it matter? He's a healthy, handsome boy."

Tony chuckled. "It looks like I already have some competition."

Jackie smiled at first, but the smile suddenly turned to a frown. "Competition? Not of the sort that I have to deal with."

Tony avoided her gaze and looked out the window. "Madame G feels no competition with you. She encouraged me to come."

"Did she? And does she expect me to come to Paris to live with the two of you? And Trey, too?"

"As a matter of fact, she does."

Jackie closed her eyes for a moment. But just as she opened them again, Trey awoke and began crying. She rocked him back and forth, then pulled her bodice open and let him suckle. "It can never work, Tony. I will not come to Paris on those terms."

Tony sighed. "Then we'll get our own apartment. I could still use the studio."

"No! You must disentangle yourself from this woman. I don't care if she continues to represent you, but—"

"She's pregnant, Jackie."

Jackie looked at him incredulously, as if he had committed a crime she had not thought he was capable of. "No, Tony. No, no, no!"

"I'm sorry. It just happened. But I can't abandon her anymore than I can abandon you."

Tears came to Jackie's eyes. She wiped one away with her free hand. "I never thought it would come to this. What is she—forty?"

"Just about."

"She could have an abortion."

"I can't ask her to do that. She had a child once and lost it. And this could be her last chance to have another."

Jackie sighed. "I can't say as I blame her. I like her, Tony. And she's been kind to me. But I can't share you with her. I just can't!"

This last outburst caused the baby to cry. Jackie rocked it back and forth until it stopped and began to suckle again.

"I'd better leave you alone now," Tony said. "We'll discuss it again later."

Jackie looked down at Trey. "There's nothing to discuss."

Tony said nothing, kissed her on the forehead and left the room.

CHAPTER 38

Rain fell steadily in London over the next few days, with temperatures in the mid-seventies. It reminded Tony of Beaufort during the summer months with daily downpours in the afternoons followed by cool breezes off the Atlantic.

But he was getting little sleep. His bedroom was just across the hall from Jackie's and he awakened whenever he heard Trey cry. Then he would step inside Jackie's room, note that she seemed exhausted, and took the baby from her as she fell back asleep. He would walk around the room with Trey cradled in his arms, humming a tune that his mother had sung to him as a child. He couldn't remember the words but the tune seemed to rise spontaneously to his lips. By this time, Trey was sleeping in a cradle that one of Lucinda's arts and crafts friends had made for him. Once Trey was asleep, Tony would carefully lay him down in the cradle and tiptoe back to his bedroom for a few more hours–sometimes only minutes–of sleep.

No more was said about Mme G. Jackie appreciated Tony's attention to Trey and his seemingly tireless efforts to comfort both him and herself. She would often stare at Tony with satisfaction and even admiration as he carried Trey about in his arms, cooing to him, kissing his little nose, and exchanging incomprehensible verbal sounds.

In any case, Tony and Jackie seemed to set aside their dispute over Tony's relationship to Mm G and what he should do about it. One day, however, a telegram came for Tony:

Paris 19 Août 17G H617Z via Calais rec'd Dover 1435h

Antonio Jones
13 Eaton Square
London UK

Madame G portrait awarded Bronze Medal STOP Much

demand for your work. STOP Return to Paris ASAP.

Dantec

"A bronze medal?" Jackie said. "That's the best except for two, isn't it?"

"Yes. Third best, not exactly a ringing endorsment of my work."

"But there must have been thousands of other candidates. You must go to Paris and get it before they give it to somebody else."

"I don't think they'll give it to anyone else as long as I claim it within a reasonable time. But Monsieur Dantec wants me to return so as to capitalize on my moment of fame."

She kissed him. They were standing in the foyer of Lucinda's house where Tony received the telegram. "Moment? No, you *are* famous. You must go!"

"But...I can't leave now."

"Why not? The baby's fine. I'm fine, and we'll be perfectly comfortable until you get back."

"I don't know when I'll get back."

Jackie's enthusiasm over the good news suddenly evaporated. "What do you mean by that?"

"I mean that once I walk into Monsieur Dantec's gallery he'll probably have a crowd of patrons there to greet me. And they're going to want paintings. My paintings. I'll be up to my neck in commissions."

"Well, that's what you want, isn't it?"

Tony put his arm around her while the telegram dangled from his fingertips. "You'll wait for me–three, maybe six months?"

Jackie lowered her eyes. "Of course I'll wait."

Tony seized her by the shoulders, forcing her to look at him. "I'll come. But then we'll pack up and return to Paris. The three of us."

"Oh, Tony–let's not–"

"What's this?" It was Lucinda, who had been looking after Trey upstairs. "Lovemaking in the foyer? What will the servants think?"

Tony chuckled. "Perhaps they'll be inspired."

"Heavens! To what? Come into the drawing room–I have something to show you."

Their curiosity aroused, Tony and Jackie followed Lucinda into the drawing room. Lucinda then stood by a tea table on which stood a telephone with an ivory bone receiver with gold-plated fittings resting on a cradle. Beneath the cradle was a white enamel box decorated with a floral design.

"I had it installed this morning while you two were out shopping for baby clothes. What do you think?"

"A telephone," Tony said. "Madame G has one."

"I assumed as much," Lucinda said. "And now that a cable has been laid between London and Paris, you and Jackie can talk anytime you like."

Tony went over to the device, lifted the receiver and put it to his ear. After a few crackles that resembled a distant thunderstorm, a feminine voice came on the line.

"May I help you?" the voice said.

"Yes, I'd like to call Paris."

"I'm afraid you'll have to come to the post office to place a long-distance call, sir. And it may take a while."

"Oh, well, thank you. I'll do that." Tony replaced the receiver on the cradle. "She says I'll have to come to the post office."

Lucinda frowned. "The telephone company didn't tell me that. What a nuisance!"

Tony laughed. "A temporary inconvenience. I'm sure that you'll soon be able to make the calls from here."

"I should hope so," Lucinda said. "But at least we can communicate whether you're in Paris or someplace else. What a marvel modern technology is!"

"I should think a telegram would be quicker," Jackie said.

"For the time being, yes," Tony said. "But neither is a solution to our problem."

"What problem?" Lucinda said.

Tony glanced at Jackie. "We can't continue to live two hundred miles apart, Lucinda. Especially now that Trey is here."

Lucinda seemed prepared for this despite her blithe denial of any problem whatsoever. "Sit down." She indicated the sofa. Tony and Jackie looked at one another and took their seats. Lucinda sat in an armchair opposite. "I've been thinking about this," she said. "The telephone, of course, is not a solution, nor did I intend it to be. It's for my own purposes for the most part. Tony, I think you should come and live with us—here. There's plenty of room and I'll keep out of your way. There's an attic room upstairs with plenty of light for your studio. And I can introduce you to a number of artists here in London, including Mr. Sargent, though he's often abroad, as well as Monsieur Monet, who I understand is presently in residence. There is no dearth of talent and resources here, I assure you. London may even surpass Paris as the art capital of the world over the next few years."

Tony fidgeted with his hands for a moment, then pulled the telegram from his coat pocket. "I just received this from my representative in Paris."

He handed her the telegram.

Lucinda read over the short message and looked up with a smile. "Congratulations! A bronze medal! That's wonderful, Tony, but it doesn't mean you have to live in Paris."

"I'm afraid it does. At least for the foreseeable future."

She handed the telegram back to him. "Well, my offer still stands. If Mr. Sargent can divide his time between London and Paris, so can you."

Tony glanced at Jackie. "That's what Jackie says. I'll certainly consider it. But as I said, I have to be in Paris for at least a few more months."

Lucinda stared at him, still smiling, and picked up a dinner bell from the coffee table. She rang it, producing the familiar tinkling sound that summoned the servants. "It's nearly teatime. Such a civilized institution we have here in England. And a respite from all the cares of the world."

CHAPTER 39

On the train back to Paris, Tony considered the situation he was in.
Nothing had changed, really, except for Lucinda's offer to house and
support him and Jackie—and Trey. But soon there would be another
child, a French child, assuming that Mme G did not face any more
complications. Then what? Would he continue to have to dash back and
forth between the two cities? Or would Lucinda welcome his French
family and support them all? This brought an amusing image to his mind
of a kind of polyglot circus with clowns bursting through windows and
children chasing them back into the house. He laughed out loud, which
drew stares from the other passengers.

Mme G would never leave Paris—she was too solidly entrenched, practically
a native...another thought emerged—what if he broke it off with Mme G?
After all, he wasn't married to her, as he was to Jackie, nor had Mme G
demanded any long-range commitment. Her main desire, it seemed, was
to have a child to replace the one that had died. This was a woman's most
powerful drive, wasn't it? To reproduce.

He came out of the station with these thoughts still swirling in his head
and hailed a cab, one of the new electric ones like those in London. He
was getting used to this type of conveyance now, whether electric or gas-
powered. However, it seemed that the electric ones were most likely to
prevail on account of their clean and noiseless operation. Manure in the
streets would soon be a thing of the past!

When he arrived at Rue de Furstemberg, J-P took his valise.

"Comment va-t-elle, J-P?"

"Elle va bien, Monsieur Tony. Sauf elle a des maux à tête le matin."

"Tous les matins?"

"Non—parfois."

"Où est-elle?"

"Dans le jardin."

J-P took his valise upstairs and Tony lingered for a moment in the drawing room gazing out the window at Mme G sitting on a stone bench staring up at the Rodin statue. She seemed very contemplative, even serene in her expression. He descended the outside stairway and approached her from behind.

"Je suis de retour, Amelia" he said.

She turned and looked at him over her shoulder. She was wearing a green taffeta dress embroidered at the hem and bodice with red and white roses.

"Bon retour, mon ami. How was your trip to London?"

"Very pleasant."

"And the child?"

Tony grinned like the proud father he was. 'Il est en bonne santé. A boy."

"I'm so glad." She patted the seat beside her. "Sit down and tell me all about him."

Tony sat down. "He's fair-skinned, like his mother. But he looks like me–I think."

"Ah, oui? And how is his mother?"

"She's doing well. A fairly easy delivery."

"Good. And his name?"

"Trey."

"Trey? What sort of name is that?"

Tony laughed. "I'm not sure. It just came to mind since his real name is Antonio Jones the Third."

"Ah. And you couldn't very well name him 'Le Trois,' like 'Napoléon le Troisième.'"

"No. He's going to be very English, it seems."

"English? They're not coming here?"

Tony sighed and looked up at Rodin's statue. "I'm afraid not. At least not soon."

Mme G put her arm in his. "Well, then. It will just be the two of us until our child is born. In the meantime, you'll have to get busy. Monsieur Dantec tells me he has customers lined up at the door clamoring for your work."

"Yes. I'll have to get busy."

"Would you like something to eat?"

"Oui. Je meurs de faim."

As it was August and rather warm in the house they ate in the garden. J-P brought a small folding table from the carriage house and set it up in front of the stone bench. Sabine served them some white wine and *amuse-*

bouches consisting of prawns and *beignets aux pommes.*

Tony noticed that Sabine was showing a bit. When she returned to the house, he said to Mme G: "J-P tells me you're having headaches in the morning."

"Did he? Well, it's nothing serious. A little morning sickness, that's all. I know what to expect. Poor Sabine, though, is having a time."

"How so?"

"Oh, vomiting and sleepless nights. I think I'll give her a week off. We should eat out more anyway."

"Amelia–"

"Yes?"

"What do you think of moving to London?"

"London? Whatever for?"

"Lucinda–Jackie's mother–has made me an offer."

"What kind of offer?"

"To move into her house in Belgravia."

Mme G remained silent for a moment. "And do you intend to accept?"

"I don't know. You see, Jackie doesn't want to come here–she seems to want to resume her acting career when the child is old enough to not need her constant attention. And Lucinda has a large attic that would serve as a studio."

"You have a large and wonderful studio here. I can't imagine a *grenier* being more suitable."

"Well, it would be a step down, so to speak. But we could all be together and–"

"Together? You mean you would expect me to come with you?"

"That's the proposition."

Mme G wiped her mouth with her napkin. "That's very generous of what's-her-name–"

"Lucinda."

"Lucinda. But I can't leave Paris. My work, my life, is here now. And our child? He'd grow up to be a stuffed shirt. Eaton, Oxford, gentlemen's clubs in Pall Mall. They're dens of conspiracies against women."

Tony laughed. "Conspiracies? Well, I suppose they're a bit old-fashioned, but I hardly think they have the power to subjugate women to the point of denying them the right to vote, for example."

"Well, they've been denying women the right to vote for the past two hundred years, and it's these so-called 'gentlemen's clubs' that have served as behind-the-scenes incubators of misogyny."

"Is it any better in France?"

"I would say so. At least women can come and go as they please here. In any case, Tony, you can tell your mother-in-law 'thanks, but no thanks.'"

That settled the question. Not that Tony expected that Mme G would accept such a proposal, but at least he had presented it.

The next morning Tony rose early and since both Mme G and Sabine remained in bed, J-P served the meal.

As it was a fine, albeit very warm, summer day, he decided to walk to M. Dantec's gallery on Rue de Rivoli. He lingered on the Pont des Arts and contemplated the Palais du Louvre, wondering if some day his paintings would be hung there. He envisioned young art students setting up their easels, as he had done years earlier, and copying 'Madame G.' But was this the goal? To achieve immortality through his art? He couldn't deny that the idea appealed to him, but was it the primary motive? It seemed somehow petty and self-serving. Wouldn't it be better to know that someone, anyone, might look at his painting and merely admire its beauty, its technique, its celebration of life?

Of course he couldn't answer these questions and he took solace in knowing that they had been asked by artists like himself for centuries with the same result: an ambiguous shrug of the shoulders.

He walked on, rounded St-Germain l'Auxerrois, and arrived at M. Dantec's gallery. It seemed to be full of people. The door was open to allow for ventilation, and he found himself surrounded by people speaking English. Some were British, some Americans, and some Germans, judging from their accents. He noticed a small crowd gathered around one of his paintings, *Les Acrobates*. M. Dantec was at the center of the group explaining something to them as if he were a tour guide in a museum. He spotted Tony and waved him over.

"Voilà l'homme lui-même!" he said. Then in English, "The man himself." He introduced Tony to the group, all of whom smiled and nodded their heads in approval.

"I say, Monsieur Antonio," said an Englishman of about middle age and voluminous side whiskers, "are these your fellow Africans? They seem as agile as monkeys."

Tony was not amused by this comparison. "I'm an American, sir. These gentlemen in the painting are, as I understand it, Frenchmen. Their agility derives from playing football in England." This was met with laughter from the group as others asked questions that seemed to him equally superficial and commonplace. He surmised that these were tourists, not serious collectors. Indeed, no one offered to buy the painting, and they eventually broke up and moved on.

Tony was left standing with M. Dantec, who patted him on the shoulder.

"Bon retour, cher ami! How was your visit to London?"

"I have a son," Tony said.

"Felicitations! Why did you not tell me? It would have made it easier to explain your absence to the judges. Nevertheless, I managed to convince them that you had pressing business to attend to and they allowed me to receive your medal. Would you like to see it?"

"Of course."

M. Dantec led Tony to his office, went to his desk, and withdrew a small box. He opened it and handed it to him. "La voilà! Very nice, don't you think?"

Tony examined the medal. It was a very pretty design with the head of a woman who he supposed was 'Marianne,' the personification of France since the Revolution, with the branch of an oak tree encircling her head like a laurel wreath and a view of Paris in the background. On the obverse side was Winged Victory carrying a rather unathletic-looking man on her back holding a torch aloft. "Very impressive. How many medals were awarded?"

"Presque quarante mille."

"Forty thousand?"

"That is, altogether. Only a fraction of that for art."

"A fraction? How many?"

"Qui sait? A hundred, a thousand. Monsieur Tanner won the silver. Interestingly, he, too, is a *nègre marron*."

"Yes. Well, he is very good. A sort of mentor of mine.'"

"I've tried to get some of his work for the gallery, but Mon Dieu! There are none to be found."

"Well, I accept it with pleasure. It's an honor to be in the same company as Monsieur Tanner."

"There have been many inquiries since the awards ceremony. Ah! J'ai presque oublié. There is a parcel for you."

"A parcel?"

"One moment." M. Dantec opened another drawer and extracted a small parcel wrapped tightly with twine. It was addressed to:

M. Antonio, aux bons soins de M. Dantec
Galerie Dantec

Rue de Rivoli, Paris

"There's no return address," Tony said.

M. Dantec shrugged his shoulders. "Peut-être que c'est une femme, non?" He grinned. "Une admiratrice qui est très timide."

"I doubt it. But I'll take it home and open it later."

"D'accord. Oh! Une autre chose. The Duke of Norfolk was here yesterday. He asked about your work. He said he would return tomorrow and would like to make your acquaintance."

"All right. I'll make a point of it. Say ten o'clock?"

"Bon. À demain."

Tony returned to Rue de Furstemberg and upon entering the house, gave the parcel to J-P, telling him that he would open it after lunch. J-P took it to the butler's pantry between the kitchen and the dining room and put it down on the counter without a second thought.

Tony went upstairs and found Mme G before her mirror, arranging her hair.

"How is Monsieur Dantec?" she said, gazing at him in the mirror.

"Quite well. He says the Duke of Norfolk has been inquiring about my work."

"Has he? I don't know him but I imagine he is quite rich. Perhaps you should raise your prices."

"That will be up to Monsieur Dantec. Oh–and he gave me this." He extracted the little box from his vest pocket and handed it to her.

She opened it. "A medal? From the Exposition?" She turned around, stood and kissed him. "That's wonderful! For which painting?"

"For *Madame G*, of course."

"My portrait? Oh, I had hoped we could keep it."

"Well, of course. But it may become very valuable, especially if the newspapers publish a photograph of it."

"Newspapers?" She examined the medal again. "I'm not sure I want it to be so public. What if–"

At that moment an explosion rocked the house.

"Oh, mon Dieu! What was that?"

Tony stood stock still for a moment. "The parcel!"

"What parcel?"

Tony didn't explain. He hastily left the room and descended to the drawing room, where he was met by clouds of dust and smoke pouring from the dining room. He pulled out a handkerchief and put it over his mouth as he made his way through broken chairs, the collapsed dining room table, and pictures strewn about the room. He heard moaning from the butler's pantry and women screaming.

Once in the butler's pantry, the dust cleared somewhat and he found J-P lying on the floor, his head bloody and his hair singed.

"Monsieur! Monsieur!" Sabine screamed. She was standing in the kitchen doorway, her hands to her face, and Eugénie behind her. "Aidez-le! Aidez-le!"

Tony knelt down and propped J-P's head up. "Comment est-ce arrivé?"

"Je ne sais pas, Monsieur Tony. J'ai mis le colis à côté de la cafetière et...je ne sais pas." His eyes closed and he seemed to lose consciousness.

Sabine knelt, her belly preventing her from going all the way down, and caressed J-P's forehead. "Jean-Pierre! Jean-Pierre! Ne meurs pas!" She burst into tears.

Tony took J-P in his arms and carried him to the drawing room. By this time, Mme G had arrived. "Put him on the sofa. I'll call the hospital."

While she was doing that, Tony laid J-P on one of the sofas. There was little blood, mostly on his forehead, but his jacket was still smoking from the heat of the blast. Tony put a pillow beneath his head. J-P opened his eyes again.

"Je suis désolé, Monsieur Tony. J'étais stupide."

"Ne t'inquiète pas, J-P. Ce n'était pas ta faute."

J-P's parents as well as Eugénie joined the assembled group in the drawing room. J-P's mother wailed in a way that Tony had never heard women do before and found it particularly annoying and unhelpful. Hasan eventually escorted her out of the room but soon returned to offer whatever assistance he could.

By the time a couple of white-uniformed young men arrived, Tony had removed J-P's cutaway jacket and scorched shirt to reveal second and third-degree burns on his chest, shoulder and neck. Eugénie, who seemed to know something about the treatment of burns, fetched a damp towel from the kitchen and applied it to the wounds. The attendants placed him on a stretcher and conveyed him downstairs to the waiting ambulance.

Sabine insisted on accompanying him but the attendants wouldn't allow it since it was not only against the rules, but they saw that she was pregnant. Tony escorted her back into the house, where Mme G took her upstairs to her room. When she came down again, Tony was in the dining room with Hasan removing debris and setting the pictures aside, which miraculously were undamaged except for a layer of soot.

"How could it have happened?" Mme G said. "There's no gas in the house."

"It was the parcel," Tony said.

"The parcel? You mean it was a bomb?"

"That's exactly what I mean. Addressed to me without a return address. Any idea who it could be?"

Mme G pulled a painting aside to examine it. "The vicomte?"

"Who else?"

"But he doesn't owe you any money. Why would he?"

"If you'll recall that little incident at the baron's soirée, he made it clear that he doesn't care much for black people."

"Ah! Well, if that's the case, then he must have lost his mind. Why else would he risk everything, his title, his estates, his freedom–just to express his distaste for people of color?"

"Bigotry is a kind of insanity."

"You're jumping to conclusions." She set the painting against the wall and slapped her hands together to remove the soot. "I seem to remember that there was a rash of bombings a few years ago. Anarchists, mostly. But there was one who the police caught and when they asked him why he did it, he said, 'to avenge the death of Napoleon.' They sent him to a madhouse."

Tony shrugged his shoulders. "Perhaps you're right. In any case, you'd better call the police."

"Better than that–I'll call the baron."

CHAPTER 40

J-P was taken to the Hôtel Dieu on the Île de la Cité, adjacent to Notre-Dame. Tony, Mme G and Sabine visited him the next day, as did Hasan and his wife later in the afternoon.

The burns were declared to be serious but not life-threatening. The doctor said that with proper care and a regular change of bandages, he would most likely not even have much scarring. He gave credit to Eugénie for quick thinking in applying the damp dish towel.

The police had arrived by the time Tony and Mme G returned to the house. Inspector Rochard introduced himself and declared that he was *un passionné* of Alphonse Bertillon, a police officer who had developed both a system of fingerprinting and handwriting analysis. Tony was skeptical because, as a close follower of the Dreyfus affair, he knew that M. Bertillon had testified as an expert witness for the prosecution in that case and falsely concluded that Dreyfus had written the note that had incriminated him. Inspector Rochard, however, dismissed this objection, saying that Bertillon had only erred in his 'presentation' of the evidence, and that his methods were sound. Though dubious, Tony was anxious to identify the perpetrator and therefore willing to give the inspector the benefit of the doubt.

Three of the forensic experts were busily sifting through the debris while Mme G and Hasan moved the paintings to the studio. Tony hovered over the investigators as one of them picked up a piece of paper with a pair of tweezers. This fragment contained Tony's name and address. Another investigator was sprinkling some sort of powder on the lid of the cardboard box that had contained the explosive. He dusted it off with a brush, pressed a thin piece of paper against it, then wrapped the lid in cloth and put it into a sack.

Tony turned to Inspector Rochard. "What good will it do to gather fingerprints if there's no one to match it with?"

"We have evidence from a previous bombing with which to compare," the inspector said, in heavily accented English.

"You mean the one meant for Baron de Rothstein?"

"Yes. And if the handwriting matches as well, we will know that the 'auteur' is the same."

Tony considered this. "But then how can you identify this 'auteur?' Especially if he doesn't have a criminal record?"

The inspector smiled. "We have our methods, Monsieur. Evidence can be obtained."

Tony took this to mean that the inspector intended to burglarize the vicomte's house. But he didn't wish to question him on this point.

After the inspector and his team had left, Mme G returned from the studio and surveyed the wreckage. "We'll have to go out for dinner."

"Where do you suggest?"

"Oh, I don't care, really. Just somewhere to get away and not think about all this for a while."

"How about Lipp? We can walk."

"Une bonne idée, Monsieur." She gave him a kiss. "Perhaps you should bring your sketchbook. There are often quite interesting people there."

"You promise not to get jealous if I decide to sketch a woman?"

She laughed. "I shall not promise you that. Jealousy is a woman's right—and her favorite pastime."

"And a man's favorite pastime is admiring beautiful women."

"Ça va, tant que tu ne touche pas!"

This sort of banter was puzzling to Tony. It seemed odd to him that she would accept his relationship with his wife but erupt into a jealous rage whenever he cast an admiring eye on a beautiful woman in a crowded theatre or restaurant. But now she claimed not to object as long as he kept his distance.

Brasserie Lipp was crowded, as usual, and they stood for twenty minutes before being seated. During this time, the only figure to catch Tony's eye was a man of sixty or so, short in stature, with gray hair and a neatly trimmed gray beard. This was President Émile Loubet, who was a champion of Dreyfus and had been struck on the head with a cane at the Auteuil steeplechase the year before by an anti-Dreyfusard. Shortly thereafter, Loubet had remitted Dreyfus' sentence and therefore saved him from being returned to Devil's Island, where he surely would have died.

Tony took out his sketchbook and began sketching the president, though it was difficult to get a clear view of him due to the constant stream of well-wishers who approached him.

Another patron of similar stature was Toulouse-Lautrec, who seemed to turn up at every watering hole in the city. He was surrounded by a bevy of beautiful women who fawned over him like mother ducks over a particularly precocious duckling. Tony wondered at his capacity to attract women and could only speculate as to what occurred in the boudoirs of Montmartre.

At last they were seated, as it turned out not far from M. Loubet's table. This gave Tony a closer look at the man, and now that most of his admirers had paid their respects, Tony was able to finish his sketch without interruption.

"You should introduce yourself," Mme G said.

"I think he's had enough hand-shaking and cheek-kissing for now and would like to eat his dinner in peace."

"Well, he might like your sketch and even give you a commission. Think of the prestige of having your work hanging in the Élysée Palace!"

"Yes...well, maybe I'll approach him after dinner."

"That may be too late. Let me see the sketch.'

Tony tore the page from his sketchbook and handed it to her.

"I think it's marvelous! Wait here." She stood.

"Amelia–"

But Mme G was at the president's table before Tony could finish his sentence. Deeply embarrassed, he put his head in his hands and stared at his dinner plate.

Monsieur Loubet seemed delighted at the approach of this beautiful woman. She introduced herself and he asked her to sit down. There were no other women at the table. After some chit-chat that Tony didn't quite catch, she thrust the sketch before M. Loubet and gestured towards Tony, who continued to stare at his dinner plate. M. Loubet craned his neck, looked at Tony, and nodded his head. He took the sketch and held it before him while he adjusted his pince-nez. Then he handed it to a colleague, who examined it and passed it on to a third gentleman. After some more conversation, Mme G returned to their table.

"Amelia, I wish you wouldn't–"

"He's a charming man. And he wants you to call his secretary to make an appointment."

"His secretary? At the Palais?"

"Of course. Where else would his secretary be? Actually, I'll do it. He asked his aide to jot down my name, but I'm not sure he caught yours."

"Of course not. It's you he's interested in, not me."

"There you go–underestimating yourself again. One must be bold if one is to be successful. Where is our waiter?"

CHAPTER 41

Madame G did indeed call the Élysée Palace the next morning and secured an appointment for Tony with the president the following week. In the meantime, carpenters and plasterers applied themselves to repairing the damage done by the bombing. This was a constant disruption for several days, during which time Mme G and Tony took their meals in the garden, or, in inclement weather, in the studio.

One morning, while they were having breakfast in the garden, Sabine ushered in Inspector Rochard. He doffed his hat, a gray homburg, and held it in both hands as he stood before them. "Forgive me for interrupting your *petit déjeuner*. But I have news."

"You have apprehended the culprit?" Mme G said.

"Alors, pas encore. But we are making progress. The fingerprints on the fragments of both parcels match."

"I'm not surprised," Mme G said. She speared a piece of melon with her fork and brought it to her mouth. "And who do these fingerprints belong to?"

"Ah, that is the difficult part, Madame. The baron has his suspicions, but we cannot invade a man's privacy without a reasonable suspicion."

"Isn't it reasonable to suspect Vicomte de Koenigsbourg?" Mme G said.

"I cannot say, Madame. However, we have obtained the fingerprints of a former employee of the vicomte."

"And?" Mme G said.

"And these prints match the ones on the parcel."

"Eh voilà! You must arrest the vicomte!"

The inspector put up his hand as if he were a policeman stopping traffic.

"Pas si vite, Madame. This employee was discharged from the vicomte's employ two months ago. And he has been arrested for burglary just recently. That is how we obtained his fingerprints."

"Well, then,"Mme G said. "It seems to be a direct link to the vicomte. Why would this employee have his fingerprints on the package if he did not act on the orders of the vicomte?"

"As I said, Madame, the employee was discharged two months ago. The parcel was delivered only last week. He may have assembled the bomb after his discharge and mailed it on his own. Or he may have merely touched the wrapping paper in the course of his duties while employed and someone else assembled the package. There are still other possibilities."

"But it is clear that the wrapping paper came from the vicomte's house." Tony said. "Isn't it?"

"It seems likely," the inspector said. "But this employee has a record of associating with criminals. It may have been one of them and the employee merely touched the paper without knowledge of its purpose."

Mme G expelled a breath of air in exasperation. "Then where does that leave us? Is this the 'progress' you spoke of?"

Inspector Rochard twisted the tip of his moustache.

"We are pursuing another avenue of investigation, Madame. That is, the handwriting on the parcel. We have samples of the vicomte's signatures on certain documents he has been obliged to file with the city. The cursive is very similar."

"Then that's it!" Mme G said. "Proof positive. You must arrest him!"

"Ah, but that is not possible just yet. The science of handwriting analysis is not yet perfected. If you may recall, Monsieur Bertillon's analysis of Monsieur Dreyfus' handwriting was proved to be false. The courts are reluctant to accept such analysis as evidence."

Mme G sighed. "Then what are we to do?"

"Patience, Madame. Patience. We are assembling more and more evidence each day. There may soon be a breakthrough."

"Well, then," Mme G said. "I must say that you and your men have not been idle. Thank you, Monsieur l'Inspecteur. We will await your next report."

"Je vous remercie, Madame, Monsieur. Bonne journée." And with a little bow, he replaced his hat and made his way back to the house.

"What does the baron have to say about all this?" Tony said. He pushed his plate aside.

"He has no doubt that it was the vicomte. And it's because of him that the inspector is devoting all of his time to the case. But I still wonder why the vicomte...Ah!"

"Ah, what?"

"It's been rumored that the vicomte is impotent."

"Impotent?"

"Yes. I'd almost forgotten. A couple of years ago–before you came–I was having lunch with the Comtesse d'Orleans and she told me that a friend of hers had had *une liaison* with the vicomte, but that he was unable to perform and went into a rage, nearly killing her."

"Nearly? How?"

"With a statuette."

"A statuette? What did he do? Hit her with it?"

"No. He forced it into her...well, her vagina. She nearly died from loss of blood, but the doctors were able to save her."

This act of cruelty brought to mind Tony's grandmother, who had been subjected to a similar assault by her half-brother when she was a slave. "Was the vicomte punished?"

"Of course not. He was a nobleman and the woman was merely the wife of a local merchant, though a prosperous one."

Tony sighed. "Interesting. But what's that got to do with the bombing?"

"Perhaps nothing. But I thought it might be productive if I invited the vicomte's wife to lunch."

"Lunch? What for?"

"I also hear, not surprisingly, that she's estranged from her husband. She may have some useful information."

"Hmm. I suppose it's worth a try. But would she accept such an invitation? If she suspects her husband is responsible, then she may be too frightened to be seen in public with you."

Mme G gave him a sly wink. "I shall be very discreet, as always."

CHAPTER 42

President Loubet suggested that his appointment with Tony take place in the afternoon, as he was busy with *affaires d'État* in the mornings.

Arriving a little before three on a sunny afternoon in late August, he stood before the impressive façade of the Palais de l'Élysée with his sketchbook under his arm and a *crayon* in his coat pocket. Mme G had insisted that he wear a navy-blue beret so as to announce to the staff that he was in fact an artist. He never liked berets, at least for himself, because he felt that they suggested the wearer was a tourist rather than an artist, especially if the wearer was a black man.

In fact, at this moment, as he stood across the street in front of a flower shop facing the grand entry with its coffered arch and spiked wrought iron gate, two policemen eyed him with suspicion. He debated whether to march straight ahead and identify himself, in which case he could be cited for blocking traffic, or to go all the way back to the corner–a good 100 meters or so–cross there and return on the other side. While he was deliberating, one of the policemen, dressed in a summer uniform of white shirt, blue trousers, and black tie, crossed the street and made a beeline towards him. He carried a pistol on his right hip.

"Monsieur? Vous avez des affaires ici?"

"Oui," Tony said. "Je m'appelle Antonio Jones. Le président m'attend."

The policeman grinned. "Il vous attend? Pourquoi?"

"Parce qu'il aimerait que je peigne son portrait."

"Ah, bon? Vous êtes artiste?"

"Oui."

"Venez avec moi."

Tony followed the policeman across the street as he put up his hand to stop traffic, which consisted of more and more motorcars. There were palace guards in very elaborate uniforms dripping with gold braid and crowned with plumed shako hats on each side of the gate, but they seemed as immobile as statues. The policeman conferred with his colleague for a moment or two, then went to a tall door adjacent to the main gate where he picked up the receiver of a telephone and spoke into a mouthpiece that Tony couldn't see. All this time, the second policeman stared at him as if he were some sort of feral animal who had just emerged from the Bois de Boulogne.

The first policeman waved him over to the door and handed him a pass. Then he pointed across the courtyard to the main entrance to the palace and instructed him to hand the pass to the doorman. Tony thanked him and passed through the gate.

The doorman was dressed much like the guards outside the wall, but without the shako hat. He smiled cordially at Tony, looked briefly at his pass and directed him to a receptionist at a desk beneath a double stairway. Each flight of the stairway consisted of risers covered with burgundy carpets and gilded bronze railings supported by stanchions in the form of fern leaves. A huge glass lantern illuminated by incandescent bulbs hung between the two wings.

Three gentlemen dressed in morning coats and silk waistcoats descended the stairs as Tony ascended. They were deep in conversation, almost whispering, and seemed not to notice him. At the top of the stairs, he saw a long hallway to his right and several doors at regular intervals of five meters or so. To his left was another hallway with a sharp turn that seemed to lead to private apartments. He went to the right and counted the doors until he came upon the Salon Doré. He thought that this must be the president's office if he had followed the receptionist's instructions correctly. He knocked.

"Entrez."

Tony cautiously peered in through the half-open door. The afternoon rays of the sun poured into the room through tall windows and lit up the gold leaf trim on the paneling that adorned the walls. This effect was further enhanced by a large gilt mirror over a marble mantelpiece. A French flag stood on one side of the central window, and another, he supposed *départemental*, flag on the other. Through the window he could see a balcony and beyond it, a wide expanse of trees and manicured lawn. Facing him, his head bowed over a sheath of papers as if in deep concentration, was Monsieur Loubet himself. A secretary, dressed in a morning suit like the men he had encountered on the stairway, stood at the side of the desk and seemed to be waiting for the president to sign one of the documents. Finally, M. Loubet nodded his head and signed the document. The secretary left without acknowledging Tony's presence.

The president looked up and smiled. "Ah! Monsieur Jones. He stood and indicated a chair. "Bienvenue. Est-ce que vous comprenez le français?"

"Oui, Monsieur le Président."

"Mais...vous êtes Américain, non?"

"Oui, Monsieur."

"Then you must bear with me as I attempt to employ my limited English. Agreed?"

"D'accord. I mean yes, if you wish."

Tony sat in a chair facing the president's desk beneath a crystal chandelier that was so large and heavy that he felt that it might come crashing down on his head at any moment. It struck him as odd that there were no portraits or paintings of any kind in the room. But considering the fact that the wallpanels were so elaborately decorated, taking up every centimeter of space, it shouldn't have been surprising. He sat rigidly in his chair as if he were about to be interrogated. Apparently M. Loubet noticed this.

"Please—make yourself comfortable, Monsieur Antonio. Perhaps you would like to sit by the window?" He indicated a pair of armchairs facing the open window.

"Yes. There seems to be a bit of breeze there." Tony rose and went to the window where he sat down and was soon followed by the president. He was a bit surprised that M. Loubet was even shorter than he appeared to be at Lipp, but also that he was powerfully built like a rugby player.

"Now, Monsieur Antonio," M. Loubet said, with his hands folded on his lap. "Madame Goldman tells me that you have recently won a medal at the Exposition."

"That is correct, Monsieur le Président."

"And she says that this painting is a portrait of herself."

"That is also correct."

Monsieur Loubet smiled and gazed out the window. "I would like to see this portrait sometime. But I'm afraid that my schedule has not permitted me to visit the Exposition since the opening ceremonies. However, Baron de Rothstein tells me that it is quite beautiful."

"You know the baron?"

"Of course. He has been very generous with his time and money. In fact, he helped to—how does one say—'extract' us from a very difficult situation after the war."

"I have been told that."

Monsieur Loubet turned and looked directly at Tony. "He also tells me that you have a very interesting history."

Tony smiled. "Nothing terribly out of the ordinary Monsieur le Président. I am really more interested in your history. I will have to have some knowledge of it before I begin work."

"Ah! But of course. Forgive me, but my own history is so boring. Politics, politics, politics! I understand that your history, on the other hand, is quite fascinating. Is it true that your grandmother was born a slave and then escaped to become a famous actress?"

"That is true Monsieur. But it is a very long story. And I understand that your time with me is limited. Perhaps—"

"Oui, oui. We should get started. Perhaps we can continue this conversation as you work." M. Loubet consulted his pocket watch. "An hour. How does one begin?"

"I'll need to do a preliminary sketch—the one I did at the brasserie was hurried and I did not have the benefit of your acquaintance at the time."

"Alors! Let us begin."

Tony, as usual, sketched rapidly, paying particular attention to M. Loubet's eyes, which were a chestnut color and seemed to convey a kindly nature. His hair was snow-white and his beard neatly trimmed, though not fastidiously so. He seemed to be at ease within himself, with the burdens of his office alleviated somewhat by his interest in others. It was this last quality that Tony wished to capture.

When the hour was up, Tony stood and offered M. Loubet a look.

"Ah, c'est bon. But you flatter me. My nose is surely larger than that."

"If you prefer, I will do it in profile and your nose will look absolutely enormous."

Monsieur Loubet laughed, and when he did his eyes sparkled. "I think you are the *artiste* for me. I value honesty in a man. When will you begin to paint?"

"As soon as your schedule permits."

"Ah, I must consult my calendar." He rose and went to his desk. "Shall we say Monday—à la même heure?"

"Perfect."

Monsieur Loubet extended his hand across the desk. "It's been a pleasure to make your acquaintance, Monsieur Antonio. À bientôt."

"À lundi," Tony said, and passed through the door just as M. Loubet's secretary was returning.

CHAPTER 43

When Tony returned to Rue de Furstemberg, he was surprised to see J-P at the door.

"Comment ça va, J-P?" he said. "Tu es guéri?"

"Oui, Monsieur. Plus ou moins. Je me sens mieux."

J-P indeed looked much better than when Tony and Mme G visited him in the hospital. He did, however, have a red burn mark on his neck that peeked out above his collar, and his eyebrows still had not grown back. But he seemed happy to be out of the hospital and back at work.

Tony followed him up the stairs to the drawing room where he found Mme G talking to Inspector Rochard.

"How did the interview with Monsieur Loubet go?" Mme G said.

"Ok. He's a very good sitter. Bonjour, Monsieur Rochard."

"Bonjour, Monsieur Jones."

"Inspector Rochard is making progress," Mme G said.

"Ah, oui?" Tony put his sketchbook down on the coffee table and sat on the sofa next to Mme G. Inspector Rochard remained standing. "In what way?"

"In actual fact," Inspector Rochard began in his stilted English, "Madame Goldman has provided us with a way of obtaining the vicomte's fingerprints."

"Really? How did she do that?"

"I had lunch with the vicomtesse today," Mme G said. "She agreed to supply us with some article that her husband has handled."

"She must really detest him," Tony said. "Does she still live with him?"

"Yes. But she sleeps in another bedroom and only has breakfast with him. The rest of the day they keep out of each other's way."

"And what if the vicomte's fingerprints are not on the parcel–or what's left of it. He might have had a servant put the bomb together, wrap it, and post it."

"That is not likely, Monsieur Jones," the inspector said. "The vicomte would not want witnesses to his scheme. More likely, he would assemble the bomb himself and once prepared for the post, given it to an assistant."

"Well," Tony said, "if he was that careful, he may have used gloves to wrap the package. Then what?"

The inspector shook his head. "That is a possibility. In which case we will have to pursue other methods."

Tony sighed "Well...it's worth a try. Bonne chance, Inspecteur."

"We will try our best, Monsieur Jones."

After Inspector Rochard took his leave Mme G asked Sabine to bring them some iced tea. Both she and Sabine were noticeably pregnant now, but neither seemed hampered in their movements, though Tony recalled that Sabine had trouble squatting down to help J-P after the bombing. He thought of Jackie–every woman he knew seemed to be pregnant. And he noticed that Mme G and Sabine had formed a closer, even intimate, relationship. In a way, he felt shut out from this developing sisterhood. Mme G, in fact, seemed less interested in sex than only a few weeks before, which was all right with him. Each time they had sex, he felt a pang of guilt, as if a triumvirate of Harpies were pointing their fingers at him, shouting "Shame!"

Mme G took a sip of tea. "Ah! That is so refreshing. It is insufferably hot. The vicomtesse and I sat outside at a little café on Rue Dauphine–at her insistence since it is virtually unknown to her social set. A narrow street with no breeze. And here it's not much better, though we get a little from the garden."

Tony didn't think it was all that hot. But ascribing that feeling to Mme G's present condition, he changed the subject. "Monsieur Loubet thinks highly of you. You very much impressed him at chez Lipp that night."

"Well, I was impressed with him, too. He seems to be very progressive in his views–unlike the average Frenchman, who wants to keep women in their place."

Tony chuckled. "Well, there are some women who will not be denied. And not just in France."

"True. When do you begin painting?"

"Monday. He gives me an hour at a time."

"Will you have to schlepp your easel and canvas to the Palais for each session?"

"No. Everything is provided."

After finishing their iced tea, they went out to the garden and sat on one of the stone benches.

"I think we've postponed the wedding long enough," Mme G said.

"What wedding?"

She looked at him as if he had been living on another planet. "Have you forgotten already? So preoccupied with your–"

"Oh, you mean Sabine and J-P. Of course–when do you think we should have it?"

"A week from Saturday. It will be a small affair, of course. And Sabine, like me, is showing. But I want her to have a beautiful wedding nevertheless. I've ordered a dress for her plus a hijab for the Muslim ceremony."

"And J-P?"

"A morning suit and a sherwani."

"A sherwani?"

"Very elegant. I'm afraid the groom may outshine the bride. I found one in a shop on St-Germain."

Tony laughed. "So they're going to have to change between acts?"

"They'll have plenty of time between the two ceremonies. I have a feeling you're not taking this seriously."

"I am taking it seriously. I'm delighted for them. I'm just not familiar with all these Muslim customs."

"Well, you should be–your African ancestors were Muslims."

"That's not true. I happen to know that most of them came from West Africa–Yoruba, Fulani, and Ibo. Tribal religions."

"How do you know that?"

"I spent a lot of time in the Harvard library."

"I forget sometimes that you are such an intellectual."

"I'm not really. In college I neglected the prescribed courses and simply focused on what interested me."

"Like art?"

"That's the one area where Harvard couldn't help me. That's why I came here."

Mme G gazed at Tony with a raised eyebrow. "At any rate, you need to learn something about Muslim rituals. We don't want to offend J-P and his parents."

"Good point."

Tony was beginning to feel that he was married to this woman. They were beginning to have these little spats that grew out of nothing. A raised eyebrow here, a curled lip there. Isn't that what married couples do? In fact, he had been living with Mme G now longer than he had with his own wife! Oh Jackie...Jackie...and his son little Trey. How could he abandon them?

Well, there was work to do. And when he was finished with M. Loubet's portrait he would go to London. But for how long? No, this situation was unsustainable. Once Mme G's child was born he would have to make a decision. Perhaps Muslims could live with two or more wives, but he was too westernized, too much a product of Anglo-American culture however mixed with African tribalism. Africa! What did he know of it? He had never set foot there. And he often neglected the fact that at least a quarter of his forebears were Connecticut Yankees.

"What are you so deep in thought about?" Mme G said, after studying his expression for several moments.

"Work. I want to paint a portrait like no one has ever seen before."

Another raised eyebrow from Mme G. "Don't sacrifice this opportunity on the altar of your artistic vanity, Tony. This is the president of France–if he rejects it, you may never get another chance."

Tony rose and went to the window where he watched the last rays of the sun dancing along the rooftops as they streamed into the *quartier*. "He won't reject it."

CHAPTER 44

Madame G had greatly underestimated the number of J-P's friends and family members. It turned out that he had several relatives in Paris who worked as servants, blacksmiths, green grocers, and cooks. Counting their families there were sixty altogether. Sabine had far fewer friends and only her sister from Montpellier showed up. Seeing that this was to be a more festive occasion than she had anticipated, she hired a group of musicians at the last minute and a caterer as well, since J-P, Sabine and Eugénie would be guests on this eventful day, not servants.

The awkwardness of two ceremonies with different costumes was resolved by allowing Sabine to wear the white wedding dress that Mme G had purchased for her, while a colorful hijab covered her head. J-P forwent the morning suit in favor of the *sherwani* for both ceremonies. Hasan, his father, turned out to be an imam, or so he claimed, and performed the Islamic service, while a Catholic priest from nearby St-Germain-des-Prés was recruited. Tony was chosen to give away the bride.

Once the ceremonies were completed, the musicians resumed play, and the guests indulged in an eclectic mix of foods, including couscous, lamb, fish, baklava and 'makroudh', a pastry filled with dates and almonds. Wine flowed freely, though some of J-P's friends abstained and drank only tea.

Tony had not had this much fun since his own wedding, though that one was marred by the rude intrusion of the Klu Klux Klan. This one was less eventful but far more joyous.

Mme G's barouche awaited the young couple in front of the house where a hired driver whisked them off to the Gare de Lyon for a honeymoon in Biarritz. But not before the guests showered them with coins.

Tony and Mme G waved at the carriage as it turned onto Rue Jacob and disappeared from sight. When they returned to the house they were surprised to find Inspector Rochard standing at the front door.

"Bonjour, Madame Goldman, Monsieur Jones. Une bonne fête, non?"

"Oui," Tony said. "Jean-Pierre et Sabine se sont mariés."

"A happy occasion," the inspector said. "Forgive me for intruding."

"You are always welcome, Inspector," Mme G said. "You have news?"

"Oui, Madame. May I have a moment of your time?"

The inspector followed them upstairs to the drawing room, where Mme G offered him a chair and she and Tony sat on a sofa. Tony felt a little tipsy from the wine and was in a good mood.

"I assume you have made progress in the investigation," Tony said.

"Oui, Monsieur. Grave progress."

"Grave? How do you mean?"

"I mean that the vicomte's fingerprints not only match the ones on the parcel, but many others as well."

"Many others? You mean other bombs?"

"Only one. The one sent to the baron. But we compared those to others we have on file and it turns out that these same prints are also found on the clothing of several prostitutes."

"Prostitutes?" Tony suddenly felt completely sober. "You mean that he—"

"I mean that he appears to be *un tueur fou*."

"A pychopathic killer?"

"I do not know the English term, but yes, something of the sort." The inspector continued. "You see, we have unsolved cases in our files involving six prostitutes, some going back to '88. Most of these women were violated in the most shocking manner and then had their throats cut. We have interrogated a score of known criminals over the years, but they either had solid alibis or the fingerprints did not match. Two were imprisoned at La Santé at the time."

"And you think the vicomte is this monster?" Tony said. "Are you sure?"

"Quite sure. But even with the matching fingerprints, it will be difficult to prove. The courts are skeptical of this kind of evidence, as I said before. In addition, the vicomte is a very wealthy and influential man. One can never be sure that a certain judge may not be compromised."

Tony and Mme G looked at each other.

"What can we do?" Tony said.

"Well," the inspector said. "First of all, you are a primary witness in your own case. If it can be established that the vicomte was the perpetrator of the attempt on your life, the court will take the other charges more seriously."

"What about the baron?" Mme G said. "He was an intended victim, too."

"That is true, Madame. But he is reluctant to testify due to his aversion to publicity. It is bad for business, you know. Especially when one is a Jew. He will be content if the vicomte is proven to be the perpetrator in Monsieur

Jones' case."

"What about Jean-Pierre?" Tony said. "He'll be on his honeymoon for two weeks."

"Jean-Pierre is not necessary for us to win a conviction, though I'm sure the judge will want to question him. He was not the target, and he hardly knew what happened, or why. However, the trial–if it comes to that–will probably not take place for a month or more."

"Well, then," Tony said, "what are we to do in the meantime?"

"Nothing," the inspector said. "Except to be vigilant and refrain from opening any parcels unless you are sure of the identity of the sender."

"That goes without saying," Tony said. "But there are other methods of mayhem, as you have pointed out in the fate of the prostitutes. How can I–or Madame Goldman–protect ourselves?"

The inspector smiled and glanced at Mme G. "The vicomte has a predilection for prostitutes–the gaudier, the better. I don't believe Madame Goldman has anything to worry about. However, I will place a guard at your door 'around the clock,' as you Americans say. As for you, Monsieur Jones, I recommend that you arm yourself whenever venturing far from home. Are you familiar with firearms?"

"Yes."

"There's a pistol upstairs," Mme G said.

"Bon. Just as a precaution." Rochard rose from his chair. "Now if there are no further questions, I must–"

"One more thing, Inspector," Tony said. "I have been engaged to paint the portrait of Monsieur Loubet, the president. Can I carry a pistol into the Palais de l'Élysée?"

"'I would think not, Monsieur. Best to declare it at the door and leave it there while you are engaged in your work."

"Yes. Of course. That makes sense."

"Now, if I may be permitted?" The inspector replaced his hat on his head.

"Of course. Thank you, Inspector."

"I will keep you informed of further developments."

CHAPTER 45

Days were cooler now as summer merged into fall. Tony enjoyed the walk from Rue de Furstemberg to the Pont des Arts, where he lingered for several minutes watching the barges ply the Seine. Most tourists had fled the city and conveyances were less crowded, including the new metro, which he caught at the Louvre and got off at the Place de la Concorde. From there he walked to the Palais de l'Élysée.

He carried his paint box under his arm and the Navy revolver in his waistband. It was heavy and tended to make his trousers sag a bit, which in turn forced him to continually pull them up. A nuisance, really.

When he arrived at the entrance to the Palais, the policeman who had admitted him the week before simply waved him through. At the receptionist's desk in the Vestibule d'honneur he presented himself, announced the time of his appointment with the president, and displayed the revolver.

The receptionist was taken aback and glanced towards a man in a suit standing next to a marble column who immediately walked over to the desk. Tony was holding the pistol by the barrel and put it down on the desk.

"Monsieur?" the man said, not really as a question, but as a rebuke.

"Je veux le laisser ici," Tony said. "C'est pour la protection dans la rue."

The man in the suit picked the gun up and put it in his coat pocket. "Je le retiens pour vous, Monsieur."

This potential crisis out of the way, Tony proceeded up the stairs to the Salon Doré, where he found Monsieur Loubet in the same position he had found him in the first day they met: pouring over some documents as his secretary stood by waiting for his signature. He looked up as Tony entered.

"Ah! Monsieur Jones. Juste à temps." He quickly signed the documents and stood as the secretary left the room.

Tony noticed that an easel was set up in a corner of the room. "Comment allez-vous, Monsieur le Président?"

Monsieur Loubet held up his hand. "Please. Only English."

"All right. Are you ready to get started?"

"Of course. I've been looking forward to it all day. Not to indulge my own vanity, mind you, but to converse with an interesting man."

Tony smiled. "You are the subject of interest, Monsieur le Président. Would you like to sit before the window?"

M. Loubet looked at the window, its doors open at about a 45-degree angle. "Why not? I see you have brought your own paints."

"And brushes. I'm very particular about the instruments of my profession."

"Ah, yes, of course. But should you need reinforcements, so to speak, we can supply you with them."

Tony put his paint box down on a console and moved the easel—it was a heavy one with a large canvas on it—to a position just to the right of the window. Then he adjusted the angle of the chair and asked M. Loubet to sit down in it, with his back to the window. The afternoon light streamed in from the garden and the draperies rustled in the gentle breeze.

Tony opened his paint box, removed the sketch he had made on his first visit, and pinned it to the top right corner of the canvas. Then he took out his palette and began mixing paints on it with a fine sable brush.

"The flags," M. Loubet said. "Are they necessary?"

"No, not necessary. But it's up to you."

M. Loubet looked at the flags on either side of him. Then at Tony. "I think it may be too formal, don't you think? And a bit of a cliché. I'll have them removed."

"Not at all necessary, Monsieur le Président. I will simply put them out of my mind."

"Well, yes—you are a man of imagination, after all."

As Tony worked, M. Loubet peppered him with questions about his experiences in America. He wanted to know if African Americans were truly free since the Emancipation Proclamation, what their relationships with their former masters were like, whether there were still laws against interracial marriage, etcetera.

"There are still places where a black person must not go," Tony said, almost absently as he began an outline of M. Loubet's face. "Restaurants, hotels, certain neighborhoods—especially in the South."

"Ah, yes—the South. I am from the South myself—the South of France, of course. It seems that people in southern climes all over the world take a poor view of outsiders, especially those who have a different complexion."

Tony found this observation both accurate and amusing. "I wouldn't say that this attitude is confined to southern climes, Monsieur le Président. Boston, for example, has its share of prejudice."

"Boston? The home of your revolution?"

"Yes. They even had slaves there once. They gave them up, not out of the kindness of their hearts, but because it was uneconomical."

Monsieur Loubet's cheery expression evaporated, at least temporarily. "Yes. I suppose one shouldn't make generalizations. Are you married, Monsieur Jones?"

"Yes, sir, I am."

"And is she, ah, of your race?"

"No, Monsieur. She is as white as you are."

This seemed to puzzle M. Loubet. "Well, then, if America restricts the movements of its black citizens as you say, then how do you and your wife get about when you are in America?"

"We are no longer in America, Monsieur le Président."

"Hmm...yes, a silly question–forgive me."

"Not at all, Monsieur le Président. We intend to go back some day and perhaps then it will be different."

"Yes...one would hope so."

Tony continued to work in his usual rapid manner, now using a fine brush, now the palette knife. Fine strokes for M. Loubet's face, broad strokes for the background.

There was a long period of silence, as if M. Loubet was loath to interfere with a genius at work. Finally, Tony put down his brush and stood back from the canvas.

"You are finished?" M. Loubet said.

"For today," Tony said. He picked up a clean cloth and dipped it in some mineral spirits. "I think I will need two or three more sessions."

"That many? Well, I suppose Rome wasn't built in a day. Excuse me–another cliché."

"Quite all right. This is not Rome, of course, but I want to get it right. If you can't spare the time–"

"No, no. I want you to 'get it right,' as you say. I am very unproductive in the afternoon, at any rate." M. Loubet stood from his chair and rubbed his thighs. "The circulation is not what it used to be. I think I'll go for a walk in the garden. But...could I see?"

Tony dropped a cloth over the canvas and conveyed the easel back to its place in the corner. "I'd rather you didn't, Monsieur le Président. It may change over the course of the next few sessions. And I wouldn't want you to become attached to a particular image before it's finished."

"No, no. I suppose that wouldn't do. When shall you return?"

"Again, Monsieur le Président, it's up to you."

M. Loubet went to his desk and checked his calendar. "Thursday?"

"Thursday it is. Same time?"

"Yes."

Tony packed up his paint box, tucked it under his arm, and headed for the door. "À bientôt, Monsieur le Président."

"À jeudi, Monsieur Jones."

At the reception desk he asked for his pistol. The man who had taken it from him did not seem to be around, and the receptionist, who called herself Claudette, opened a drawer and handed it to him. Tony opened the chamber and saw that it was empty.

"Ah!" Claudette said. "Les balles." She scooped up the six cartridges and dropped them into Tony's outstretched palm.

"Mercie, Madame."

"Quand est-ce que vous revenez, Monsieur?"

"Jeudi."

"Bon. Veuillez décharger les balles la prochaine fois."

"D'accord, Madame."

It seemed reasonable that he should be required to remove the bullets before entering the Palais. Rather than put them back into the chamber, he dropped them into his pocket, put the pistol into his waistband, and made his way to the street, where the policeman simply nodded.

As he strolled along Rue de Rivoli, enjoying the sun on his face and the children playing in the Jardin des Tuileries, he thought how ridiculous it was for an artist to be carrying a gun, especially in Paris. Not that Paris has not known violence, but in this day and age it seemed to be the most civilized of all cities. The vicomte, if he indeed was a murderer, was an anomaly. And besides, he seemed to prefer knives and explosives to firearms.

As he took his seat on the metro, the pistol dug uncomfortably into his abdomen. He took it out of his waistband–to the alarm of a middle-aged man seated next to him–opened his paint box, put the pistol in it, and snapped the lid shut.

Henceforth, he would leave the pistol at home.

CHAPTER 46

While Tony was preoccupied with his portrait of M. Loubet, Inspector Rochard was not idle. He persuaded a judge to allow him to search the vicomte's house in Neuilly-sur-Seine and his detectives came away with boxes of evidence over the strenuous objections of the vicomte, who promised to take up the issue with the préfet de police. Sifting through this evidence was painstakingly slow even though Inspector Rochard assigned half-a-dozen of his men to the task.

But after two weeks of this process, the inspector felt confident enough to turn all of the evidence over to a *procureur*, who filed charges against the vicomte, including, but not limited to, attempted murder and murder. Due to his high position and–he claimed–failing health, he was spared imprisonment in the infamous La Santé, and put under house arrest until the trial was completed.

In the meantime, J-P and Sabine returned from their honeymoon in Biarritz and the household at Rue de Furstemberg returned to its normal routine. Or, nearly normal. When Tony returned from the Palais de l'Élysée one afternoon, he found Mme G and Sabine hovering over the dining room table unpacking baby clothes. They held up the garments one by one, examined each, giggled, and then moved onto the next item. They were becoming like sisters. The lectures Tony had endured earlier from Mme G about maintaining a certain distance between master and servant seemed to no longer apply. His announcement that he was nearly finished with the president's portrait fell on deaf ears.

After failing to get their attention, he went upstairs and sat at his desk, where he went through a stack of correspondence that included dinner invitations, letters from young women wanting to marry him, an art critic for *Le Figaro* wanting to interview him, and a summons to appear in court. This last one was somewhat disturbing even though he was anxious to see the vicomte prosecuted because he didn't quite know how the publicity would affect his career. What if the vicomte were acquitted? Would he,

Tony, then be seen as a charlatan, a shameless self-promoter, reckless in his quest for fame?

And there was one more letter–from Jackie.

> *Dearest Tony,*
>
> *Trey is growing fatter every day. He is quite robust and pink-cheeked and grasps for everything in sight. But he calls for his papa, and his papa is not there. I am afraid that he is beginning to think Alastair is his papa, for Alastair is always present and even changes his nappy whenever Stephanie is not available.*
>
> *Can't you come to visit us soon? I see in the papers that some French aristocrat has been charged with the most horrific crimes and that he even sent a bomb to Madame Goldman's house that injured one of her servants. Were you acquainted with this man?*
>
> *I also see that your reputation as a painter is growing. That is wonderful– but can't you tear yourself away from Paris for even a short visit? I would come to you with little Trey, but the doctor says cases of influenza have been reported in northern France and that it would be too much of a risk for us to travel.*
>
> *Please let me know if you can come. I miss you.*
>
> *Your loving wife,*
> *Jackie*

Tony put the letter down and considered his options. He could not leave Paris as long as this trial was going on. And the president's portrait? Well, he would soon be finished with that and M. Loubet may not even like it. But if he does, it could create a demand for his work that would far eclipse his little bronze medal from the Exposition.

And Jackie–why can't she come to Paris? His work was here, his career. The 'influenza scare' was just an excuse. He hadn't even heard anything about it till now. Jackie seemed to want to have her way. She prefers London to Paris, and no doubt wants to raise little Trey as a proper Englishman.

For himself, he felt more like a Frenchman every day. His influence was growing. His friends were either Frenchmen or American expatriates.

Which reminded him—what has become of Nat? In spite of his profligate ways and impetuous behavior, Tony still considered him a friend. And with new commissions coming in every day, he didn't really need the money Nat owed him.

He put the letter away in the same drawer as the revolver. Should he shoot himself? He laughed. The only time in his life that he seriously considered suicide was at Harvard, where he felt isolated and ashamed that he had betrayed the hopes and sacrifices of his parents who had sent him there. But it turned out that having a son with a Harvard diploma was less important to them than his own happiness. They were incredibly loving and tolerant parents.

Which brought him back to Trey. His son! Jackie was right—he must not neglect his only son. As soon as the portrait was finished he would go to London. And the trial? No telling how long it might last, but his role in it would be very limited. The inspector was rightly more concerned with putting away a serial killer.

He opened the drawer again and took out a sheet of stationery:

Dear Jackie,

I will come to London as soon as circumstances permit. That is, in the next few weeks. I will send you a telegram the moment I am free.

As far as the vicomte is concerned, he has been charged but no one knows how long the trial may last. I am a witness because the bomb he sent to Madame Goldman's house was intended for me. No one knows what his motives may have been, though I suspect he is bent on cleansing the earth of blacks, prostitutes, gypsies and Jews. Fortunately, he is under arrest now and will most likely spend the rest of his life in prison.

Kiss little Trey for me—everyday. I will soon be there to do it myself.

Your loving husband,
Tony

CHAPTER 47

On his way to what he hoped would be the last session with M. Loubet, Tony altered his usual route slightly and crossed the river on the Pont Neuf where he lingered for a few minutes and gazed at the Palais de Justice. Like many Parisian institutions, it was clad in a neoclassical facade, with statues of Roman statesmen and mythical ladies representing Truth and Justice atop Doric columns. He hoped to be spending as little time there as possible.

He stopped again at the newly opened metro entrance at Châtelet to admire the Art Nouveau design of M. Guimet, with its glass canopy, green wrought-iron supports and script-like lettering. He wondered at M. Guimet's talent and even more at the Public Works Committee's acceptance of such a design that radically broke from tradition. Why couldn't New York approve such a design?

He descended the stairs to the platform and was surprised to see an old friend: Nat. He had set up his own gallery of sorts with about a half a dozen canvases against the wall and was sitting in a folding chair as commuters examined his work while they waited for the trains.

"Tony!" Nat stood from his chair, rushed over to shake his hand, and clapped him on the back. "We keep running into each other. You know, we should get together for an *apéro*." He indicated his paintings with a sweep of his arm. "What do you think? I haven't sold one yet, but it's only a matter of time."

Tony looked at the paintings. There were actually more than six, some stacked behind the others. Of those that he could see, two were of Marie-Louise, paintings that Nat had done while they both were living in the studio on Rue de Fleurus. The other four were of the metro station, two of the entrance and two of the trains coming and going, belching white smoke ventilating through the gratings overhead. "Rather interesting, Nat. I mean the ones of Monsieur Guimet's entrances. You may be the first to paint them."

"Well, not really. There are a number of artists doing the same thing at other stations. I managed to run one of them off who was decamped here this morning and now I have it to myself."

"How much are you charging for them?"

"Ten francs each. So far, no takers."

"Well, just as you say it's a matter of time. What about the ones of Marie-Louise? Nudes always sell."

"Thirty francs for those. By the way, Marie-Louise and I are back together again."

"What happened to Carlotta?"

"She ran off with the others to Spain. Safer for gypsies, you know."

"Ran off? But she's your wife."

"Gypsy marriages aren't recognized in France. Not unless you go to a *mairie* and fill out the forms. Our marriage was just symbolic."

"And the dress? You invested a small fortune in that dress."

Nat shrugged his shoulders. "She took it with her. Along with 2,000 francs."

"Two thousand francs? She robbed you?"

Nat shrugged again. "What could I do? The police would never find her. Besides, she needed the money more than I did. A kind of settlement, you might say. Which reminds me, I was going to pay you back with that money, but what happens, happens. I'll be getting another dividend cheque next month and I'll pay you back then."

At that moment, a middle-aged man wearing a navy-blue beret like Tony's approached them.

"Combien ça coûte, Monsieur?"

"Dix francs, Monsieur," Nat said.

"Chacun?"

"Oui."

The man pointed to one of the paintings of the metro entrance. "Et celle-là?"

"Dix francs," Nat repeated.

The man shook his head and held up five fingers. "Cinq francs."

At that moment the shriek of a whistle pierced the air and a train came coasting to a stop at the platform. A conductor opened the door nearest them and passengers began to stream into the car.

"Cinq francs, Monsieur," the man said. "Pas plus."

Nat sighed. "D'accord. Cinq francs."

The man put a few coins into Nat's hand, tucked the painting under his arm and boarded the train just as the conductor was closing the door.

"It's better than nothing," Nat said. He looked at Tony's paint box as if noticing it for the first time. "And where are you headed, Tony? I see you won a medal at the Exposition."

"Well, yes, it's helped me get a commission or two. In fact, I'm just on my way to see a sitter."

"Yes, that's the way to make money. Say, if you get more than you can handle, could you send them my way?"

"I'll do that, Nat." Another train screeched to a stop at the platform. "I've got to go, Nat. Good seeing you." Tony hurried off to the car nearest him.

"Come see us!" Nat shouted. "Marie-Louise is learning how to cook!"

On the way to the Palais de l'Élysée Tony felt a bit guilty for brushing Nat off like that. Certainly he would recommend him for a portrait. Nat was actually a pretty good draughtsman. But he lacked originality. His best paintings were of the Old Masters that he copied in the Louvre.

When he arrived at the Salon Doré, M. Loubet was pacing back and forth before the window with his hands clasped behind his back. His secretary was not present. He merely looked up when Tony appeared at the door without saying anything.

Tony saw that he was deep in thought and so went to the corner where the easel was located and moved it to its usual position. He removed the cloth covering the painting. "Monsieur le Président?"

M. Loubet continued pacing, his head down. Then he stopped before the window, looked out for a few moments, and turned on his heel to face Tony. "Qu'est-ce que vous pensez de la peine de mort?"

"Capital punishment?" Tony said. "Well, Monsieur le Président, I have to confess that I'm very biased on that issue."

"Biased?"

"Partial."

"Ah, yes. Well, sit down for a moment, Monsieur Antonio."

Tony put his brushes down and sat in a chair facing the president's desk. M. Loubet sat as well.

"Perhaps you can tell me why you have this 'bias,' as you call it."

"Monsieur le Président, I am a black man. In my country, since the Civil War, there have been hundreds, if not thousands, of my brothers lynched for no other reason than the color of their skin."

"Lynched?"

"Lynché."

"Ah, yes. Un mot apparenté. My English fails me at times. Well, what about criminals? I mean ones that are found guilty of crimes *odieux*?"

"I suppose that's where my bias carries over to the death penalty in general. Even among white people in America, many innocent people are executed each year. And the percentage of blacks in that category is even higher. In the end, whether the accused is guilty or not, it seems to me that the death penalty does not serve as a deterrent."

M. Loubet stroked his chin. Then he rose and handed a document that lay on his desk to Tony. "Read the first paragraph or two, if you please."

Tony read these paragraphs. It was an application for clemency for a man convicted of killing his wife as well as his own mother. The weapon used was a carving knife. His wife's head was nearly severed in the process, while his mother was stabbed multiple times.

Tony replaced the document on the desk. "Quite gruesome murders."

"Oui. *Macabre*, as we say in French. What would you recommend I do?"

Tony wondered at this question. Here he was a painter, little more than a household servant in the Palais de l'Élysée, and the president of France was asking him for his recommendation regarding an important *affaire d'État*?"

"Well, Monsieur le Président," Tony said, "you already know my opinion on the question of capital punishment. However, I know little about the case at hand beyond what I have just read."

"Then you recommend clemency?"

"For what it's worth, I do."

"All opinions are valuable," M. Loubet said. "A head of state should not make momentous decisions without consulting others. However, if I were able to consult all the people of France, they would object to your reasoning, Monsieur Antonio. You are in a small minority."

"I've always been in a minority, Monsieur le Président. Though not necessarily a small one. In any case, I am not a French citizen. Perhaps you should consult your staff."

"I have. They are of the same opinion as the vast majority of my countrymen. If I grant this disturbed young man clemency, there will be an outcry."

Tony felt helpless. And yet he wished to help. "In my country, Monsieur le Président, there was once a man in a position very much like yours."

M. Loubet's eyes opened wider. "Yes?"

"His name was Abraham Lincoln."

"Ah, yes. A great man."

"He was very unpopular even on the eve of his election. He was even more unpopular when he issued a proclamation freeing the slaves. And yet he did the right thing. And history has vindicated him."

"Oui, oui. C'est vrai." M. Loubet began pacing again. Then he seemed to have an idea. He stopped and turned to Tony. "You were the intended victim of a murderer, were you not? I have read about it in the newspapers."

"That's true, Monsieur."

"And if this man, this so-called vicomte, is convicted and sentenced to death, would you recommend clemency?"

"I would, Monsieur le Président."

M. Loubet regarded him with a stern look, as if dubious of his response. "You know also that the vicomte is accused of a string of murders, of women that he mutilated in the most horrible manner?"

"I do, Monsieur."

"Same answer?"

"Yes."

"Hmm." M. Loubet faced the window and looked out again. "Qu'on est bien ici...c'est magnifique!" He turned again to Tony, then pulled out his pocket watch. "Mon Dieu! We have squandered half of the hour."

"I shall not need much time today," Tony said. "I'm nearly finished."

"Bon," M. Loubet said with a broad smile. "I am anxious to see the final result." He took his seat by the window and it suddenly seemed that he had not a care in the world.

Tony worked more quickly than usual in consideration for the president's time, but there were only a few areas on the canvas that he felt needed more attention. When he put down his brushes, he stood back and assessed his work.

M. Loubet looked up. "C'est fini?"

"Oui," Tony said. "Unless you are not satisfied. Would you care to look?"

M. Loubet rose from his chair, circled around his desk, and stood next to Tony. He lifted the pince-nez that dangled on a black ribbon from his waistcoat to his right eye. "Mon Dieu! Is that me?"

"You do not like it?"

M. Loubet stepped closer to the canvas. "Like it? Well, I think it is a very pretty thing. But again, I think you flatter me."

Tony chuckled. "That was not my intention, Monsieur le Président. I merely tried to capture your spirit, your personality, but most of all, your character."

"Caractère? Ah, yes–well and good. But...let's see what my staff thinks.

He went to his desk and pressed a button. Then a second, then a third.
In seconds, his secretary entered the room followed by several other aides,
around ten altogether.

M. Loubet indicated the painting. "Qu'est-ce que vous en pensez?"

The staff members crowded around the easel and scrutinized the
painting. Some, like the president, applied a pince-nez to their eyes.
Others, especially the women, came closer at first then stepped back for
a broader perspective. One gentleman even put his thumb up and closed
one eye, presumably to block out some feature of the portrait, then
dropped the thumb and shifted his position for another view.

"Donc?" M. Loubet said.

"C'est bien ça!" the secretary said.

"C'est vous, Monsieur le Président!" a woman said.

M. Loubet smiled, nodded in affirmation and excused them. After
they had all filed out the door, he turned again to Tony. "Then it is
done, Monsieur Antonio. It will be hung in the Salon de Portraits if the
Ministry of Finance approves. I would hang it in here, but I don't know
if I could bear to be presented with such a stern image of myself each
morning. C'est splendide, Monsieur!" He then kissed Tony on both
cheeks. "Continuez sur la même piste!"

Tony packed up his paints and brushes and took one last look at his
handiwork as M. Loubet returned to his desk.

Apparently word traveled fast in the Palais, for when he passed through
the Vestibule d'honneur on his way out, the receptionist stood and
clapped as did several others.

"Bravo, Monsieur Antonio, bravo!"

CHAPTER 48

While Tony awaited the approval of the Ministry of Finance and having no idea what his compensation would be, the trial of the vicomte was underway. Tony was called as a witness, but could offer little useful testimony, as he had had no contact with the vicomte other than at the baron's soirée the previous winter. As for motive, he was reluctant to claim that the vicomte had targeted him merely because he was black, for fear that he would appear to be one of those minority people who ascribe all their misfortunes to racism. And yet there was no other motive that he could think of, and he said so.

The vicomte's defense attorney scoffed at this statement, pointing out that the vicomte employed several black servants and not one had a negative thing to say about him. As for the handwriting on the package, the defense attorney demonstrated the ease with which a man's handwriting and signature could be duplicated by presenting to the judges an example that he had written himself. And fingerprints? An inexact science at best, and a quack theory at worst.

The prosecutor countered these arguments by showing that fingerprints had in fact been used to identify individuals as far back as the Babylonians in 200 BC, and perfected by science in recent years by both British and French researchers. He then called his star witness: Inspector Rochard.

Inspector Rochard sat in the witness box with a copy of E. R. Henry's *Classification and Uses of Fingerprints* on his lap. He explained the evolution of the science, noting Henry's improvements on Bertillon's system and that metropolitan police departments the world over used the method with signal success.

While the inspector admitted that the prints on the parcel fragments collected at Madame Goldman's house were somewhat smudged and indistinct, the prints found on the bloody clothing of the prostitutes were clear and matched the vicomte's exactly. He went on to say that no two human beings on earth had the same fingerprint patterns, not even twins.

Following Inspector Rochard's testimony, a string of other witnesses was called, mostly servants in the employ of the vicomte, who admitted that the vicomte was arrogant and often used abusive language in dealing with them but had never employed physical force or excessive penalties against them for dereliction in their duties.

By far the most interesting aspect of the trial–to Tony–was the interrogation of the vicomte by the president of the judicial triumvirate, who seemed to have extraordinary powers as compared to his American counterpart. The judge acted as the prosecutor-in-chief and though this role seemed extremely prejudicial to the defendant, the judge nevertheless appeared to be only interested in eliciting the truth.

And it worked. After a series of questions regarding the vicomte's experiences as the French consul in Guinea, he suddenly exploded with a rant against the conspiracy of Jews and blacks to emasculate white European men.

"Émasculation?" the judge said. "Comment?"

The vicomte then claimed that these two groups were often seen in the company of white women who bestowed their favors upon them in proportion to the size of their penises. And as everyone knows, the vicomte said, Jews and blacks were of two primitive races that had failed to evolve as white Aryans had, who, in the process of evolution, had had the blood of their lower bodies diverted to the brain for its higher development, thus diminishing the size of their penises, which were now only as large as needed to produce children. Thus, as women gravitated to these inferior men with large penises for their own pleasure, fewer and fewer white men would be able to reproduce and soon the Aryan race would die out.

The judge, along with everyone in the courtroom, sat aghast and in silence at this diatribe. Then he looked at the defense counsel, who seemed to be preoccupied with some document. "Alors–Monsieur?"

The defense counsel looked up as if the judge had raised a minor point of law. "C'est tout, Monsieur le Président."

"Donc," the judge said. "À demain."

French jurisprudence is quick but efficient. Monsieur Vicomte de Koenigsbourg was found guilty of the murder of two of the three prostitutes, as well as mailing the bomb intended for Tony. This second, lesser verdict, seemed to be influenced by the vicomte's outburst on the penultimate day of the trial. In addition to a sentence of twenty years imprisonment for attempted murder, the vicomte was ordered to pay 10,000 francs to Mme G to compensate her for the damage done to her house. But the prison sentence was made moot by the death penalty imposed for the two murders.

However, the vicomte's defense attorney immediately filed an appeal with the *Cour de cassation*, the Court of Appeals for criminal cases. Unlike the *Cour d'assises*, as Tony soon discovered, the appeals process could be lengthy, as much as two or three months.

In the meantime, the newspapers were having a field day. And the vicomte found this to be to his advantage. Against the advice of his attorneys, he welcomed interviews and took the opportunities to express his theories of white supremacy and racial conspiracies. These pronouncements were made on the doorstep of his mansion in Neuilly-sur-Seine, as the judge allowed him to remain under house arrest until the appeals court rendered a judgment.

While waiting for this second verdict, Tony was notified by the Bureau du Président de la République that his portrait of President Loubet had been rejected by the Ministre des Finances–not based on its merits, of which it offered no opinion, but the price that was suggested by M. Loubet himself: 15,000 francs. There was a silver lining, however–M. Loubet offered to buy the painting with his own funds and ship it to his home in Montélimar.

This was a major windfall to Tony and, his presence no longer needed in Paris at the moment, he decided to pay a visit to his wife and son in London.

Arriving on the kind of dreary day that drives Londoners into their pubs and dimly lit offices, Tony regretted that he had not brought an umbrella. He did have a fedora that Mme G had bought for him, saying that homburgs and top hats were going out of style, even in London. However, when he got off the train at Victoria Station, the only people he saw wearing this style of hat were women! Nevertheless, the wide, down-turned brim kept the rain out of his face.

He took a hackney cab–the old-fashioned horse-drawn kind–to Eaton Square and pressed the bell. Alastair answered the door, welcomed him as if he were an old friend, and ushered him into the parlor. There he found Jackie, Lucinda, a woman whom he had not met before but who looked familiar, and little Trey. Trey was about six months old now and standing on his own two feet, albeit with the assistance of his mother. He had short blond curls and was wearing a sailor suit. He stared at Tony as if he were a strange creature from the wild and turned his face into the folds of his mother's dress.

"You've come!" Jackie said. She ran her hands through Trey's tousled hair. "It's your papa, Trey! Say hello to your papa."

Trey cautiously turned his head and again stared at Tony.

Tony knelt down to his level and stretched out his arms. "Come to Papa, Trey."

Trey didn't budge.

Tony, not wanting to force himself on the child, stood up and embraced Jackie, who seemed hesitant at first but then burst into tears.

"Oh, Tony!" she said. "We thought you'd never come." She quickly wiped away her tears, seemingly embarrassed and confused by her display of emotion.

"Welcome, home, Tony," Lucinda said. "Allow me to introduce my friend, Madame Bernhardt."

Tony stared at Madame Bernhardt as Trey had stared at him, and with the same sense of wonder. He had seen her on the stage, but in person she appeared much older, though she had a magnetic quality that belied her age. She wore a broad-brimmed hat with an ostrich feather secured by a scarlet *foulard* tied beneath her chin. She extended her hand.

Tony kissed her hand, in the French manner. "Enchanté, Madame. Je suis ravi de faire votre connaissance."

"Enchantée, Monsieur. May we speak English?"

"Of course. I've just come from Paris where I saw you in *L'Aiglon*. You were magnificent!"

"Thank you, I owe much of the play's success to my good friend Monsieur Rostand, who wrote the play for me. And this is why I'm here: Miss LeRoux is to produce it here in London next year."

"Well, Lucinda," Tony said. "This will be quite a coup for you. The production in Paris was wildly–"

"Are you an actor, Monsieur?" Miss Bernhardt said. "You have the fine features and robust physique required for the role of *Othello*."

"Unfortunately, Madame, I am merely a painter."

"A painter? Then you must paint my portrait."

"I would be honored, Madame."

Madame Bernhardt put her long white gloves on and walked to the door. "My agent will contact you. In the meantime, I must be going. Lucinda, ma chérie–" She hugged Lucinda and kissed her on both cheeks. "I will see you at the theatre tomorrow. Jacqueline–" She performed the same honors with Jackie. "A delight to make your acquaintance. When little Trey is a bit older, you must return to the theatre. Your talent must not be wasted in child-rearing. That's what governesses are for." She bent down to kiss Trey. "Au revoir, mon petit garçon. Tu es très mignon!"

And with a flourish, scarlet *foulard* trailing, she left the parlor followed by Alastair, who draped a blue cape with an ermine collar over her shoulders and opened her umbrella.

When she was gone, Tony turned again to Jackie. "Well, the little fellow doesn't know me? We'll have to get acquainted." He bent down and picked Trey up, raising him high above his head. This delighted the child and he chortled with the thrill of soaring aloft. Tony then cradled him in his arms.

"Trey, my good man, what shall we do today?"

Trey looked at his father in wide-eyed wonder.

"He still hasn't figured this out," Jackie said. "But he likes you."

"We'll play some games." Tony looked out the window. "Indoors, of course. Has it been raining for long?"

"For days," Lucinda said. "Typical English weather. But all the more reason for people to go to the theatre."

Tony looked at Lucinda. She was in her fifties now, about the same age as Mme Bernhardt, and like her, still attractive though she had gained a bit of weight since her boar hunting days in South Carolina. "It's sunny in Paris and people still go to the theatre. Madame Bernhardt's play has been a roaring success."

"And it shall be here as well," Lucinda said.

There was no dearth of games available in the nursery, but Trey wasn't quite old enough to tell the difference between a game and simply knocking things over. And this he was very good at. Jackie joined in, and she and Tony sat on the floor as Trey crawled among the wooden blocks, push toys and stuffed animals. He finally sat on his bottom and clutched a rag doll.

"A doll?" Tony said. "Shouldn't he be playing with something more... more–"

"For boys?" Jackie smiled. "He doesn't really make any distinction. He's as apt to play with the bear."

Tony noticed the stuffed bear in the corner. "No, I guess it doesn't make any difference at this stage. Whatever he likes."

"Tony–"

"Yes?"

"I've been reading in the papers about that horrible man who tried to kill you."

"Yes, well, it seems that he will either be sent to prison for the rest of his life or executed."

"I understand, I think, why he killed those poor prostitutes. But why did he try to kill you? Did you know him?"

"Not really. Only briefly at a party."

"'Then why would he send a bomb to you?"

"He apparently was disturbed to see me with Madame G. In addition to having a problem with prostitutes, he is convinced that Jews and blacks are out to get him. And Madame G–who isn't really Jewish–set him off, it seems. He probably hoped that the bomb would kill both of us."

They sat in silence for a few moments, their eyes on Trey.

"Tony," Jackie said, "you've become quite successful now."

"I would say things are going well, but I wouldn't say that I'm successful yet."

"Well, you're financially successful, at least."

"So far."

"Then can't you tear yourself away from Madame Goldman and set up your own studio?"

Tony sighed and leaned back on the palms of his hands. "I can 'tear myself away,' as you say, anytime I want. But Madame G's studio is a nearly perfect workplace. The light is perfect, the space is perfect, the location is–"

"And the woman who provides you with all this–is she the perfect woman?"

Tony frowned. "All right, Jackie. I see what you're driving at, but the answer is no. She is not the perfect woman for me–you are. And after some doubt, I admit, I have come to believe that you are the only woman for me."

Jackie looked skeptical. "Then why–"

"Don't I leave Paris and come to live with you in London? Because, as I've told you before, my career is in Paris. And besides, I'm old-fashioned enough to believe that a woman should follow her husband wherever he goes, not vice-versa."

"And I'm old-fashioned enough to believe that a marriage is between two people–not three."

Tony lay on his back and closed his eyes. "All right. I will leave Madame G's studio–and her house."

"And Madame G herself?"

He sat up and looked at her. "And Madame G herself."

"When?"

Tony paused to consider this. "When you and Trey come to Paris."

"Promise?"

"Promise."

"The first of the year, then. Trey will be walking by then and it will be easier to travel."

"The first of the year. Agreed."

CHAPTER 49

Tony spent two weeks in London, during which time the weather cleared up and the temperatures fell. It was now fall, and the English were spending more time outdoors, as did Tony and Jackie. They went horseback riding in Hyde Park and boating down the Thames to the Queen's House in Greenwich.

It seemed, however, that Mme Bernhardt forgot all about her desire to have Tony paint her portrait, and soon Tony dismissed her offer as simply an effort to be polite. When he brought up the subject with Lucinda, she said that Mme Bernhardt had already had dozens of portraits made of her and was prone to lose track of them.

And so Tony returned to Paris.

Commissions were streaming in. This was all fine and well, but Tony was beginning to tire of painting portraits. He wanted to do something different, something new, something experimental. Of course he could do this regardless of the subject matter, but his patrons usually expected a portrait that was realistic and, of course, flattering. In between commissions, he roamed the streets of Paris, sometimes at night, looking for subject matter and inspiration.

All the nightlife of Paris—at least for the adventurous—seemed to be concentrated in and around Pigalle. This was a long way from Rue de Furstemberg, and the new metro lines did not extend to Montmartre yet. So Tony solicited the services of J-P as both driver and companion, to convey him to this *quartier* of the city. One of the first stops was Le Moulin Rouge, where Toulouse-Lautrec had established his headquarters. It was a laboratory of human behavior, where top-hatted aristocrats mingled with stone masons and courtesans. Artists were in abundance, all with the same idea as he had, though he was skeptical that their interest was entirely professional. He would have liked to have J-P accompany him inside, but somebody had to stay with the carriage and the horses.

Toulouse-Lautrec was, in fact, present at this time and holding court at his usual table. Tony went over and paid his respects, as did others, while

M. Toulouse-Lautrec entertained his courtesans and quaffed his peculiar mixture of absinthe and cognac.

"J'ai vu votre oeuvre, Monsieur," he said, as Tony reintroduced himself. They had been briefly acquainted in the early '90's, but as Toulouse-Lautrec's fame soared, Tony assumed that he had forgotten about him. "Je suis ravi de votre succès. Asseyez-vous."

Tony sat down as the courtesans–there were five of them, drinking at Toulouse-Lautrec's expense–regarded him with interest. One of them put her arm around his neck and drew catcalls from the others. Toulouse-Lautrec ordered one of his *Tremblements de terre*, or 'Earthquake Cocktails,' for him. But Tony countermanded him and asked for a glass of red wine.

There were several of Toulouse-Lautrec's posters mounted on the walls of the establishment. Tony admired these and said so.

"Est-ce que vous en aimeriez un?" Toulouse-Lautrec said. "Take your pick."

Tony scanned the posters on the wall until his eyes settled on one of several top-hatted gentlemen at a table with three women, one of them with bright-red hair, her back to the viewer. There were other women in the background, some dancing on the stage, others conversing with gentlemen of varied dress. It seemed to portray precisely what he was seeing around him.

"Celui-là," Tony said, pointing at the poster.

"Excellent!" Toulouse-Lautrec said. He signaled the bartendress, pointed at the poster, and she went into a back room to retrieve one. When she arrived at their table with the poster rolled up with a ribbon tied around it, Tony pulled out his wallet.

"Non, non!" Toulouse-Lautrec said, pushing his hand away. "You are my American friend. C'est gratuit."

Tony protested, but Toulouse-Lautrec would have none of it. "Danse-toi avec Noémi," he said, indicating the woman who still had her arm draped around Tony's neck.

Tony looked at her more closely. She was red-haired, like the woman in the poster, and had a faint pattern of freckles that covered her nose and cheeks. Green eyes, heavily made up, and bright red lipstick applied liberally. "Pourquoi pas?" He put his arm around her waist and led her to the dance floor.

The rest of the evening was a blur. Tony returned to the table after a couple of dances with Noémi, quaffed a *Tremblement de terre* that Toulouse-Lautrec had ordered for him, and returned to the dance floor with another one of the women named, if he recalled correctly, Fanny. By this process, he danced with all three women and consumed as many cocktails.

He woke up the next morning with a horrendous headache. He wasn't sure where he was. It was a hotel, apparently. The room was small, with a single light bulb suspended from the ceiling that burned with what seemed an uncanny brilliance for such a small device. He looked over his shoulder to see a woman's head buried in a pillow, her back partially exposed, her brightly painted toenails peeking from beneath the sheet. He couldn't remember her name, but she was a brunette, so it wasn't Noémi or Fanny, who was a blonde.

The only decoration in the room was a collection of Toulouse-Lautrec's posters. At least that was some aesthetic relief. But there was no relief from this headache! It was as if someone had cleaved his skull with a meat axe.

He sat up slowly, a feat in itself. There was a window, with an oilskin shade pulled down over it that admitted a little light at the edges. He stood on rickety legs and made his way to the window and raised the shade. This was a bit of a shock, and he immediately pulled the shade down again. The woman, awakened by the sudden flood of light, turned and looked over her shoulder.

"Qu'est-ce que tu fais?" Then she closed her eyes, rolled over and went back to sleep.

Tony raised the shade again and looked out the window. The sky was a slate gray, though the sun's rays penetrated the clouds through spidery intervals. He looked down into the street and saw Mme G's carriage, with J-P sleeping on the back seat.

Despite his splitting headache, he dressed quickly, gathered his belongings, which included his wallet, his cravate, his wristwatch–what time was it? Ten a.m.–and the poster that Toulouse-Lautrec had given him. He dropped a couple of five-franc notes on the battered dresser and left without the woman–whoever she was–stirring.

He passed a tall, thin well-dressed man with a monocle on the stairs who was headed in the same direction but struggling, it seemed, with a cane. At the bottom of the stairs was a sort of lobby–he didn't remember any of this–and a sleepy-eyed desk clerk reading a copy of Le Petit Journal. When he emerged on the street the clouds seemed to have lifted and the sun prompted J-P to open his eyes and sit up.

"Monsieur Tony–est-ce que vous allez bien?"

"Pas mal, J-P. On y va!"

J-P stood, looked around as if he weren't sure where they were either, but getting his bearings, climbed into the driver's seat and snapped the reins as the horses came alive after having slept standing up.

When they arrived at Rue de Furstemberg, J-P put the carriage away, fed the horses and retired to his room. Tony made his way to the backstairs, his head still throbbing, clutching the poster under his arm. At the top of the stairs stood Mme G with her arms folded between her swelling belly and equally enlarged breasts, scowling at him like a mother whose child has violated his curfew.

"Where have you been?" she said.

"Pigalle," Tony said.

"Pigalle? You look like you slept in the gutter. What were you doing there?"

"Looking for something to paint."

"Like what? Prostitutes?"

"Possibly. Monsieur Toulouse-Lautrec has made a good living doing just that."

"Well, that may be fine for him, but–"

"He gave me one of his posters." Tony unfurled the poster and showed it to her.

Mme G examined the poster. "He does have a certain flair, doesn't he? I've been meaning to purchase one of his paintings, but not of prostitutes. There's one of the circus in Monsieur Dantec's gallery."

"Then I suggest you buy it. It will be very valuable someday. Now if you'll excuse me, Amelia, I'm very tired." He brushed past her and encountered Sabine, who was dusting some furniture in the hallway. "Bonjour, Monsieur. Puis-je vous apporter quelque chose?"

"Non, merci. J'ai besoin de dormir."

Tony continued to his room and collapsed face down on the bed.

CHAPTER 50

Despite the onset of cooler weather—or perhaps because of it—the Exposition of 1900 continued to attract visitors at a record pace.

Having recovered from his hangover, which lasted nearly forty-eight hours and prompted him to swear off any liquor stronger than wine for the rest of his life, Tony still found it difficult to concentrate while in the studio. Mme G was nearly due at this point and seemed unwilling, or unable, to venture out of the house. And she was becoming increasingly irritable and given to 'spells' during which she complained about nearly everything.

So Tony decided to find some escape by returning to the Exposition. The Palais des Illusions was particularly attractive to him, with its creation of optical illusions through mirrors and lighting effects. He was also intrigued by the Palace of Electricity with its gigantic fountain, which was illuminated at night by colored lights. But he always gravitated to the Grande Roue de Chicago because it lifted him high above the city where he could meditate on the life of the vibrant metropolis below—and his place in it.

One afternoon, upon stepping off the Ferris wheel, he came up behind a man who had ridden in the car just ahead of him. He recognized the profile and the walk. "Inspecteur! Bonjour."

Inspector Rochard stopped, turned around and greeted him. "Monsieur Jones! Comment ça va?"

"Très bien. Et vous?"

"Ça va. You are interested in the machines?"

"Machines? Well, certainly the Ferris wheel."

"Ferris?"

"The name of the man—an American—who invented the *Grande Roue*."

"Ah, oui. A marvelous invention. But I am particularly interested in the *motrices*—how do you say in English?"

"I suppose you mean locomotives," Tony said.

"Yes. And the motorcars, of course."

They walked along together for a few minutes and stepped onto the moving sidewalk.

"This is a still more useful invention," the inspector said. "Imagine if the whole city were to adopt these conveyances. There would be no need for trams or taxis."

"The expense would be prohibitive, I'm afraid."

"More expensive than the métro? I think not."

Tony laughed. "You have a point, Inspector."

As they got off the sidewalk at Les Invalides, the inspector adjusted his hat, which had nearly fallen off as they sped along, and tapped his cane on the cement sidewalk as if to assure himself that it was stationary. "I must return to work now. My superiors frown on these little excursions while on duty. But I find it clears the mind."

"Good to see you, Inspector," Tony said. "But tell me—how is the vicomte's appeal going?"

The inspector shook his head. "I'm afraid there is interference."

"Interference? What kind of interference?"

"The vicomte has powerful friends. They are endeavoring to have the sentence overturned on account of the vicomte's unstable mental condition."

"Well," Tony said, "he *is* mentally unstable."

"Yes, I agree. But the law is not clear on this point. He may be retried, or the sentence may be commuted to life imprisonment, or he may be committed to—how do you say—*une maison de fous*."

"A mental institution."

"Yes. From which he could eventually be released."

"When will we know?"

"December, perhaps. Well, Monsieur Jones, I must be off. À la prochaine!"

Tony walked across the Pont des Invalides and stopped at the new aquarium, where he watched the exotic sea life for a while, at one point locking eyes with an octopus that clung to a rock as if defending his property. He felt an odd kinship to this creature with its intelligent eyes and sense of isolation from the other sea animals, who swam above and around him as if he were as inanimate and of no more consequence than the rock he was perched on. Even the name of the creature was reminiscent of a term that was often applied to himself: *octoroon*.

The octopus seemed to win the staring contest, so Tony left the aquarium and climbed the stairs to the street. He then continued to the Place de la Concorde, where he descended underground again at the metro station. When he arrived at the Louvre, he was not really surprised to see Nat camped out on the platform with his paintings set up against the wall. But this time Marie-Louise was with him, playing a guitar and singing a song.

"What's this, Nat?" Tony said. "An art gallery with music?"

"You laugh, Tony," Nat said, "but Marie-Louise is getting their attention. They put a few sous into her cup and then linger a while to look at the paintings. I've sold three already this morning."

"I'm not laughing. It seems to be working. I have to say you're very resourceful."

All this time Marie-Louise continued singing as commuters dropped coins into the cup. She seemed not to notice Tony.

"By the way, Tony." Nat opened a cigar box, revealing wads of cash. He took a note out. "I can pay you back a little of the money I owe you. Here's fifty francs."

Tony stared at the note for a moment. "Fifty francs? Nat, you owe me a thousand."

Nat shrugged. "I'll pay you what I can. Those fifty francs represents a morning's work."

Tony sighed and put the note in his pocket. "All right. At least you're making the effort. What about the proceeds from the settlement of your father's estate?"

"The lawyers are still working on it. My brother is the executor and occasionally sends me a check, but I think he's trying to grab it all for himself."

"Well, again, I appreciate the effort, but–"

"Say, Tony–what's going to happen with this crazy vicomte that tried to kill you? I read that he's insane and they're going to send him to the nut house instead of the guillotine. If you ask me, he's faking it."

"He may well be. The trouble is the French courts don't quite know how to deal with insanity pleas. And as grisly as his crimes were, I'd just as soon not see him executed."

Nat rolled his eyes. "You always were a soft-hearted soul. And a bit naïve, it seems to me. Even if he's not faking it, he's a dangerous character. Better to make sure he can't ever do it again."

"Maybe you're right, Nat. We'll see what the judges say. Anyway, thanks for the fifty francs. I've got to be going now. Au revoir."

"À plus tard." He turned and shouted at Marie-Louise. "Chérie! Ne peux -tu chanter pas autre chose?"

When Tony returned to Rue de Furstemberg, he found J-P and Sabine in the kitchen. Sabine was just buttoning up her blouse as J-P stood by grinning.

"Monsieur?" Sabine said. "Avez-vous faim?"

"Oui, Sabine. Un jambon-fromage, s'il te plaît. Et du vin rouge."

"Tout de suite, Monsieur!"

"Où est Madame Goldman?"

"Elle est allée chez le baron."

"Chez le baron? Pourquoi?"

"Je ne sais pas, Monsieur."

As Tony climbed the stairs to his bedroom, he wondered at Mme G's frequent visits to the baron. A business deal, she said. But how many meetings does it take to consummate a business transaction? Granted, purchasing or merging one bank with another could be complicated, especially across national borders, but this deal seems to have been in the works for months.

He tossed his beret on to the dresser, took off his shoes, and lay on the bed with his hands folded behind his head. Ah, well, the child would be born soon, and then he would have to inform Mme G that Jackie was moving back to Paris and that...what? How could he keep his commitment to Jackie to leave Rue de Furstemberg to live with her and thus abandon not only Mme G, but his second child?

He closed his eyes. He would worry about it later.

CHAPTER 51

The Cour de cassation issued its ruling on the vicomte's case in early December. It affirmed the verdict of the Cour d'assise in its entirety.

The date of execution was fixed for the second Monday in January. The vicomte was immediately transferred from his home to La Santé prison in the heart of Montparnasse.

It was rumored that though the vicomte was well-connected by friends in the Ministry of Justice, his influence was trumped by the even more powerful influence of Baron de Rothstein.

Inspector Rochard, upon hearing the news, sat in his office at the préfecture de police and stared at a photograph of the président de la république, Émile Loubet. Could it be true? The président was known to be against capital punishment. Of course it was possible that he would commute the sentence, though he would do so at grave political risk. For the moment, Inspector Rochard was satisfied.

Tony, for his part, was both saddened and relieved. Saddened, because of his general opposition to capital punishment. Relieved, because this monster, the vicomte, could never kill again. But the guillotine, with its association with the excesses of the Revolution, seemed particularly barbaric. Especially since the execution was to be carried out in public. He could envision a circus atmosphere as all the worst elements of Parisian society turned out to celebrate the spectacle, which reminded him of lynchings in the South.

Mme G seemed to be in agreement with the inspector. Why shouldn't such a fiend be put to death? "After all, Tony, he tried to kill us. You, me, J-P, Sabine–any of us or all of us could have died. And these poor prostitutes–they're used like raw liver to pleasure the men who frequent them and what do they get? Beatings, scorn, ridicule, and yes–murder. Think of how many of them have had their throats cut and were left to die in cheap hotel rooms as their killers walked away as calmly as if they had just decapitated a chicken. The vicomte would never have been brought to justice had it not been for the baron's influence!"

Tony thought of his own encounter with the prostitute in Pigalle. He felt a little guilty, though he had not mistreated the girl, and his only concern had been the thought that he might have contracted a venereal disease from her. "Chopping his head off is not going to deter others like him," he said. "The prostitutes need to be diagnosed, inspected by health authorities, and protected by the police."

Mme G, her belly leading, embraced him and kissed him. "You're a sweet man, Tony. Unfortunately, though, a bit idealistic. Or maybe it's not unfortunate–an artist *should* be idealistic."

"I suppose we're like children–naïve and unworldly. Is that it?"

Mme G smiled. "Naïve–no. Unworldly...I would say 'other' worldly. And I hope you remain so."

Later that same day, Mme G began to complain of abdominal cramps. At first she thought it was simply indigestion, but then they became more severe. She instructed Tony to call the Hôtel Dieu to send a doctor. Within an hour a woman arrived carrying a black valise.

Madame Bonnemort–she never offered her given name–was about fifty years old, wore a black dress that resembled a priest's frock, and wore her graying hair pulled back in a bun. She wore little or no make-up and had a bit of a mustache that contrasted with her pale blue eyes. She was apparently well-educated because she spoke grammatically perfect English. When Tony remarked on this attribute, she said, "I was a governess in London. Of course I was a mere child at the time and had no foreknowledge of my true calling. Where is the expectant mother?"

"Upstairs," Tony said, rather cowed by this woman's air of authority. "Follow me."

When they arrived at Mme G's bedroom door, Tony knocked and they heard a muffled moaning followed by, "Entrez."

They discovered Mme G lying on her side in a fetal position with a pillow pressed into her face. After a moment, she pushed the pillow away and opened her eyes. She stared at Mme Bonnemort with a bemused expression.

"Vous êtes médecin?" she said.

"Non, je suis sage-femme."

"Ah, bon. Pour un moment, je pensais–"

"I speak English, Madame. If you are more comfortable in that language."

Mme G seemed even more bemused. "English? Why, yes. I should be happy to–Oh!" She clutched at her abdomen and again buried her face in the pillow.

Mme Bonnemort pulled up a chair and gently put her hand on Mme G's belly. "How long have you felt these contractions, Madame?"

"Oh...off and on now for about an hour. They started just before my...my friend Antonio called the hospital."

Mme Bonnemort regarded Tony with a censorious eye. "You are the father?"

"Yes," Tony said.

"Well, then, you can be of assistance. However, I think it will be some time before the child is born. You may tend to other business for the time being–if you have any."

Tony did not like the tone she was taking with him. "I am an artist."

"Indeed? Well, painting is an excellent way to occupy yourself for the next several hours."

Tony could not decide whether Mme Bonnemort was dismissing him as a feckless lover or she simply did not like the color of his skin. "I'll be in my studio if you need me." He gave Mme G a kiss on the forehead and quietly left the room.

Alone in the studio, he stared for some time out the window. Snow was beginning to fall. It occurred to him that he had never painted a snowy scene before. Of course Beaufort had rarely seen snow when he was growing up and even at Harvard, though there were often piles of snow in the Yard, at that time he was more interested in portraiture. He admired the wintry scenes of Pissarro and Monet, with their eerie mists of snow and refracted light. There was a sense of all shapes, human, animal, and inanimate, being insubstantial with no defining edges or separation, only a merging of form with the elements. Why couldn't he do something like that? After all, life was amorphous, always changing, never definitive.

He put a fresh canvas on the easel and broke out his paints. Then he went to the window and looked out again. The Rodin statue was now covered with a light dusting of snow, as were the trees. The borders of the pathways, the hedges, the brick walls enclosing the garden, were melting into one another. The darkening sky was turning gray and provided the only contrast with the whiteness of the objects in the garden.

He went back to his easel and began to paint.

After about an hour, he heard a knock on the door. "Entrez."

Still absorbed in his winter scene, he applied more white to the lower half of the canvas and black to the upper half. Then he began to mix the two.

"Monsieur?"

Tony had almost forgotten that anyone had knocked. He turned around to discover J-P standing about ten feet away with a grave expression on his face. "Oui?"

"Sabine–je pense qu'elle est entrée en travail."

"En travail? Maintenant?"

"Oui."

"Où est-elle?"

"Dans sa chambre."

Even though J-P and Sabine were now married, Sabine continued to sleep in the same bedroom in the main house that she always had in order to better serve Mme G's needs.

"Est-ce que Madame Bonnemort en sait?"

"Qui?"

It was obvious that J-P wasn't even aware that Mme Bonnemort was in the house. Tony threw down his brush and rushed out the door, followed by J-P, who was now truly alarmed. When he arrived upstairs, he knocked on Mme G's door. There was no answer. He started to move on to Sabine's room, when the door opened slightly and Mme Bonnemort stuck her long thin nose into the crack.

"What is it, Monsieur?"

"It's Sabine," Tony said.

"Who is Sabine?"

"The maid. Next door. She's going into labor."

Madame Bonnemort stepped into the hallway and closed the door behind her. "I heard someone moaning–I thought it was Madame Goldman at first, but she's asleep. Show me the way."

Tony led her down the hall. Mme Bonnemort knocked on the door. She was answered by a loud cry. Then she opened the door and rushed to Sabine's bedside, followed by Tony and J-P. She pulled the sheet back and placed her hand on Sabine's belly. "Get me some hot water. This young lady is already in advanced labor."

Tony and J-P nearly knocked each other down in an effort to get the hot water. Realizing, however, that J-P was better suited for the task, Tony returned to the bedside.

"What about Madame Goldman?" he said.

"Fortunately, her contractions have subsided and she's resting. But this woman–what is her name?"

"Sabine."

"Well, Sabine needs all of my attention now. Who is this J-P?"

"Jean-Pierre. Her husband."

"Well, at least someone in this house observes Christian principles. Are there towels in the loo?"

"I think so. I've never been in–"

"Get them. As many as you can."

A few minutes later, J-P arrived with a bucket of hot water and Tony emerged from the loo, as Mme Bonnemort called it, with a stack of clean towels. Mme Bonnemort had found a shallow porcelain bowl and filled it with the hot water. Then she banished the men from the room. "It won't be long," she said.

Tony stopped by Mme G's room, saw that she was sleeping, and closed the door. He and J-P descended the backstairs and Tony noted that there was a large pot of steaming water on the stove.

"We might as well make use of it," he said aloud in English, as much to himself as to J-P. "On fait du thé, J-P. Pour nous deux."

J-P made the tea and Tony invited him to sit down with him in the drawing room. J-P was reluctant, aware of its impropriety, but finally settled into one of the armchairs that he was normally forbidden to sit in.

As they sipped their tea, Tony noted that there was still a red mark on J-P's neck, where he had been injured by the bomb. "Ça va?"

"Pardon?"

"Ta blessure."

"Ah oui, Monsieur Tony. Ça va bien."

The two men exchanged small talk until they heard a loud cry followed by a softer one—an infant's.

They put down their teacups and rushed upstairs. Tony knocked on the door.

"Entrez, Messieurs."

They entered the room and found Sabine cradling the child in her arms and smiling down on it.

"It's a girl," Mme Bonnemort said, wiping her hands with a towel. "An easy delivery. Now, Monsieur Jones, I will attend to Madame Goldman, whose delivery may not be so easy."

Tony followed Mme Bonnemort to Mme G's room, where they found her still asleep.

CHAPTER 52

The house on Rue de Furstemberg was beginning to resemble a maternity ward.

Tony sat up most of the night listening to the cries of Sabine's child, interspersed with the moans and occasional shrieks of Mme G. When he heard the latter, he would rush to her door, only to be told to go away by Mme Bonnemort. It was nerve-wracking. He couldn't tell whether Mme G was truly in distress, or whether the contractions were simply more severe than normal. At times, he thought she must be dying.

After three or four of these episodes, he fell asleep on his bed, exhausted. It was as if he were the one having the baby. Finally, at around four a.m. there was a knock on the door. Accustomed now to sleeping lightly, he jumped up and went to the door. Upon opening it, he saw Mme Bonnemort standing there with a big smile on her face.

"It's a boy," she said.

Tony blinked. "A boy? Is he…"?

"Perfectly healthy. I must say I had my doubts, given Madame Goldman's age and the difficulty of the delivery, but the child seems as healthy as Sabine's, only considerably larger. I'd say about eight and a half pounds."

Tony brushed past her and went to Mme G's room, where he found her in virtually the same position Sabine had been hours earlier, cradling the child in her arms and smiling down at it as it suckled at her breast. He sat down at the side of the bed. "Are you all right?"

"I'm fine," Mme G said. "It was painful, but worth it. Look, isn't he beautiful?"

Tony now looked at the infant more carefully. He was quite red, with wet black hair that curled around his forehead like the spit curls in portraits of Napoleon. His eyes however, seemed sealed shut. He looked up at Mme Bonnemort.

"Why doesn't he open his eyes?"

"He will," Mme Bonnemort said. "In fact, they were wide open before you came in. I think he's had his fill for now and simply wants to rest for a moment. It's been a long and difficult journey for the little bugger."

'Little bugger,' Tony repeated to himself. Mme Bonnemort has obviously spent too much time in England. "Well," he said, turning back to Mme G, "what shall we call him?"

At this point, as if wanting to be included in the debate, the child opened his eyes and looked at Tony. Tony smiled. The child smiled back.

"Why not Antonio, III," Mme G offered.

The child looked up at his mother as the smile disappeared from his face.

"I don't think he likes that one," Tony said. "Besides, two Antonios are enough. He needs something of his own, something more distinctive."

"How about Sebastian?" Mme Bonnemort said.

Both Tony and Mme G looked at her as if to say, 'butt out, Madame.'

"Why Sebastian?" Tony said.

"Because it's a pretty name. Also the name of a saint."

Tony looked at Mme G and shrugged his shoulders.

"I was thinking of Alexandre," Mme G said. "A conqueror."

Now it was Mme Bonnemort who shrugged.

"Alexandre it is," Tony said. "Sorry, Madame Bonnemort, though I agree that Sebastian is a pretty name, too."

"Yes," Mme Bonnemort said with a frown, "they both are. But Alexandre was a heathen. And slaughtered who knows how many people. St. Sebastian was known for saving lives, not taking them."

Tony looked at Mme G. "She's got a point, Amelia."

Mme G sighed, but with a smile said, "Why not call him 'Sebastian Alexandre,' and let him decide which he prefers when he's old enough?"

Tony laughed. "Spoken like a true diplomat. Madame Bonnemort?"

"A just compromise," Mme Bonnemort said. "After all, it's his name, and certainly distinctive. I doubt there are many boys in France with both names."

After Mme Bonnemort packed up her equipment and Tony paid her for her services, she left and he went down to the cellar to pick out a bottle of champagne to celebrate. But as he was choosing a bottle, it occurred to him that the child, though red with the afterbirth, was rather fair-skinned. How was it that he, Antonio Jones II, widely considered a mulatto, could father not one, but two, children who appeared to be white?

He shrugged this off as being one of the mysteries of life and picked out a bottle of Veuve Clicquot Ponsardin, Vintage 1893. He knew nothing about Champagne but was attracted by the yellow label. Mme G certainly knew what she was buying.

Passing through the kitchen, he found J-P and Eugénie discussing the new additions to the family and invited them both upstairs to celebrate.

During the course of the festivities, it was decided that Sabine's child would be named Amélie, after her employer, who, she said, was like a second mother to her.

After the celebration, Tony returned to the studio, but found that in his present, slightly inebriated state that he could get nothing done. He simply stared at the painting for a while, then went to the window where the night sky was studded with bright stars and the garden was covered with a white mantle. The snow had stopped and the scene was quite different than it had been a few hours earlier. This change provided thoughts of the ephemeral nature of life, but the transcendence of beauty as well.

He realized that he had been up for the better part of 24 hours. He was tired, but not exhausted now, and felt a sort of tranquil melancholy. Best to get some sleep.

Thus, he returned to his bedroom and slowly undressed, replaying the events of the day in his head. What now? He had two children to support, though Mme G was more than capable of supporting Sebastian Alexandre without his help. In fact, she was supporting *him*, which enabled him to save most of the money he had earned from his commissions. All well and good, but what about Jackie and Trey? They would be arriving soon and he would have to tell Mme G that he was moving out. A delicate task, to say the least.

After removing his shoes and socks, he put his trousers away and noticed an envelope on the dresser. It must have been put there by J-P sometime that afternoon, and in the excitement over the dual births, forgot to tell him about it.

From Jackie?

He picked the envelope up and noted the return address—42 rue de La Santé. No name. He slit open the envelope and extracted a single plain sheet of paper. It read:

Monsieur Jones:

> *I am writing to you in English to ensure that there is no misunderstanding. The explosive device that injured one of your servants was not sent by me, but one of my own servants who sought to incriminate me out of spite.*

> *Furthermore, I have been unjustly condemned to death for the murder of two prostitutes with whom I was never acquainted. It was all a conspiracy against me on the part of three judges, two of whom are Jews. They, of course, like Monsieur Dreyfus, take their orders from the baron, who detests me because of the purity of my Aryan ancestry.*

> *I have nothing against the members of your race. Though I consider you an exception—it is clear that you are quite talented—your African cousins*

*are backwards and incapable of such conspiracies as the baron directs
on a world-wide scale.*

*To prove that I have no hard feelings towards you, I propose that you visit
me at La Santé, at a time of your choosing. In fact, I would like to have you
paint my portrait as a gift and legacy to my nephew and his descendants.
As you know, I have no children of my own, though that is no fault of mine,
but of my wife's, who prefers the company of low-born men.*

I await your reply,

*Jean-Louis Raynouard
Vicomte de Haut-Koenigsbourg*

Tony didn't know whether to throw the letter into the trash or forward it
to the Cour de cassation as additional evidence of the vicomte's unstable
mental condition. But he was too tired to think about it. He put the letter
aside and fell back onto the bed. He was asleep in seconds.

CHAPTER 53

The snow was already melting when Tony rose the next morning and looked out his window onto the square in front of the house. It was a bright, sunny day and unseasonably warm.

Well rested, he dressed quickly and looked in on Mme G and the baby. Both were still asleep. J-P had risen even earlier and was preparing breakfast, while Eugénie and his mother camped out at the bedsides of Mme G and Sabine. As everything seemed to be under control, Tony descended to the dining room, ate his breakfast, and went into the studio. He stood at the window for a few minutes, studying the effect of the sunlight on the snow, and the emergence of the shrubs and trees from the white mantle that had covered them completely the night before. Then he began to paint.

He was finished by noon. Standing back from the canvas, he liked what he saw. At first he was tempted to alter some objects in the garden, like the Rodin statue–did this work of another artist upstage his own work?–but decided that it was a part of the inspiration, and besides, what could be more natural than statuary in a garden?

After lunch, he wrapped the painting in a heavy cloth, tucked it under his arm, and headed for M. Dantec's gallery. He had not offered M. Dantec a new painting for some time, as he had mostly been working on commissioned portraits. M. Dantec would no doubt be delighted to have something new to offer to his customers.

On the way back from the gallery, he stopped at the préfecture de police and called on Inspector Rochard. He showed the vicomte's letter to him and asked what he should do about it.

"I am not sure, Monsieur Jones," the inspector said as he handed the letter back to him. He rose from his desk and looked out over the Seine. "The sentence has been appealed and the lower court's decision affirmed. It seems to me to serve no purpose to submit additional evidence."

"I'm of the same mind," Tony said. "It doesn't really change anything. The vicomte still insists on his innocence, as he did throughout the trial. And the judges rejected the notion that he is insane and therefore not responsible for his actions."

"Exactly."

"But what about this request that I come to La Santé and paint his portrait? Is that wise?"

Inspector Rochard remained at the window, his hands clasped behind his back, still looking out. "Portrait? Oh, yes. A strange request. A strange request indeed for a man in his position." He turned around. "But then he is a strange man. Are you asking me if I think it's safe?"

"Yes—I suppose so."

The inspector shrugged his shoulders. "I don't think there's any danger to your *personne*. But the—how do you say in English—the *dispositions*—"

"Arrangements."

"Oui. 'Arrangements.' The authorities there may not be keen on the idea. But why do you wish to expose yourself thus? Do you need the money?"

"No. I don't need the money. I'm just curious, I guess."

The inspector smiled. "How do you Americans say? 'Curiosity killed the cat.'"

Tony laughed. "Yes, an old saying. But I suppose it's true. In some cases, at least."

"Well, Monsieur Jones—I will contact the director of the prison. He is an old friend of mine. Perhaps he can find a secure room for your interview. But will you need to pay more than one visit?"

"No, I don't think so. I won't be taking an easel and paints. I'll simply sketch his portrait while we talk. I can do the painting at home."

"When will you want to see the vicomte?"

"Oh, say, Saturday."

"There is an execution scheduled for Saturday. Many spectators. How about Monday?"

"That would be better."

The inspector picked up the phone and asked for La Santé.

When Tony returned to Rue de Furstemberg, he was surprised to see Sabine up and about, performing her duties as if nothing out of the ordinary had happened. "Ça va, Sabine?"

"Oui, Monsieur," she said, her maid's uniform a little tight around her belly. "Ça va. Amélie dort bien. Est-ce que vous voudriez du thé?"

"Oui, merci."

Tony then went into the dining room where he was even more surprised to see a large fruit basket with a soccer ball prominently displayed in the middle.

"Qu'est-ce que c'est?"

"Un cadeau de Monsieur le Baron," Sabine said, who had followed him into the room.

"De Monsieur le Baron? Il était ici?"

"Non, Monsieur. Il a envoyé un domestique."

Tony picked up the card that was attached to the basket. It read:

> *Félicitations! Un garçon. C'est formidable!*
> *Votre ami dévoué,*
> *Alphonse*

He put the card down and picked up the soccer ball. Though he knew of the game that the French called 'football,' he had never seen a game, or handled one of the balls they used. Rather heavy, round, with several patches of leather sewn onto a rubber bladder. He chuckled. It would be some time before Sebastian Alexandre could even lift the ball, much less kick it.

"Et madame–est-elle au courant?"

"Non, monsieur."

Tony decided to have Sabine take his tea upstairs while he visited Mme G. He found her sitting in a rocking chair nursing the baby in her arms, gazing out the window.

"Are you all right?" he said, upon entering.

"Of course I'm all right," she said. "And Alexandre is growing fatter by the minute!"

Tony sat down on the bed. "Don't you think it's a little soon for Sabine to be returning to her duties?"

"I didn't ask her to do anything. She volunteered. And I suspect she's a little bored."

"Who's watching Amélie?"

"J-P's mother. She's been very helpful."

Tony stared at the child for several moments. "I think he looks like you."

Mme G looked down at the child and smiled. "He has my eyes. But that could change."

"The baron has sent you–and Sebastian–a gift."

"Oh?"

"Yes. A fruit basket as big as a washtub. And a football for Sebastian."

She laughed. "A football? Men–must you all think that boys will want to kick a silly ball around instead of say, painting a picture?"

Now Tony laughed. "I think the ball will have more appeal to him–at least in the beginning. Maybe he'll pick up a paint brush when he's older."

"I certainly hope so. I don't intend to raise a little savage."

About this time, Sabine arrived with a tea tray.

"Pose-toi le plateau sur la table, Sabine. Ça va?"

"Oui, Madame. Juste un peu fatiguée."

"Donc, vas te reposer et occupe-toi de votre bébé."

"Oui, Madame. Merci beaucoup."

By this time little Sebastian Alexandre seemed to have had his fill and dozed off to sleep. Mme G buttoned up her dress and sipped her tea.

"Are you painting?" she said.

"I have been, actually. I just dropped off a new landscape at Monsieur Dantec's gallery."

"Any new commissions?"

'Well, there may be one."

"And who is that? You know, the baron might want you to—"

"The vicomte."

Mme G's eyes widened and she put her cup back into its saucer. "The vicomte? You can't be serious."

"I am serious. I received a letter from him yesterday. It seems he wants a portrait of himself to hand down to his heirs."

"What heirs? He has no children."

"He has a nephew."

"Tony—you can't accept it. It's blood money."

"I'm not interested in the money, really. Besides, his money is inherited. I was thinking of donating my fee to a relief organization."

"What kind of relief organization?"

"I don't know, exactly. Perhaps one that helps prostitutes."

"A fine thought. But prostitution is regulated by the police—you might as well give it to them."

"Then a health clinic, perhaps."

Mme G sighed. "They're already inspected twice a week—at least the ones who are registered are. But Tony, how are you going to get the vicomte to sit for you? Will the prison authorities allow it?"

"I've already arranged for that through Inspector Rochard. It's set for Monday morning."

Mme G picked up her teacup again and took a sip. "Is it dangerous?"

"I don't think so. There'll be guards standing by and he'll be searched coming and going."

"Strange," Mme G said, now staring out the window.

"What is?"

"That the vicomte would choose one of his intended victims to paint his portrait. They're thousands of artists in Paris. Why not one of them?"

Tony shrugged his shoulders. "I've wondered the same thing. It makes me curious."

"Well, you know what they say—curiosity killed the—"

"Cat. Yes, I know. That's what the inspector said."

"Maybe you should take the pistol."

"The prison authorities wouldn't allow it." Tony leaned over and gave her a kiss. "Don't worry, Amelia—I'll be safer at La Santé than I am walking the streets of Paris. Will you be coming downstairs for dinner?"

"Why not? I'll show Alexandre his new world." She looked down at the child and smiled. "A new world for all of us."

CHAPTER 54

On Monday morning, Tony had breakfast with Mme G and set off for La Santé. Armed only with a sketchbook, he walked to Boulevard St-Germain and caught an omnibus at Boulevard St-Michel. La Santé was only a kilometer or so south of the Luxembourg Gardens.

It was a massive, forbidding sort of building, with high walls composed of crushed rock and masonry. The only windows visible from the street were tall, narrow casements framed in limestone, resembling the kind of portals that one associates with fortified castles, just wide enough to shoot arrows through. But the truly grisly feature of La Santé lay outside the prison, at the corner of Boulevard Arago and Rue de la Santé–the guillotine.

It was a peculiarly sinister looking piece of machinery. A vertical frame with a heavily weighted oblique blade that now, while not in service, rested within a yoke to immobilize the victim. Dried blood stained the fine-grained wood. It seemed like a barbaric device left over from medieval times, yet it was relatively new, having been invented just before the Revolution. Viewed objectively, it was probably more humane than say, hanging, which, along with the firing squad was still used extensively in the United States. A lynching, by comparison, could inflict great pain on the victim as it was often a matter of slow strangulation.

However, there was something extremely unsettling about the thought of losing one's head.

Tony walked around the corner and along Rue de la Santé to the front entrance. Unlike other monumental buildings in Paris, there was a rather nondescript door without ornamentation or entablatures of any kind. But craning his neck, he could make out the words high above the door, just under the eaves: *Liberté, Égalité, Fraternité*. It seemed a cruel joke on those who dwelled within its walls.

There was no guard or policeman outside the door. There was, however, a button with a small plaque over it that said, 'Appuyez Pour Service.' He pressed the button and waited.

After two or three minutes, an eye in a peephole appeared.

"Vos affaires, Monsieur?"

"J'ai un rendez-vous," Tony said.

"Votre nom?"

"Antonio Jones."

After another minute or two, the door slowly opened to reveal the man behind the eye. He was a stout chap, perhaps in his sixties, with white hair stuffed into a *képi*, and sideburns that joined with his moustache above a clean-shaven chin. Tony guessed that he was a veteran of the Franco-Prussian War of 1871.

"Par ici," he said.

Tony followed his instructions as the man closed the heavy door behind him. He found himself in a courtyard facing a building that seemed to be the spoke of a wheel, with other buildings radiating from it. These other buildings were three or more stories, with the same sort of narrow windows as those in the external wall, only smaller. He approached this main building and discovered another button with an even briefer message than the one on the street: 'Appuyez.'

He pressed the button and the door immediately opened. Another guard appeared, this one a younger man without a cap, and clean-shaven except for a thin mustache. He said nothing, but indicated a desk with a bald official sitting behind it. There was an open ledger before him.

"Signez ici," the bald man said.

Tony signed his name and put the time of arrival next to his signature.

"Videz vos poches, s'il vous plaît."

Tony emptied his pockets, which included his sketchbook. "J'ai besoin de mon carnet à dessins."

"Tenez. Bloc 'A.'"

Tony took back his sketchbook and followed another guard to a door marked 'A.' The guard led him down a hallway past several doors, then opened one with his keys. After they entered the room, he locked the door behind him.

The room was rectangular, about ten meters long and half as wide. The guard indicated one of the chairs opposite the middle of a long table divided by partitions that rose to just below eye level. Tony sat down and waited.

After a minute or two, a door on the other side of the room opened and the vicomte appeared. He was wearing dungarees surmounted by a smock, the kind that laborers wear when doing particularly messy work. His hands were manacled, not with chains, but with a single iron rod welded to the clamps around his wrists. His ankles, on the other hand, were chained together so that he could walk.

He stared at Tony with a piercing gaze but said nothing. The guard that had ushered him into the room roughly pushed him down into the chair on his side of the table. Then he returned to the door with his back to it.

The vicomte's hair and beard, which had always been meticulously trimmed, was now longer and unkempt. He sat with his manacled hands on the table, still staring at Tony.

"You have come," he said.

"Yes."

"You accept the commission?"

"On one condition."

"And what is that?"

"That you donate my fee to the *Croix-Rouge*."

"And your fee is..."

"Ten thousand francs."

The vicomte's eyebrows arched. "Ten thousand? Monsieur Jones—I could obtain the services of Monsieur Monet himself for ten thousand francs."

"That is my fee."

The vicomte looked around the room as if looking for a means of escape. "D'accord. When do we begin?"

"Now." Tony extracted his sketchbook from his jacket along with a pencil. "Where are your paintings? Your easel?"

"No need for that here. Besides, the prison authorities wouldn't allow it. I will do the painting at home."

"Will you need to come back?"

"Possibly. But I think one interview should suffice."

The vicomte looked around again, this time at the guards. "These men are pigs...the scum of Paris. I think that one—" he indicated the guard at the door— "is a Jew. The one behind me is Aryan, but an imbecile. Can't we dismiss them?"

"I don't think so."

The vicomte sighed, apparently resigned to these indignities, at least for the time being. "They won't allow me a razor. Nor scissors. The barber comes only once every two weeks and cuts hair like a field laborer threshing grain."

"I can adjust for that." Tony started sketching. "But tell me, Monsieur le Vicomte—why did you choose me to paint your portrait? As you say, Monsieur Monet might charge the same fee—and he is an Aryan like yourself."

"Because I wish to show Monsieur Loubet that I am not prejudiced."

"Ah, but the sentence is final. Monsieur Loubet cannot—"

"My lawyers have already submitted an application to him for a pardon."

"A pardon? On what grounds?"

"That I am innocent."

"Oh. I see."

Tony continued to sketch the vicomte's face. He was a thin man with somewhat delicate, boyish features. If the beard were removed, he would look ten years younger. A straight, narrow nose, large blue eyes, and a weak chin. His beard, once a Van Dyke, was now a bushy woodsman's. His hair, which must have been blond in his youth, was reddish brown.

"You will dress me?" he said suddenly.

"What?"

"Dress me. That is, in the portrait."

"Oh. Yes, I can do that."

"And don't forget the medal. I am a Chevalier de la Légion d'honneur."

"Ah, yes. The medal. I remember you wearing it around your neck at the baron's soirée last year."

"Of course I regret having ever attended the soirée. The baron is the worst kind of Jew."

"The worst? In what way?"

"He sucks the blood from gentile women. Like a vampire."

"And how does he do that?"

The vicomte found this question amusing. "You are young and naïve. How would you know? The Jews appoint a leader every year, 'le Grand Loup,' to seduce as many gentiles as possible. In this way, he contaminates their vaginal fluids, which in turn produces imbecile children."

Tony found himself sketching dark, sinister-looking eyebrows, turned up at the ends. "How do you know this?"

"It is quite obvious. One only has to look at the many *bâtards* sired by the baron. They are all drooling idiots."

Tony suppressed a chuckle. "And where may they be found?"

"In the baron's châteaux. Many are his servants. And I hear another is on the way. Madame Goldman, who is a gentile despite her name, is pregnant."

Tony stopped sketching and looked up. "Madame Goldman?"

"Yes. It is common knowledge. I know that you live with her, but as a servant. Whatever the relationship is between you, it is well-known that she visits the baron with regularity, on the pretense that she has business with him."

Tony continued sketching, shading in the brows and the beard. He didn't know what to think about the vicomte's assertion that the child–Sebastian Alexandre–was in fact the baron's. It was entirely possible. He had often wondered why Mme G visited the baron so often without any results in regard to their bank merger. As a former banker himself, he knew that such negotiations took time, but not that much time. It had been going on for over a year.

Tony put down his pencil. "That will do for today."

"May I see?" the vicomte said.

Tony flipped the cover of the sketchbook over. "I'd rather you not see it at this preliminary stage. I'm a bit superstitious about that. You will see the final oil version and if you're not satisfied, I will make changes."

"Fair enough," the vicomte said. "You won't forget the medal?"

"I wouldn't think of it." Tony stood and indicated to the guards that he was ready to leave.

Once out on the street, he brooded over the vicomte's claim that the baron had fathered Sebastian Alexandre. Of course the vicomte was insane–or perhaps incredibly clever at feigning insanity. But could it be that in this one instance he was telling the truth?

As he sat on the omnibus on the way home, he considered the best way to find out. A direct question to Mme G would be extremely insulting. Besides, she would probably deny it whether it was true or not. So what was the alternative? Stealth...he could rummage through her correspondence when she was out of her room, or perhaps grill J-P about what he knew of their meetings since he often drove her to the baron's house.

But he didn't like this kind of sneaking around, as it often led to lies and mistrust. And what if she caught him reading her mail?

As he ascended the stairs at Rue de Furstemberg, he laughed out loud to himself. Here he was playing the role of the jealous husband. Again. But Mme G was not his wife, Jackie was. So what if the baron had fathered the child? It would actually give him the excuse he'd been looking for to break off the relationship before Jackie arrives. And yet, the child…

Upon entering the drawing room, he found Mme G rocking Sebastian Alexandre in her arms and singing to him in French. She looked up. "What were you laughing about on the stairs?"

"The vicomte. He's quite a comedian."

CHAPTER 55

Christmas was fast approaching and it was snowing nearly every day.

Tony sat in his studio–or rather Mme G's studio–and alternately stared at a half-finished portrait of the vicomte and the falling snow in the garden.

He longed for Jackie more than ever. She said that she would be coming with Trey in January. So how would he be spending Christmas? With Mme G, apparently, and Sebastian Alexandre. Should he wait till after Christmas to confront her with the vicomte's accusation?

He turned his attention once again to the portrait. Perhaps the vicomte was just trying to get under his skin. A Machiavellian character, insane or not.

If he were honest, Tony surmised, he would paint the vicomte in the dark, venomous colors that he deserved. But it was a commission. If the vicomte rejected the portrait, *La Croix-Rouge* would lose a sizable donation. He continued to paint.

After an hour or so, as he was nearing completion Mme G walked into the studio.

"My goodness," she said. "That is truly frightening. Do you think he will actually pay you for that?"

"You don't think it's a good likeness?"

Mme G sat down on the divan and continued to stare at the painting. "Likeness? I don't know. It's a bit abstract, almost a caricature."

Tony put his brush down and wiped his hands with a cloth. "After all, he is a murderer. I've tried to capture the evil demon inside of him rather than the outward appearance."

"Well, you've certainly done that."

Tony stood back from the easel and tried to assess his work. "Perhaps I've gone too far. What do you think?"

Mme G remained silent for several moments as she continued to stare at the portrait. "I wouldn't say that you've gone too far. It's probably the essence of the man. Still, it's frightening to look at."

He turned to her. "We had a long conversation as I was sketching him."

"That must have been interesting."

"It was. Even alarming in many ways. He said something about you."

"Me? What did he say about me?"

Tony steeled himself for what might come next. "He said that it was 'common knowledge,' as he put it, that your meetings with the baron were about more than just business."

"Did he? How would he know what our meetings were like?"

"Servants," he said. "Gossip."

"Well, then, that's all it is–gossip."

Tony came and sat down on the divan beside her. "I will not take the word of a madman over yours, Amelia. And if it weren't for Sebastian Alexandre, I would say it's none of my business. You've never claimed that our relationship was exclusive. But I have to know–is Sebastian my child or the baron's?"

Mme G stared at him for a moment, then looked away at the falling snow outside. "I don't know."

Tony put his hands on his thighs, stood, and began pacing in front of the divan. "Then what are we to do?"

"Do? Well, nothing. That is, if you are so wounded by my discreet encounters with the baron, then you can simply abandon the child–and me–and I will raise little Alex myself. I don't need your help."

"No, you don't. But what about the baron? Is he prepared to acknowledge the child as his?"

"I doubt it." She laughed, as if at a private joke. "His wife would divorce him. Or failing that, would go abroad, perhaps."

Tony considered this and scratched beneath his chin, which had a bit of stubble on it that he had missed shaving that morning. "The child has none of my characteristics, you know."

"I wouldn't say that. His hair is curly like yours. And his eyes are brown, like yours. The baron's eyes are blue."

"But his skin is white."

"So is Trey's, as I understand it."

Tony was getting frustrated, even angry. Not with Mme G, but himself. He slapped at the canvas and knocked it to the floor.

Mme G remained on the divan with her hands folded in her lap.

Tony stared out the window for a moment and then picked the canvas up and replaced it on the easel. "Jackie's coming soon. After Christmas."

"And when she does, what do you intend to do?"

"I don't know. Obviously, I will have to move out."

"I'll be sorry to see you go. Our relationship has been a good one."

He turned and glared at her. "Has it? Your sneaking about and–"

"I've never 'sneaked about.' I made it clear that I had a relationship with the baron and never said otherwise. Have I ever reproached you for your relationship with Jacqueline?"

"No, not with Jackie. But I seem to recall a few instances when you flew into a rage when I even looked at another woman."

"That was in the early days of our relationship. I was just getting to know the baron. He taught me something about *les affaires de cœur*."

Tony thought about this. "You and the baron live on a different plane than Jackie and I. Almost a different planet. I guess it's something the very rich have in common–a different sort of morality."

She smiled that enigmatic smile of hers. "Not so different, really. You were content to have two women for a time, and now you reproach me for having two men. Aren't you being a bit hypocritical?"

Tony, now calmer, sat down again next to her. "I suppose I am. It's hard for me to see things the way you do. Jackie and I, though we were brought up in vastly different circumstances, nevertheless share the same sense of values."

Mme G suppressed a laugh. "Excuse me, but there you go again talking about 'values,' or 'morality,' as you would have it. As far as I'm concerned, the only 'values' are honesty and kindness."

Tony sighed with a certain resignation. "You are an extraordinary woman, Amelia. But we still haven't solved the problem. What are we to do about Sebastian Alexandre?"

"Love him. Care for him. I think Jackie will understand, eventually. And you can come and visit him any time you wish."

"I'll have to tell her, of course."

"Of course."

Tony rose from the divan and went back to the easel. "The man *is* evil, you know."

CHAPTER 56

Tony took the finished painting to La Santé with some trepidation. As Mme G said, it was frightening to look at. But he felt that it was an honest portrait.

When he was ushered into the interview room, the vicomte was sitting at the table waiting for him. He smiled, expectantly, as if looking forward to seeing an old friend. He had also had a haircut, and his beard was once again neatly trimmed.

Tony placed the painting on the table and sat down. It was covered with wrapping paper and secured by twine.

The vicomte couldn't take his eyes off it. "It is finished?"

"Yes. Though you may want some alterations. It's up to you."

"Eh bien! Let's see it!"

Tony stood and removed the wrapping paper. The guards came a little closer and craned their necks to see.

The vicomte's smile evaporated, replaced by a frown. "What is this? A joke?"

"I try to paint what I see," Tony said.

"And what do you see when you look at me?"

"'I see a deeply conflicted man, an angry man. A dangerous man, both to himself and to others."

The vicomte stared at Tony with the same fierce hatred that appeared on the face of the figure in the painting. Then, after a moment, he looked at the painting again. "You think I am insane?"

"I don't know. Again, I only paint what I see."

If his hands had been free, the vicomte would have stroked his beard. He continued to stare at the painting. "Dangerous, you say?"

"That's what I see."

"The medal—you forgot the medal."

"Non, Monsieur. C'est là."

The vicomte leaned forward and squinted at the portrait. "Ah, oui. I see it. But can you make it a little larger? And the ribbon—it should be red, not blue."

"Red? My mistake. I can easily change that."

"Bon."

"Is that all you want? No other alterations?"

"No. It will do. Except for the ribbon."

"Then I will return tomorrow for your final approval."

"Yes. Tomorrow." He rose from the table and nodded to the guard standing behind him as if nodding to a servant to carry out his command.

The interview was over.

Tony was left alone in the room except for the other guard standing at the opposite door. He was a bit dazed at the vicomte's reaction to the portrait. He had fully expected him to angrily reject it–which he did at first–or at least demand major alterations, which Tony was prepared to reject himself. It would be no loss to him if the commission were canceled.

He wrapped the canvas up again and secured the twine around it. The guard escorted him out the door and into the reception area. Along the way he said, "Il est fou furieux!" Or in plain English, "He's as mad as a hatter!"

Tony returned to Rue de Furstemberg and made the change in about five minutes. Mme G again entered the studio to find out how the interview went.

"That's all?" she said.

"That's all he requested. The color of the ribbon has to be right."

"Extraordinary. Now what?"

"Tomorrow I'll take it back to him for his final approval and then deliver it to his house in Neuilly-sur-Seine, where his secretary will give me a cheque."

Mme G shook her head. "I think he's using you somehow."

"I know he is. He thinks that by employing me that he will show President Loubet that he is not prejudiced against blacks, and therefore he will pardon him."

"Do you think that will work?"

"No. But Monsieur Loubet is against capital punishment. He may commute his sentence or possibly recommend that he be transferred to an asylum."

"That's where he belongs."

"I agree. But then there's the chance that he could escape or use his influence to be released altogether."

Mme G sat down on the divan as Tony covered the portrait.

"There's a telegram for you," she said. "I put it on your dresser."

"Telegram? From whom?"

"I don't know. There's no return address on the envelope."

"Perhaps another commission." He sat down next to her.

"Perhaps. Tony—"

"Yes?"

"The baron has invited us to his Christmas party."

"Has he?"

"Yes. Do you want to go?"

Tony considered this. "My first instinct is to say no. But I'm not inclined to challenge the baron to a duel. And I think he regards me as a domestic servant with a paint brush."

Mme G laughed and put her hand on his knee. "He doesn't regard you as a domestic servant. In fact, he thinks very highly of you."

"Well, he has invited me, hasn't he? I suppose it would be rude to decline."

"Yes, it would. You'll see—we'll all have a fine time."

"And Sebastian?"

"Alexandre. Tony, we must settle on a single name. It's too confusing."

"All right. How about 'S.A.'"

"Ugh That's not a name."

"Well, there's J-P."

"That somehow has a ring to it."

"Okay. How about Alex?"

Mme G brightened. "Alex. All right. That's what I've been calling him, anyway."

"That's settled. Now the next question: is Alex invited, too?"

"He's a bit young. Though the baron would like to—" She stopped herself.

"See his son?"

"We must humor him."

"You know, don't you, Amelia?"

Mme G kept her poker face. "What does it matter? Neither of you will be here for Alex's daily upbringing. He'll think of you as kindly uncles who occasionally come around with candy and footballs."

Tony put his arm around her and kissed her on the cheek. "We'll do more than that. I intend to teach him how to play *American* football."

She laughed. "And the baron?"

"He'll teach him how to make money."

"I'd rather you teach him how to paint and the baron how to be a gentleman." She put her head on his shoulder.

"A gentleman? Am I not a gentleman?"

"You are a 'gentle man,' not a gentleman."

Tony sighed as he stroked her hair. "Just my luck."

Later, Tony went up to his room and picked up the telegram on his dresser.

London S.W. 1   *9:12   3 12 1900*

Antonio Jones
6 Rue de Furstemberg
Paris

Arriving Paris 8-1-01 with Trey STOP Xmas with Lucinda STOP Secure apartment STOP Merry Christmas

Jackie

Rather business-like, he thought. 'Secure apartment.' No terms of endearment. Well, at least there would be no clash of the two families. Was that what it had come to? Two separate families?

He folded up the telegram and replaced it in the envelope, then stared out the window into the square below. A single soul sat on a park bench, covered with snow. Like a statue. It was impossible to tell whether it was a man or a woman. A vagabond? Whoever it was could freeze to death. Or perhaps they already had.

Just as he was about to rush downstairs to be of assistance, the figure stood and shook off the mantle of snow. It was a woman. A man in an overcoat with a fur collar arrived and they embraced, oblivious to the cold.

She was hardly a vagabond. He could see now that she was well-dressed, as he was. What was the story? Husband and wife? No, not husband and wife. Only lovers would have a tryst in a secluded park in a snowstorm.

He watched as they walked away, arm in arm.

Could love be so simple?

CHAPTER 57

The vicomte approved the final version of the portrait and gave Tony a note instructing his secretary to issue him a cheque, which he had the power to sign in the name of his employer.

He took the painting under his arm and caught the metro to Porte Maillot, where he followed the vicomte's directions to his house.

As he stood before the mansion, a château nearly as impressive as the baron's, he hesitated before knocking on the door. Would the vicomtesse be there? And if so, what was she to think of the portrait? Mme G had said that she was estranged from her husband and she even helped to provide the evidence that incriminated him. Tony had only met her once, at the baron's country estate the previous year, and had hardly spoken to her. And now that her husband was a convicted murderer, what was she to do? Well, he would find out.

He approached the massive oak door and, as there was no buzzer, used the heavy iron knocker, which was in the shape of a lion's head. After a few moments, the door opened and a liveried servant admitted him. He was instructed to wait in the vestibule.

Tony gazed around this room, which was nearly the size of the entry to the Petit Palais on the Champs-Élysées. There were frescoes on the ceiling that would have made Michelangelo proud. And who knows? Maybe Michelangelo himself—or one of his pupils—did the painting. The vicomte said that the château was over three hundred years old and had been in his family for six generations.

A man in a striped business suit appeared and without introducing himself, instructed him to follow him down a long corridor filled with portraits of distinguished-looking men and women. Gainsborough came to mind. Or perhaps Reynolds.

At the end of the corridor, the man, presumably the vicomte's secretary, knocked on a tall mahogany door.

A woman's voice barely penetrated this thick door.

"Entrez."

The secretary opened the door and stood aside to allow Tony to go first.

Then he followed.

Standing in the middle of the room, which appeared to be a library, though the books seemed to take second place to statuary and other objets d'art, was the vicomtesse. She was dressed in a silk robe de chambre, as if she were still attending to her toilette, though it was eleven o'clock in the morning. Thin, rather tall, with black hair streaked through with premature gray, she was the very model of an aristocrat.

She extended her hand. "Enchantée, Monsieur Jones. It has been some time since we last met."

"Yes," Tony said, somewhat surprised that she spoke English much like Mme Bonnemort, only with more precise elocution. "I remember our meeting at the baron's soirée last year. Unfortunately, we had little opportunity to talk."

"That was because my husband was busy insulting you. I apologize for that. Won't you sit down?"

Tony said he would, but wasn't sure what to do with the painting.

"Bertrand," the vicomtesse said. "Prenez le tableau et entreposez-le."

"Oui, Madame."

After Bertrand took the painting, which was again covered with wrapping paper, Tony said: "Don't you want to see it?"

"Not really," the vicomtesse said. "I assume that it's another tribute to my husband's vanity."

"It's hardly flattering," Tony said.

"Then I commend you for your artistic integrity. But do sit down, Mister Jones. Madame Goldman tells me that you have a most interesting history. I would like to hear it."

Tony was a bit tired of being asked about his 'history.' But he did the best he could, recounting his early life in South Carolina, growing up on an isolated island that was predominately black, being regarded as black himself in spite of having two white parents who he assumed had adopted him until he found out the truth as a young man.

"But how could that be," the vicomtesse said, "if both of your parents were white?"

"Well, actually my father only passed for white–his mother, who also passed for white, was a former slave."

"How very interesting. And so they sent you off to Harvard?"

"That they did. But Madame la Vicomtesse, I am curious about your own history. How did you come to marry the vicomte?"

The vicomtesse sighed and gazed out the window. "That is a story not so interesting as yours. My parents and the vicomte's parents were friends. The vicomte–very young at the time and always in debt, even then–asked for my hand in marriage because my father was a successful manufacturer.

But he had no title. And he was ambitious in that way. So the marriage was arranged."

"You had no say in the matter?"

"I suppose I might have. But I was only sixteen and idolized my father. I wanted to please him."

"And the vicomte–how did you feel about him?"

"Well, he was quite handsome in those days. I hardly gave a second thought to his character, though there were always rumors."

"What kind of rumors?"

"Wild parties, gambling debts, debaucheries. I thought–and my father thought–that it was just a passing phase. 'Sowing his oats,' as the English say. But of course it never stopped."

"And now this."

The vicomtesse closed her eyes for a moment as if to blot out the past, then opened them again. "Yes–and now this."

"What will you do now?"

"Go abroad, I suppose. I went to an English boarding school when I was a girl. I detested it, but I still have friends there." After staring dreamily into the distance for a moment, she said: "I will miss Paris."

"Must you leave?"

She turned to him. "You have no idea how intolerable life has become for me here. Daily threats–from the political left as well as the right. There are those who believe that I am just as depraved as my husband and even encouraged him. No, life for me now in Paris is impossible."

Tony felt almost ashamed of his role in this sordid affair, though he had done nothing wrong. He felt an urge to tell the vicomtesse that he was not benefitting in any way from the commission, but he didn't want to suggest that he was making excuses.

The vicomtesse stood up. "This has been a most pleasant interview, Mister Jones. I am only sorry that it had to concern a most unpleasant subject. Please give my love to Madame Goldman. She has been my only friend in this affair. And tell her I will keep in touch." She extended her hand and Tony kissed it.

"I will do that, Madame la Vicomtesse."

"Stop next door and Bertrand will give you your cheque."

"Thank you, Madame. Au revoir."

"Au revoir, Monsieur."

When Tony stopped at the secretary's office he was asked to whom to make out the cheque.

"La Croix-Rouge," Tony said.

CHAPTER 58

Christmas was a bitter-sweet affair for Jackie, who wondered the whole time what Tony was doing. He had sent a parcel containing gifts for both herself and Trey: a robe de chambre for her, and a hand-painted spinning top for Trey.

Lucinda threw a party for her theatrical friends, who arrived at intervals as they made the rounds throughout the day. But Jackie did not venture out, even though the weather was very mild with cloudless skies and only traces of snow on the streets.

"You should go out," Lucinda said, as she donned a new pair of leather gloves and a smart hat. "This is the most festive time of the year for Londoners. And everyone is in a fine mood."

"I can't leave Trey, and I'm afraid he'll catch cold if we go out," Jackie said.

"Pshaw! The child has the constitution of a horse. But you could leave him here with Sybil. Alastair's off today, but Sybil has nowhere else to go."

"Then Trey and I will keep her company."

Lucinda buttoned up her coat. "All right. Have it your way. I do hope you will attend tonight's performance of *A Christmas Carol*. It's become a tradition, you know."

"I suppose I can entrust Trey to Sybil for that. Besides, he'll be asleep by eight o'clock."

Just then, a horn was heard coming from the street.

"That's Johnny and Gertie in their new motor car. This one seats four very comfortably. Too bad you won't be joining us."

"All the more room for you."

"What's that supposed to mean?" Lucinda looked down at her waist, which had expanded over the past year.

"I mean that they must have gifts to deliver along the way."

Lucinda went to the window and pulled aside the curtain. "You're right. There's a pile of them in the back seat. I'll have to squeeze in. Well, I'm off."

Jackie remained in the drawing room, sitting beneath the Christmas tree amidst an array of wrapping paper, open boxes, and a tangle of ribbons. Trey sat on his bottom, bewildered by all the fuss, but apparently enjoying it. The top was especially fascinating to him, though he was unable to set it spinning himself. This Jackie did for him to his endless amazement.

Sybil, who had been cleaning up in the kitchen after the mid-day festivities, came into the room and asked if she could entertain Trey for a while.

"That would be delightful, Sybil," Jackie said. "I don't know how many more times I can spin this top without going mad. Trey seems to never tire of it."

Sybil laughed and sat down in front of Trey. "I used to do this for my little brother, though his top wasn't so fancy as this."

"Your little brother?' Jackie said. "And where is he now?"

Sybil frowned as she wound the string around the top. "He died of a fever, ma'am."

"Oh, I'm so sorry."

"That's all right, ma'am. It's been quite a while now, but I do miss him."

"Do you have any other siblings?"

"Well, there's Angela, but she ran off with a sailor who shipped out to Australia and hasn't been seen since."

"Oh. Where is she now?"

"Last I heard, ma'am, she was in Newcastle and took up with a coal miner. That's five years ago, I reckon."

"And your parents?

"Dead, ma'am. Dad drank himself to death when I was still a lass, and Mum had the fever like my brother."

Jackie was now sorry that she had been so inquisitive. "Well, you have a home here now."

"Yes, ma'am. Miss Lucinda is like a second mother to me. I can't complain."

Sybil continued to entertain Trey while Jackie went to the foyer and put on her overcoat. "I think I'll go for a walk, Sybil. You're sure you can manage with Trey for a while?"

"Oh, yes, ma'am. He's a gay little lad. But he'll be tired soon and I'll put him down for his nap."

"That's a good idea. I won't be out for long."

Jackie stepped out onto the front steps and watched the carriages as they drove by, along with an occasional motorcar. The air was crisp, but not too cold, just enough so that she could see her breath. She pulled her fur cap down over her ears and set off along Eaton Square where children were building snowmen and throwing snowballs at each other although much of the snow was already melting.

As she walked, not really knowing or caring where she was going, she thought of the upcoming move back to Paris. If anything, her French was worse than before as she had not kept in practice. But she was not concerned so much with that as she didn't intend to continue acting. Tony was apparently earning a good living now, and she could afford to stay home with Trey. But she couldn't spend all of her time with the child, could she? And what would be Tony's relationship with Madame Goldman after he moved out? She liked Mme G, but she couldn't bear the thought of her and Tony carrying on an affair right under her nose.

As these thoughts ran through her head, she suddenly found herself in the middle of Sloane Square. This was a busy meeting place, with shops that catered mostly to the wealthy residents of Belgravia and Chelsea. She looked into these shops rather absently, not really interested in buying anything, and besides, many of them were closed for the holiday.

Her attention, however, was drawn to the Royal Court Theatre, where the playbill announced a performance of Shaw's latest play, *Captain Brassbound's Conversion*. It seemed odd to her that Lucinda had not mentioned it. Perhaps she had had a falling out with Shaw, who had recently formed his own company with Granville-Barker. In any case, it intrigued her.

As she walked back to Eaton Square with her hands in her muff, she felt a sense of violation somehow. 'Violated' in the sense that she was being pulled away by Tony from her true vocation as an actress. 'True vocation?' A few moments earlier she had rejected acting as a career. But now she felt that she really couldn't live without it. Life on the stage was not just one life, but many. Each role was a new adventure. How could she confine herself to only one role, and a dull one at that, as a wife and a mother?

As she ascended the few steps to Lucinda's front door, she felt suddenly dizzy and grabbed the railing to steady herself. It recalled the feeling she had when she and Tony sat on the stern of the prince's yacht, sailing away from Savannah Harbor and watching the shoreline disappear beneath the watery horizon. It was a feeling of being wrenched away from something you know and love, never to see again, something that couldn't be helped. One had to move on in life.

But move on to what?

CHAPTER 59

The Baron's Christmas party was more an affair of state than a private gathering. Indeed, his mansion resembled the Élysée Palace in both size and design. Situated at the northeast corner of the Place de la Concorde on Rue St-Florentin, carriages disgorged their owners at the gate and returned to the Place, where the drivers parked in semicircles around the frozen fountains and huddled beneath blankets for warmth.

The baron, as he did at his soirée the previous year at la Ferrières, stood at the main entrance receiving his guests and calling them by name–all 250 of them. Tony noticed that the baron was wearing the red ribbon and breast badge of the Grande-Croix, the highest order of the Légion d'honneur. This particular honor outranked the vicomte's by a factor of four.

There was a towering Christmas tree in the ballroom decorated with the usual tinsel and cloth ornaments, but also with electric lights. This created a spectacle that Tony had never seen before. Liveried servants circulated with silver trays ladened with *lait de poule* and *canapés au caviar.*

Absent guests who had attended the previous year's soirée included the vicomte, of course, his wife, as well as the prince and Loïe Fuller. Tony was surprised to see, however, le président de la république and felt instinctively that he should greet him as an old friend, but then was restrained by Mme G, who noted that Monsieur Loubet was deeply engaged in conversation with the British ambassador.

As he sipped his *lait de poule*, which he discovered was ordinary eggnog laced with cognac rather than bourbon, he gazed around at the extravagant furnishings and suddenly felt that he had no business being there. He was put at ease, however, upon spotting a group of black men that included Henry O. Tanner. Tanner, like himself, was very light-skinned, but the two men he was talking to were as black as coal and wearing heavily decorated uniforms. He assumed these were ambassadors of African states.

As he was observing the animated conversation of these men, Mme G nudged him in the ribs.

"Ah," she said, "here comes Monsieur Loubet. Apparently, he wishes to speak to you."

Tony turned his head in that direction and found himself face-to-face with le président.

"Comment ça va, mon ami," M. Loubet said, extending his hand.

"Ça va bien, Monsieur le Président," Tony said, shaking his hand. "I believe you have met my friend Madame Goldman."

"Bien sûr." M. Loubet kissed Mme G's hand. "Enchanté de vous revoir, Madame."

"Moi aussi, Monsieur le Président," Mme G said, with a little curtsey.

"Alors, let's not speak French with so many Americans and Englishmen about. Besides, I need the practice."

Madame G laughed. "It seems you need very little practice, Monsieur. Your English is flawless."

"Oh, not flawless. In fact your friend here, Monsieur Antonio, has had to teach me a few phrases of your native country. I still have trouble with this word, 'yawl.'"

Tony laughed. "Did I teach you that?"

"Oh, yes. My difficulty is, to whom is it addressed? To one person or two?"

Tony explained this colloquialism as best he could, but M. Loubet had trouble with the concept of addressing an invisible person.

They went on chatting about such things as the weather and the success of the Exposition, along with its long-term benefits for the city of Paris. They were soon joined by M. Loubet's wife, Marie-Louise, who spoke only in French.

The baron then appeared after having greeted all the guests and announced that as Hanukkah and Christmas coincided, there would be celebrations and toasts to both. At that point, the electric lights on the tree dimmed and candles on several menorahs around the room were lit, while a group of children trooped in from a side door. At the baron's signal, they began to sing a medley of Christian and Jewish songs, in both French and Yiddish. At the end of this performance, the lights on the Christmas tree were turned up again, and the children began playing a game called 'dreidel,' which consisted of spinning brightly colored tops shaped like cubes with Hebrew letters inscribed on them.

Tony was curious about the tops, especially the significance of the letters on them. He was informed by Mme G that they were, when viewed in the right order, an abbreviation for the Hebrew words, 'A great miracle happened here,' referring to the miracle of the oil that took place in Israel before the time of Christ.

"Miracle of the oil?" Tony said. "What oil?"

"Olive oil," Mme G said. "After the desecration of the temple, there was a revolt by the Jews and a rededication of it. There was only enough oil to burn the lamps for one night, but the lamps burned for eight days. That was the miracle."

"Oh," Tony said. "Well, as miracles go, that's one of the more plausible ones. Christ rising from the dead. Now *there's* a miracle."

"I get the feeling you don't take religion seriously."

"That's a fair assessment."

"Didn't you go to church as a child?"

"Sure. On St. Helena Island there was a black church where my mother and I went from time to time. My mother was a teacher in the school across the street, so it was natural for her to attend though she was often the only white person there."

"And did you enjoy it?"

"Oh, yes. It was very entertaining. People singing, shouting, and stomping their feet, some passing out from the excitement."

Mme G laughed. "It sounds very theatrical."

"It was. Ever since, I've considered organized religion to be another form of theatre. Like what we just witnessed, only this is much more subdued."

M. Loubet listened to this conversation with intense interest, as if taking notes.

When the children grew tired of playing at the 'dreidel,' several of the adults showered them with what looked like gold coins, but which turned out to be chocolate wrapped in foil. This, according to Mme G, was called the 'gelt.'

"For a gentile," Tony said, "you seem to know a lot about Judaism."

"My husband insisted that I convert, so he hired a tutor to prepare me for it."

"So what did that consist of?"

"The Torah and the Talmud. I thought it was very interesting."

"But you didn't convert."

"No. As we became more estranged, I drifted away from my studies. And then little Willie was born."

"And so you sent him to a Christian school?"

"No. I sent him to a public school."

"And on Sunday?"

Mme G smiled wistfully. "We played tennis in the park."

"Where will you send Alex?"

"I don't know. France is a Catholic country. All the schools are–"

Monsieur Loubet interrupted. "Madame, France will soon have a system of secular education."

"Ah, oui?" Mme G said, despite M. Loubet's preference for English on this occasion.

"Yes. The priests in this country have constructed a barbarous system of indoctrination that demands rote memorization and crushes the spirit. We will change that. And by the time your child is old enough for school, we will have a first-rate educational system that will rival that of Britain and America."

Tony and Mme G were somewhat taken aback by this sudden passion of M. Loubet.

Just then it seemed that the British ambassador had been eavesdropping and challenged le président on his assertion that the French system could rival the British. This conversation became very esoteric and while they were thus engaged Tony and Mme G drifted away towards the dining room.

There was no announcement for dinner as it was a buffet style with one long table laden with platters of roast goose, turkey, ham, lobster and other delicacies. About thirty tables or so were set up for ten diners each, covered with white tablecloths. At the far end of the room was an elevated box, or balcony, where a string quartet played selections from Mozart, Bach, and Vivaldi. The baron interrupted them for a moment, apparently to give instructions. They resumed playing as the baron made his way through the crowd, briefly chatting with each guest and encouraging them to partake of the buffet.

When the baron approached them, Tony wasn't sure how he should receive him. Should he be jealous, congratulatory, aloof? He had never been in a situation like this.

"Greetings, my friends," the baron said, kissing Mme G's hand. "I am so glad you were able to come. And how is little Sebastian Alexandre?"

So at least he knows the name of the child, Tony thought.

"Quite well, Alphonse," Mme G said with a warm smile. "And growing fatter every day."

"Mon Dieu! Not too fat, I hope. One would hope that he would be an athlete on the playing field–if he's so inclined."

Mme G laughed. "It's a bit early to tell. But he's fascinated with the football you sent him. That may be a sign."

The baron turned to Tony. "I am a frustrated athlete, you see. Like many fathers, I encourage all my children to excel where I could not."

This statement stymied Tony. Was he acknowledging his paternity of Alex? Or was he just making a general statement of his attitude toward raising children? For once, Tony had little to say.

"Enjoy yourself, my friends," The baron said, patting Tony on the shoulder. "And Merry Christmas!" Then he moved on and stopped to speak to M. Loubet and his wife.

"Is he always like this?" Tony said to Mme G.

"Like what?"

"This 'bonhomie.' I know it's Christmas and he wants to entertain his guests. But can he be so *insouciant* about a child he just fathered out of wedlock?"

Mme G frowned. "I told you—I don't know who the father is. And certainly he doesn't. We may never know. But it doesn't matter."

"Certainly it matters. The child, if no one else, has a right to know!"

"Don't get angry."

"I'm not angry."

"All right. The way I see it, the baron will take responsibility for Alex's schooling and when he's old enough, employment. That is, if he wants to be a banker. You will be responsible for teaching him how to be a man."

"Me? But what if he doesn't acknowledge me as his biological father? How will he even know who I am?"

Mme G smiled and put her arm into the crook of Tony's. "We'll wait to see if he prefers the football or a paint brush. Then we'll know. I'm hungry. Let's eat."

CHAPTER 60

On the 8th of January Tony stood on the platform at the Gare du Nord waiting for the train to arrive. It was very cold, but the steam from the trains raised the temperature somewhat so that he unbuttoned his overcoat. J-P waited in the carriage in the plaza outside the station.

Tony was not sure what to expect. Jackie had sent another cryptic telegram informing him of the train number and time of arrival, but little else. It was as if it were a business appointment.

Nat had informed him of an apartment that was available on Rue du Luxembourg, right around the corner from his loft on Rue de Fleurus. It was spacious and on an upper floor with a fine view of the Gardens. There was little room for his paintings, however, and he had had to leave most of them with Mme G in the carriage house. The idea was that he would continue to use the studio but live with Jackie on Rue du Luxembourg. He was a little uneasy about whether Jackie would accept this arrangement. An advantage, however, was that he would be able to see little Alex on a regular basis.

It was late in the afternoon and in the gray mist the exiting passengers resembled a mass of rodents abandoning a sinking ship, so anxious were they to get home or to a hotel. It was typical of Jackie to sit in her seat on a crowded conveyance until everyone had departed.

At last she appeared, a welcome contrast to the other passengers who all seemed to be clad in black overcoats. Jackie wore a light beige camel-hair coat with a broad, upturned collar. Her blond hair had grown out a bit and filled the spaces between the collar of the coat and her neck. A fedora like the one in the play of the same name, was pulled smartly over one eye.

Little Trey stood on his own two feet at her side, holding his mother's hand. He wore a miniature navy peacoat and a sailor's hat.

Tony made his way through the swarming crowd.

"Only one bag?" he said.

"The porter's bringing the others. How are you, Tony?"

"Well. Quite well. And you?"

"Very well, thank you." She put her valise down on the platform and picked up Trey in her arms. "Can't you say hello to your papa, Trey?"

Trey looked a little bewildered. "Papa?"

"Yes," Jackie said. "This is your papa. Don't you remember?"

Trey looked again at Tony, who drew closer to him and tugged on his sailor's cap. Trey smiled and chortled a bit, but no other word came out of his mouth. Tony rubbed his nose against Trey's and he chortled again, apparently receiving it as a friendly tickle. "Papa," he said again.

Tony raised the brim of the hat and kissed Trey on the forehead. "He knows me."

"I think he does. Do I get a kiss?"

Tony looked into her deep blue eyes and realized how much he missed her. It seemed that he knew no one else in Paris who had blue eyes. He leaned forward slowly and kissed her on the lips.

"Pardon, Madame. Est-ce que vous voudriez un taxi?"

It was the porter, who had pushed a dolly up beside them. There were a half a dozen suitcases, in addition to a steamer trunk.

"Non, merci," Tony said. "Nous avons une voiture. Suivez-nous." Then to Jackie: "What have you brought with you? Your trousseau?"

Jackie laughed. "As a matter of fact, yes. That and a few other things."

"I'll take Trey," Tony said, and plucked the child from her arms. "Can you handle the valise?"

"Of course. You two need to get to know one another a little better."

Tony led the way to the main entrance to the station amidst a cacophony of whistles, brakes screeching, and arrival and departure announcements over the loudspeaker. J-P leapt down from his perch, greeted Jackie with the few words of English that he knew, and helped the porter with the luggage.

"Where are we going?" Jackie said, as they pulled away from the station.

"Rue du Luxembourg, right around the corner from Rue de Fleurus."

"Rue de Fleurus? Isn't that where Nat's studio was?"

"Still is. Nat and Marie-Louise have gotten back together. He told me about the apartment. It's quite nice–you'll see."

"Oh, Tony–I don't know if I want to be so close to them. They're so, so–"

"Bohemian? Yes, they are. But we don't have to socialize with them if you'd rather not. Besides, I'll be very busy."

J-P pulled onto Boulevard Haussmann.

"What's that?" Jackie said, just as she was about to voice further objection to living near Nat and Marie-Louise.

"That's the Galeries Lafayette. A new department store. I'm sure you'll be spending some time there."

"Goodness! It's huge."

"And planning to get even huger. They're buying up all the commercial space available."

"I've only been gone a year and everything is already looking different."

"The Exposition has pumped millions into the economy. It's a good time to be here."

They rode a little further down Boulevard Haussmann until they came in view of the Opéra House, where icicles were hanging from the roof.

"Oh, Tony—we must go to the Opéra. Can we afford it?"

Tony chuckled. "Yes, we can afford it. We can afford a lot of things we couldn't before. But we can't overdo it. The art market is a fickle thing."

"Like the theatre. Tony—do you think I could perhaps land a minor role in some play or other?"

"I thought you had given up acting."

"I did. But now I'm getting the itch again. Do you think we could afford a nanny?"

"A nanny? I suppose so. You're serious about this?"

Jackie sighed. "I suppose I am."

They rode on for a while, turning down Avenue de l'Opéra towards the river. At the Place du Châtelet, Jackie stood up again—Tony was still carrying Trey in his arms—to get a better view of the Théâtre Sarah Bernhardt. "Miss Bernhardt—is she still starring in *L'Aiglon*?"

"I believe she is," Tony said.

"Oh, I hope so. I'd like to see her performance before she moves on to London."

"Now, that could really be expensive. I've heard that standing room only tickets are 100 francs."

"One hundred francs? My goodness. Maybe you could approach her and—"

"Ask for a discount? I'm not sure she remembers me."

Jackie sat down. "Or me, either, for that matter. Well, I'll give Lucinda a call. Do we have a telephone?"

"Not yet. But I could call from Madame G's."

Jackie, bubbling with enthusiasm until now, suddenly pouted. "Madame G? I thought you had made a clean break with her."

"I never said that. I've moved out, that's all. So we could have a place of our own. But she still has about a hundred of my paintings lying about. Jackie, you have to remember Madame G launched my career. And she's still a good friend."

Jackie continued to pout.

At the Luxembourg Gardens J-P parked the carriage in front of the apartment building and began unloading Jackie's luggage. It was getting dark now, and there was little contrast between the sky and the snow-covered tops of the trees. Snow was also piled up along the sidewalk and in the gutters. Jackie stared at this scene for a few moments and then with Trey in her arms followed Tony and J-P up the stairs to the third floor.

"Oh, my goodness!" she said upon entering the apartment. "Are you sure we can afford this?"

"Unless there's a collapse of the art market. Even if there is, I've saved quite a bit of money over the past year thanks to Madame G."

"What do you mean? She didn't charge you rent?"

"I offered to pay, but she wouldn't hear of it."

"Well, she is very rich."

Tony took her on a tour of the apartment, which consisted of three bedrooms, a study, a small kitchen, a separate dining room, and two bathrooms, one the 'salle de bain,' and the other a 'salle d'eau,' or shower room.

"I'll use the second bedroom as my studio," Tony said, "since it faces the Gardens. It's small, but the light is good, especially in the spring and summer. Is that okay with you?"

"What? Oh, certainly." They were now back in the drawing room, which had two floor-to-ceiling *portes-fenêtres* side by side that opened out onto a wrought iron balcony. But the thing that had really commanded Jackie's attention was the elegant furnishings, which consisted of Louis XVI chairs and sofas, and end tables of the same period. The drapes were of a green moiré silk, and a Savonnerie carpet covered most of the oak flooring, which was laid out in a herringbone pattern.

"This must be very expensive, Tony. If your savings run out–"

"I'll sell more paintings. I forgot to tell you–President Loubet commissioned me to paint his portrait. That alone brought in 15,000 francs."

"Goodness! But who is your landlord? He–or she–certainly has good taste."

"I don't know who the owner is–I dealt with the property manager."

"Oh. Well, it must be someone who cares about beautiful things."

Trey, who had been dozing against Jackie's shoulder, suddenly began crying.

"I need to change his diapers. Where–"

"The laundry room is probably best," Tony said. "There's a table in there."

While Jackie was changing Trey's diaper, Tony gave J-P a five franc note and asked that he bring some of his things from Rue de Furstemberg back to the apartment. After J-P had left, he went to a window and looked out, first at the snow that covered the balcony, then at the trees in the Gardens.

Well, now–had he arrived?

CHAPTER 61

Rather than go to Mme G's house to make a telephone call to her mother in London, Jackie decided to approach Miss Bernhardt herself. She entered the Théâtre Sarah-Bernhardt on a Monday afternoon with some misgivings and sat in the back of the theatre during a rehearsal for *L'Aiglon*. Miss Bernhardt, who played the title role of Napoleon's son, was busy with the other actors, alternately praising them and scolding them.

At a break in the rehearsal, Miss Bernhardt noticed Jackie sitting alone.

"La répétition est à huis clos, Mademoiselle."

Jackie stood and started to go, convinced that Miss Bernhardt did not remember her.

"Mademoiselle! Un moment." Miss Bernhardt continued up the aisle in her military uniform, white with tight breeches, a red sash at the waist. She strode like a man, deliberate and authoritative. "Est-ce que nous nous connaissons?"

Jackie, now more intimidated than ever, managed a faint smile. "Oui. À Londres, chez ma tante."

Miss Bernhardt broke into a broad smile. "Ah, yes! Madame LeRoux. That is, Lucinda LeRoux. But you are—"

"Jacqueline. Jacqueline Jones."

Miss Bernhardt, still playing the part of the young duke, kissed her hand. "Delighted. Absolutely delighted. What can I do for you, Mademoiselle Jones?"

"Well, I thought...that is, as I now live in Paris—"

"Ah, oui?"

"Yes. I've just moved here to be with my husband. He's an artist, you know."

"Yes, yes. I remember him well. A handsome black man. And your husband—forgive me, 'Madame.'"

"That's all right. Well—"

"I'm sorry to say that I did not have time to sit for my portrait. And soon I will be off to London again, and then New York."

"I was wondering…"

"Yes?"

"Well, I've had a great deal of experience with acting–"

"Eh bien. You are quite young."

"Yes, but I've had some success in the West End."

Miss Bernhardt now looked her up and down. "Yes, now I remember your aunt telling me so. You were with child then. He is born?"

"Yes."

"And now you are here. Because of your husband."

"Yes."

Someone called to Miss Bernhardt from the stage.

"Un moment! Je suis occupée!" She turned again to Jackie. "It just so happens that one of my actors is–how do you say–*enrhumé*."

"He has a bad cold."

"Yes. The role is a small one, that of a page. Do you mind playing the part of a boy?"

"No, not at all. Do you think I look young enough?"

Miss Bernhardt smiled. "With your hair under a cap–you will have to cut it–no one will be the wiser. Wait here until the *répétition* is concluded. I will show you your cues. You know a little French, it seems."

"Yes. I mean, un peu."

"Bon. Attendez."

Jackie was giddy with excitement as she left the theatre and decided to walk home rather than take a taxi. The weather had cleared and though still cold, seemed invigorating. Now Tony would see that she was as capable of earning bread for the table as he. Of course this minor role, not even a speaking part, would pay very little. But to act in the same play with the great Sarah Bernhardt!

She lingered for a moment at the Théâtre de l'Odéon to examine the playbill, which announced an upcoming performance of Sardou's *Tosca*. Old stuff! Miss Bernhardt had played the title role at the premiere in–when was it–the late 80's as she recalled. But *L'Aiglon* was new and bold, with Miss Bernhardt playing the dashing young Duke de Reichstadt, son of Napoleon I.

Jackie continued to the apartment on Rue du Luxembourg, anxious to inform Tony of her good fortune landing a role in the French theatre. Of course, they would have to hire a nanny right away for Trey. And perhaps a tutor for herself so that she could improve her French. Suddenly, Paris seemed to be her oyster!

When she arrived at the apartment, she found Tony tossing a ball to Trey, who inevitably failed to catch it and chased it under a sofa.

"Trey!" she said. "He'll get hurt–not to mention the furniture as well."

"You can't protect him against everything. Let him bump into a few things and find out for himself what to pursue and what to be careful of."

Jackie went to the sofa and pulled Trey out from under it by his legs. Trey came up triumphantly with the ball in his hand.

"See?" Tony said. "He got it–and no worse for wear."

Jackie scooped Trey up and into her arms. "Don't listen to Papa, Trey–you'll hurt yourself."

Trey looked bewildered for a moment, then tossed the ball to the floor and with one bounce, it landed on the coffee table and knocked over a flower vase which in turn fell to the floor and smashed into smithereens.

"Now look!" Jackie said. "See–I told you so."

Tony went to the coffee table and began picking up pieces of the porcelain vase. "All right. Maybe it's not such a good idea playing ball in the drawing room. But he's a boy–he needs room to play."

"Then take him to the park across the street."

"It's too cold."

"Now who's overprotective? Can't he wear his peacoat?"

Tony sighed as he collected the last piece of the vase. "Okay. You win. How did the interview go?"

Jackie sat down on the sofa with Trey in her lap and blew into his ear, which the child seemed to regard as a form of tickling. He laughed and blew back with little effect. "Very well. Miss Bernhardt remembered me–and you–and gave me a part."

"A part? A speaking part?"

"Well, no. But it's a start. By the time the play has run its course, my French will be better."

"I hope so. We'd better get a nanny."

"That's what I was thinking. The sooner the better."

Tony paced the floor. "Let's see...how does one go about finding a reliable nanny? And one that Trey gets along with?"

Jackie bounced Trey on her knee. "I don't know. Is there an employment service here?"

"I suppose so. I could ask Madame G."

"Hmm. Well, she should know. Oh, Trey's wet again. I'll do it this time, but Tony, you need to learn how to do it for when I'm not here."

"Me?"

"Yes, you. Come into the laundry room with us."

This was a task Tony thought he would never have to perform, but under the circumstances, he had no choice. He followed Jackie into the laundry room. As he watched her change the diaper, disposing of the dirty one in a hamper to be washed later, he thought of another time-saver. "We need to get a telephone. I'll apply at the SGT tomorrow."

"The SGT?"

"La Société Générale de Téléphone."

"Oh."

Tony looked down at Trey, who seemed happier now that he had a fresh diaper on. "How long is this going to last?"

"What?" Jackie said. She pinned the diaper up and sat Trey on the table.

"This diaper thing."

"Oh, for a few months. But first we'll have to toilet-train him."

"Oh, boy."

Jackie laughed. "It's not so bad. And you'll be glad when Trey can do it himself." She put Trey down on his feet. He stood by himself, a bit wobbly, then clutched his mother's knee. "He'll be walking by then without our help."

"Jackie–" Tony put his arm around her waist.

"Yes?"

"I'm glad you're here. I've missed you."

Jackie looked at him as if to assess his sincerity. "I've missed you, too. Now I'm sorry I ever left."

"Well, maybe it was for the best. A test of our marriage."

"And did we pass the test?"

"What do you think?"

Jackie looked at him with less suspicion now but was still unsure. "I'd like to think so."

"But you don't?"

"I don't understand your relationship with Madame G."

Tony dropped his hands. "There's nothing to understand. She's a business partner. And a friend."

"And do you still make love to her?"

Tony sighed and replaced his hands around her waist. "No. It's purely platonic now." He started to kiss her, but she pulled away.

"Then we'll know if we passed the test in good time."

She led Trey out of the laundry room and left Tony standing there, wondering what 'good time' meant. After a few seconds he decided that she was right to be skeptical. And it would be 'good time' before even he knew whether his affections for Mme G had become purely platonic.

CHAPTER 62

L'Aiglon continued its successful run in Paris and then moved to London as Miss Bernhardt said it would. This left Jackie with the dilemma of whether to follow Miss Bernhardt, who suggested that she could be a backup for another actress with a speaking role. In the end, she decided to stay in Paris, rather than once again breaking up the family.

Tony, for his part, kept busy painting, often at Mme G's, but more and more at the new apartment. The second bedroom was a bit small, but the light was good and the view of the Gardens with the snow melting away offered new subject matter.

One morning in the middle of February, with the sun shining into the new studio where Tony often took his coffee before beginning to paint, he read in *Le Figaro* that a young artist in Montmartre had shot himself in a popular café. It seems that he was spurned by the object of his affections, who refused to marry him.

Tony put down the paper and gazed out the window, where the trees in the Luxembourg were beginning to show some signs of rejuvenation. Children, though bundled up in sweaters and jackets, were taking advantage of the milder weather, playing at hoops and football.

Why does a man commit suicide? In this case, an artist like himself. And over a woman. As much as he loved Jackie, he couldn't imagine killing himself if she left him again. But the fact that the man was an artist was disturbing. Some even thought that artists were more subject to depression than other people, and that this very depression gave rise to creativity. Was it necessary to be deeply unhappy to be a successful artist? He didn't think so.

He picked up the paper again and turned to another page. More depressing news. The vicomte had exhausted all of his appeals, including his application for clemency, and was scheduled to be executed at La Santé on Saturday.

Tony had thought that M. Loubet, with his passionate crusade against the death penalty, would at least commute his sentence to life imprisonment. Which, incidentally, might have been a more severe penalty for a man like the vicomte. There was even some talk that he would be murdered in prison on account of his aristocratic *hauteur*. In any case, Tony did not plan to attend.

Done with his coffee, he put his newspaper aside, put on his smock, and began painting over a sketch he had done the previous day. Jackie had left early to attend classes at the Sorbonne in order to improve her language skills. They had decided that a private tutor was too expensive and not necessary. As for a nanny, Tony had asked Mme G to recommend someone, but as yet she had been unable to locate anyone suitable. In the meantime, he would have to look after Trey himself, which wasn't too difficult since Trey tended to sleep a lot and once Jackie had fed him in the morning, he usually went right back to sleep.

After painting for about twenty minutes, Tony heard an unfamiliar ringing sound. At first he thought someone was at the door, but then he realized that it was the telephone. This was the first time anyone had called since it was installed.

He put down his brush and went to the phone, which was in the hallway in an alcove that was originally designed to display objets d'art. He picked up the receiver and put it to his ear.

"Vous êtes bien chez Jones," he said.

There was a woman's laughter at the other end.

"Tony! You don't have to be so formal on the telephone. A simple 'Allô' will do."

"Amelia?"

"Oui. Ça va?"

"Ça va. What's up?"

"I just got a call from Monsieur Dantec."

"Dantec? What does he want? More paintings?"

"As a matter of fact he does. I'm not sure which ones he's talking about, or which ones you want to send over. You'll have to come and see."

"All right. Anything else?"

"No...oh, yes. Inspector Rochard called."

"What did he want?"

"I don't know. He just asked that you call him. Here's the number."

Tony wrote down the inspector's number. "How's Alex?"

"He's fine. But he keeps calling for his papa."

"Uh, oh."

"Tony, you've got to at least pretend you're his father. Or *oncle*. He just needs a male presence."

"What about J-P?"

Mme G sighed. "J-P's sweet, but he's not exactly a good example for a young gentleman."

"I thought you said I was only 'a gentle man,' not a gentleman. What about the baron?"

"Don't be silly. The baron has no time for him even if he dared to visit us. Which he won't."

"All right. I'll stop over later this afternoon."

"Bon. And don't forget to call the inspector."

"I won't. À plus tard." Tony placed the receiver back in its cradle. Then he picked it up again and dialed the inspector's number.

"Rochard."

"Monsieur l'Inspecteur? C'est Antonio Jones."

"Ah, oui. Monsieur Jones. English, please. I need your assistance."

"Certainly. How can I help you?"

"The vicomte's execution will take place on Saturday."

"Yes, I just read about it in the newspaper."

"Can you attend?"

"Attend? What for?"

"A new procedure. There must be two witnesses."

"Two?"

"Yes. One must not be a police officer."

Tony sighed. "What time?"

"Six o'clock."

"In the morning?"

"Yes. To minimize the number of spectators."

"All right. I'll be there."

"Merci beaucoup, Monsieur Jones."

"De rien." Tony hung up. He stood in the hallway for a few moments contemplating this event. He had never seen a man decapitated before. He wondered if he would have nightmares about it later. Possibly even for the rest of his life.

He went to the bedroom and looked in on Trey. Sound asleep. The kid sleeps at least 12 hours a day.

Just as he was about to return to the studio, the phone rang again.

"Allô?"

"Tony–c'est moi. I think I've found a nanny for you."

"Good. Who is she?"

"Sabine's sister."

"Her sister? Where did she come from?"

"Montpellier. She just arrived and needs a job."

"Well...send her over. But wait till after lunch–Jackie will be here by then."

"D'accord."

Tony went back to the studio and stared out at the Gardens. So serene, so still, except for a few children playing. Painting such a scene seemed to be almost a lie. Paris was beautiful, but there was so much that was ugly teeming beneath the surface. What was the purpose of art? To make people more miserable than they already were? Or to lift their spirits, if only for a few moments?

He picked up his brush again and began painting in the broad, bright colors that he preferred.

CHAPTER 63

S abine's sister, who was barely sixteen, was a pretty but very shy girl who nevertheless seemed to get along with Trey. She had, like her sister, run away from home as soon as she was old enough to gain the confidence to do so. The fact that her father was in jail made her escape a little easier.

Tony rose early Saturday morning while it was still dark, dressed, caught a tram on Boulevard Raspail, and met Inspector Rochard at Place Denfert-Rochereau. From there they walked to La Santé. When they arrived at the corner of Boulevard Arago and Rue de la Santé, there was already a crowd forming. The guillotine was set on a scaffold with several steps leading up to it. There was a man on the scaffold wearing a black mask and a workman's jacket, as there was a bit of chill in the air. The sun was rising over the rooftops to the east and there was a line of ravens along La Santé's high wall peering down as if in anticipation of a free meal.

Several people in the crowd began moving forward to secure a ringside seat. It consisted of men and women, mostly over fifty, though there were a few boys carrying book bags, apparently intent upon an entertainment before school.

"The usual crowd," the inspector said. "I see the same faces each time."

A door opened on Rue de la Santé and a procession filed out, led by a priest. Several officials followed him. As the procession approached the site of execution, Tony could make out the vicomte, his hands secured behind his back. He was no longer dressed in his own attire as he had been at the portrait sittings, but in dungarees and the smock that he wore at their first meeting. His hair was close-cropped, as was his beard, and his expression morose.

It was a long walk. When they arrived at the guillotine, two guards led him up the steps of the scaffold as the crowd erupted into cheers and whistles.

"Assassin!"

"Sale bâtard!"

"Salaud privilégié!"

This last insult was the only one that got the vicomte's attention. First he searched the crowd to identify the heckler, then when he made eye contact, he broke into a broad grin, as if giving his approval to this characterization.

The priest recited passages from his prayer book as he led the procession up the steps of the scaffold. The vicomte paid no attention to him, still grinning at the crowd as if enjoying the spectacle. This unsettled the crowd a bit, and they grew quiet.

When the priest had finished his recitations, he crossed himself and stepped back. The executioner pushed the vicomte face-down onto the *bascule*, strapped him to it, and closed the *lunette* over his neck. Then he went to the *déclic*, which was the delicate trigger-like mechanism that was set to release the weighted blade suspended above his head.

Suddenly another official appeared, having pulled up the rear without anyone noticing. He was a large man, broad-shouldered and pot-bellied, huffing and puffing, as he had been running. He raised the palm of one hand. "Arrêtez!"

The executioner, his finger poised at the *déclic*, desisted.

"Le Président a commué la peine!" the warden said.

"Pourquoi? Il est meurtrier!"

"Corruption!"

"Erreur judiciaire!"

The warden stepped forward into the crowd and shouted at them. "Rentrez chez vous! C'est terminé! Allez-y!"

The crowd slowly dispersed amidst grumbling and catcalls until Tony and Inspector Rochard were the only ones left aside from the prison officials. The warden acknowledged the inspector with a somewhat sheepish nod, shook his head and returned to the prison yard through the same door from which he had emerged. The executioner, though his face was covered, appeared to be indifferent to the outcome and released the vicomte from the *lunette*.

The vicomte stood rather stiffly, looked up at the sky as if to thank God for his deliverance, then gazed at Tony and smiled.

The guards led him down the steps and back to the entrance to the prison.

"I didn't think he'd do it," Tony said.

"The commutation?" The inspector spat on the cobblestones. "It does not surprise me. Le Président is too soft in the heart, as you say. This is the second commutation in the past six months."

"He obviously struggled with this one," Tony said.

A man approached the inspector and identified himself as a reporter for *Le Figaro*. While he was thus engaged, Tony took his leave and headed back to Rue du Luxembourg.

When he arrived at the apartment, he found Jackie feeding Trey in the kitchen.

"They called it off," he said.

Jackie, suspending a spoon in mid-air, looked up. "The execution?"

"Yes. The warden arrived with a commutation from Monsieur Loubet at the last minute."

Jackie placed the spoonful of apple sauce into Trey's mouth. "Thank goodness. The guillotine is a barbaric relic of the past."

"I don't know that it's all that barbaric. It's quick and efficient."

"Still..."

Tony sighed and took off his overcoat. "I don't like capital punishment any more than you do. But I'm afraid that the vicomte may somehow contrive to escape punishment altogether."

"How?" Jackie wiped some of the apple sauce from Trey's mouth.

"I don't know. But he's still rich and has friends in the government. Maybe those same friends pressured Monsieur Loubet."

Jackie shrugged. "It's beginning to sound like Dixie politics."

"It does, doesn't it? Where's Camille?"

"She'll be here any minute. I've got to go to class."

Tony lifted Trey from his highchair and entertained him in the drawing room while waiting for Camille to arrive.

Camille was somewhat shorter than her sister, but also blonde and very pretty. At first Jackie seemed to balk at having her in the apartment all day while Tony went about his work in the studio. But Camille won her over by her quiet earnestness and especially her almost instantaneous rapport with Trey. And she was industrious. When she arrived at the apartment, she immediately took charge of Trey, led him to the toilet, changed his diaper, and set about cleaning the apartment, which hardly needed it.

With Jackie gone, Tony retired to the studio and gazed out over the Gardens before getting started on his painting. He couldn't help thinking of the vicomte and the grisly murders he committed in Pigalle. The man was a monster—shouldn't he be put to death, if for no other reason, to prevent him from killing again? He, Tony, might have to reconsider his position on capital punishment.

As he was thus contemplating philosophical and moral issues, he noticed a group of small boys in the Gardens choosing sides for a football game or what the Americans now called soccer. The tallest boy held the ball under his arm, while the others looked on and stepped to one side or the other as they were chosen by the captains. The snow had mostly melted away and the field of play looked rather soggy. Tony had never played this game. On St. Helena Island, where he grew up, he and his friends played the American version of the game, which was most closely related to rugby. At any rate, as he watched the boys play, he was fascinated by what these young boys could do with their feet. Never touching the ball with their hands, they passed the ball from one to another with an amazing degree of dexterity and ultimately scored by kicking the ball into a makeshift goal of fish netting. After an hour, they were covered with mud.

Thus began certain alterations to the painting he had started a few days earlier, which he now called 'The Game.'

Trey was walking by his first birthday and eager to join the growing number of boys who were playing football in the Gardens. Of course he was still too young, but Tony would take him out to watch and occasionally the bigger boys would let him make an attempt at kicking the ball, laughing when he inevitably fell down. But Trey felt no shame or embarrassment and got up and tried again.

As for Alex, Tony visited the house on Rue de Furstemberg about once a week and often found J-P out in the garden kicking the ball while Alex chased after it. J-P proved to be adept at this game, and Tony felt that he could contribute little to it, though J-P taught him a few of the basics.

But what was he to do as Alex got older? He couldn't keep dividing his time between the two households. Jackie, who had apparently decided that Alex was Mme G's child and thus her responsibility, acted as if he didn't exist. She had said nothing about him since she arrived in Paris.

By this time, Jackie's French had much improved. She landed a role at the Comédie-Française, partly through a recommendation by Miss Bernhardt, who was touring in America. The play was Molière's *L'École des femmes*, or the School for Wives. It was a minor role but signaled the fact that her French was at least passable.

One morning in September, Tony was reading in *Le Figaro* about the attempted assassination of President McKinley. It wasn't clear how seriously injured the president was, or if he would survive. Tony had voted for him in '96, based on McKinley's promises to appoint blacks to cabinet posts and to stamp out lynchings in the South. These promises, however, had not been fulfilled, or at least fell far short of expectations. If McKinley died, Theodore Roosevelt would succeed him as president. Roosevelt, young and energetic, seemed more vigorous and committed to racial justice than McKinley, but it was too early to tell what would happen.

As he put his paper down and Camille took away his breakfast tray, Tony prepared for the day's work. The weather was clear and a bit cooler as fall approached, and he decided to move his easel to the Gardens to paint. But as he was packing up his paint box, the phone rang. Camille answered with the very formal 'Vous êtes bien chez Jones' that Mme G had admonished him for a few months earlier.

"Pour vous, Monsieur Tony," she said.

Tony put down his easel and paint box and took the receiver.

"Monsieur Tony?"

Tony recognized the voice. "Oui, J-P."

"Madame Goldman–elle a disparu."

"Disparu? Qu'est-ce que tu veux dire?"

J-P went on to explain that Mme G had taken Alex out for a walk in the square early that morning and had not returned.

"Cela ne fait pas longtemps," Tony said. "Peut-être qu'elle sera bientôt de retour."

"Non, Monsieur. De la fenêtre, je les ai vus sur la place ce matin. Un homme les a abordés."

"Un homme?"

"Oui, Monsieur."

J-P explained that the man, a big man, he said, seemed to argue with Mme G, then grabbed her roughly by the arm and began dragging her away with Alex screaming and trying to follow. J-P immediately ran down the stairs to prevent him from doing so, but by the time he got there, they were gone.

"Disparus? Tous les trois?"

"Oui, Monsieur."

"Tu as appelé la police?"

"Non. Monsieur. J'ai voulu vous appeler d'abord."

Tony told J-P to sit tight while he called the police. He reached Inspector Rochard after waiting on the line for several minutes.

"Enlevée?" the inspector said. "Madame Goldman?"

"Oui. Ce matin."

"Êtes-vous sûr?"

"Oui. Sûr et certain."

Then, in English: "I shall be there in fifteen minutes. Do not allow anyone else in."

"I no longer live with Madame Goldman, Inspector. But I can meet you there."

"Bon."

Tony rushed out the door and hailed a taxi. He arrived at Rue de Furstemberg ahead of the inspector and J-P met him at the door.

"Ils ne sont pas encore rentrés?"

"Non, Monsieur."

Tony walked to the little square and noticed the soccer ball that the baron had given Alex resting against the trunk of a tree. He picked it up and bounced it on the pavement. Then he walked to the far end of the street, looked up and down Rue Jacob, and returned to the square. At this point, a police vehicle pulled up and Inspector Rochard got out.

"You are playing football?" the inspector said.

"It belongs to her son. He disappeared with her."

The inspector looked up and down the street. Then he instructed the driver, who had just stepped out onto the pavement, to search the area.

"Did anyone see this happen?" The inspector said.

"J-P, the chauffeur, but he was in the house looking through a window. By the time he got downstairs, they were gone."

"How many men?"

"Only one."

"One? Someone from *le quartier*?"

"J-P had never seen him before."

"I must talk to J-P."

They met J-P at the door, who had been watching from the foyer. Once upstairs, they were met with Sabine and Eugénie, who could be of little help. The inspector, after a more extended interrogation of J-P, turned to Tony.

"Madame Goldman is a very rich woman."

"That's true."

"Does she have enemies?"

"None that I know of."

The inspector sat down on one of the sofas, pulled out a notebook and began jotting down notes. "As I understand it, she is married. But not to you."

"That's true also."

"Then to whom?"

"An American. His name is William Goldman. But as far as I know he is in San Francisco."

"San Francisco? A long way away."

"Yes."

"Do you know him?"

"No."

"He and Madame Goldman are, how do you say–*séparés*?"

"Estranged? Yes. As far as I know, they haven't seen each other in years."

The inspector closed his notebook and put it in his pocket. "This makes things very difficult, Monsieur Jones. A husband living 10,000 kilometres away, no enemies, an unknown man, ordinary in appearance but tall and broad in the shoulder. It could be any number of criminals in the area. There are certain *extorqueurs* and *maîtres chanteurs* known to us. And of course he may have taken the child for insurance. Perhaps he intended to kidnap the child only, but Madame Goldman got in the way. Who knows? We will do our best to find them."

"Is there any chance that the vicomte was involved?"

"The vicomte? I doubt it. What would be his motive? He is richer than she. And it would be difficult to manage in his present situation in any case. Leave *le travail de détective* to me, Monsieur."

Tony smiled for the first time since he arrived. "Yes, Inspector. I will leave it to you. But you will keep me apprised of the situation?"

"Apprised?"

"Informed. Au courant."

"Informed. Yes, I will call you on the telephone if anything 'turns up,' as you Americans say. Au revoir, Monsieur."

"Au revoir, Inspecteur."

Tony sat down on the sofa and suddenly realized that he had been clutching the soccer ball all this time. He looked at it, spun it on its axis as if searching for a clue, then finding none, bounced the ball on the floor.

He stood up. "J-P!"

After a few moments, J-P appeared.

"Oui, Monsieur?"

Tony passed the ball to him, and J-P, though surprised, caught it. "Tiens! Garde-le! Alex le voudra quand il reviendra."

"Oui, Monsieur."

As Tony descended the stairs to the street, however, he wondered if Alex would ever return to play with the ball again.

CHAPTER 65

President McKinley was dead. A hundred thousand people were said to have passed by his open casket in the Capitol Rotunda, many waiting in the rain. The newspapers, including the ones in Paris, generally praised the deceased president, though the more radical papers denounced him as an imperialist.

Tony was anxious to see what the new president, Theodore Roosevelt, would do.

But he was even more anxious to find out what had happened to Mme G. And, of course, Sebastian Alexandre. Were they even still alive?

He often stood in the hallway and stared at the telephone, expecting Inspector Rochard to call at any minute. But he didn't call.

How could they have vanished without a trace? A couple with a small child, of course, was a common sight at railroad stations.

The inspector had alerted customs authorities at Calais, Le Havre, and Marseille in case the kidnapper attempted to flee the country. But as passports were not required, the authorities at those ports could only rely on a description, which fit thousands of travelers. And what about Belgium, Germany, Switzerland, Spain? Their only hope was if the kidnapper were a common criminal in the Paris area. But so far there had been no demand for a ransom.

Tony sat in his studio and, as was his custom, stared out the window into the Gardens for a while before getting down to work. But these days it was harder to get started.

At noon, when Jackie returned from her class at the Sorbonne for lunch, he had accomplished little.

"What is that?" Jackie was at the door, looking in.

Tony didn't turn around. "Ochre."

"I know what the color is, but what is it supposed to represent? Just that one color?"

Tony stared at the canvas. "It represents a mood, that's all."

Jackie came into the room. "A mood. All right. Can you give me a clue as to what mood?"

"I'm not sure I can explain it. It's just a mood."

Jackie put her hand on his shoulder. "You shouldn't worry so much about Madame G. There's been no demand for a ransom. I think her husband dragged her away and she eventually agreed to return to San Francisco with him."

"She detested him. And she showed no signs of wanting to return to San Francisco—ever. She had just about consummated a deal with the baron to sell him a majority stake in the bank when it happened."

Jackie stroked his shoulder and gave him a kiss on the cheek. "I know you care about her, Tony—and you should. But leave it to Inspector Rochard to do all the worrying. He'll eventually find out what happened. N'est-ce pas?"

Tony smiled and kissed her hand. "Ton français s'améliore."

"S'améliore? I don't know that one."

"Is improving."

"Ah—je comprends. I know the word—it's the pronunciation that confuses me sometimes."

"How's the play going?"

"Fine. I don't have to say much but listening to the other actors is a great help. Oh—Trey is calling me. I'd better see."

Tony went back to his easel and contemplated this new painting. It was, in fact, about mood. He hadn't planned it that way—he only dragged his paintbrush back and forth until the entire canvas was this one somber color. It would have to be more than that, wouldn't it?

Perhaps not. This new young painter—the one whose friend shot himself in Montmartre a few weeks ago. Picasso. He had created a minor stir with his dark blue canvases, though those did contain human figures. Should he follow suit? Perhaps fill in the ochre with a figure of a woman holding her child's hand. No, too obvious. Even if no one else recognized Mme G and Alex, Jackie would. Jackie was right—he should let Inspector Rochard worry about them and move on with his work.

As he was thinking, or rather trying to envision what the painting would look like if he added another color, the phone rang. Camille answered.

"C'est l'Inspecteur," she said.

Tony went to the hallway and took the receiver from her.

"Allô?"

"C'est moi, Rochard."

"Ah, oui, Monsieur l'Inspecteur. Qu'est-ce qui se passe?"

"I fear I have little to tell you, Monsieur Jones. But I thought that you would like to know that the case is still open."

"So, there are no leads?"

"Leads?"

"Pistes."

"Ah, yes. 'Clues,' as you say. I'm afraid not. At least nothing of substance. However, as there has been no demand for ransom we assume the culprit is a foreigner–Madame Goldman's husband, perhaps."

"I already assumed as much."

"We have discovered that this Monsieur Goldman has recently been released from prison in California."

"Prison? What did he do?"

"It seems he was in the habit of forging cheques."

"Ah. Anything else?"

"Yes. He purchased a train ticket and arrived in New York 9 August. From there he boarded a steamer that disembarked at Le Havre 1 September. At that point we can only assume that he traveled by train to Paris, but we do not know where he stayed once he got here."

"Can't you check with the hotels?"

"Monsieur, there are over a thousand hotels in Paris. Of course we contacted the major ones but they have no record of a Monsieur Goldman."

"He registered with an alias, perhaps."

"Possibly. But what alias?"

"What about the cheques he forged?"

"We thought of that. But the authorities in California will not release that information. It is confidential, they say. The banks will not allow it."

Tony sighed in resignation. "Well, I appreciate your efforts, Inspecteur. You will keep me informed if there are any new developments?"

"Of course."

Tony went back to his easel.

CHAPTER 66

Jackie sat attentively in a front row seat at the Comédie-Française one morning watching the rehearsal of *L'Ecole des femmes*. Though she had memorized her part, that of Georgette, a servant, she still had trouble understanding what the other actors were saying. At the moment, two of the principal actors were rehearsing a scene between them while Monsieur Béjart, the director, watched, cajoled and otherwise bullied them into performing in the way he envisioned.

Seated beside her was a young French actor named Armand, who played the lead character's valet, a counterpart to her own role. Armand was about twenty-five, nearly ten years younger than she, with chiseled features and dark intense eyes that unsettled her a bit. He sat in his chair with his right arm over the back of Jackie's and his left elbow poised on the back of the chair in front of him, his thumb and forefinger beneath his dimpled chin. His legs extended to the space in front of her so that she was forced to sit with her feet tucked under her own chair. He seemed completely unaware that he was making her uncomfortable.

"Merde!" Armand said. "Monsieur Béjart ne connaît nullement Molière."

Jackie understood enough French to realize that Armand did not think much of Monsieur Béjart's directing abilities. "Pourquoi tu penses que oui?"

This question elicited a torrent of French that Jackie failed to understand a word of.

"Chut!" Monsieur Béjart said, turning around briefly to silence him.

Armand muttered a few more words under his breath and turned to Jackie, who returned his gaze with a blank stare. He smiled at her. "You didn't understand a word, did you?"

"I'm afraid not."

"You were awarded the role of Georgette because you are quite beautiful, but not as beautiful as Monsieur Béjart thinks Agnès should be—nor as young."

Jackie felt like slapping his face, but he said it with such aplomb and without malice, simply as an observation, that she restrained herself. Besides, he was right.

"I should say," Armand said, whose English was flawless, "that I disagree with Monsieur Béjart on that point—you are more beautiful than Clara," who played the ingénue, Agnès. "Far more."

First he insulted her and then, almost in the same breath, flattered her. What was she to make of him?

She walked home after the rehearsal as it was a beautiful day, and as was her custom, stopped at both the Sarah Bernhardt Theatre and the Odéon to see what was playing. She wondered when Miss Bernhardt would return. She seemed to have an inexhaustible store of energy and was on her fifth or sixth tour of the Americas. Miss Bernhardt was also nearing sixty, but still played both male and female characters who were forty years her junior—and to wide applause. How dare Armand say that she, Jackie, was too old to play an ingénue!

She continued along Rue Vaugirard, past the Palais de Luxembourg, and onto Rue du Luxembourg, which bordered the Gardens. How pleasant this neighborhood was! "Qu'on est bien ici!" as the French say. She suddenly felt very glad that she was back in Paris. It was beautiful where London was merely 'stately,' with massive but uninteresting buildings and monuments everywhere. The French embellished their buildings with intricately carved friezes and stylized flora and fauna, always experimenting with new styles. She loved Art Nouveau!

And of course her husband was an artist. Though she hated to say it—it was cruel of her, but she couldn't deny it—she was glad that Madame Goldman had disappeared. Of course she hoped that the poor woman had come to no harm, nor her child.

As she climbed the stairs to the apartment, she thought of Armand. So handsome! And very talented. It would not be long before he would move up to leading roles and even stardom. Miss Bernhardt had not seen him yet, but when she did, she would recognize his talent and steal him away from the Comédie-Francaise. And perhaps even become his lover!

This thought amused her as she opened the door to the apartment and saw Camille with Trey in her arms.

"Bon retour, Madame!" Camille put Trey down and he ran, a bit unsteadily, but ran all the way into Jackie's arms.

After giving him a hug and a kiss, she put him down and looked in on Tony, who was so absorbed in his painting that he didn't respond at first when she announced herself and then only muttered, "Qu'est-ce qu' on va déjeuner?"

After lunch with Tony on the balcony, Jackie returned to the Comédie-

Francaise for the final dress rehearsal. She did so with some trepidation, not because opening night was near, but because she was having mixed feelings about Armand. He was extremely attractive. But how could she even think of such things? True, Tony had been unfaithful to her and even had a child by another woman. Or so it seemed. There was some speculation in the tabloids–which she could read now–that the father was not Tony, but Baron de Rothstein. Oh! She should stop reading these gossip rags. *Le Petit Journal*, though the worst offender, was the easiest to read. It carried all of the most sensational stories, including the kidnapping of Madame Goldman and her relationship with Tony. One headline, 'l'Amant nègre de la américaine' immediately caught her attention at one of the kiosks. It was full of lies and exaggerations, but some indisputable facts, too. Oh, the French! They loved scandal, especially of the amorous kind.

She arrived at the theatre ten minutes late because of a carriage accident on Rue de Rivoli and was scolded by Monsieur Béjart. The tyrant! He accepted no excuses. When she went backstage to the dressing rooms, she encountered Armand, who was already dressed in his 17th century servant's costume. Somehow he looked more like a cavalier than a servant. He was really miscast. Alain, the servant, was supposed to be meek and subservient. Armand exuded confidence and good breeding.

"Well, my little coquette," he said, "so you've tasted the lash of Monsieur Bégart's tongue as well, eh?"

"I am not your coquette, Armand," she said. "And I wish you would treat me with more respect."

"Respect? I respect you immensely. So what if you are married to a *nègre*? It took courage to defy the prejudices of your countrymen."

"To me, he's not a *nègre*. He is a wonderful man and a brilliant artist."

"An *artiste*. Yes, I have seen some of his paintings. All of Paris is talking about him. Not to mention his *liaison amoureuse* with the American heiress."

"That's none of your business. Besides, she's gone now. Please let me pass."

Armand, who was blocking her path to the dressing room, dropped his arm and stepped aside. "I would not dream of preventing you from going anywhere you wish, *mon amie*. I can't wait to see you in full costume."

Jackie brushed past him and found a chair in front of the mirror. She sat down and began putting on her make-up. Clara was seated beside her.

"Fais comme s'il n'était pas là." Clara said. "Il traite de toutes les femmes comme ça."

Ignore him? thought Jackie. How could she ignore him?

Besides, a little thrill coursed through her veins whenever he was near.

CHAPTER 67

$\mathcal{A}$ year passed without any news of Mme G or Sebastian Alexandre. A policeman reported seeing an abandoned child at the St. Lazare station the day of the kidnapping, but when he turned his back to break up a fight between two passengers, then turned round again, the child was gone. Initially, he thought it was likely that the child's mother had only neglected him for a moment to purchase a ticket, but later reported the incident to the *préfet*. Belgian, German, Swiss, Spanish, and Italian authorities found no 'Goldman' on passenger lists or hotel registers.

The San Francisco police, however, reported that William Goldman was now listed as chairman of the Bank of Northern California. Yes, it was that same William Goldman, but police could find no evidence that he had violated any laws since he was released from prison. He, in fact, had recently been elected to the Board of Supervisors. When questioned by the police at the urging of the French authorities, he claimed that he had never left the country.

As for the house on Rue de Furstemberg, the baron continued to pay the staff and the taxes in the event that Mme G should return. Tony visited often to use the studio and to check up on J-P and Sabine, and their daughter, Amélie. J-P was beginning to see himself as master of the house, but Tony gave him a gentle reminder now and then that Mme G could return at any moment.

Privately, Tony thought that Mme G was either dead or kept as a prisoner in the basement of William Goldman's Nob Hill mansion.

Tony's sales were lagging. After a flurry of commissions once the news of his portrait of M. Loubet got out, interest in his work waned. Younger painters, like Picasso and Braque, were commanding the attention of art critics, who flocked to their studios and reported on their often startling experiments. Tony, still not forty years of age, was associated with the 'old school.'

Jackie's career, on the other hand, was on the ascendancy. She was becoming fluent in French and her youthful beauty and obvious talent was winning her more substantial roles. Miss Bernhardt, on her return from America, insisted that she remain exclusively with the Théâtre de Sarah-Bernhardt, but Jackie had already committed to roles at l'Odéon and others. This caused a falling out between the two, but Miss Bernhardt soon relented and amended her contract so that Jackie could accept roles in other theatres.

Armand, whose career was on the ascendancy as well, seemed to have a knack for getting himself into the newspapers, especially the tabloids. His numerous affairs were common knowledge, and one husband had even challenged him to a duel. Though illegal in France, the two met on private property, where Armand managed to disarm his opponent, drawing blood from his wrist, at which time the duel was stopped. Armand was fined fifty francs, the cuckolded husband thirty.

Jackie read an account of the duel with a mixture of admiration and disgust. Disgust that Armand would agree to such a barbaric ritual, and admiration, of course, for his courage and skill. After all, he was well versed in the art of fencing as part of his training as an actor.

And he still pursued Jackie.

Currently, they were both starring in a revival of Rostand's *Cyrano de Bergerac* at the Théâtre de la Porte Saint-Martin.

The critics praised Armand for his swashbuckling panache as Cyrano, but singled Jackie out as a particularly beautiful and skilled actress. Her performance was favorably compared to that of Miss Bernhardt's, who, for all her talent and popularity, was clearly too old now for the part.

"I saw your husband in the audience,'" Armand said backstage after a matinée performance. "He stands out in a crowd."

"That's because he's so handsome," Jackie said, who had learned to needle Armand where his vanity was concerned.

"I was referring to the color of his skin," he said.

"That, too," Jackie said. "A lovely café au lait, don't you think?"

Armand leaned against the door of her dressing room, which was open. "I fail to see what you have in common."

"You would, wouldn't you? He has a brilliant intellect and a highly refined sensibility–something that you seem to lack."

"Aucune sensibilité? Moi?"

"Oui–toi. Now please let me pass."

"Bien sûr, ma belle Roxane. Will you and your husband dine with me this evening?"

"Dine with you?"

"Yes. I have reserved a private room at the Café de la Paix. All the cast is invited, of course. But you and your husband will be seated at *la place d'honneur*."

"That must be very expensive, Armand."

Armand shrugged. "C'est peu de chose." He flicked his wrist as if to dismiss the thought. "Une bagatelle."

"Well...I'll ask my husband. Here he comes now."

As Tony approached, Armand stood up straight and addressed him: "Monsieur, I must commend you on your good taste. Madame's extraordinary talent is exceeded only by her beauty."

Tony chuckled. "I'm afraid I had little to do with her good qualities. I was simply lucky to be in the right place at the right time. Your English, sir, is as impeccable as your acting. And with an American accent. Where did you learn it?"

"My father is a former ambassador to the United States. That's where he met my mother."

"Ah! That explains it. Then you were born in America?"

"I was."

Jackie was tiring of this mutual admiration. "Armand has invited us to dinner, Tony. But I am afraid it will make us too late to relieve Camille so that she can go home."

"Camille will stay until we get there. And she can sleep in the nursery if she's too tired to go home. We'd be delighted to join you, Monsieur Rougier."

"Please call me Armand."

"And I go by Tony."

Jackie wasn't sure whether this bonhomie between the two men was a good thing or not. But she was relieved that Tony would be there to protect her.

After she and the other actors had changed into their street clothes, they all met outside the theatre and hailed several cabs, which took them to the Cafè de la Paix.

Some of the actors declined Armand's invitation for one reason or another so that there were only about a half dozen of them, along with spouses and friends. As promised, Jackie and Tony were seated next to Armand, with Jackie between the two men. M. Béjart, the director, had declined to attend since he had himself presided over a full cast dinner after the première and considered Armand something of a strutting peacock who attempted to upstage the other actors at every opportunity. Had Armand not lately become the darling of the theatrical press, he would have fired him long ago.

"Tell me, Armand," Tony said to his host as the waiters bustled around them in their long white aprons, "how long did you live in America?"

"Only until I was seven," Armand said, "At which point my father was recalled to Paris. He was sent to Switzerland, where I went to the lycée, and then back to Paris, where I went to the *Conservatoire*."

"Do you have any siblings?"

Armand laughed. "I have nine–some of whom I haven't even met."

Tony, having been an only child, as was Jackie, found this circumstance intriguing. "How could that be?"

"My father," Armand continued, "has been married three times. My mother was twenty years younger than he. He was fifty when I was born."

"Is he...still alive?"

"Oh, yes. I recently gave him a drool cup for his seventy-fifth birthday."

Tony didn't know whether Armand was joking or not, and said nothing.

Armand continued. "He's back in Switzerland at a sanatorium. He has the dropsy."

"What about your mother?"

"Oh, she's with him. Sort of. She has an apartment there and visits him from time to time. That is, when she and her lover are not skiing in the Alps."

Tony, who had been craning his neck over the head of Jackie in order to converse with Armand, decided that he had perhaps intruded too far into the young actor's personal life. But Armand was not deterred from returning the favor.

"And you, Monsieur Tony–how did it happen that you obtained that lovely *café au lait* complexion, as your wife so charmingly put it?"

Tony glanced at Jackie, who smiled a little uncertainly. "I suppose Jackie can fill you in on the whole story. Basically, my grandmother was born a slave."

"Ah!" Armand said. "That explains it. But aren't there laws in the States against–what do they call it–miscegenation?"

"I don't care for that word, Armand, but–"

"Sorry. I don't know the proper term."

"I'm not sure there should *be* a term for it."

Armand stared at Tony for a moment as if trying to determine the exact admixture of his blood. "It is strange, isn't it? And rather arbitrary. Ah–here's the champagne." A waiter filled his glass and he stood from his chair. "Je porte un toast à Monsieur et à Madame Jones, qui sont des artistes extraordinaires!"

"À votre santé!" came the reply, and everyone drank.

Armand sat down and turned to Jackie. "Forgive me–I forgot to mention that you are far more beautiful than your husband."

Jackie glanced at Tony, who was grinning at her, then back at Armand. "Why do Frenchman persist in telling a woman how beautiful she is? It sounds hollow after a while."

"Hollow?" Armand said. "I say it only because it's true. And I have never known a woman to object until now."

"Well," Jackie said, a bit on the defensive. "I don't want to sound unappreciative, but…"

"But what?"

"It's a form of flirting. And it's not right for men to flirt with married women."

Armand laughed and downed the rest of his champagne. "There's not a woman in France, my dear Jacqueline, that objects to flirting. It's a national past-time. There's no harm in it."

Jackie glanced again at Tony, who simply smiled and shrugged his shoulders.

CHAPTER 68

Newspapers proliferated during *La Belle Époque* and Tony read nearly all of them at one time or another. But lately he had come to rely more and more on *Le Temps* for its objectivity and thorough reporting.

One spring morning he and Jackie were having breakfast on the balcony off the drawing room and he came across an article that disturbed him:

Le Vicomte Raynouard de Köenigsbourg est Transféré à Charenton

The article went on to say that a special court of inquiry had determined that the vicomte was delusional but not violent and therefore would be better served—as would society—if he were transferred to the asylum at Saint-Maurice, just outside of Paris.

"Not violent!" Tony exclaimed. "He murdered at least two women and even mutilated them!"

"Tony—not so loud," Jackie said. "People in the street can hear you."

Tony ruffled the pages of the paper and folded it up. "I don't care. How can they send this maniac to an asylum with minimal security where the inmates put on plays to entertain themselves?"

"Put on plays?"

Tony took a sip of his coffee and opened the paper again. "Yes. They say it's some kind of therapy. Well, the Marquis de Sade directed his own plays there for twelve years and he showed no signs of rehabilitation."

"Really? What were his plays like?"

"Sadistic. The very word that carries his name. I read a couple of them when I was at Harvard. It's the worst kind of pornography."

"I've never seen you so angry."

Tony sighed and put the paper down. "Well, I should be. Everyone should be. The man is a menace. The inspector was right—the vicomte has friends in high places that can get him out of anything."

"But why would his friends want him to go free?"

"I have no idea. Of course he's not really free. But this move to Charenton seems to be just one more steppingstone to freedom."

Camille came to collect their dishes.

"Did the marquis ever escape?" Jackie said.

"No. He died there."

"Well, maybe the vicomte will, too. Camille–où est Trey?"

"Dans le studio, Madame."

"Le studio? Qu'est-ce qu'il fait là?"

"Peignant, Madame."

"Peignant?"

Tony looked up from his newspaper. "Comment est-il peignant?"

Camille held up one hand and spread her fingers apart. "Avec les doigts."

Tony and Jackie looked at each other blankly.

"Let's have a look," Tony said.

"I told you he'd take after you," Jackie said.

Camille smiled and took the dishes away while Tony and Jackie rose and went into the studio. There they found Trey on the floor with both hands covered with paint and smearing them across a piece of kraft paper that Camille had laid out for him. He looked up and smiled, obviously proud of his work.

"Qu'est-ce que c'est, Trey?" Tony said.

"Un tableau, Papa."

"So it is," Tony said. He knelt down to examine this first effort by his son. "C'est magnifique!"

Trey beamed.

"It looks like one of your abstract paintings," Jackie said. "Like that one– in the corner."

Tony looked at the painting she indicated, then at Trey's rendition of it. "Pas mal, mon fils. Not bad at all."

Clearly pleased with this approval from Papa, Trey went back to his *oeuvre*.

Camille appeared at the door. "Je suis désolée, Monsieur. Vous n'êtes pas fâché avec moi?"

"Au contraire, Camille. Je suis ravi!"

Jackie laughed. "A chip off the old block."

"I'd almost forgotten the expression." Tony turned to Trey again. "We'll paint together, old man. And don't forget–we must speak English from time to time."

"Anglais?" Trey said.

"English," Tony said.

Trey looked confused for a moment, then said, "Yes. English. Look, Papa!" And he went back to his finger painting.

As Tony slipped on his smock, he had an idea. "Camille–pourrais-tu le faire une blouse?"

"Oui, Monsieur."

"Bon." Then to Trey: "Well, sport—I might even buy you a beret. Then we'll be a pair!"

Jackie laughed. "Well, I'll leave you two to your work. I'm off to the theatre."

"Which one?"

"Miss Bernhardt's. She's back and wants to produce a new play by Sardou. She says there's a role in it for me."

"Good. By the way—is Armand trying out for it?"

"I don't know. Why?"

"Just wondered."

Jackie stared at him for a moment as he turned away and picked up a brush. She shook her head. "À tout à l'heure."

"Right," he said.

As she walked around the Gardens on her way to the theatre, Jackie wondered at Tony's rather cryptic 'Right,' when she said goodbye. He was suspicious, jealous of Armand. That was clear. But he had no reason to be! Everyone knew that Armand was a flirt and a self-styled Don Juan. Most did not take him seriously.

He was a fine actor, though. There was no doubt of that. His spontaneity, his ability to improvise, his subtle gestures pregnant with meaning.

She paused at the Odéon and noticed that they were holding auditions for a new play based on a novel by Balzac. She hadn't read anything by Balzac since she was a girl at the lycée in Charleston, but she knew that Balzac created wonderful female characters. Sardou's women, on the other hand, tended to be rather melodramatic and conventional though she would never say that to Miss Bernhardt, who loved Sardou's work and had had great success with it.

At the Théâtre de Sarah-Bernhardt she encountered Armand in the lobby.

"Ah, ma cherie Jacqueline," he said. "Tu deviens plus belle chaque jour!"

"Et tu," she said, "devient plus vaniteux."

"Vain? How can you say that when I adore only you? I dissolve in your presence. I become nothing."

"Please, Armand—I'm not in the mood."

"Ah. I see that you have had a falling out with your husband."

This observation startled her. She had not had a 'falling out' with Tony, but they had just parted with an unspoken distancing between them. "Why do you say that?"

"I would say a little bird told me, but I don't know any talking birds. I can see it in your face, your demeanor."

"Hmph," she said. "Well, are you here to audition for a part in *La Sorcière*?"

"I am indeed. There are several good roles, but I prefer that of the Grand

Inquisitor."

"I don't know the play," Jackie said, "but I suspect that you're too young for the role."

"Too young? Make-up can do wonders. I once played King Lear in a production at my lycée."

Jackie laughed. "And I once played Lady McBeth in a production at *my* lycée. Adult audiences are a little more discerning, Armand."

Armand shrugged his shoulders. "Tell that to Mademoiselle Bernhardt."

"Faites bien attention!" It was Miss Bernhardt, standing in the doorway to the theatre, as if Armand had conjured her up. "Tout dedans le théâtre pour les auditions!"

"We'd better go in," Jackie said.

As it turned out, Armand was awarded the lead role of Don Enrique, the young lover of Zoraya, the Moorish woman who is deemed a sorceress by the Christian authorities. Zoraya, of course, was to be played by Miss Bernhardt herself, notwithstanding the fact that she was some thirty years Armand's senior. Jackie was awarded the part of Joana, daughter of the governor of Toledo.

After this initial rehearsal, Armand invited Jackie to have an *apéro* in the café across the street. She agreed, since other cast members were also headed there. She and Armand sat at a tiny table next to the window.

Armand ordered a bottle of wine and sprawled his arms and legs out over table and chair in his usual manner. "How do you like that?" he said with a laugh. "I wanted to play the old man and she casts me as her young lover!"

Jackie smiled. "I wasn't surprised. You're obviously perfect for the part of Don Enrique. And she'll play young women–and men–until she's ninety."

Armand chuckled. "Yes, she is eternally vain–far more so than you seem to think I am. But her audiences adore her and care not a whit whether she plays a princess or an old dowager. We should be so lucky!"

The waiter arrived with their wine and Jackie took a sip. "This is very nice–what is it?"

"The wine? Oh, that's from my father's vineyard. One of his hobbies. Now that he's unable to attend to it, I suppose one of my elder brothers will take over."

"Where is it? The vineyard, I mean."

"Bourgogne. Chambertin. He only owns a piece of it. At any rate, the old man has good taste in wine as he does in everything else."

"I suspect you have not always seen eye-to-eye with him."

Armand seemed thoughtful for a moment, then took a sip of his wine. "I suppose you're right. He's always favored my stepbrothers. I was a sort of afterthought. *Un aprés coup.* I was always trying to get his attention as a child. I suppose that's why I became an actor."

"And your mother?"

"She also had little time for me, even though I was her first-born. Diplomatic receptions, soirées–parties were her passion. Pregnancies were a nuisance and an embarrassment to her. My sisters got even shorter shrift than I did."

Jackie was beginning to see Armand in a different light. "I suppose all actors have some sense of having been neglected in childhood."

"And you? Were you neglected?"

Jackie thought back to her childhood in South Carolina. "I wouldn't say 'neglected.' I was an only child, after all. But I was raised by my aunt, who for a very long time I thought was my mother."

Armand sat up straight and poured some more wine into each of their glasses. "You *thought* she was your mother? Why were you told that?"

"It's rather complicated. My real mother had me–well, she wasn't married. I was an embarrassment to the family. So Lucinda–my mother–was packed off to England and my aunt pretended that she was my mother."

Armand stared at her for a moment. "How extraordinary. And so you felt neglected?"

"Again, I didn't know anything about the actual situation. My adoptive parents were very attentive. But I always felt that something was amiss–a comment here or there that made me feel like a foreigner."

"Hmm," Armand murmured. "Une étrangère. Yes, I know the feeling."

They lingered over their wine for several moments, both consumed with their own thoughts of childhood. Then, as if suddenly jolted back to reality, Armand called the waiter over.

"Would you like something to eat?"

"I don't think so. My husband's expecting me for dinner."

"Yes, of course." Armand put a few francs on the table. "Should I call for a cab?"

"Oh, no–that won't be necessary. It's a short walk."

"Then I will escort you. Where do you live?"

"Rue du Luxembourg."

"Ah, yes. I know *le quartier*. Shall we go?"

They walked along the Seine and lingered for a few minutes on the Pont au Change, watching the barges and cruise vessels pass underneath. It was dusk and lights were coming on all over Paris.

"It's beautiful, is it not?"

"Yes. Very beautiful."

"And romantic. Look at those two lovers on the embankment. Anytime now–yes, he looks into her eyes, she at him–*voilà*! They kiss."

Jackie laughed. "It's hardly a rare occurrence."

"No, but it happens in Paris as in no other city in the world. It's as if Aphrodite herself were watching over young lovers with an approving eye, saying, 'Do not miss this opportunity–it will make you immortal!'"

"You've missed your calling, Armand. You should have been a poet."

"I *am* a poet. Would you like to see some of my verses?"

"Some other time. I need to get home."

Armand, who had been leaning with his elbows on the bridge, pulled himself away and began walking again. "I may have misjudged you. You have no sense of the romantic. Like most Americans."

This statement offended her. Nevertheless, she followed him. "Americans are just as romantic as the French–they just aren't so public about it."

"Ha! I know both. Americans are like the English–puritanical. *Amour* is a commodity to them. They barter and exchange it like so much cattle–or cotton. Of course, there are exceptions."

"Am I one of the exceptions?"

"I don't know. We'll have to see."

Jackie was a little more stung by Armand's characterization than she let on. There was some truth in what he was saying. Though Lucinda lived in England, she took on lovers like bonbons, kept them if they were sweet to her taste, and cast them aside if they weren't. Her aunt Edwina, who raised her, was just the opposite–strait-laced and almost virginal. And speaking of virgins, she, Jackie, was a virgin well into her twenties until she met Tony.

They continued across the Île de la Cité and on to the Place de l'Odéon, where Armand took a keen interest in the playbill announcing Balzac's *La Rabouilleuse*.

"Ah, Balzac," he said. "I would love to play one of his characters. He is the French Dickens, only better."

"Why don't you audition?"

"Perhaps I will. But when is it? I'm afraid it will conflict with *La Sorcière*."

"It says the play won't open until the fall. *La Sorcière* may not last that long."

"Well, yes. It's a possibility."

They walked on and soon arrived at the door of Jackie's apartment building. It was now dark.

"Thank you, Armand, for walking me home. Even Paris can be a bit dangerous for a woman after dark."

"You can be assured that I would defend you with my life."

She smiled, almost as if indulging a child. "Yes, I'm sure you would."

"Jacqueline–"

"Yes?"

"I want you to be my mistress."

She laughed, a bit nervously. She hadn't expected him to be so blunt. "I'm very flattered, Armand. But I'm afraid that's impossible."

"Why impossible? Your husband ignores you."

"I wouldn't say that."

"No? I observed him at our dinner at the Café de la Paix recently. His eyes were on every woman there but you."

This statement rattled her. "Well—he's a man, isn't he? And an artist. He appreciates feminine beauty."

"No one appreciates feminine beauty more than I do, and you are without peer."

Now she was blushing. "Armand—"

But he interrupted her by putting his hand over her mouth. "Speak not another word." Then he slowly removed his hand and pressed his mouth against hers.

They were just inside the entry to the building where it was out of the way of passersby. She felt his lips against hers, soft, not hard, as she expected. It was, in fact, a tender kiss. She pulled away, her hand pushing against his chest.

"That was very nice, Armand. But I can't allow you to do that again—except perhaps on stage."

"Then we will meet on stage, live on stage, breathe the same air on stage. Jacqueline—you must believe that I am madly in love with you. All the others till now meant nothing. It's hopeless—I am lost!"

Jackie laughed, again somewhat nervously. "You'll never be lost, Armand. You know what you want. And it's not me. Good night."

She pushed the door open and quickly ascended the stairs.

CHAPTER 69

That same day Tony paid a visit to M. Dantec carrying two of his most recent paintings with him. M. Dantec did not greet him with his usual good cheer, but with a somber expression invited him into his office.

Tony proudly displayed his paintings against the backs of two chairs and then sat down in a third before M. Dantec's desk.

"What do you think?" Tony said.

Monsieur Dantec seemed distracted at first, reviewing some papers on his desk, then looked up at the paintings. "Hmm? Oh, yes, very nice. What do you call those?"

"I don't have titles for them yet, but the one on the left I'd say falls roughly into the Impressionist category, and the one on the right I'd call…well, 'supra-impressionist,' for lack of a better term."

"Supra-impressionist? Never heard of it. What is the point?"

"Well, it's an attempt to expand the boundaries of Impressionism. I've ignored the usual fidelity to realistic lighting and flattened the perspective a bit. And of course color takes a prominent role."

Monsieur Dantec adjusted his monocle and squinted at the painting in question. "Something like Gauguin's work, eh?"

"Who?"

"Paul Gauguin. A strange character. He's abandoned France for Polynesia and occasionally sends a batch of his paintings to my colleague, Vollard. But Vollard can't sell them and convinced me to take a couple of them on consignment. There's one on the floor that you can see. But I'm afraid it's hopeless."

"Hopeless. Well, I'd like to see it."

"Yes. Well, Monsieur Antonio, I'm afraid that your paintings aren't selling at the moment, either. These younger painters–Picasso, Braque, Derain, Matisse–are all the rage now, and my clients are clamoring for their work."

"Yes," Tony said. "I'm familiar with their work–at least that of Matisse and Picasso. But they're not much younger than I am. It took Monet and Cézanne thirty years to be recognized for their talent."

"Yes, but I can't wait thirty years to sell my paintings, Monsieur Antonio.

And these younger artists are knocking down the doors of the establishment. I want to 'get in on the ground floor,' as you Americans say."

Tony stared at M. Dantec for a few moments, then glanced at the two paintings he had set on the chairs. "Then you don't want to take these–even on consignment?"

"I already have four of your paintings on the floor, Monsieur. And they're not selling. I'm sorry."

Tony forced a laugh. "You realize, Monsieur Dantec, that the painting on the right falls into the avant-garde style being pursued by Matisse and Picasso. Perhaps not as extreme. Or as completely abandoned from that of our predecessors, but more or less along the lines of what I call 'supra-impressionism."

"'I'm sorry, Monsieur. Business is business."

Tony packed up his paintings, took his leave of M. Dantec, and left the gallery, but not before pausing to examine Gauguin's painting of two Tahitian women, bare-breasted, one of them holding a bowl of fruit, or perhaps some exotic flowers–it was hard to tell. But he liked it, the contrast of bright and dark colors, especially. And the perspective was flattened, like the one he had presented to M. Dantec. If Gauguin was somehow 'persona non grata' at the moment then he, Tony, was glad to be in his company.

He strolled home at a leisurely pace, watching the *bateaux* making their way up and down the Seine. And beyond, perhaps. Some of them plied the waters of the upper Seine well into Bourgogne. It occurred to him that he had not been out of the city in years except to visit Jackie when she was living in London. It was time.

At the last minute, having just crossed the river on Pont Neuf, he decided that he might as well deposit the paintings at Rue de Furstemberg. His studio at the apartment was getting crowded, and there was plenty of space at the carriage house. Though he still had a key, he didn't like to barge in on J-P and Sabine, so he pressed the bell. J-P came down the steps and opened the door.

"Comment ça va, J-P?"

"Ça va bien, Monsieur Tony," J-P said. "Puis-je vous aider?"

"Oui. Je veux déposer des tableaux."

"Bon. Je les prends."

"Merci."

J-P took the paintings and Tony followed him up the steps.

"Et Sabine," Tony said. "Elle va bien?"

"Oui, Monsieur. Elle est enceinte de son deuxième enfant."

"Bravo! Félicitations!"

"Merci, Monsieur."

After they reached the drawing room, J-P continued to the carriage house where he deposited the paintings. Sabine appeared from the kitchen and greeted him. She was not yet showing.

"Félicitations, Sabine!" Tony said.

"Merci, Monsieur Tony. Il y a une lettre pour vous."

"Une lettre?"

"Oui. Je vais la chercher."

She went into the butler's pantry and retrieved the letter. "La voilà."

"Merci." Tony took the letter and sat down on a sofa. The postmark was San Francisco. It was addressed to 'M. Jones, 6 Rue de Furstemberg, Paris, France.' Could it be–? No. Probably from the police. Perhaps they had a lead of some kind.

He opened the letter.

Dearest Tony,

I know you are surprised to hear from me. Did you think I was dead?

I almost thought I would be. My husband, as you may have guessed, abducted me on that day that now seems like an eternity ago. He silenced me with chloroform, and when I developed a certain resistance to that, morphine. He was easily able to get me past the authorities since we are still legally married and have the same surname.

Once we arrived in San Francisco, he locked me in my room—the only window is high above the street—and starved me until I agreed to sign over my shares in the bank to him. As a convicted felon, he could not risk forging my signature again.

He now sends a servant to my room with food, but she has been instructed to lock the door when she leaves. I am still a prisoner, but she—at great risk to her position—has agreed to post this letter for me. She has also agreed to help me escape.

And my poor Sebastian Alexandre! I do not have a clue as to where he may be. Bill claimed that he wandered off at St. Lazare and was lost in the crowd. I'm sure that is not true, since Alex was too young and too frightened of strangers to have wandered far from me. Do you have any information as to his whereabouts? I do hope—though I know it's a foolish mother's wish—that you or Inspector Rochard have somehow located him. Oh, I hope with all my heart that he is safe!

So, I must return to Paris. But as I mentioned, I am penniless. I cannot ask the baron for money since he must think I somehow planned all of this to deceive him. He has already lost a great deal of seed money for our proposed venture. Bill has simply pocketed that money.

Can you, dear Tony, send me 1,000 dollars? That would be enough to get me to Paris. I have an account with the Banque de France, but I cannot access the money from abroad. I can pay you back when I arrive.

Je t'embrasse,
Amelia

P.S. See the wiring information below. Note that the correspondent bank is The Bank of California, not The Bank of Northern California.

Tony folded up the letter and sat in a sort of daze. He was relieved to hear that she was alive and safe, but—was the letter genuine? It was hard to imagine Mme G asking him for money. And why can't she access her account from abroad? Surely the bank would have some way of verifying her identity. Then it occurred to him that her husband had forced her to write the letter, just as he had forced her to sign the bank shares over to him.

What was he to do?

He put the letter in his jacket and let Sabine know he was leaving. When J-P appeared again, he asked him to call him if anyone other than tradesmen came knocking on the door.

Then he retraced his steps to l'Île de la Cité and paid a visit to Inspector Rochard.

The inspector always received him cordially and set aside whatever business he had unless it was an emergency. But of course, there were often emergencies.

"The murder rate has gone up," he said. "As it does every year. But violent crime otherwise has gone down. What can I do for you, Monsieur Jones?"

"I have received a letter, Inspector. The writer appears to be Madame Goldman." Tony handed him the letter.

The inspector read it over. Then he sat down at his desk, picked up a magnifying glass, and examined the postmark. "It is indeed from San Francisco. Do you have a sample of Madame Goldman's handwriting?"

"I'm afraid I didn't think to bring one."

"Does it appear to be genuine to you?"

"It does."

"Then why do you doubt that it is genuine?"

Tony sighed. "Partly because she's never asked me for money before. And partly because I would think that she could easily contact her bank here and have them transfer money from her account."

The inspector put the letter down. "Have you ever wired money abroad, Monsieur? Or received it?"

"Well, no."

"It can be quite a difficult and lengthy process. And banks usually require the physical presence of the account holder to initiate the transfer. In addition, of course, they must have the account number."

"Well, she would certainly be able to supply them with that."

"Do you know *your* account number?"

"Mine? Well...I'd have to look at my cheque book."

The inspector leaned back in his chair and clasped his hands behind his head. "And do you think Madame Goldman would have had her cheque book with her the day she was kidnapped?"

Tony chuckled. "I see your point, Inspector. I'm afraid I would not make a very good detective."

"Experience, Monsieur Jones. Experience. However, it is possible that her husband forced her to write this letter. But how would he know my name? And why would he further incriminate himself by mentioning the chloroform and the morphine? Even husbands are not permitted to drug their wives for illicit purposes."

"Well, then, you believe the letter is genuine?"

"I don't know for certain. But it seems so to me." The inspector stood again and returned the letter along with the envelope. "One more thing–an extortionist would likely ask for a larger sum than one thousand dollars. That is what–five thousand francs? No, he would demand ten times that and expect to settle for half. One thousand dollars would be just enough to cover Madame Goldman's travel expenses and no more. I suggest you wire the money to her and take the chance that it may be a–how do you say in English? *Escroquerie?*"

"Escroquerie? I'm not familiar with that word."

"Ah...your language is so rich in argot. How does one say, *tromperie?*"

"A swindle."

"Yes. That's it. At any rate, I would advise you to send the money. In the meantime, I will contact my counterpart in San Francisco and ask him to keep an eye on Monsieur Goldman. Such men often reveal themselves in unintended ways."

Tony left the inspector's office still troubled by the letter. Certainly he would send the money. But should he inform Jackie of this turn of events? Not that she ever wished that any harm should come to Mme G, or her child, but there was no doubt that she saw her as a rival. And he suspected that Jackie suspected him of pining away for Mme G and hoping she would return.

And the child–Sebastian Alexandre. What has become of him? He still wasn't sure whether little Alex was his or the baron's. In any case, he hoped some kindly woman at St. Lazare recognized that he was lost and took him home with her. But if that were the case, why didn't she notify the authorities? There have been women, he knew, who were childless, and snatched up abandoned children and raised them on their own. If so, at least the child would be safe and well-fed.

As he turned onto Rue du Luxembourg, he saw a man leaving the apartment building who looked familiar. The man turned the corner and quickly disappeared down Rue de Fleurus. Nat? No, it was a younger, more athletic-looking man. Like...Armand.

CHAPTER 70

Tony went to the PTT (Postes, télégraphes et téléphones) the next day to wire Mme G the money. The inspector had suggested that this could be quicker than through the banks, so Tony withdrew the funds from his account at Crédit Lyonnais and carried the cash to the PTT office.

It was a windy spring day and Jackie was more on his mind than Mme G. He asked her the night before about the man he saw leaving the building and she said it was indeed Armand and that he had walked her home from the rehearsal. This seemed innocent enough, but he was suspicious. Armand was a notorious womanizer, and it was unlikely that he would walk a beautiful woman home out of chivalry alone. And in fact, Armand saw more of Jackie these days than he did.

And what was he to do if, as M. Dantec said, his paintings fail to sell over the next few months? Or even years? Jackie, of course, was beginning to make some money in the theatre, but her situation was just as precarious as his. If something didn't turn up, they would have to return to South Carolina. At least he had some experience in banking, though it was very limited compared to that of Mme G, much less the baron's.

Painting suddenly seemed like a frivolous thing for a grown man to spend so much time doing. He chuckled at the thought that Trey might sell one of his paintings before he did. Well, then, it was all about play, wasn't it? The strange thing was that people were willing to pay good money to see adults indulging their childish impulses on the stage, in the studio, or at sporting events. Were artists and athletes simply children who refused to grow up?

But he was not in the mood to play at children's games. Thinking of Nat, he realized that he hadn't seen him for months even though he lived just around the corner. And Nat still owed him money. Even another 100 francs would be helpful. He turned into Nat's building on Rue de Fleurus.

He waited after pressing the bell and looked around the neighborhood. The buildings on either side had been refurbished and looked prosperous, more upscale. Only Nat's building still looked a bit shabby, but there was some scaffolding set up with a couple of painters at work on the second floor. 'Painters.' That made him think that he might be better employed on the more practical side of the profession.

"Tony, old man!"

He looked up and saw Nat's head sticking out of his atelier window.

"Come on up. I'll buzz you in."

A buzzer sounded–a new and convenient device–and Tony entered the building and climbed the stairs to Nat's loft. He pressed a second button and Nat opened the door. He immediately gave him a big bear hug along with a pat on the back.

"Long time, no see!" Nat said. "And to think that we're neighbors. Where have you been?"

"I was about to ask you the same thing." Tony stepped inside and looked around. Many of the same paintings that he had seen before were still hanging in their places, with a few new ones standing against the walls on the floor. These were departures from his earlier work, which was more representational and, frankly, rather prosaic. The new ones, though, were bold, even crude, abstractions.

"I see you've been at work," Tony said. "Interesting stuff."

"You think so? Well, once you've seen the kind of things that Sérusier and Derain are doing, there's no turning back. What do you think of this one?" He pulled a canvas away from the wall and set it on a chair. It was a mass of bright yellow and red, with no discernable structure other than some vertical lines in black. "It's called *Synthétisme*."

"It's actually been around for a while, Nat."

"Has it? Well, it's new to me. I just saw—"

"I like the colors, but...what does it represent?"

Nat laughed. "Represent? Why, nothing, nothing at all. That's the idea. We're no longer to be slavishly tied to representational forms. Just color and random shapes and *feeling*. That's the most important part."

"I understand that. But what 'feeling' exactly are you trying to convey here?"

Nat looked at the painting for a moment, then at Tony and shrugged his shoulders. "Who knows?" He laughed and then put the painting back against the wall. "How about a glass of wine?"

"Sounds good."

They spent the next half hour discussing Synthetism, Cubism, Fauvism and other 'isms' that had recently arrived on the scene. Tony was not sure he could subscribe to any of them, while acknowledging that he had experimented with what he continued to call 'Supra-impressionism.'

"And what is that?" Nat asked.

"I'm not sure exactly. I suppose I mean a transitional phase between Impressionism and whatever comes next."

Nat laughed. "Then why don't you call it 'Supra-Guess What?'"

Tony found this amusing and admitted that he didn't know where his own painting was going, only that he felt it was too soon to completely abandon the immense gains art had made over the last half century. Impressionism would remain the foundation of fine painting for many years to come.

As they were about to open another bottle of wine, the door opened and in walked a young woman carrying a bag of groceries. Tony was struck by her appearance, which was not only one of beauty but of race. She was as black–even more so–than he. He guessed that she was about twenty-one or twenty-two.

"Vivien," Nat said, "I want you to meet my best friend, Tony Jones."

Vivien stopped and stared for a moment. "Let me put the groceries down first." She went to the kitchen and set the groceries down on the counter. After removing a few items and storing them away, she returned to the main room. "Enchantée, Monsieur."

She said this with the slow, careful enunciation of a first-year French student.

Tony stood. "Enchanté. Mademoiselle. Comment allez vous?"

"Bien, Monsieur. But I'm afraid that's the limit of my French at the moment. Nat's a good teacher, though."

"I keep telling her to speak only French," Nat said. "But she persists in breaking into English, just like she did now. Tu ne dois pas parler en anglais, Vivien."

"Well, how else am I going to get to know your friend here?" Vivien said. "It would take hours if we spoke only French."

Tony laughed. "She's right, Nat. Give her a break until we get to know each other better."

"Pourquoi pas?" Nat said. "Juste pour cette fois-ci."

"I got the 'juste pour cette' part," Vivien said. "What's 'fois-ci'?"

"This once," Nat said.

"Oh. Well, Mr. Jones–I hope you'll stay for dinner."

"That's very kind of you, Vivien," Tony said, "but I'm expected home."

"I thought you said Jackie was at rehearsal," Nat said. "And you've got that nanny–what's her name?"

"Camille."

"Right. Say, why don't we go around the corner and pop into the new cabaret?"

"A new one?" Tony said. "What's it called?"

"Le Café de la Rue Madame. They've got a *chanteuse* that's terrific!"

"Let me change," Vivien said.

"Don't bother, Viv," Nat said. "It's very casual."

Vivien nevertheless went upstairs to freshen up a bit. While she was gone,

Tony plied Nat with questions.

"How did you meet her, Nat?"

"At the Académie Julian. She's studying art there and was living at the American Girls Club until I convinced her to move in with me."

"Where is she from?"

"From your neck of the woods, actually. Charleston."

"Well, what do you know. She's very pretty."

"You bet. She knocked my socks off when I saw her."

"Kind of a whirlwind romance, no?"

"Well, it hasn't been as easy as that. I asked her to come look at my paintings. Later, I asked her to go to the opéra with me. She liked that. Then–"

Vivien appeared again at the top of the stairs. She was wearing a silk taffeta dress, midnight blue, and she had pinned her hair up. Large hoop earrings dangled from her lobes.

"I thought we were going to be casual," Nat said.

"I like to look my best when I go out. Calico is for grocery shopping."

"Well, you look terrific whatever you're wearing. Shall we go?"

At the Café de la Rue Madame, they found a table in the corner near a window. It was early and the *chanteuse* would not go on until nine o'clock. This gave time for Tony to find out more about Vivien.

"How did you end up in Paris?" Tony said, as they waited for their drinks.

"Oh, my father is a photographer," Vivien said. "Mother teaches at a local school. They both urged me to come."

"That's interesting. Did you go to your mother's school?"

"Oh, yes. It's a small school. A finishing school for young ladies."

"A finishing school. For black girls?"

Vivien bristled at the question. "Of course. Why not?"

"I didn't mean that there was anything wrong with that, just that it seems rather unusual."

"I guess it is. But why shouldn't black girls have the same opportunities as white girls? My mother thought good manners and elocution were the only difference between us. So she went to some investors who agreed with her and started the school."

"Ah!" Nat said. "Here come our apéros. You'll like this, Tony. Specialty of the house."

Tony did indeed like the specialty of the house, which was a combination of champagne and crème de cassis. But he was still focused on Vivien.

"So you took art classes at your mother's finishing school?"

"Well, yes, but there was only one art teacher, and she was kind of limited, I guess you'd say. So I went to Philadelphia to art school. And from there to here. But I want to hear about you, Mr. Jones. I understand that you won a medal at the Exposition."

"Please, Vivien—call me Tony."

"Tony."

"That's better. Yes, I did win a medal, but I can't say that it's helped me that much. My most important commission was a portrait of Monsieur Loubet."

"Monsieur Loubet? Who's he?"

"Only the president of France," Nat said.

"The president?" Vivien said. "That's fantastic. What's he like?"

"A very nice man," Tony said. "Perhaps too nice. At any rate, the government wouldn't pay for it so he bought it himself and sent it off to his residence in Montèlimar. I'm afraid only his family members will see it."

"Oh, that's too bad. But it's a feather in your cap, isn't it?"

"I suppose so."

The conversation shifted to Nat and his work, which Vivien seemed to regard with some awe. Nat regaled her with his adventures among the gypsies, failing to mention his 'marriage' to Carlotta. After a while Tony began to get the peculiar feeling that Nat and Vivien's relationship was not what it appeared to be. For one thing, Vivien would sometimes refer to him as 'Mister,' as she had with him. For another, she talked of returning to the Girls' Club the next day, where she still had a room.

At last the *chanteuse* appeared on the small dance floor and sang some familiar French songs. Nat seemed mesmerized, but Tony paid little attention and took the opportunity to converse further with Vivien. He was impressed with her intelligence and apparent good sense, but he was still puzzled as to why she had moved in with Nat. They seemed to keep each other at a distance.

At the end of the evening, Tony announced that he was already out later than he had planned and needed to get home. He was a little tipsy from the four or five rounds that Nat had ordered and gave Vivien a kiss on the cheek. She simply smiled and did not return the gesture. When he got back to the apartment, he found Jackie waiting for him.

"Where have you been?" she said sternly, which evoked memories of Mme G's admonishment of him the night of his debacle in Pigalle.

CHAPTER 71

Several weeks passed and there was no sign of Mme G. Tony had informed Jackie of her desperate situation and his wiring of the money. She was very skeptical, and it seemed that her skepticism was well-founded. No word.

In the meantime, Jackie's star was ascending. *La Sorcière* was a success, and though she had a minor role, the critics singled her out for praise. Miss Bernhardt was a little annoyed at this, but Jackie made sure that she did not upstage her mentor, and their relations remained cordial, if not warm.

Another bit of luck came in the form of a successful audition at the Odéon. She and Armand won the lead roles in *La Rabouilleuse*. *La Sorcière's* final performance would take place a few weeks before the première of the adaptation of Balzac's novel. Jackie was unusually busy.

Armand's campaign to win Jackie's affections did not abate. During rehearsals he was the model of professionalism and restraint, but afterwards he showered her with gifts–mostly flowers–and invitations to his father's townhouse, which was in La Place des Vosges, site of many distinguished residences, including one that was the home of Victor Hugo. She declined all of these, but consented to tête-à-têtes at local cafés, ostensibly to discuss their roles.

Rather than arouse Tony's suspicions, Jackie gave the flowers away to startled strangers on her way home. Sometimes she threw them into the Seine.

She noticed that Tony was spending more and more time at Nat's atelier. At first she thought they must be collaborating on an art project. Or that Tony was running out of space in his tiny studio in the apartment and needed a larger space–she was relieved that he frequented Mme G's house less often even though she wasn't there.

But one day she received a telephone call from M. Dantec, saying that a customer had purchased one of Tony's paintings and wanted to see more. She thought this was urgent enough to deliver the news to him right away, and she knew he was at Nat's. Nat didn't have a telephone, so she decided to walk around the corner and give him the good news.

She pressed the buzzer, waited a few moments, heard the reply, and pushed the door open. The foyer was recently refurbished, with an antique console against the far wall and a gilt mirror hanging above it. This was a far cry from the shabby appearance of the entry when she and Tony had lived there with Nat a few years earlier. She ascended the four flights of stairs and passed some workmen who were in the process of installing an elevator. Well–that would be a most welcome convenience!

And she was in for another surprise. When Nat opened the door to the atelier, wearing a paint-smeared smock, she looked over his shoulder and saw Tony at an easel, standing as was his custom, and peering over the canvas at a beautiful young black woman seated on an armchair, dressed in an elaborate costume with a headdress adorned with pearls. Or at least they appeared to be pearls. Costume jewelry, perhaps. Large hoop earrings dangled from her earlobes.

"Jackie!" Nat said. "What a surprise. Come in and see what your husband and I are doing."

Jackie cautiously entered, knowing that Tony hated to be interrupted when he was painting. He turned to look at her briefly, said nothing, and turned back to his work.

Nat whispered to her as if she had just walked into a theatre in the middle of a performance and he was an usher guiding her to her seat. "This was Tony's idea. Exotic, don't you think? We rented the costume–and those are real pearls, believe it or not. Come on and have a seat. I'll introduce you to Vivien as soon as they take a break."

Jackie took her seat and continued to stare at Vivien. Nat went to the kitchen and broke out a bottle of wine.

After a few minutes, Tony put down his brush and told Vivien to relax–they would take a break. Then he turned to Jackie. "Trey all right?"

"He's fine," she said. "Camille took him out to play in the Gardens."

"Then what is it?"

She resented his curt response and wasn't sure whether it was because of the interruption or that it was a sign of his suspicions regarding Armand.

"I've got a message from Monsieur Dantec," she said.

"Oh? That's enough for today, Vivien. Why don't you get out of that costume–it must be hot–and join us for a glass of wine? I can see that Nat's wasting no time breaking out the libations."

"Juste un peu d'apéro," Nat said, noisily uncorking the wine.

Tony walked over to Jackie and gave her a peck on the cheek. "I'm glad you came. I want you to meet Vivien."

"Don't you want to know what Monsieur Dantec wanted?"

"Oh. I forgot. What is it?"

"He says a customer is interested in your work. He wants to see more."

"Good. It's about time. Does he want me to come to the gallery?"

"He didn't say. You'd better call him."

"All right." Tony sat down at the table–there had been no change in the 'decor' of the atelier since Jackie had last seen it. Nat brought some glasses along with the wine. Vivien was still upstairs changing out of her costume.

"Who is this girl?" Jackie said.

"Vivien?" Tony said. "She's Nat's uh–"

"Kind of a live-in model," Nat said. "We have an arrangement. Let me show you the ones I've done of her." He went to the far wall where he had set up his own easel and turned it around. It was indeed a portrait of a black woman, but it hardly resembled Vivien. It was disjointed, fragmented, rather a horror–or so it seemed to Jackie.

"Don't look for any familiar signposts," Nat said with a laugh. "This is the new style. It represents the violence of Africa as well as the beauty."

"What do you know about Africa, Nat?" It was Vivien as she descended the steps from the loft. She was wearing a robe de chambre with a sort of batik pattern of leaves and animals.

"Just what you've taught me," Nat said. "Especially the violence part." He laughed uproariously at his own remark.

"Vivien's from South Carolina, Jackie," Tony said. "Charleston."

Jackie stood as Vivien approached. "Really? How do you do, Vivien."

"Enchantée," Vivien said with a smile.

Nat poured the wine. "You see how her French lessons are paying off."

"Don't make fun of me, Nat," Vivien said.

"Fun? I'm perfectly serious. Je suis à votre service, Mademoiselle." He handed Vivien a glass. "Un verre de vin?"

"Merci, Monsieur," Vivien said.

"Bon." Nat presented Jackie and Tony with their glasses and offered the customary toast. "À votre santé!"

After an initial awkwardness, Jackie and Vivien seemed to hit it off. Jackie, of course, had gone to a similar finishing school in Charleston, but had been unaware that there was one for black girls. Like the *lycée*, Vivien's school, the Academy for Young Colored Ladies offered French as well as classes in geography, history, literature, and homemaking. Vivien's parents, she discovered, were both descendants of free blacks, her father the son of a prosperous dry goods merchant, her mother, the daughter of a Philadelphia attorney.

After finishing her glass of wine, Jackie declined Nat's offer of a refill and said that she had to be at the Odéon at five o'clock. She gave Tony a perfunctory kiss on the cheek and excused herself.

On the way home, she wondered about this girl Vivien. Was she Nat's lover? Apparently so, since she was living with him though only part-time. An odd arrangement, she thought. Two or three days with Nat, and the rest of the week at the Girls' Club. She wondered what sort of policy they had at the Club, which was after all, designed to offer a safe and secure sanctuary for young art students from abroad. Chastity seemed not to be one of their concerns. But then that's the French for you!

After looking in on Trey, who had by this time come back in from the Gardens with Camille, she spent a half hour or so reading over her lines for the play. She had trouble concentrating, though. Tony seemed a little too interested in Vivien, it seemed to her. All through their little tête-à-tête he took every opportunity to praise her intelligence, her talent (what evidence was there of that?), and of course, her beauty. And what were they doing now in Nat's atelier since she left? Why didn't Tony accompany her home? He was finished for the day, wasn't he?

These thoughts plagued her all the way to the Odéon.

CHAPTER 72

The vicomte gazed out the window of his cell–he preferred to call it his apartment–at the pastoral scene that lay before him: the Bois de Vincennes.

His 'apartment' was possibly the best in the hospital thanks to his friend, Comte d'Oise-Montmorency, who despite his aristocratic title, served in the Chamber of Deputies.

There was no censorship here as there was at La Santé, and he had little to fear from the other inmates, though some were extremely annoying. He, in fact, was allowed to have whatever reading material he wanted, and being familiar with the history of Charenton and its most famous inmate, he obtained a volume of *Justine*.

This was most interesting reading indeed. He fully subscribed to the marquis' philosophy of absolute freedom, but he objected to extending this freedom to *la racaille*; i.e., 'the rabble.' Nor did he approve of the marquis' sexual assaults against children–though he defined 'children' as those under the age of twelve.

The idea of writing and performing plays in the common areas appealed to him. He had written some poetry in his youth and even once wrote a one-act play that his father read and severely punished him for when he was about eight or nine. He couldn't remember exactly what the play was about, but he remembered the beating his father gave him and he vowed to get his revenge. But being mortally afraid of his father, he directed his rage against some animals he had trapped on the family's heavily wooded property. He remembered fondly the satisfaction he got in one instance where he managed to capture a squirrel, tied him spread-eagled to a wooden stake, and slowly eviscerated him with his pen knife.

Revenge was sweet, even if extracted from a surrogate.

He was sitting in a leather armchair reading *Justine* and smoking his long-stemmed pipe, when he heard a knock at the door.

"Entrez," he said.

The door slowly opened and a short, pot-bellied man of about forty-five entered the room. This was Dr. McCool, who was the interim director while a search went on for a permanent one. Dr. McCool had some impressive credentials, having been educated in Scotland and studied psychiatry in Vienna with Dr. Freud.

"Comment allez-vous aujourd'hui, Monsieur le Vicomte?"

"Très bien," the vicomte said. He regarded Dr. McCool as the manager of an inn who was unused to catering to aristocrats. "Asseyez-vous."

"Non, merci. Je n'ai pas le temps. Mais–"

"Speak English, man. I like to hear that Scottish lilt. My grandmother was Scottish, you know."

"Yes, I am aware of that, Monsieur le Vicomte. We know quite a lot about you, you know."

"Hmm. Well, what is it?"

"I am afraid that the committee has denied your request to stage theatrical performances in the common area. I personally have no objection, but they feel that it would be disturbing to the other residents."

"The other residents are already disturbed. An entertainment may distract them from their monotonous lives."

"True. But your suggestion of reviving the plays of Monsieur de Sade, complete with scenes depicting sexual intercourse and whippings, seems to them somewhat provocative."

"Well, of course it would be provocative, although I prefer the word 'stimulating.' That's just what these degraded misfits need–something to revive the fires within that have been all but extinguished by society's arbitrary rules. They are animals, after all, and must express their carnal impulses–in a healthy way, of course. I witnessed Monsieur Trintignat masturbating on his little window perch the other day, as we all did. Think if he could actually participate in sexual intercourse with the actors! He might even recover his sanity."

Dr. McCool tugged on his goatee and seemed to consider the proposal. "I'm afraid that there is no clinical evidence to support your theory, Monsieur le Vicomte. However, I will pass it on to the committee for their consideration. In the meantime, I would recommend some more salubrious reading material–like Victor Hugo, for example. We have a complete set of his works in the library."

"Hmph. I read all that rubbish as a child. And now, 'Le Docteur,' will you be so kind as to leave me in peace?" He tapped the bowl of his pipe into an ashtray at his side. "I seem to be out of tobacco. You will send someone with a fresh packet, won't you? Cavendish. I'm sure you are familiar with the brand."

"I'll see what I can do, Monsieur le Vicomte."

"Good. Now go away." The vicomte went back to his reading.

CHAPTER 73

As the years went by, Tony wondered if Mme G had been swallowed up by the San Francisco earthquake. Certainly she would have left San Francisco before then–if she had been able. Perhaps her husband had intercepted the money he had wired her and again locked her in her room. It was reported that more than 80% of San Francisco had been destroyed and 3,000 lives had been lost. The authorities had been unable to identify more than a fraction of the dead.

Jackie's career had taken off with the success of *La Rabouilleuse*. She and Armand were the darlings of Paris' theatrical scene. They were thought to be lovers and the impresarios did nothing to discourage this notion. Tony had his suspicions that the rumors were true, but then Jackie suspected him of having an affair with Vivien, who was now living alone in the atelier while Nat was in America attending his brother's funeral–and collecting his share of their inheritance.

Tony, in fact, had been faithful to Jackie and she to him. Nevertheless, they continued to uncover–they thought–evidence of betrayal. Jackie had not visited the atelier since that first meeting with Vivien, but Tony had frequented it because it was larger than his studio at home, and the light was better. It didn't help his case when he brought a painting home to the apartment that depicted an only slightly abstracted image of Vivien in the nude.

For her part, Jackie had a hard time explaining why she had visited Armand's townhouse at the Place des Vosges and didn't return until seven o'clock in the morning. "A cast party," she said without further explanation or apology.

They were beginning to act like some of the middle-aged couples of Paris they knew who, being long estranged and either unable or unwilling to divorce, lived together under a truce like two armies at a stalemate.

Trey, now six years old, seemed to regard them not as parents, but as a kindly aunt and uncle, devoted to him but content to leave his daily care to Camille, who he began to regard as his real mother. And as he was speaking French most of his waking hours, he also began to regard English as a foreign language.

Almost as a corrective measure to this condition, it so happened that Tony's mother, Georgia, decided to visit Paris on one of her husband's buying trips to stock up on the latest fashions. Georgia cared little for *la haute couture*, but she ardently wanted to see her grandson.

They arrived in Paris one breezy autumn afternoon and put up at the Bristol, where Hiram was well-known to the staff. After getting settled, they hired a carriage, eschewing the proliferating motorized taxis, and arrived at Tony and Jackie's apartment just as the sun was setting over dappled leaves in the Gardens.

Georgia, as unpretentious as any rural schoolteacher could be, was nevertheless giddy with excitement over her first trip abroad, and especially with Paris.

"The women here!" she exclaimed after the usual exchange of greetings and kisses. "They dress to go grocery shopping as if they were attending a ball!'

Jackie laughed, but not so loudly as to appear haughty. She always had liked her mother-in-law and found her refreshing in her simplicity. "They do so not to impress, but because they appreciate beautiful things—especially in day-to-day life. They're the same way about food—the poorest working woman will spend half a day scouring the markets for the freshest food. It's all about making the most of daily life."

"Well said," Hiram said. "That's what I've been trying to impress upon Georgia for years, but you've put it so much better. She hasn't worn half the dresses I've bought for her since we were married; they collect dust in the cupboard."

"That's not true, Hi," Georgia said. "I just save them for special occasions."

"Like Christmas and Easter," Hiram said with a laugh. "Why not when you go shopping—like the French?"

"Mama's a practical woman," Tony said. "And thrift is a virtue that she learned during the war."

"Well, of course," Georgia said. "We had to save every scrap of cloth to make our own dresses. And food! There were no grocery stores or open-air markets like they have here with every imaginable fruit and vegetable. We grew all our own food."

"Those days are gone, Mama," Tony said. "And I should think you would be glad."

"Of course I'm glad. The war was horrible. But some lessons are hard-learned and difficult to unlearn. And what if there's another war? Or hurricane, for that matter?

"They don't have hurricanes in France, Georgia," Hiram said.

"But they do have wars,' she said. "Goodness! Wars with Germany, wars with England, wars with Spain—who knows when the next one will be?"

"Not likely, my dear," Hiram said. "The last one was in 1871. The French and Germans are quite friendly now."

Tony stood. "Enough talk of war. Can I get you anything, Mama? Some more wine?"

"Oh, I don't think so. I'm already feeling a bit tipsy. We even had champagne for breakfast! And where's little Antonio? I'm dying to meet him."

"He's out in the Gardens with Camille," Jackie said. "But they'll be coming in at any moment. He's anxious to meet you, too."

When Camille returned with Trey, Trey politely shook his grandmother's hand and stared at her with a sense of wonder.

"Are you from America?" he said in English. He had been warned that his grandmother spoke no French.

"I am indeed, little man," Georgia said. "And in fact, I've brought you something."

"Qu'est-ce que c'est?" Trey said.

"Speak English, Trey," Tony said.

"Okey-dokey, Papa."

Georgia picked up a box that she had brought with her and placed it on the coffee table. It had a red ribbon around it and a tag marked 'To Antonio III, from your Grandmama.'

Trey hurriedly tore off the ribbon and removed the lid. He peered into the box with a dubious expression on his face. "Des plumes?"

"English, old man," Tony said.

"Feathers?"

"It's a headdress," Georgia said. "Like the Indians in North America wear."

Still puzzled, Trey lifted the headdress out of the box and stared at it for a moment. Finally he realized it was to be worn and placed it on his head. He ran to a mirror in the hallway. Then he came back into the drawing room, beaming. "Papa—Je suis un Amérindien!"

"English," Jackie said.

"Oh, don't keep correcting him," Georgia said. "I only had a little French in high school, but I understand what he's saying."

All laughed at this while Trey ran around the room whooping like the Indians he had heard about. While Tony had shown him an illustrated copy of Cooper's *Last of the Mohicans*, he learned that Indians 'whooped' from his classmates at the *école communale*.

"Careful, Trey," Hiram said. "You may start another war between America and France."

"I'm afraid he's not familiar with the French and Indian War yet, Hi,"

Tony said.

But by this time, Trey wasn't listening and had run down the hall to terrorize Camille.

After dinner, Trey was put to bed and the two couples went for a stroll in the Gardens, which now had electrically lighted streetlamps. Jackie and Georgia walked ahead, and Tony and Hiram lagged some two or three meters behind.

"I understand you won a medal at the Exposition," Hiram said.

"Oh–that was some time ago, Hi. Things have been a bit slow since."

"Well, if you're struggling, I'd be glad to–"

"That won't be necessary, Hi. But thanks anyway. Jackie's making more than enough to pay the rent. In the meantime, I'll just have to keep my nose to the grindstone."

They walked a little further in silence.

"How's the Emporium doing?" Tony said in an effort to change the subject.

"Quite well. Business is booming as a matter of fact. That's why I'm here–to stock up on the latest fashions while people are still buying. Your mother's right. There could be another war at any time despite what I said about the Germans. I was just trying to put a lid on that kind of talk."

"I'm glad you did. But it does seem that there's a lot of bellicose rhetoric coming out of Germany these days."

"They're a warlike nation. They have this notion of 'lebensraum' that they think entitles them to other people's property."

"Yes, I've heard that. But Hi, tell me what's happening in the States."

"Well, nationally, Roosevelt's quite popular and is breaking up the big trusts and rooting out corruption. But in South Carolina, I'm afraid to say, it's more of the same old cronyism and promotion of the myth that the war was about Northern aggression and states' rights." Hiram chuckled as they paused before a miniature replica of the Statue of Liberty. "And as I'm a Yankee carpetbagger myself, I can't say as I agree."

"You're no carpetbagger, Hiram. You helped my people and always treated blacks and whites alike."

"Well, I've tried to. But I'm a businessman, too. And it gets harder and harder to convince my white customers that there's no risk of disease in sharing a dressing room with blacks. Many of them are going to my competitors."

Tony laughed. "What competitors? The Emporium is famous for its goods and services. Where else can they go?"

"Oh, there are others cropping up. But we still dominate the market for quality goods. It's mostly Confederate veterans and their families who get indignant."

"And the others?"

"They tend to be indifferent towards blacks at best. But there are murmurings all the same. And I'm afraid our governor isn't helping any."

"Governor? Who is he?"

"A fellow named Hayward. You know the family. Wants to revive the Confederacy. And I'm afraid his successor will be no better."

After a tour around the basin with its illuminated fountains, the two couples returned to the apartment.

"How long will you be here, Hi?" Tony said, as Hiram and Georgia prepared to leave for their hotel.

"About two weeks," Hi said.

"I want to see the Ferris wheel," Georgia said. "And the Petit Palais. Isn't that where your paintings are, Tony?"

"Yes. A couple."

"Including one of one of his mistresses," Jackie said.

Everyone looked at her in astonishment.

"Jackie–" Tony began.

"Why not be honest about it?" Jackie said. "They want to know how we live in Paris. Well, this is it. Tony has his lovers and he–at least thinks–I have mine. That's the way of the French. Now if you'll excuse me, I need to look in on Trey. It's been a lovely evening."

Their eyes followed her as she left the room.

"She's been under a lot of strain lately with non-stop performances," Tony said.

Georgia and Hi seemed not to know what to say.

"We'll get together again in a day or two," Tony said. "She'll have settled down by then."

Georgia gave Tony a hug and a kiss on the cheek. "If you need someone to talk to, Tony, you know where to find us. I know it's hard to be living abroad and so far from your family. But remember, I'm your mother and I love you."

Tony gave her a kiss and shook Hiram's hand. "Thank you both for coming. And don't worry about us. Just one of those spats that's probably long overdue. Good night."

CHAPTER 74

$\mathcal{N}$ow truly estranged from Jackie, Tony turned more and more to Vivien for solace and as a confidante. And since he had confessed that he had had an affair with Mme G years earlier and Mme G's whereabouts were unknown, he assumed that Jackie's recent outburst was occasioned by his attention to Vivien. The irony of it was that though he often painted Vivien in the nude, there had been no physical relationship between them. Not that he wasn't tempted, but she seemed to exhibit no romantic interest in him whatsoever. She even brought around a male student from the Académie Julian once and introduced him to Tony as if he were her avuncular mentor.

As far as Jackie's relationship with Armand was concerned, he had his doubts despite the newspapers' almost daily revelation of their *liason amoureuse*. He knew Jackie, or at least he thought he did. Notwithstanding her halting adaptation to French *moeurs*, she was very conservative at heart, at least regarding sexual matters. Her time at the girls' lycée in Charleston, her upbringing by her Aunt Edwina, who she believed to be her mother for so many years, and her fierce protection of her virginity right up until weeks after they were married, all seemed to confirm this notion. However, he couldn't be sure. In many ways, especially since she had returned to Paris and her career had blossomed, she was a changed person. And Armand was handsome, talented, and persistent.

One morning, while having breakfast on the balcony overlooking the Gardens, Tony decided to test this hypothesis. After the usual interlude of silence, he put down his newspaper and turned to her. "Why don't you invite Armand over for dinner?"

Jackie looked at him as if he had just proposed adopting a vicious dog. "Armand? Are you serious?"

"Of course I'm serious. He's obviously a good friend of yours and a partner in the theatre. I imagine this play of yours will be ending soon and it would be a shame if we never see him again."

Jackie regarded him with suspicion. "Why wouldn't we ever see him again?

He's not going anywhere."

"Exactly. That's why we should invite him over. We need to let him know he's welcome here even though the play has completed its run."

Jackie took a sip of her coffee and replaced it in its saucer. She gazed out over the Gardens. "And who else would you invite? Vivien?"

"That's an idea. She's developing into a first-rate artist. Even won a ribbon recently at a student competition at the Académie. You need to get to know her better."

Jackie said nothing as she tried to penetrate Tony's mind. He was usually forthright, not given to devious stratagems, but who knows? They both had changed over the past few years. And she couldn't help thinking that he was an intriguing, multi-faceted, highly intelligent man who she had found fascinating and irresistible from the beginning. Armand was a child by comparison, transparent in his motives and self-absorption.

"All right," she said. "So when should this soirée take place? And will we invite your mother?"

"I think we'll wait until they leave, which will be next week. You might invite some of your fellow thespians, though. And Vivien might want to invite some of her student friends as well."

Jackie turned her gaze again to the Gardens. "How about the Saturday after Georgia and Hi leave?"

"Perfect," Tony said.

That afternoon at a rehearsal for the final performance of *La Rabouilleuse*, Jackie informed Armand of Tony's invitation.

"He's going to kill me," Armand said.

Jackie laughed. "He's not going to kill anyone. He hesitates to kill insects."

Armand was dubious. "He is a large man. Does he fence?"

"Fence? I don't know. Maybe when he was in college. But Armand, he has no intention of harming you. He wants to be your friend."

"Hah! When the newspapers daily trumpet that he is a cuckold? He has been publicly humiliated. Why would he not want to kill me?"

"He doesn't pay any attention to what the newspapers say. And besides, we both know that he isn't a cuckold."

Armand came closer to her and put his arms around her waist. They were backstage in the hallway between their dressing rooms. "Chérie, you have resisted my advances from the beginning. But you have allowed me to kiss you, to fondle you–you have even slept in my bed. Is it not time to tell your husband the truth?"

"What truth?"

"That we are in love and that nothing will keep us apart–not even the sacrament of marriage."

Jackie gave him a kiss on the forehead. She was actually two inches taller than he. "You're a sweet man, Armand, for all of your posturing. But I don't love you."

"No?"

"No. I love my husband, though he makes me wild with jealousy at times."

"Jealous? Of whom?"

"Of every woman he takes a second look at. And especially the models."

"The models? For his art?"

"Yes. There's one now–"

"I don't care to hear it. If he has betrayed you, then he doesn't deserve you. If he makes you sad, then I detest him. I will come to your party. And when I arrive, I will challenge him to a duel."

"A duel? Oh, my, you can't be serious."

"Have I not fought duels before? And I am always victorious. When is the soirée?"

Jackie reluctantly informed Armand of the date, but then regretted it when she was walking home. A duel? It was true that Armand had fought a duel some years earlier, but it ended without serious injury. But what if he did challenge Tony to a duel? Would Tony accept? Probably not–he would laugh it off. But what if Armand persisted and even slapped his face? Tony was a peaceful man but he had his limits.

She reproached herself for relishing the prospect of two men fighting a duel over her. How barbarous! How ridiculous! But... how deliciously romantic!

CHAPTER 75

When Jackie informed Tony of Armand's reaction to her invitation, as she predicted, he laughed it off.

"'He's serious, Tony," she said. "You know that he fought a duel with that what's-his-name a few years ago."

"Yes, I remember that. I also remember that as soon as his opponent suffered a minor cut to his wrist, the duel was called off. He's not a killer like the vicomte."

"But he still might be dangerous. I think we should call the party off."

"Why? It might liven things up if he challenges me to a duel around the time everyone is getting bored with the usual small talk.'

"Be serious. He may not even wait till some appointed time and place. What if he gets angry when you laugh at him–and I know you will–and he feels he must avenge his honor then and there?"

"Not likely. I don't suppose he'll bring a rapier with him, which is his weapon of choice. And he's not as strong as I am. I'll simply throw him out if it comes to that."

They were again sitting on the balcony having their breakfast as the weather continued to be ideal. Jackie finished off her *fraise à la crème*, which was especially delicious this time of year. "I don't want to see a brawl in my own home. Besides it would probably get in the papers."

"You worry too much. It'll be a wonderful party."

Jackie wasn't so sure, but she offered no further objections. The truth was that not only did she like the idea of the two men fighting over her, but she saw their confrontation as a way of testing Tony's commitment to her. Of course he would laugh at Armand's challenge should he make one. But would he defend her honor? That is, would he laugh at the suggestion that she had been unfaithful to him, or demand that Armand withdraw the charge? And what would Armand say? 'Everyone knows that I've been sleeping with your wife'? Taken literally, it was true. But as a metaphor for sexual intercourse, it was not. Well...she would wait and see.

Georgia and Hiram said their goodbyes on the Thursday before the party was to take place. Hiram presented them with an elaborate gilt mirror that they mounted over the fireplace in the drawing room.

With the in-laws gone, Jackie set about the preparations for the party.

When six o'clock Saturday evening arrived, the guests began to trickle in. First, Vivien arrived dressed in an African-inspired dashiki, or kaftan, with bold colors, predominantly red, with a *décolleté* bodice embroidered with stylized animal figures. She was what many would call a full-figured woman, and Jackie immediately took umbrage at this display of sexuality. Vivien was accompanied by two friends from the Académie, a man and a woman. The man was white, a tall slim American from Kansa City dressed in a white painter's smock with a red bandana tied around his neck; the young woman, black like Vivien, only of a darker hue, was more demurely dressed in an emerald satin evening gown, which Jackie estimated to cost at least 500 francs. She said she was from Senegal and was fluent in French.

Several actors from the *La Rabouilleuse* cast arrived after the first group, but Armand was not among them. There were the usual libations and cocktail chatter before Armand finally arrived–alone. He paid his respects to Jackie with a prolonged kiss of her hand, and brushed by Tony, who was standing next to her, with a curt, "Bonsoir, Monsieur Jones."

The party, now composed of a dozen people, including Tony and Jackie, moved to the dining room where Camille and Sabine, recruited for the purpose, served the meals. Champagne was poured, toasts were offered by various cast members, and finally Armand stood and offered his:

"À Jacqueline, la coqueluche de la ville!"

Everyone clapped and Jackie was at a loss as to what 'coqueluche' meant, so she whispered the question to Tony.

"He says you're the darling of Paris. Roughly speaking."

"Roughly?"

"'Heartthrob,' whatever. It looks like he's working up to a declaration of some sort."

Jackie stared at Tony for a moment, unsure if he meant that Armand was about to issue his challenge. But then Armand surprised them both. Raising his glass again, he said in English:

"The newspapers lately have charged that Jacqueline and I have been having an affair. Nothing could be further from the truth. We have become fast friends during our theatrical adventures, nothing more. So, I offer this toast to the health and happiness of our American friends. À votre santé, mes amis!"

Jackie and Tony looked at each other, somewhat astonished, but then Vivien stood and astonished them even more.

"I want to thank Tony and Jackie for this lovely party, first of all. Merci beaucoup, Jacqueline et Tony." Everyone clapped. "Second of all, I want to thank Tony, especially, for teaching me about line and color in a way that none of my previous teachers have been able to get through my thick head." Laughter all around. "And finally, I want to announce that I am pregnant."

Everyone was silent for a moment, then broke out into applause. "À votre santé! Félicitations!"

This left Jackie, drawing the obvious conclusion, furious. She glared at Tony, and was about to rise from her chair, when Vivien, who remained standing, spoke again:

"One more thing. Nat and I will soon be getting married."

Now, as half of those present did not know who Nat was, and those who did had not seen hide nor hair of him for over a month, there was no applause or toasting. At first. Then one of Vivien's friends from the Académie raised his glass and broke the ice with a toast to the two of them.

Vivien, seemingly unaware that there was any need for explanation, simply thanked everyone and sat down again

"What does this mean?" Jackie whispered to Tony.

"I haven't the faintest idea," Tony said. "I suppose they could have slept together before he left for the States. But I haven't heard anything from him since then. Apparently, Vivien has."

After dinner, Tony kept a careful eye on Armand, unsure of his intentions. The man seemed unpredictable, alternating between outbursts of passion and quiet reserve. Tony noticed, however, that his attention had shifted from Jackie to another member of the cast, a pretty young French woman more nearly his age.

Tony made a point of not staying too close to Vivien, who nevertheless sought him out as she was about to leave.

"It was a lovely party," she said. "I hope I didn't shock you too much with my announcement."

"Well," Tony said. He glanced at Jackie, who was paying close attention. "I must say it caught me by surprise. When is Nat returning to Paris?"

"Next week," Vivien said. "I'll tell him to drop by to see you."

"Please do. I need to talk to him about other matters."

"Oh—if you're worried about the money he owes you, don't. He's cleared up his brother's estate and since his brother had no children, he's the only heir."

"I see. Well, there's no hurry. Thanks for coming, Vivien."

After Vivien left, Armand approached with the young French woman on one arm and Vivien's friend from Africa on the other. He kissed Jackie on both cheeks and extended his hand to Tony.

"Merci, Tony. Fantastic party. Would you consider painting my portrait some day?"

"Yes, of course. Just let me know when you're ready."

"I will. Ciao!"

Tony was left more bewildered than ever.

Jackie sidled up to him and put her hand on his shoulder. "It seems that Armand has decided that two women are better than one."

"Disappointed?"

"What? Because he's given me up without a fight?"

"Yes."

"A little. What would you have done if he *had* challenged you to a duel?"

"I don't know. I know nothing about dueling. I don't even remember being in a fist fight."

"But you shot a wild boar once."

"Actually, your mother shot him. Or at least she administered the *coup de grâce*."

"Well, then–we'll never know whether you would have been my hero, my champion!" She said this with an ironic smile and kissed him on the cheek.

"Pity," he said

"By the way," Jackie said after the last guest had departed, "what does 'chow' mean?"

"I have no idea."

CHAPTER 76

When Nat returned to Paris, he seemed to be a changed man. He dressed differently, forgoing his beret and his generally Bohemian attire in favor of business suits and a homburg, as well as a cane. That is, when he ventured outside of the atelier, which wasn't often. He seemed to have rededicated himself to his work. In fact, he was becoming a prolific and well-regarded artist—even M. Dantec took on several of his paintings.

Most surprising of all was that he came around to the apartment on Rue du Luxembourg shortly after he arrived and paid Tony the balance of the money he owed him. Tony could only attribute this change in behavior to Vivien, who continued to work in the atelier with him, side by side. She, too, was beginning to gain some recognition.

Tony's career, on the other hand, was flagging. This was not due to lack of industry on his part, but to the vagaries of the art market. Tony felt that he was doing the best work of his life. He had settled into his own style, which he once described as 'Supra-Impressionism' and was now called, at least by one critic, "post-Impressionism.' Tony found himself being grouped with such artists as Pierre Bonnard, Edouard Vuillard, and Camille Pissarro—who he had always admired—while Nat followed the lead of Cézanne and the young Picasso, who leaned more to symbolism and cubism.

Jackie's career seemed to be on a slow but steady upward trajectory. This was in no small part due to her association with Miss Bernhardt, who between tours of the Americas, cast her in plays at home in roles that complemented her own without competing with her.

Trey was now fourteen and enrolled in a lycée in the 7th arrondissement in the shadow of the Tour Eiffel. This school was chosen partly due to its long-standing reputation and partly because it was a state school and therefore cheaper than some of the private lycées. Tony also liked the fact that though like most French schools it was associated with the Catholic Church, it no longer had a formal connection to it. But what he didn't count on was the influence the nearby *École Militaire* would have on his son. Trey was enamoured with the impressive uniforms worn by the students he saw on parade in the Champ de Mars on special occasions and admired their self-assurance as he encountered them on Rue St-Dominique after school. They never bullied him as did some of the older students at the lycée did and seemed above all petty preoccupations such as the cinéma and football.

So both Tony and Jackie were shocked when he declared that he wanted to be a soldier. This was all the more disturbing due to rumors of war with Germany and perhaps Austria-Hungary as well.

"What happened to your painting?" Tony asked at the dinner table one evening when Trey announced his intentions.

Trey looked down at his plate. He was already nearly as tall as his father but had the blond hair and fair skin of his mother. His hair tended to be curly, which he hated as a sign of femininity and was often the source of bullying at school. For though Trey was taller than his peers, he had not yet filled out and knew he was weaker than they. His artistic inclination also contributed to his being subject to ridicule.

"I can always pursue my artistic career after the military," Trey said, still staring at his plate. "Besides, an artist–a really great artist–needs to have experience of the world."

"You can have plenty of experience of the world in other ways," Tony said. "Like taking a year off after the lycée and going to America. If it's adventure you want, you can go out West and live with the Indians. Remember the war bonnet your grandmother gave you a few years ago? That could be your entrée."

"That was for children, Papa. The war bonnet doesn't even fit me now. The Indians would laugh at me like the bullies at the lycée. But they wouldn't laugh at me if I were a lieutenant in the dragoons!"

"I think you exaggerate about the bullying at the lycée. What about your friend Jacques? He likes to draw–I've seen some of his work. He's quite good at it."

"Jacques is stronger than me. And he plays football. No one dares bully him."

"Well, what about Florent? He writes poetry."

"His father drives a train."

"What's that got to do with it?"

"He lets some of them in the cab with him at Gare Montparnasse."

"So what?"

"Then he lets them toot the horn and even drive it onto another track when they're in the switchyard. They don't want to be left out of that."

"Tony," Jackie said, "don't interrogate your son. If he wants to be a soldier, let him take the exam for the École Militaire. And then we'll see."

Tony grumbled and finished off his *coq au vin* with a swallow of wine. "You'll get yourself killed, Trey. There's nothing glamorous about war. I wish your grandfather were still alive so he could tell you what it's really like."

"Grandpapa? The one in the American Civil War?"

"Yes. He once saw one of his men get his head blown off. There was nothing heroic about it."

"But he helped defeat the forces of slavery, didn't he?"

"Well, yes, but–"

"That's what I want to do–help defeat the Germans."

"They don't own slaves."

"But my *professeur* in history class says they will enslave Europe if we let them!"

"Touché," Jackie said.

"You're not helping, Jackie. Do you want your son to become a soldier?"

"I want him to follow his own star," Jackie said, with a doting smile directed towards Trey. "Like you did."

"Touché, Papa!" Trey said with a triumphant air.

"All right," Tony said. "I know when I'm outnumbered. But you've got another year at the lycée, Trey. We'll talk about it when you graduate."

"I'll have to take the exam before then."

"Fine. Take it. But in the meantime you'll have plenty of time to think about it."

"Je suis fatigué de parler en anglais," Trey said. Then he stood up and performed a rather questionable salute to no one in particular. "Vive la France!"

After he left the dining room Tony looked at Jackie with a hangdog expression. "We've created a monster."

CHAPTER 77

The vicomte had reason to believe that Dr. McCool had poisoned his food. There was an odd taste to it. Something like arsenic. No, he was sure it was arsenic. But why would Dr. McCool want to poison him?

To make sure, the vicomte decided to put a small portion of his meal—in this case, an apricot—and take it to the common room where the other patients spent most of their time. There was one fellow, a former government official of some sort, who was obviously a glutton. It would be easy to persuade him to eat the apricot and then the vicomte would watch and see what happened.

After the day of this experiment, it became clear that the apricot had no effect on the glutton. So the vicomte, who refused to eat anything during this time, brought him a biscuit, a portion of meat, and a pudding in its porcelain bowl. The glutton gobbled all of this down with apparently no ill effect.

The vicomte decided that he must devise another strategy. It was possible that the glutton had some sort of immunity to arsenic. There was a cat that prowled the halls of the sanitarium more or less at will. Nobody seemed to own it. He decided to follow this cat the next time it appeared at his door. But first he must gain his trust. A saucer of milk would do the trick. Heretofore, he had ignored the cat, who sometimes paused at the door, looked in, meowed as if begging for something, and then moved on.

On this day, the vicomte put the saucer of milk at the door—he never drank milk himself—and the cat lapped it up. It was evident there was no arsenic in the milk. The cat then waited for a few minutes, hoping for something more substantial, but when this failed to appear, moved on. The vicomte followed.

The cat stopped at each of the rooms on the floor, meowing in expectation of a treat. Most often, he was disappointed. Occasionally, a scrap of meat would be thrown out into the hall, which the cat sniffed at and then ignored. Like all cats, he was partial towards fish, and he would settle for nothing less.

At the end of the hall was one of the common rooms where no meals were served, but where many of the patients often brought snacks from their breakfast or lunch trays as did the vicomte himself on the previous day when he initiated his first experiment. The cat strode boldly in, no doubt thinking that this was the mother lode of comestibles. The vicomte followed and sat in a chair just inside the door and watched.

The cat approached first one patient, then another. Most ignored him. Finally, one–known to all as Napoleon–picked the cat up and put it on a table. He addressed it as if it were one of his officers and launched into his plans to attack Russia.

The cat seemed to listen attentively. At the end of Napoleon's spiel, he gave the cat a treat. It was a sardine. The cat gobbled this down in one bite and then waited for more.

At this point, Dr. McCool entered the room and, having seen the incident, went over to Napoleon and gently admonished him for bringing food into the common room. Napoleon seemed not to comprehend and started waving his arms about, declaring that the attack would take place at dawn.

Dr. McCool smiled, picked up the cat and while petting it, left the room. He seemed to ignore the vicomte.

This was telling. The vicomte concluded that the cat was a demon in disguise and that Dr. McCool was the Devil. This was obvious because the cat took orders only from him, and his orders were to infiltrate the ranks of the 'patients' and report back to him. The cat would know which foods the patients preferred and which they rejected, and thus Dr. McCool would poison only the foods they preferred. And Dr. McCool now knew not only that Napoleon had no use for sardines, but that he preferred apple tarts, for that was the item Napoleon popped into his mouth upon finishing his spiel.

How does one kill the Devil? Impossible. The Devil had always been around, since the beginning of time, when God cast him out of Heaven. Then what was to be done? He, the vicomte, could not abstain from eating much longer. Well, at least he knew the sardines and the milk were safe. But he couldn't stand either. Even the foods he liked were poorly prepared at Charenton and he only consumed them in order to stay alive. Maybe he could convince Dr. McCool that he detested poached salmon or Boeuf Bourguignon, two of his favorites. In the meantime, he would have to find a way to kill the doctor. What other solution was there? So what if no one had ever done it before? He, le Vicomte Jean-Louis Raynouard de Koenigsbourg, was not to be trifled with, not even by the Devil.

As there were none of the conventional weapons available, one would have to improvise. Swords, pistols, bombs–all out of the question. Garroting? A possibility. Stabbing? Knives were not allowed, but one could improvise here as well. A spoon could be fashioned into a dagger of sorts. He had observed this at La Santé. Arsenic? If he could turn Dr. McCool's weapon of choice on himself, what sweet revenge! What irony! But where was he to get arsenic? Mushrooms? There were plenty in the woods behind Charenton, but he had no idea which ones were poisonous and which were not.

A stake through the heart? No, that was for vampires. Besides, he didn't believe in vampires.

Back to everyday items. That was the most practical. Scissors! There must be several pairs among the maids and laundresses. He had only to sneak into one of their workrooms, chat up the silly woman, even flirt a bit, and slip a pair into his pocket while she was distracted.

Scissors it would be.

Back in his apartment, the vicomte settled into his armchair and lit his pipe. That was fine tobacco that Dr. McCool had supplied him with. No doubt to put him off his guard. Odd that he would be allowed to have matches–none of the other patients were. Perhaps Dr. McCool acknowledged that he was a gentleman who had certain needs that the others didn't. In any case, he could not allow sentimental notions to get in the way of his plan. The Devil was shrewd. No one had ever been able to outwit him, other than God. But then God was dead, according to the philosophers. He had always thought so himself. Who was to replace Him? Why not himself? Who else was there? And think of the service he would be doing to mankind if he dispatched the Devil! The source of all man's ills, all his miseries. Without the Devil, life on earth would be a paradise!

Perhaps he could learn something from Napoleon. Not that idiot in the common room, but the real Napoleon. When to attack, when to retreat. Retreat? Never! But even Napoleon did retreat sometimes as a part of his stratagem. One needed to always keep the ultimate goal in mind.

Napoleon. He would have to visit the library tomorrow and obtain a book on the Great Man.

CHAPTER 78

With both Nat and Vivien working together in the atelier, Tony felt that his presence would be a bit intrusive and, besides, there was less and less space available due to the proliferation of paintings stacked against walls, resting on furniture, and even on the kitchen counter. So he continued to work in his own cramped studio, while occasionally transporting canvases to Rue de Furstemberg where there was still ample space.

One fall day, as the leaves began to change and temperatures were dropping, Nat showed up at the apartment dressed in a tweed jacket, a homberg, and corduroy trousers. The cane, made of ebony with a sterling silver *repoussé* handle, evoked an English banker or member of parliament rather than an artist. He was even cultivating a handlebar moustache which he kept pointed at the ends with bee's wax.

"I've come to ask a favor, old man," Nat said, as he sat on a chair while Tony painted. "By the way, that's an intriguing piece of work you have there. What is it?"

"I don't know yet. A memory from childhood, I think. What favor?"

"Well, you see, I've had a visit from Carlotta."

Tony stopped painting and turned to look at him. "Carlotta? I thought she was in Spain."

"She was, but she's back. She somehow got wind of my recent good fortune. And she wants money."

"She's already made off with that wedding dress you bought. What more does she want?"

"Half. Half of everything I've got."

"And how much is that?"

"I don't know exactly. Around a million dollars, I reckon. Six million francs."

Tony let out a whistle. "And what if you don't give it to her?"

"She'll tell Vivien for one thing. And she could take me to court."

"But the marriage wasn't legal, was it? She has no standing."

"No, but she can make a mess of things. She's already made a mess of me. I don't know what I'd do if Vivien left me."

"You're really in love with her, aren't you?"

"Madly."

"Well...what can I do?"

"Back me up. If it goes to court, testify that the gypsy wedding was a lark. A gala event but of no significance, merely an artistic exhibition."

"Which is what it was. Sort of."

"Yes. But I also need for you not to mention it to Vivien. Not to even breathe Carlotta's name."

"I wouldn't think of it."

"Good."

After Nat had gone, Tony picked up his brush and started to paint again, but he paused. What if Vivien was a gold digger, too? She seemed not so interested in Nat at first, treating him more like a mentor than a lover. Well, that was Nat's problem, a problem that only rich men had. Still, he didn't want to see Nat taken advantage of. For all his foolhardiness–or was it foolhardiness? Perhaps it was a willingness to take risks, to plunge ahead into new adventures–a quality that some of the greatest artists shared. And he, Tony, what risks had he taken lately? This idea so depressed him that he put down his brush and stared out the window for a half an hour.

When Trey came home from school, he looked at the painting in progress.

"Qu'est-ce c'est, Papa?"

"I don't know," Tony said. "We speak English at home, remember?"

"Yeah, okay. But what is it?"

"I told you–I don't know. I'm trying to reach back into my childhood. You're a child–maybe you can tell me."

"I'm not a child. I'm almost fifteen."

"Sorry. You're already a young man. But tell me what you see."

Trey stepped closer to the canvas and squinted at it. "I see...red and yellow."

"That's obvious. What else?"

"A kind of dream."

"Ah! Now we're getting somewhere. What kind of dream?"

"Something scary. Like a scene from Hell."

Tony was somewhat taken aback by this observation. He came off his stool, which was at an oblique angle to the painting and looked directly at it. "From Hell? You mean like fire and brimstone–because of the colors?"

"Some. But those black streaks–they look like people, people in agony from the flames."

Tony studied the painting even more closely. "Now you're scaring me. Do you believe in Hell?"

"Sure. We've been reading Dante's *Inferno* in school. There're all different circles, depending on how bad you've been in life. The inner circle's the worst."

"Know any candidates for the inner circle?"

"Hmm. Well, there's Kaiser Wilhelm."

"Who else?"

"Then there's the slave owners, like the ones in America who owned Grandpapa."

"Great grandmama, you mean. Grandpapa was a free man."

"Right. Well, then there's murderers like the Vicomte Raynouard de Koenigsbourg."

"The...who? What do you know about him?"

"It's in all the *journaux*. Didn't you read about it?"

"I didn't have time this morning. What did it say?"

"The vicomte is this crazy man in the madhouse at Charenton. He stabbed one of the doctors to death."

Tony was speechless.

"Papa? Are you all right? You look as white as a ghost. And with your complexion–"

"Yes, I know what I must look like, Trey. Fetch me the paper, will you? I think it's in the drawing room."

Trey retrieved the newspaper and Tony unfolded it.

"Page six," Trey said.

Tony opened the paper to page six:

*Le Vicomte Raynouard de Königsberg poignarde
à mort un médecin à Charenton*

The article went on to say that the vicomte had attacked the doctor with a pair of scissors in his office. The Préfecture de police was called and a detective was sent to investigate. The detective, Inspector Rochard, gave few details, but said that the vicomte would be returned to La Santé, the maximum-security prison where he was first sent and condemned to death before his sentence was commuted.

Tony handed the paper back to Trey.

"Did you know this man, Papa?"

"I'm afraid so. He tried to kill me once."

Trey's eyes opened wider. "Kill you? Why?"

"He objected to...well, it's a long story. Let's just say that he was a very disturbed man who committed some very serious crimes."

"Then why wasn't he executed?"

"Because Monsieur Loubet, the president at the time, didn't believe in capital punishment. I didn't either, really."

"And now?"

"And now I don't know. Had his sentence not been commuted…"

"Wait till I tell my friends at the lycée about this!"

"Try to restrain yourself, Trey. This is a very serious matter. Rumors circulating around your school won't help. They may think I had something to do with this."

"Oh. Well, I see what you mean. But Papa, why did this, this vicomte want to kill you? I want to know."

Tony looked at his son with his blue eyes and curly hair, which was now a light brown. "He's a racist, Trey. Like the ones in the American South. I attended a ball once with a white woman, not your mother, and he was outraged. As time went on, his mental condition deteriorated. Unfortunately, the French judicial system doesn't know what to do with such men."

"What should they do?"

"I don't know. Lock them up in a more secure facility than Charenton, obviously. Beyond that, I'm not sure."

Trey drew the edge of his hand sharply across his neck. "The guillotine. That's the answer."

"Perhaps. Now, don't you have some schoolwork to do?"

"I can do it later. But Papa, I hate to see you looking so sad. Are you sorry for this man?"

Tony thought for a moment, then looked out the window. "No, Trey, I'm not sorry for him. But I'd like to know more. I think I'll pay a visit to Inspector Rochard. Tomorrow."

The next morning, Tony received a call from M. Dantec, who said he had just sold two of his paintings to a couple of American tourists, and he needed two more to replace them.

"Something along the lines of your earlier work," M. Dantec said. "Americans like the Impressionist style more than *le genre en vogue.*"

Tony agreed and picked out a couple of conventional scenes of Paris, one of the Pont Alexandre III at night and one of the Roue de Chicago. After delivering the paintings to M. Dantec, he stopped by the Préfecture of police and visited Inspector Rochard.

"What happened?" Tony said as he sat down in a not very comfortable chair in front of the inspector's desk. The inspector remained standing.

"The *journalistes* are rather careful–how do you say–*circonspect?*"

"Circumspect," Tony said.

"Of course–how stupid of me. Almost an exact cognate, like *journaliste.* You are my best teacher, Monsieur Jones. I've missed your presence these last few years. How is your artistic career? Ça va bien?"

"Pas fameux. You were saying about the journalists…"

"Oh, yes–they are very reluctant to report the details of a gruesome murder. Except for the tabloids. But it is my opinion that the public has a right to know. When they are made aware of the full horror of such crimes they are less likely to be sentimental about the fate of the perpetrator."

"And what is the 'full horror'?"

The inspector went to the window and clasped his hands behind his back. "The vicomte 'purloined'–is that correct?"

"Yes."

"From *purloigner*, I think. Old French. Or perhaps Norman."

"Go on, Inspecteur…"

"Hmm? Oh, yes. The vicomte purloined a pair of scissors from one of the maid's work rooms and managed to break the two halves apart so that they were essentially a pair of daggers with very sharp edges. Together, you see, they would have been less useful. Then he went to the doctor's office and politely knocked on the door. The doctor admitted him and listened for a while to his incoherent ramblings–I don't know exactly what he said, though a nearby employee heard it as indistinct mutterings since the door was closed–and at the end of this rambling produced one of the daggers and plunged it into the doctor's heart. This not being enough to satisfy him, the vicomte stabbed him some twenty times more. And as if this still were not enough, he proceeded to disembowel him, cutting off his penis in the process. The employee, a custodian, heard nothing during this time. But to his horror, when the vicomte walked out of the office, his dressing gown was covered with blood. He then alerted the assistant director, who entered the office and discovered the mutilated body."

Tony put his head into his hands and could think of nothing to say.

The inspector turned away from the window. "So you see, Monsieur Jones, why I was most disappointed when the order of clemency arrived at the last minute as we stood together so many years ago waiting for the sentence to be carried out at La Santé."

Tony looked up. "What will happen now?"

"The case will be brought to the Cour d'assises as with the earlier case. And as before, they will most likely convict him. No doubt the vicomte's lawyers will appeal the verdict to the Cour de cassation, but they will likely confirm the lower court's decision unless there is a judicial error. And the current president is not likely to issue a commutation as did Monsieur Loubet."

Tony recalled that dreary morning of the vicomte's scheduled execution, the fine-tuned but simple mechanism of the guillotine awaiting its victim, the crowd clamoring for the sentence to be carried out, and the delight on the vicomte's face when it wasn't. "Will you be present at the execution?"

"I wouldn't miss it for all the world," the inspector said, with nearly the same expression of delight that the vicomte had shown that wintry morning. "I will still need a witness. Will you join me?"

Tony considered this. "Yes. I believe I will."

"Bon," the inspector said, obviously pleased. "Oh–I almost forgot. I received a telegram from my counterpart in San Francisco recently. Let's see–I have it in my file here somewhere."

Tony stood and watched with anticipation as the inspector went to his filing cabinet and opened a drawer. "About Madame Goldman?"

The inspector plucked a manila envelope from the drawer and opened it. "Not exactly about Madame Goldman. About her husband." He handed the telegram to Tony:

San Francisco, California *Paid 9G73*   *Oct 15 9:18am*

Det. Rochard
Préfecture de Police
Paris, France

Body of Wm Goldman found in rubble of destroyed home no sign of Mrs. Goldman sorry for delay we have our hands full here.

McFarland

Tony handed the telegram back to the inspector, who put it back in his file. "Do you think she died, too?"

"It is impossible to know for sure. I would say it is highly unlikely she survived the earthquake. They are still clearing the rubble years after the event."

Tony sighed. "I suppose that's the end of it. Thank you, Inspector, for all your trouble."

"De rien, Monsieur Jones. I will keep you informed of the case against the vicomte. Oh, by the by–I saw your wife at the Odéon the other night. She is a marvelous actress! And her French is impeccable. Like a true native."

"Thank you, Inspector. I'll be sure to relay the compliment to her. Adieu."

CHAPTER 79

In June of that year, a young man named Gavrilo Princip assassinated Archduke Franz Ferdinand of Austria in Sarajevo. By August, all of Europe was at war.

Trey had recently been admitted to the École Militaire and was scheduled to begin classes that same month. However, there was some confusion as to whether young men of his age should be allowed to continue their education or be conscripted. It was finally decided to limit conscription to those above the age of twenty, so Trey was allowed to enter the École with the expectation that the war would be over by the time he was commissioned.

Trey was sorely disappointed.

"I'm tall for my age, Papa," he said one morning at breakfast. "I could pass for eighteen. Maybe twenty."

"You should thank your lucky stars that you're too young. This is going to be a bloodbath."

"Your father's right," Jackie said. "There will be nothing glamorous about this war."

"The dragoons, your favorite corps," Tony said, "are outmoded now by mechanized infantry. Men on horses will be useless."

Trey brooded over this. "Jean-Paul has already signed up. His older brother, too. They'll be combat veterans while I'm still in school."

"And we hope they'll come home in one piece," Tony said. He ruffled the newspaper rather noisily. "You're mother's right, Trey. There will be no glamour in this war. And there's nothing to fight for. No principal like the American Civil War, which was to end slavery. This is about pride and saber rattling."

"But what if the Germans invade France?" Trey said. "What if they come to Paris? Won't that be something to fight for?"

Tony sighed and glanced at Jackie, who smiled. "Yes. That will be something to fight for. But it hasn't happened yet. And maybe it never will."

Trey looked dubious. "You sound like a pacifist, Papa."

"I'm not a pacifist, Trey. I just told you that I believe there are some things worth fighting for. This just isn't one of them."

"May I go now?"

"Of course you can. We're not holding you prisoner."

"I feel like one." Trey rose from the table and threw his napkin down. "Vive la France!"

"Vive la France," Tony said without enthusiasm.

After Trey left the table, Tony and Jackie looked at each other as if they had somehow failed their only son.

"I think we should leave," Jackie said.

"Leave? You mean leave Paris?"

"I mean leave France. We haven't been home in years. We're Americans, Tony. This isn't our fight."

Tony put his newspaper aside. "No, it isn't. But Trey is half French. Sometimes I think he's all French. Or at least *he* seems to think so. He never speaks English outside of the apartment."

"Which is all the more reason to acquaint him with the country of his origins. He's never even met his grandparents–my parents, that is."

"No, he hasn't. But, Jackie, this war could be over in a few months. There's no sense in uprooting ourselves–"

"That's what they said about the Civil War. It went on for four years. It devastated the South. This one could devastate France."

Tony sighed and started to take the last sip of his coffee, but finding it cold, put the cup down. "What about your career?"

"We could go to New York. As Miss Bernhardt's protégée–at least one of them–I would have an immediate entrée."

"Hmm. Yes, that's a possibility. There's an art scene there too, though it's rather primitive compared to Paris."

"Primitive? Sargent has done some of his best work there, and St. Gaudens has made a big splash with his statues going up all over Manhattan. There's the Metropolitan–"

"All right, all right. I get the point. I'll think about it. The greatest advantage, though, would be to get Trey out of the École Militaire. I've never liked the idea of his going into the military."

"Do you think I was happy about it? But we can't forbid him to–he would just be more determined."

"No doubt." Tony stood. "Well, I've got work to do. What will you do now that *La Rabouilleuse* has run its course?"

"I don't know. There aren't any new productions scheduled that I know of. The theatres may shut down."

"I could use a model."

"Oh, Tony–be serious."

"I am serious. Have you ever posed in the nude?"

"You know I haven't."

"There's always the first time."

"Now I know you're joking. I'm forty—well, forty-something."

Tony laughed. "There's no age limit. You're still beautiful, Jackie. And you've kept your figure. Would you rather I recruit Vivien?"

"Of course not."

Tony smiled, a familiar gleam in his eye.

"Oh, no."

"Oh, yes." He took her in his arms and gave her a passionate kiss, a kiss like the one he gave her as they dallied along the Quai Voltaire fourteen years earlier.

"C'est Paris, ma chérie."

CHAPTER 80

The German army moved quickly into Belgium and then into Northern France by the end of August. But in the first week of September the Allies won their first victory and forced the Germans back to the Marne, then the Aisne, where both sides dug into trenches and fought to a stalemate.

In late September, Nat paid a visit to Tony while he was working in his studio.

"We're getting out," Nat said, as he watched Tony paint.

"Out? Now?"

"Yes. Before it's too late. And I think you and Jackie should, too. I've booked passage on a steamer out of Le Havre. It may be the last one for a while."

"But the Germans have been pushed back. The British have weighed in. The Russians, too. The war could be over in a few weeks."

"Don't count on it. In the meantime, nobody's buying artwork. The American tourists have fled. Monsieur Dantec is talking about shutting down his gallery."

"As long as there are a few francs to be made, Monsieur Dantec will stay open."

Nat seemed frantic, "How can you be so calm? The Germans have the most efficient war machine in history. The French and British armies are no match for them, and the Russians are on the verge of civil war. Eventually, they will all converge on Paris and the city will be a burned-out shell— uninhabitable!"

Tony continued to focus on his painting, the one of Jackie, that he had been working on for a month. "I think you're overstating the case, Nat. The French army just showed its mettle at the Marne. In any case, Jackie and I have decided to stay. Trey is determined to get his commission at the École Militaire. We can't leave him here."

"Okay. It's your funeral. When we get settled in Boston, I'll send you my address. We might move into my family's summer home on Martha's Vineyard. It's peaceful there."

"I'll keep you posted on events here."

Nat emitted a nervous laugh. "Assuming there's any mail service from Europe by that time. Well—" He extended his hand. "It's been a great time for both of us, old chum. I hope you'll come see us when you finally come to your senses."

Tony shook his hand, then gave him a hug. "You're my best friend, Nat. Take care of yourself. And Vivien, too."

"Will do."

After Nat left, Tony began to feel that he was right. Was it foolish to stay? He and Jackie probably would have left already if it weren't for Trey.

He went back to his painting, which only needed some finishing touches. This portrait was similar to the one he had done of Mme G years earlier and which won him a medal at the Exposition. But it was in a more abstract vein, with flatter planes and thus very little depth. The idea was more of a universal woman, alluring but flawed, mysterious yet accessible. Or at least that was the intention.

Jackie knocked on the door, then entered without waiting for a response. "What did Nat want?"

"He and Vivien are leaving. Headed for Boston."

"I'm not surprised. Do you think she will be accepted in Nat's social circle there?"

"I don't know. He says they might go to Martha's Vineyard for a while. Perhaps to give his family a chance to get used to the idea that he's brought a black bride back from Paris."

"Poor Vivien. I wonder if she knows what she's in for."

"She's a tough *fille*. I wouldn't worry about her."

Jackie moved closer and stared at the painting. "Is that really me?"

"It's you, and Vivien, and Madame G rolled into one. And maybe Camille, too."

"And here I was thinking that you were out to flatter me."

Tony laughed. "You don't think it's flattering?"

Jackie squinted. "Why are my breasts so large? I have small breasts."

"Have you looked at them lately?"

"No. Why would I? But I suppose you're a connoisseur."

Tony put down his brush. "What's that supposed to mean?"

"You know what I mean. All your philandering."

"Philandering? I've only strayed from your arms once, remember? And that's ancient history."

"Hmph. I hope so."

Tony put his arms around her and kissed her. "Jackie, you're my only love and you always will be. Other women are simply potential subject matter for my work."

She kissed him back. "A likely story. But I have to say you've been a good boy lately. By the way, there's a letter for you on the credenza in the dining room. It has a rather fancy return address."

"Hmm. No name?"

"None."

"I don't like letters like that. The last time I got a parcel with no sender's name it was a bomb."

"This is a letter. A bomb wouldn't fit."

"Well, I'll get it when I'm finished. Where are you off to?"

"Shopping."

"Shopping? For what?"

"Food. Stockings. Underwear. We need to stock up in case the Germans reach Paris."

"I was just having this same conversation with Nat. It'll never happen."

"Let's hope not. À tout à l'heure!"

Tony continued working after Jackie was gone until he felt satisfied with the painting. Then he washed up, went to the dining room, poured himself a glass of brandy, and picked up the letter. He took it out onto the balcony, settled into a chair and took a closer look at the return address: 2, rue St-Florentin.

He slit open the envelope with a butter knife from the table and read the contents:

My Dear Antonio,

I am writing to inform you that I will be closing the house at Rue de Furstemberg as it is no longer economical. I understand that you have a number of paintings there. Can you pay me a visit so that we can decide what to do with them?

I will soon be removing my household and staff to the château at la Ferrières until I feel that Paris is safe again.

Please let me know when you can visit me. However, it must be before my departure date, which is the 14th.

Your obedient servant,

Alphonse de Rothstein
Tel. 1245

Tony folded up the letter and put it back into the envelope. He looked out over the railing of the balcony at the trees in the Gardens, which were just now beginning to change from green to red and yellow.

Well, it seems as if even the baron has given up hope that Mme G is still alive. No doubt it has been very expensive keeping up the house over the years, not to mention salaries for J-P, Sabine, and the rest of the staff. What will happen to them now? He wished he had the financial resources to keep them employed. Well, they were skilled and dependable servants. They would find other jobs. But the paintings? Perhaps he could store them at Nat's atelier. He would have to write and ask his permission.

He went to the hallway and picked up the phone. But when the connection was made, he found that the speaker at the other end was not the baron but his secretary.

"Je suis Antonio Jones. Je réponds à la lettre du baron de Rothstein."

"Oui, Monsieur. Quand pouvez-vous venir?"

"Demain. À dix heures?"

"Bon. Il vous attend."

Tony hung up the phone. A dark cloud seemed to settle over his head.

Closing the house at Rue de Furstemberg was tantamount to declaring Mme G dead.

CHAPTER 81

The new line 4 of the metro was the first to connect the left bank with the right, passing through a tunnel under the Seine between Raspail and Châtelet. Tony was now able to get on at Carrefour de l'Odéon and change at Châtelet for la Place de la Concorde, which was just a few steps from the baron's townhouse.

It had been years since he had visited the baron's palatial residence, the occasion being a Christmas party, as he recalled. He had attended with Mme G, who was as beautiful as always, and they were received by the baron cordially, even though there was some dispute as to whose lover she was. The baron was always a consummate gentleman, unflappable no matter what the circumstances.

A doorman showed him in and directed him to the secretary's office, who received him graciously and led him to the baron's study, though the baron was not there. The secretary bade him take a seat and left the room.

As Tony sat in a not so comfortable Louis XIV chair, his eyes roamed around the room. There was, in fact, one of his paintings hanging over the marble mantelpiece, just above a gleaming brass clock with a hand-painted enamel dial. This was his portrait of Mme G, the one that had earned him a medal at the 1900 Exposition.

As he stared at the painting, recalling the circumstances under which it was painted, a door opened. It was concealed in the wood paneling and seemed part of a bookcase. Through it stepped the baron.

"Welcome, my good friend!" exclaimed the baron in his impeccable English.

Tony stood and almost bowed his head as if in the presence of royalty but caught himself in time. "How are you, Baron?"

The baron reached towards him and took Tony's hand in both of his. "At my age, there are always minor ailments, but on the whole I have been blessed with good health. And I must say you seem to retain your youthful looks with great ease. How do you do it?"

Tony flushed a bit at this compliment. "Well, I suppose it's from a great deal of walking. Since the opening of the metro I never take a cab."

"Ah, yes–the metro. I am afraid my business contacts would refuse to receive me if I came by metro. One must arrive with great pomp and circumstance, you see, or they do not take one seriously. Please–sit down."

Tony sat down again while the baron went behind his ornate desk, donned a pair of ordinary reading glasses, and perused some papers before taking his seat.

At that point, there was a knock on the door, the main door.

"Entrez," the baron said.

It was the secretary. He said nothing but went directly to the baron's desk and presented him with a single document.

The baron adjusted his glasses and read the document. "Douze millions de francs! He must be joking. We need not bother to answer."

The secretary nodded, picked up the document and left the room.

The baron removed his glasses and looked up. "Forgive me, Monsieur Antonio. These intrusions are unavoidable at times. Now–where was I?" Oh, yes–we need to make a decision concerning your paintings at Rue de Furstemberg. Would you be interested in selling them?"

"Well...of course."

"None that you would like to keep?"

"Um...perhaps a few."

The baron looked up at the portrait of Mme G. "I have always admired your work, Monsieur Antonio. Of course I am partial to the more representational style such as this portrait of Amelia." He looked wistful for a moment or two. "I would like to see more like that."

"Well, we could meet at Rue de Furstemberg and if there are any you like, I would be glad to offer them to you."

The baron replaced his glasses and opened a drawer. "I'm afraid that I have no time for that. But suppose you go and pick out the ones you wish to keep and I will buy the rest." He extracted a cheque book from the drawer and picked up a pen.

Tony gripped the arms of his chair. "All of them? Sight unseen?"

"Yes. All but the ones you choose for yourself, as I just mentioned. I trust your good taste–and your talent. How many are there?"

"Oh, I'm not sure. At least one hundred and fifty."

"Good. And how much would you offer them for, say, at Monsieur Dantec's gallery?"

Tony emitted a nervous chuckle. "Well, the market is depressed, and likely to go even further south until the war is over. I would say, on average, let's see...possibly 2,500 francs each."

"Twenty-five hundred francs times one hundred fifty–and how many would you like to keep?"

"Oh, I'd say only a half a dozen or so."

"One moment." The baron made a quick calculation with a pencil. "Minus the six—three hundred sixty thousand francs. However, I believe you are in the habit of underestimating your own work. Let's say 400,000 francs. Is that agreeable?"

Tony nearly gagged. "Most agreeable."

"Good." The baron wrote out a cheque for the amount, ripped it out of his cheque book and rose from his desk. Tony rose as well.

The baron came from behind the desk and handed him the cheque. "Now, I have other business to attend to. Don't forget that you must retrieve the paintings you wish to keep before the 14th."

"No. I won't. I will go over there tomorrow."

"Good." Then, almost as an afterthought, he said, "By the way, if you would be so kind as to wait here for a few moments, there is someone who would like to see you."

"To see *me*?"

"Yes." The baron again extended his hand. "Well, Monsieur Antonio. It has been a pleasure doing business with you. Good luck and don't hesitate to call on me if I can be of any assistance during these troubled times."

"No...no, I won't, Baron. Thank you."

The baron then left the room.

Tony, somewhat dazed, sat down again in his chair and stared at the cheque. It was more money than he had ever seen in his life. Even as a banker back in Beaufort, South Carolina, he had never handled a transaction of this amount. As he was thinking of what he could do with the money the concealed door adjacent to the bookcase opened. And through it walked Mme G.

In her fifties now, she was still beautiful. She had lost weight, however. The cheeks were sallow, her eyes appeared larger, her breasts smaller. But there was an elegance about her that wasn't there before. She was dressed in a silk taffeta dress, cut higher in the bodice than those she used to wear. A diamond necklace around her neck sparkled in the sunlight streaming in through a window.

"Tony," she said simply and reached out her arms as if to embrace him, but instead grasped his hands and kissed him on both cheeks. "How good it is to see you."

Tony was speechless at first, as if having witnessed an apparition. "Amelia. I thought I'd never see you again."

"That was a distinct possibility. Please—sit down."

She led him to a divan beneath the window. They both sat, while she continued to hold his hands.

"What happened?" Tony said.

She smiled. "It's a very long story, I'm afraid. And very unpleasant–at times. After the earthquake, I woke up and found myself in the parlor of our house, directly below the bedroom where my husband kept me prisoner. I looked around, pushed some debris aside, dusted myself off, and stood. Or at least I tried to stand. I fell back into the pile of debris. My leg was broken, I had lacerations to my face and arms. I remained there for a day and a half until rescue workers discovered me. Bill was found much later buried under tons of debris in the basement. I spent the next six months in a hospital in Sacramento, where I went in and out of consciousness. I remember very little of that time."

"My poor Amelia! What happened after that? The earthquake was in '06–"

"I went back to San Francisco and tried to see about Bill. He was buried in a mass grave in a cemetery in San Bruno. Or so they said. There were no names on the crosses. Next I went to the bank, which had somehow survived, though it was badly burned. It attracted looters, of course, but they were unable to crack open the safe which was of hardened steel and partially underground. I tried to contact the other directors, but they were either dead or fled the city."

"So the bank–and the safe–are still there?"

"Yes. But the city imposed a moratorium on all banking transactions. Auditors and inspectors were sent in and they finally opened the vault, but found no gold, no cash, only worthless securities. That's why the surviving directors fled. They had no money to meet the demand of depositors who made a run on the bank once the debris had been cleared."

"So you were penniless."

"Yes. Again."

"My God, Amelia–why didn't you wire me for help?"

"I had already imposed upon you once–I didn't want to become a pest."

"You could never have been a pest. Besides, you supported me, encouraged me,"–he kissed her hands– "and launched my career. All you had to do was–"

"I reached out to the baron instead. His resources are infinite."

Tony looked around the room at its lavish furnishings, then at Amelia again. For the first time, he noticed that she was wearing a platinum ring with a large diamond mounted in the center. "You're married!"

"Yes. The baron's wife died just three years ago. Of an embolism. He was lonely. I was lonely–and I did not want to come between you and Jacqueline. So we had a very quiet wedding at la Ferrières."

"Well...are you happy?"

"I think so. The baron is very kind. But Tony–have you heard anything from your detective friend about Alex?"

Tony sighed. "I'm afraid not. Nothing. He seems to have simply vanished."

"I asked the baron to try to find him. Of course he's very busy, but he hired a private detective. There seem to be no clues, no witnesses."

"That's what inspector Rochard says. I'm afraid they have put the file into some dusty storage room at the Préfecture."

Mme G released Tony's hands and put them to her face. "I know he's still alive. I just know it!" She lowered her hands and tears streamed down her cheeks.

Tony reached out for her hand again. "There's no reason to think he's dead. And he was old enough at the time to remember you. He'll turn up one of these days."

"Oh, I hope you're right. Well, Tony–" She stood. "I must not keep the baron waiting too long. Give my love to Jacqueline. And oh! Your son, Trey. How is he?"

"Doing well, thank you. But I'm afraid he's determined to get into this war. He's a cadet at l'École Militaire."

"Oh, my goodness. Well, I'm sure he'll make a fine soldier. And we'll need as many as we can get to defend Paris."

"If it comes to that. Au revoir, Amelia." He kissed her hands again.

"À plus tard, mon cher. Stay in touch."

Tony merely smiled, knowing that he wasn't likely to see her again, at least not for some time. He took one last look at her portrait and left the room.

CHAPTER 82

Trey's matriculation at l'École Militaire was delayed somewhat due to the initial German bombardment of Paris. These initiatives were sporadic and largely ineffective and ceased for a time after the Battle of the Marne and the German army was pushed back to the Aisne. Nevertheless, Parisians were nervous, unsure of what to expect. These fears, however, were allayed somewhat when General Gallieni requisitioned private vehicles, including six hundred taxicabs, to carry 6,000 soldiers to the front at Nanteuil-le-Haudouin. The result was a defeat for the Germans and a tremendous boost in morale for the people of Paris.

Trey wore his cadet uniform every day even though he was not officially a student at the École. He even began addressing his father as 'Monsieur.'

"I have a mission for you, Cadet Jones," Tony said at breakfast.

"Oui, Monsieur?" Trey said, brightening.

"Oui. I have to go over to the studio at Rue de Furstemberg to collect some paintings. I don't know exactly how many. Do you think you can spare an hour or two?"

Trey's face fell. "Tableaux? Pourquoi?"

"The baron's closing the place up and taking most of the paintings with him to his country estate. Do I need to order you to help me?"

Trey pouted. "Non, Papa. Je viens."

"Bon."

Jackie seemed amused by this conversation and wisely stayed out of it. After breakfast, she straightened Trey's tie and gave him a kiss.

It was a short walk to Rue de Furstemberg, during which Trey regaled Tony with the exploits of General Gallieni and his strategic genius. He was particularly excited about the general's placement of machine guns and a cannon on the Tour Eiffel to defend against aerial attacks.

When they arrived at Rue de Furstemberg, they found J-P and Sabine packing up furniture and collectibles.

"Qu'est-ce que tu vas faire maintenant, J-P," Tony said.

"Nous allons au château de Ferrières, Monsieur Tony."

"Au château? Avec le baron?"

"Oui. Nous travaillons pour lui maintenant."

"Tous? Eugénie et vos parents aussi?"

"Oui."

The baron's generosity seemed to have no bounds. Not only did he buy out nearly the whole stock of Tony's paintings, but he was employing five additional servants that he probably didn't need in order to ensure that they didn't starve during the war.

He led Trey to the studio over the carriage house and began sorting out the paintings.

"I didn't know you had so many, Papa." Trey said. Suddenly he was speaking English, perhaps because he was now in his father's world. "Did you paint all these before I was born?"

"Most of them."

Trey looked out through the big Palladian window into the garden, with its perfectly manicured hedges and statuary. "Did you sculpt the statues, too?"

"No. Those are copies of Monsieur Rodin's work. Signed by him, I might add."

Trey continued to stare at the garden. "I would like to have a studio like this."

Tony stopped what he was doing and looked up. "You're thinking of taking up painting again after the war?"

"That was always the plan, remember? But I think I might like to be a sculptor. Do you know Monsieur Rodin?"

"I run into him at exhibitions from time to time. Perhaps I could arrange for you to meet him."

"That would be great."

Tony finally picked out seven paintings he wanted to keep, including three of his early paintings of Mme G. He hesitated to keep them for fear of alienating Jackie, but they were among his favorites and he had no intention of banishing Mme G from his life, even though, or especially because, he might never see her again. Jackie would just have to get used to her presence, if only in portraiture.

They took a cab back to the apartment during which time they heard explosions in the distance.

"They're coming closer," Trey said, looking out the window.

"On the contrary," Tony said. "I think they're being pushed back. At least for now."

When they got to Place St-Sulpice, just north of the Gardens, they were forced to stop as a herd of cattle was being driven through the square.

"Mon Dieu!" Trey exclaimed. "Qu'est-ce que c'est?"

"They're called 'cows,'" Tony said. "In case you've forgotten the word in English."

"Très drôle," Trey said. "I know the word. But what are they doing in the middle of the street?"

"Meat," Tony said. "In case the Germans lay siege to the city."

In a few minutes, the cattle cleared the square and they continued to Rue du Luxembourg.

Tony paid the driver and they took the paintings upstairs to the apartment in two trips. Once they were stacked against the wall of the studio Tony stood back to examine them.

Jackie looked in. "Did you have to keep *three* of her?"

"Maybe I'll sell one or two. I think they're among my best paintings."

"Well...then keep the one where she has her clothes on. I know how much she means to you, but I don't want to see you panting over her body every day."

"Who is she?" Trey said.

"A friend of your father's," Jackie said, folding her arms over her chest.

"And she posed naked for you, Papa?"

"She was my patron, Trey. And she was a very good model. Though not as good as your mother."

"Hah!" Jackie said.

Tony chuckled. "I'm serious, Jackie. You were very good. More patient and composed than Madame G."

"Well...are you going to hang it in the drawing room over the mantelpiece? Or in the dining room where—"

"It'll stay here in the studio–facing the wall, if you like."

Trey seemed to pick up on the tension between his parents. "Well, I think I'll change out of this uniform and see if I can get up a game of football in the Gardens. I'm sick of being stuck inside all day."

"Do it while you can," Tony said.

After Trey was out of the house, Tony and Jackie sat down in the drawing room and Camille brought them some tea. Camille had moved in now that she had no place else to go.

Tony picked up his cup and blew the steam off the surface. "Est-ce que tu veux aller à Montpellier, Camille?"

"Non, Monsieur. Je me plais beaucoup ici."

"Bon. Tu peux rester tant que tu veux."

"Merci, Monsieur." And with a little curtsy, Camille left the room.

"Not to mention she has a boyfriend here," Jackie said with a wink.

"Does she? And who is he?"

"Bernard. He's a waiter at Café de la Rue Madame."

"Really? We haven't been there for a while. We should drop in so I can meet him."

"Tony…"

"Yes?"

"When you went to the baron's yesterday–did he have any news of Madame G?"

Tony put his cup down. "Now that you mention it, yes he did."

"And is she …alive?"

"Very much so."

"Where?"

"Here. In Paris. Though they're moving to la Ferrières to wait out the war."

"They?"

"Madame G and the baron. They're married."

Jackie sat with her mouth agape.

"So you see, Jackie–you don't have to worry about her coming back into my life anymore. She's alive, but as good as dead to me."

"Oh, Tony–don't say that. I never wanted her to die. I like her very much. Couldn't we see them socially?"

"Not likely. The baron, for all his forbearance and Old-World manners, doesn't want to see me around. He essentially bought me off. Besides, they move in a rarefied social circle where we'd be out of place."

"Out of place? But we've known princes and celebrities–like Miss Bernhardt."

"They just toy with us. Shiny baubles that they tire of easily and then discard. Forget it, Jackie. Class consciousness is one thing in Europe that is here to stay."

They remained quiet for several minutes. Then Jackie spoke:

"I'm thinking of volunteering for the Red Cross."

Tony sat up in his chair. "The Red Cross? Are you serious? They'll send you to the front."

"Of course they will. That's where I'm needed."

"Jackie, Jackie–have you thought this through? What about your career?"

"The theatres are all closing–or at least most of them. I'll be out of a job, anyway. And I'd like to help."

"And what am I supposed to do? Sit here alone while you and Trey win the war?"

Jackie smiled. "You could join, too. Maybe drive an ambulance."

"I don't know how to drive an ambulance."

"I'm sure you could learn."

Tony sighed. "Well, I suppose I should contribute somehow."

"Everyone will have to contribute."

"I think there's a law against whole families going to war."

"We won't be going to war–we'll just be helping those who do."

Tony pushed his chair away from the table. "I'm afraid the Germans won't be making distinctions between combatants and medical aides."

"Perhaps you're right. It was just a thought."

CHAPTER 83

The Cour d'assises continued to function normally into the winter of 1914-1915 as the city no longer seemed to be threatened. Among other cases that were considered was that of le Vicomte Raynouard de Koenigsbourg.

There was no doubt as to the vicomte's guilt. The problem was, now that he had been tried and convicted of murder for the second time, what was to be done with him? He was obviously insane, but he just as obviously could not be sent back to Charenton, which was simply not equipped to deal with such violent inmates. Nor did the judges think it advisable to send him back to La Santé, which was not equipped to deal with the mentally ill.

A solution was proposed: Why not send him to Devil's Island off the coast of French Guiana? One of the three judges suggested that this would be tantamount to a death sentence, while they were prevented by law to execute him at home. Another objected that the vicomte would be a danger to the other prisoners, but the other two observed that the prisoners of Devil's Island were in fact mostly murderers who were quite capable of defending themselves, and in any case, death was probably preferable to living out the remainder of one's life in such a harsh environment.

So the vicomte was sentenced to life imprisonment and packed off to Devil's Island.

Inspector Rochard was once again sorely disappointed.

"Still, Monsieur Jones," he said the morning the sentence was announced, "justice is not done."

Tony was walking with the inspector along the Quai des Grands Augustins opposite l'Île de la Cité. Despite the fact that large chunks of ice were bumping up against their hulls, *bateaux de charbon* plied their way along the Seine to deliver much-needed fuel to heat Parisian homes and places of business.

"What good would it do to execute him?" Tony said.

"The 'good' is quite obvious in my opinion," the inspector said. "It would ensure that he would not kill again. For thirty years I have been dealing with murderers of all kinds. Some kill out of passion—these often make model prisoners and if they are incarcerated until middle or old age, make model citizens when released. Others kill for the pure pleasure of it, to satisfy their blood lust, as a man may lust after women and cannot be stopped but by disease or infirmity in old age. This is the case of the vicomte."

They stopped for a moment and placed their elbows on the stone parapet overlooking the river.

"But the judges," Tony said, "determined that the vicomte stabbed Dr. McCool because he thought he was the Devil. In his mind he was simply defending himself."

"They naïvely believed the vicomte's attorneys, who by the way are among the best that money can buy. Did the vicomte believe that the women he murdered in '97 and '98 were the Devil? I think not. He simply wanted to see their blood flow. Like a vampire, he will seek out other victims when he reaches Devil's Island. Appropriately named, I may add."

Tony stared into the water, now swirling in eddies beneath the bridges as the barges passed underneath. "Well, Inspector, I can't say as you are wrong. It simply seems to me that executing a human being because he might kill again is not sufficient justification. Who knows what is in the mind of a man like the vicomte? You say he is a sort of vampire. What could cause a man to believe that of himself? Why not isolate him in a secure environment and subject him to a thorough psychiatric examination? Perhaps a cure could be found."

The inspector smiled ironically. "Do you suggest that we call in Dr. Freud?"

"Why not? I'm sure he would find it an interesting challenge."

"And who would protect Dr. Freud during this examination? I can't spare the men."

Tony laughed. "I think we must agree to disagree, Inspector. There seems to be no acceptable solution at present. But the vicomte's fate is not what I wished to see you about."

"Oh? And what is that?"

"Madame Goldman's—now Madame Rothstein's—child. Is it impossible to find him?"

"The child? That was long ago, Monsieur Jones. What—fifteen, twenty years? No, it's not impossible, but extremely unlikely unless the child—now a young man if he's still alive—comes forward and wishes to solve the mystery himself. No evidence, no witnesses, much time passed—the police can do nothing at this point. Why are you so interested? Ah! You believe the child is yours."

Tony turned away from the river and leaned with his back against the parapet. He could see the steeple of St-Germain-des-Prés, within a stone's throw of Rue de Furstemberg. "I don't know. It's possible. In any case, Alex is Amelia's child. I know that she would give anything to find him and I'd like to help her do that if I can."

The inspector, who now walked with a cane, tapped it against the pavement as if to signal an announcement. "I will recover the files from our *fichier enterré*. If there are any clues that we missed so many years ago, we will find them. Time can sometimes provide one with a fresh perspective."

"I would greatly appreciate that, Inspector. Now, could you tell me where I can find the office of la Croix-Rouge?"

CHAPTER 84

The war went on...and on...and on...the Germans did not succeed in getting any closer to Paris over the next few months, though there were occasional aerial bombardments from aircraft and on one occasion in early 1916, a Zeppelin, which was successful only because a dense fog prevented it from being shot down.

Jackie applied to la Croix-Rouge and was hurriedly trained as a nurse. As women were not sent to the front except in unusual circumstances, she remained in Paris, which needed as many volunteers as possible. There were food shortages, injured and dying citizens and many, many wounded soldiers returning from the front. Most of her work was in the Hôtel Dieu on the Île de la Cité, but she was also sent to suburban hospitals when needed.

Tony learned to drive an ambulance and was sent to the front first at the Marne, then later at the Aisne near Soissons.

Trey continued his studies at the École Militaire, where the officers' program was accelerated so that he would receive his commission in early 1917. The Germans' increasingly successful use of airplanes prompted the French to step up the training of pilots and Trey was accepted into this program as well.

Tony followed the line of battle as it moved from Soissons along the Hindenburg Line towards Arras and Ypres. When soldiers were not seriously wounded, he would take them to nearby field hospitals, but the ones who were but had some chance of survival would be taken all the way to Paris, where he was able to remain for a day or two.

"What's it like at the front, Papa?" Trey said one morning as they were eating in the dining room. The sky outside was a featureless gray and snow piled up on the sidewalks since there was no one to clean them off. At least the cold suppressed the stink of uncollected garbage.

"It's not pretty, Trey," Tony said. "You should probably drop in on your mother at the Hôtel Dieu sometime to see what high-speed metal can do the human body."

"Tony!" Jackie said. "Don't try to frighten Trey. He's–"

"I'm not frightened, Mama. I'm a soldier now. In three more months I'll have my wings."

"At least that will keep you out of the trenches," Tony said. "As I've said before, there's nothing glamorous about it. I've seen grown men, strong men, crying and shaking uncontrollably. I just hope by the time you get your wings the war will be over and you can describe lazy eights in the sky to your heart's content."

Trey looked at his plate. "Can't we find something better to eat than pig's feet?"

"We're lucky to have that, Trey," Jackie said. "Meat is scarce at the moment. How about some more potatoes? We have plenty of that."

"I'm sick of potatoes," Trey said. "And beets. That's all we get at school. Some chicken now and then."

"You're eating like a king compared to the troops in the trenches. They're eating cold rations–sardines and sausages. I think they were left over from the last war."

Trey pushed his plate away. "I'm not hungry anymore."

"Trey," Tony said with a stern look. "You're acting like a child. You're seventeen now and you'll have to make sacrifices like the rest of us."

Trey looked up from his plate. "You should see what they get in the officer's mess. Steak. Caviar. Champagne."

"How do you know that?" Tony said.

"They took us out to the new training field at Étamps. We went for a ride, then had lunch with the pilots."

"Well," Tony said, "that's something to look forward to. In the meantime, you'll have to settle for what the rest of us earth-bound types eat."

After dinner, Tony announced that he was going to Nat's studio to see if there were any of his paintings that could be transferred to the apartment. Nat had left him a key to occasionally check up on the place. Trey was recruited to help.

As they approached the front door of the building, Tony looked up and noticed that the lights were on. He must have forgotten to turn them off the last time he was there three weeks earlier. Now he would have to reimburse Nat for the enormous electric bill that was sure to come.

When he and Trey approached the door of the atelier, they heard music. Clapping, dancing. Someone was in there. Rather than open the door with his key and burst into who knows what, he knocked. Silence.

"What's going on here?" Trey said

"I don't know," Tony said, "But I'd wager a guess that it's an old friend of Nat's."

The door slowly opened, light streamed into the hallway and a large bearded man appeared. "Oui?"

"Je suis Antonio Jones. Qui est vous?"

The burly man puffed out his chest. "Cela ne vous regarde pas!"

Just as the man was about to slam the door in Tony's face, a woman appeared and gently pushed him aside. It was Carlotta.

"Monsieur Tony! C'est vous?"

"Oui, Carlotta. Je suis venu récupérer mes tableaux."

"Entrez."

Tony and Trey entered to find a dozen gypsies scattered about the room, some sitting in chairs, others standing who had apparently been dancing. One of those sitting had a guitar in his lap, another an accordion strapped across his chest. They simply stared as Tony nodded and went about his business of searching out his paintings.

The men eyed Trey with suspicion as he was wearing his cadet uniform. Sensing their fear and respect, he regarded them as miscreants whom he might arrest at any moment. He was unarmed, but ready for any sign of aggression.

"Où est Nathaniel?" Carlotta said as Tony picked out a couple of paintings.

"Il est aux États-Unis," Tony said. "Attendant la fin de la guerre."

"Vraiment?"

"Oui."

They collected six paintings and were about to leave when Carlotta approached Tony and whispered:

"Cet appartement–c'est à moi."

Tony said nothing and opened the door.

"Vous n'appellerez pas la police?"

"Non, Carlotta."

They left and before they had reached the ground floor, they heard the music and the dancing again.

"Who *are* those people, Papa?" Trey said, as they trudged through the snow on the way back to the apartment.

"Gypsies. The one named Carlotta thinks she's Nat's wife and is entitled to the atelier as well as half of his fortune."

"Why don't you call the police?"

"It would do no good. They apparently have no place else to stay, and there's a war going on. Eviction proceedings would probably be stretched out for weeks or even months, anyway."

"But what about Mr. Holmes? When he comes back–"

"He'll have to deal with it–if they're still there. Gypsies aren't city dwellers. They're more comfortable in the country–in makeshift camps. And since Carlotta must know she can never prevail in court, she'll probably abandon the atelier as soon as it's safe to leave."

"Why don't they leave now? Isn't it safer in the country?"

"At the moment, no. The gendarmes are rounding them up and deporting them. In the city the police have other priorities."

"They ought to just lock them up somewhere."

Tony stopped suddenly and glared at Trey. "They're not criminals, Trey. At least not as far as I know. Don't talk of locking people up because of the way they look."

Trey seemed taken aback. "I didn't mean that, exactly. It's just that gypsies are always stealing stuff and–"

"Again, you don't know that. If they've committed crimes, they'll be charged and tried if there's enough evidence. Got that?"

"Sure. You don't have to get so defensive about it."

They walked on.

"Sorry, Trey. It's just that I want you to have a sense of justice. I come from a place where justice depends on the color of your skin."

"Oh… yes, Papa–now I get it."

CHAPTER 85

In April, Trey graduated from l'École Militaire and simultaneously was awarded his wings. Unfortunately, the Germans had opened a new fighter training school at Valenciennes and stepped up both their recruitment and their manufacture of the latest aircraft. For the first few months of 1917, they dominated the skies, inflicting major losses on the British and the French. Trey, as a rookie pilot, was assigned to reconnaissance during the Battle of Arras.

It so happened that Tony's Red Cross unit was sent to Arras about this time. Though the British succeeded in pushing the Germans back to the Hindenburg Line, the result was another stalemate. Casualties on both sides were heavy.

Tony and his team made repeated forays into the trenches to evacuate the wounded. This was a nearly impossible task, as they were understaffed and the casualties were so massive that they had to leave the less seriously injured groaning and wailing in their agony, while evacuating the ones with mortal injuries, who were curiously quiet. A field hospital was set up to the west of Arras and a permanent hospital was available in Amiens. The noise of exploding artillery shells was constant, though the soldiers in the trenches played cards and wrote letters, seemingly unconcerned with the possibility of a direct hit.

On one of these forays, the sixth of that day, Tony, exhausted but determined to evacuate as many as possible before nightfall, wound his way through a trench nearly knee-deep in mud. He led the way looking for soldiers most in need of medical attention. As he rounded a corner, trying to avoid losing a boot that had come untied in the deep mud, he saw a boy about Trey's age lying on his back staring straight up into the dun-colored sky. He was wearing a French uniform, helmet-less, and shaking. Slightly dark-complected, Tony thought he must be an Arab. His left leg was shattered, the bone sticking out near the knee. He appeared to be in shock. His comrades, attentive to their own wounds, paid no attention to him.

Tony stopped, as necessarily did his companion at the other end of the stretcher. He knelt down to the boy and put his hand on his shoulder, gently lest he have a wound there as well.

"Comment vous appelez-vous, soldat?"

The boy said nothing but turned his head towards Tony and stared.

"Vous êtes blessé," Tony said. "Votre jambe."

"Ma jambe?"

"Oui. On va vous amener à l'hôpital."

"'L'hôpital?'"

"Oui." Then to his partner at the other end of the stretcher: "Faites attention!"

They picked him up, careful not to move his leg any more than necessary and loaded him onto the stretcher. The soldier did not complain. Then they made their way through the labyrinthine trench until they emerged at the other end where the ambulance was parked in a clearing that miraculously still had some grass on it.

"À Amiens!" Tony said to his comrade.

Along the way to the hospital, the boy's leg started bleeding again. Tony tightened the tourniquet that he had applied earlier and the boy suddenly cried out. Tony loosened the tourniquet, but the blood again spurted out.

"Tenez!" Tony said. "Nous y arriverons bientôt!"

Once in the hospital, he and his comrade, Philippe, carried the boy on the stretcher into a hallway strewn with wounded soldiers. No nurse attended them, so Tony used his pen knife to cut away the boy's trousers. The bone was now protruding above the knee, apparently having been aggravated during the bumpy ride to the hospital. The boy was now screaming in pain.

"Morphine!" Philippe called out to a passing nurse.

The nurse stopped for a moment, looked at the boy in his agony, and said: "Il n'y en a plus."

"Trouvez-en!" Tony shouted at her.

The nurse looked startled, then went off into another room. In a minute or two, she came back with a vial of morphine and administered it. The boy almost immediately stopped screaming and soon closed his eyes.

Tony noticed his dog tags dangling from his open shirt and picked it up. The name was clear:

Dufy, Sebastian Alexandre
16ème Régiment d'infanterie
756173

"Sebastian Alexandre," he muttered to himself. Can it be? No...Dufy... but of course if it was Alex, he probably would have taken the surname of the woman–or man–who raised him. Or, if he was brought up in an orphanage, he might have invented the name himself.

As Tony considered these possibilities, a doctor appeared, examined the wound, and ordered Sebastian Alexandre to be taken to an operating room. As it was the last sortie of the day into the trenches, Tony decided to remain in the hospital until the operation was performed.

"Je suis fatigué," Philippe said. He was a bit younger than Tony, a Belgian with a ruddy complexion and a cheerful countenance except when he was exhausted, as he was now. "Je vais dormir dans l'ambulance."

"D'accord," Tony said. Though exhausted as well, he waited in the corridor on a wooden bench with his back against the wall. He nodded off and lost track of the time. He was awakened by the surgeon, who asked whether he was the boy's father.

"Moi?" Tony said. "Pourquoi me posez-vous cette question?"

"Parce que le garçon appelle son 'Papa.' Vous n'êtes pas son père?"

"Non. Il n'est pas mon fils."

The doctor, himself exhausted, sighed. "Bon. Néanmoins, il faut le voir."

Tony thought this was an extraordinary request, but he in fact did want to see the boy.

The doctor directed him to the ward where Sebastian Alexandre lay, alongside a dozen or more young soldiers. He seemed to be asleep.

Tony went to the boy's side and pulled up a stool. After waiting a few minutes, he decided to try an experiment:

"Sebastian Alexandre Goldman."

The boy slowly opened his eyes and looked at Tony intently. "Qui êtes-vous?"

"Tony. Monsieur Tony–un ami de Madame Goldman."

The boy's eyes grew wide. "C'est impossible! Où est ma mère?"

"Elle va bien. À Paris."

It was indeed *that* Sebastian Alexandre. He had only a vague recollection of Tony, thinking that he was a household servant of his mother's. "Monsieur Tony–est-ce que vous êtes mon papa?"

Tony didn't know how to answer this. He really didn't know himself. "C'est possible. Dis-moi ce que tu te souviens."

Alex recounted that wintry afternoon long ago when he was a toddler, yet the event was burned into his mind like a red-hot branding iron. He remembered kicking the soccer ball about the little square on Rue de Furstemberg and when he turned around, a man was dragging his mother off as she screamed for help. He ran after the two of them, but the man swatted him away. He picked himself up and continued to follow them until the man stopped a cab and forced his mother into it. When he reached the door of the cab, his mother reached out to him, and the man, apparently fearful of calling too much attention to the three of them, grabbed him by his coat collar and dragged him into the cab. He clung to his mother's bosom, but the man put a handkerchief over her mouth. Then she seemed to fall asleep.

"Tu te souviens de la gare?"

"Oui."

Alex explained that at the train station, the man supported his mother, though she was groggy and wobbly on her feet. Other passengers stared at them but did nothing. Then, when the train came, the man pushed his mother into a carriage, but suddenly turned and pushed him back onto the platform. Then the train pulled away in a cloud of steam and he ran to catch up but fell down on the platform in a flood of tears. After a minute or two, he looked up and a woman with a kind face picked him up and that's all he remembered.

"Cette femme," Tony said. "Qui était-elle?"

"Elle était ma mère adoptive. Madame Dufy."

Alex then closed his eyes and fell into a deep sleep.

The next morning Tony awoke in the ambulance to the sound of distant explosions, a sound not unusual in itself, but notable because they seemed to be receding and less frequent. He and Philippe made two runs before noon, delivering four soldiers to the field hospitals and two to the hospital in Amiens. While he lingered in the hallway waiting for news of Alex's condition, the doctor who had performed the surgery came up to him and informed him that Alex had developed gangrene and would have to be transferred to Paris as soon as possible if he were to avoid amputation of the leg. The infected area would have to be debrided, and though a relatively simple procedure, there was no time for him to attend to it, nor were there sufficient antiseptics available in Amiens.

Tony went to his superior and received permission to convey Alex to Paris as long as he returned within 48 hours. When told this, the doctor took the opportunity to add three more patients to the trip and off they went, with Tony doing his best to avoid bomb craters and potholes while Philippe tried to keep the wounded stable and hydrated along the way.

In Paris, Tony navigated the ambulance through streets strewn with debris and garbage until they arrived at l'Hôtel Dieu where they unloaded the soldiers with the help of other volunteers. Tony asked that Jackie be notified of his arrival and to meet him in the emergency ward.

"What is it?" Jackie said.

"This boy needs special attention—he's got gangrene and if he has to wait any longer he could lose his leg."

Jackie examined the leg, pulling back the bandages, and concurred. Then off she went to find a doctor who she knew was experienced in such cases.

The doctor had Alex transferred to a ward with about twenty others. He examined the leg and announced that he would have to debride the wound immediately. Another transfer was made to an operating room.

Tony and Jackie waited outside the door.

"What's so special about this soldier?" Jackie said. "There are hundreds of boys who need–"

"He's Madame G's son," Tony said.

Jackie looked stunned. "How do you know?"

"He answered to 'Sebastian Alexandre Goldman,' in spite of his dog tag saying his surname was Dufy. Then he told me about the kidnapping, which is still burned into his brain as if it were yesterday."

Jackie leaned her head against the wall and closed her eyes for a moment. Then she opened them again. "Is he your child, too?"

"I don't know," Tony said. "I honestly don't."

"You'll have to contact her," Jackie said. "She has a right to know."

"Of course. But I don't have time. I have to get back to the front. You'll have to do it."

"Me? No–I can't."

"Why not? The baron's phone number at la Ferrières must be in the book."

Jackie looked him in the eye, then put her hand to her brow and looked away. "All right. I'll do it. When are you returning?"

"I don't know. Have you heard anything from Trey?"

"Yes. They've transferred him to Ypres, where he says the next big push against the Germans will take place. Oh, Tony–I'm so worried that he'll get himself killed."

Tony stroked her hair. "Trey's an excellent pilot, they tell me. And the tide's beginning to turn in our favor."

"And what about that mutiny in Soissons? The French army seems to be falling apart!"

"That's over. Nivelle's been relieved and Pétain has restored morale. Besides, that was just a small portion of the infantry. Trey won't be affected. And the Americans will be ready soon. We'll win–you'll see."

She put her head against his chest as tears ran down her cheeks. "Oh, I hope you're right." Then she pulled herself together. "Is there any chance you'll get to see Trey at Ypres?"

"Possibly. It's not far from Arras."

At this point the doctor appeared and began removing his surgical gloves.

"Vous êtes encore là?" he said. "Bon–il ne faut pas amputer la jambe. Il dort maintenant."

"Merci beaucoup, docteur," Jackie said.

"C'est mon travail," the doctor said. "Alors–venez avec moi. J'ai besoin de votre aide."

Jackie gave Tony a kiss, which seemed to surprise the doctor, but he kept on walking.

"I love you, Tony," she said.

"I love you, too, Jackie," Tony said. "You won't forget to contact Madame G?"

"No. I won't."

Tony lingered for a moment outside the ward, then pushed open the door to see if he might have one last look at Alex.

CHAPTER 86

Jackie didn't know what to expect as she waited in the lobby of l'Hôtel Dieu for Mme G to arrive. She hadn't seen her for years and their last parting had been a bit tense. At the time, she thought she had lost Tony to her and might not see either of them again.

As she sat on a bench in the hall entrance that had been chiseled out of stone centuries earlier, she gazed out through the portals of the building and saw a maroon Rolls Royce pull up and a uniformed chauffeur open the passenger door. A lady in a tweed sporting jacket, split skirt and broad-brimmed straw hat stepped out. It was unmistakably Mme G. She was thinner than Jackie remembered her, and she had streaks of gray in her hair, but she moved with the poise of a natural aristocrat. She was wearing goggles and a veil to protect her eyes from road dust.

Jackie stood and waited, feeling that her nurse's uniform with its small white cap pinned to her blond hair, frizzled due to long hours at the hospital, somehow put her at a disadvantage.

As Mme G ascended the steps to the front entrance, she removed her goggles and pulled back the veil. Jackie remembered the penetrating black eyes that now seemed to search her out amid the bustle of other nurses and visitors.

Mme G removed her kid gloves and extended her hand. "How are you, Jacqueline?"

Jackie shook the hand, hardly conscious she was doing so. Mme G looked so elegant, even with a layer of road dust on her hat and clothes. "I am well, Madame Rothstein."

"Oh, please, you know me better than that. Call me Amelia, as you used to."

"Well, yes, Amelia, you're looking quite well."

"Thank you. I'm a bit older and subject to all manner of infirmities, but for the most part, I can't complain. You, of course, haven't aged a bit!"

"Well, now—"

"No, I'm serious. I saw you in a play not long ago at l'Odéon. What was it? An adaptation of one of Balzac's novels."

"*La Rabouilleuse.*"

"Yes, that's it. You were stunning!"

"Well, thank you. But of course that's ancient history now. Would you like to follow me upstairs to the rehabilitation ward?"

"Oh, yes. I'm anxious to see Alex. If, of course, it is indeed Alex. I can't help thinking that this is some kind of cruel joke."

"Oh, no–it's no joke. Tony is quite sure that he is your son." Jackie stared at Mme G–now Rothstein–for a moment as if to look behind those dark eyes to determine whether Alex was *only* her son and not Tony's.

"Well, shall we go?" Amelia said.

"Yes."

They climbed the ancient stairs and arrived at the first floor, where the staircase opened onto a long corridor illuminated with sunlight streaming through Gothic windows. The doors at the end of the corridor were open and they walked into the ward. This room was a sanctuary from the cacophonous sounds of the rest of the hospital, with its nurses, doctors, and orderlies rushing to and fro. Jackie led Amelia to the bedside of Alex, who was propped up with a pillow, his injured leg suspended by a complicated apparatus of ropes and pulleys. She pulled out a cane-backed chair from the wall for Amelia and stood silently by with her hands folded over her apron.

Alex, who had been reading a book of poems, set the slim volume aside and gazed up at Amelia. "Qui êtes-vous?"

"Je suis...Émilie," Amelia said, using the French version of her name. "Émilie Goldman."

Alex looked at her wide-eyed. "Goldman? Maman?"

"Oui." Amelia put her hand on his. "Je suis votre mère."

Alex, who had not been warned of his mother's arrival by her own request, seemed dumbstruck. "Non–c'est impossible!"

"C'est vrai, Sebastian Alexandre Goldman. Nous sommes enfin réunis!"

Alex nearly leapt out of the bed to embrace her but was restrained by the pulley apparatus.

"Non, non, mon chéri," Amelia said. She rose and kissed him on the forehead. "Tu dois te reposer. Il faut penser à ta jambe. Do you speak English?"

"Anglais? Un peu."

"Bon. Now, can you tell me what happened at the railway station that day we were separated?"

As Alex began to tell his story, his childhood memories informed and stimulated his English. His adoptive mother, Madame Dufy as he called her, was a former model of the painter Raoul Dufy and she had a romantic relationship with him, but he spurned her and she was returning to Le

Havre at the time, where they had both grown up. Realizing that she could not have children, she discovered Alex abandoned at the railway station and decided to make him her own, giving both of them the name of Dufy. His adoptive mother then looked for modeling jobs in Le Havre, with only sporadic success. She filled in the gaps with waitressing and factory work at a nearby textile mill but continued to struggle to make ends meet. She also had several lovers, who treated her badly and had no time for the boy. At last, because of his name, he was admitted to an art school, but could not keep up with the tuition payments. Finally, he left the school and joined the army.

"And your adoptive maman," Amelia said. "Where is she?"

"I heard she died," Alex said in suddenly unaccented English. "A friend in the army from Le Havre said she was in a train accident. But he was always telling stories."

Amelia's eyes began to water and she wiped the tears away. "You must come and live with me."

"With you? Where?"

"At la Ferrières. But after the war we will return to Paris."

"Ah–and where is la Ferrières?"

"Not far from Paris. It's very peaceful there. You'll see."

"And what about Papa? Monsieur Tony?"

Jackie cringed at his question and had been on the verge of tears herself when she heard it.

"Tony is not your papa," Amelia said gently.

"Non? Donc–qui est-ce?"

"Tu vas voir."

This puzzled Jackie, though she was relieved that Amelia had not named Tony as the father. But then Alex's response in French echoed in her own mind– 'then who is'?

CHAPTER 87

Alex remained in the hospital for another two weeks, during which time Amelia came to visit every day. She brought him books–some of which he requested–as well as fresh fruits from the baron's orchard and cakes from the chateau's larder. All of this largesse made Alex very popular among the other patients and he distributed it liberally.

Once his leg healed enough for him to stand on it, he took daily walks around the hospital and its courtyard. Amelia brought him an elegant cane made of ebony with a carved ivory elephant's head that he was somewhat embarrassed to use. The other soldiers joked that Amelia was really his lover and was masquerading as his mother.

Finally, his discharge came through and Amelia arrived in the Rolls to take him home to la Ferrières.

"Mama," Alex said as the Rolls pulled out of the Parisian traffic and onto a country road. "Is the baron my papa?"

"The baron *will* be your papa," Amelia said. "He has agreed to legally adopt you."

Alex remained silent for a mile or so, then said, "Does he have other children?"

"Yes, but they're grown and gone away now. You'll meet them soon enough."

Alex remained silent for another mile. "Am I never to know who my real papa is?"

Amelia patted him on the knee. "Perhaps. But does it matter? The main thing is that you now have a mama and a papa who care about you and who will give you a home. Would you like to go to university after the war?"

"University? I don't know. Does the baron speak English?"

Amelia laughed. "He does speak English–and better than you or I."

The chauffeur pulled the Rolls into the long drive and parked it parallel to the steps that led to the chateau. Two liveried servants met them at the steps, one of whom was J-P, who took Alex's duffle bag, which contained all of his earthly possessions. Still in his uniform, Alex commanded respect from the servants, who escaped military service due to the baron's connections.

"This is his house?" Alex said in amazement, as his eyes took in the three-story edifice, with its towers at each corner and its central double staircase that led to the colonnaded entry.

"This is *your* house," his mother said. "At least for now. When the baron dies it will belong to your brothers and sisters as well as you, but as they are much older than you, it may be all yours someday."

"What would I do with so many rooms?" Alex said.

Amelia laughed as she opened her parasol and looked up at the gray clouds, which were beginning to dispense droplets of rain. "You'll need to marry and have lots of children. Let's hurry–how is your leg?"

"A little stiff, but I can manage."

The front door opened as they approached. An elderly man with gray side whiskers and a slightly stooped posture appeared.

"Is that the baron?"

"It is indeed," Amelia said. "He's anxious to meet you."

They ascended the steps and the baron greeted Amelia with a hug and a kiss, then turned to Alex with outstretched arms. Alex balked, not expecting such a warm embrace. The baron kissed him on both cheeks and patted him on the shoulder.

"Bienvenue, mon fils! Ça va bien? Comment va ta jambe?"

"Ça va. Je suis ravi de faire votre connaissance, Monsieur le Baron."

"Allons, donc, tu es mon fils maintenant! Nous devons nous tutoyer."

"D'accord."

"Do you speak English like your mama?"

"Yes, sir. It was my first language."

"Then we shall speak English." The baron stood aside and with a sweep of his arm indicated that he and Amelia should enter. "Make yourself at home! Jean-Pierre, porte les baggages de Maître Alexandre en haut."

As J-P escorted him upstairs, Alex got the uncomfortable feeling that this liveried servant was watching his every move. Of course he noticed that J-P was a North African and had a complexion similar to his own. Alex had always thought that his bronze coloring came from Algerians who emigrated to southern France sometime in the mid-19th century. At other times, however, he thought that his father was Tony, who he had only a vague recollection of before their encounter at Arras. But the idea that he was descended from slaves did not sit well with him, and he was somewhat relieved when his mother declared flatly that Tony was not his father.

"Bienvenue, Maître Alexandre," J-P said after putting the duffel bag down and opening the curtains. "Désirez-vous autre chose?"

"Non, merci, Jean-Pierre."

J-P did not move, but stood stock still like a soldier on parade, staring at him.

"C'est tout, Jean-Pierre," Alex said.

"Monsieur—"

"Oui?"

"Puis-je vous poser une question?"

"Oui."

J-P seemed to dither about for a moment, as if unsure of the propriety of the forthcoming question.

"Alors?" Alex said, expectantly.

"Est-ce que votre père…"

"Oui?"

"Est-ce que votre père est Monsieur Tony?"

"Non. Je ne sais pas qui est mon père."

"Ah. Je suis désolé, Maître Alexandre. Je vous ai connu quand vous étiez jeune. Vous ne vous souvenez pas de moi?"

"Non, Jean-Pierre. J'étais trop jeune."

"Ah, oui. Donc…ça ne fait rien. Merci. Appelez-moi si vous avez besoin de quelque chose."

"D'accord."

After J-P had gone, Alex sat down on the bed and pondered this curious exchange. Why was J-P so interested in who his father was? Considering his stature now as the son, albeit adopted, of a baron, it seemed to him a rather impertinent question. What was it to him?

But this conversation was soon forgotten as Alex looked around the spacious room that was now his. A fifteen-foot coffered ceiling with plaster florettes, gold trimmed paneling to the tops of the walls where they arched towards a Venetian chandelier of cut-glass, portraits of very staid-looking ladies and gentlemen of past centuries curiously mixed with post-Impressionist paintings. The bed was covered with a *couvre-lit* of intricately figured silk. He dropped his cane to the floor and leaned back into a pile of voluminous pillows.

It crossed his mind for a moment that he had died. For it seemed that he had been delivered from the trenches of Arras to a place that surely must be Heaven.

CHAPTER 88

Jean-Louis Raynouard de Koenigsbourg did not study engineering at l'École Polytechnique for nothing.

True, he did not graduate, but that was due to a completely false accusation that he had cheated on his final exam. And that was of course made by a fellow student who was jealous of his aristocratic breeding, as people of the lower sort always are. He made short work of this fellow in the dormitory later that night by stabbing him with his penknife, but unfortunately the blade only penetrated the fleshy portion of his midriff, just below the diaphragm. The boy squealed like the pig he was, but the screams alerted the others and Jean-Louis was expelled from school even before the academic committee issued a ruling on his case.

But no matter. Now he was in a position to resume his scientific studies. The so-called *Île du Diable* was a paradise! The vicomte had his own little thatched hut on a promontory only a few meters from the ocean, with gentle windward breezes, steady enough to blow the mosquitoes away. This splendid isolation was designed by the authorities to separate him from the other prisoners, on the premise that he was too dangerous to be held in close proximity to them. Ridiculous! What did he have to do with them? In any case, it gave him the privacy and seclusion he desired, as well as the time to pursue his studies.

Although this situation was pleasant, it was by no means ideal. He would have liked to move freely about, perhaps visit the mainland, even do some gambling in Paramaribo. Also, the food was execrable, and he often dreamed of gourmet dining in Paris, or even in his home in Neuilly-sur-Seine. Ah! How he missed the old chateau!

But to work. It seemed to him that if he could contribute somehow, in some significant way, to the war effort he could appeal to the French legislature—never mind the imbecilic and corrupt judiciary—or perhaps even the president and obtain his release. But how to do this?

The project he settled upon was suggested to him in a dream. He dreamed that he was underwater, swimming about without need of an external apparatus for the purpose of breathing and spotted a submarine coming his way. This submarine, it seemed, was unusually long and shaped exactly like a penis. He found this somewhat disturbing at first but decided to hitch a ride. He clung to an antenna that protruded from the conning tower and trailed along effortlessly until the submarine suddenly transformed itself into a woman! This was even more disturbing, especially since the woman resembled his wife.

He woke about that time and so was deprived of the opportunity–if there had been one–of somehow destroying his wife, er, the submarine.

But what if he could devise a method, a weapon, that would finish the job? At present, so far as he knew, there was no defense against submarines. They roamed at will beneath the waves, torpedoed Allied shipping, and disappeared into the inky-black depths of the sea.

He sat at a table, rather roughly fashioned by ignorant savages, no doubt, and stared at a blank sheet of paper that was allowed by the prison authorities. He had asked for, and received, a compass–with a blunt point, but it would serve as well–and a slide rule. This last instrument he had slipped into his pocket when he was first interviewed by the warden, a stupid man who fancied himself a mathematician, when he turned his back. The fool did not suspect him–perhaps he hadn't even missed it to this day, for what would he use it for? Calculating the price of mangoes?

The vicomte stared at this blank sheet of paper for a while, then, quite aware of the way geniuses work, simply started drawing. A horizontal line here, an oblique line there. Soon he had something he could work with. A little motor with a propeller at the end of one line, a steam-driven catapult on top of what now looked like the deck of a ship. The drawing was becoming more complex. He took some measurements and added more decks below the waterline.

A catapult! An ancient device for launching missiles of all sorts, beginning with rocks and now even airplanes, as he had seen in photographs of American battleships. Well, this was a start. But how would this missile, as it were, be guided to its target, a target that was submerged?

As he was pondering this difficult problem, he heard a knock at the door. Suspecting it was the warden, he removed the slide rule from the table and finding no better place to hide it quickly, slipped it into his waistband. It was awkward and uncomfortable, but it would have to do.

"Entrez."

The vicomte remained seated as the door was pushed open–there was no lock, only a latch that didn't really work–and the warden appeared. He was a short, balding man with a powerful build which was somewhat intimidating to most, but not to the vicomte. He knew that there were ways of defending himself against stronger men–he had done it many times in his life. One had only to distract them by some ridiculous ruse, like, 'Regardez là-bas!' and then thrust home with a knife, a fork, even a kick in the groin.

"Bonjour, Monsieur le Vicomte," the warden said.

"Bonjour. Qu'est-ce qu'il y a?"

"Désolé de vous déranger, mais il y a des détenus qui se sont échappés de l'Île."

"Échappés?" This was both alarming and encouraging to the vicomte at the same time. Alarming because escaped prisoners–most of whom resented him for what they regarded as special treatment–and encouraging because it showed that it was possible to escape this dreadful island even though he sometimes thought of it as a paradise. "Quand?"

"Ce matin. Vous n'avez vu personne par ici?"

"Non. Personne à part toi." The vicomte always asserted his superiority over underlings like the warden, even though the latter was nominally his master, by using the familiar 'toi.' The warden, on the other hand, always addressed him as 'vous.'

"Bon. Vous m'avertirez si vous voyez quelqu'un?"

"Oui."

"Merci beaucoup."

The warden pulled the door to and left.

What a fool the man was! Two or more prisoners, vicious murderers no doubt, simply walk off right under his nose! Of course the island was small, the currents treacherous, and the water infested with sharks, especially this time of year. There was little chance that they would escape.

Mais, un moment! The warden had left him exposed. What if these degenerates were to descend upon his little hut? He rose from his chair abruptly, only to have the slide rule stab him in the groin. He cried out in pain, but quickly suppressed it. Then, after throwing the device against the wall, he went to the door and secured the latch as best he could. Useless! As he looked around for some tool, some method of securing it, he heard horses. Apparently, the warden was not alone–there was a sort of posse.

A disadvantage of this hut, aside from the flimsy latch, was that there were no windows on the leeward side. There were two on the windward side, overlooking the rocks and surf below, one on each side of the door that led to his little veranda. And of course no one was likely to approach from that side. But on the leeward side, how was he to know if anyone approached?

Ah–an alarm system. Easy enough. He rummaged about his meager belongings and could find nothing of use. But then he had an idea–the drawstring in the waistband of his trousers, which were actually pajamas. He pulled it out and found that it was quite long enough. Then it was only a matter of collecting the tins that his food was delivered in and that the guards were stupid enough to leave with him.

In a matter of fifteen minutes he had a first-rate alarm system.

CHAPTER 89

When Tony returned to Arras, he discovered that the battle was moving north towards Ypres. He had no idea why this was happening, but he did know that Trey was now flying missions out of a makeshift airfield at a farm near Messines, south of Ypres. As there was little to do in Arras save delivering bandages and medicines to the hospital, he drove up to Messines and introduced himself to the French commander at the airbase.

Capitaine Bertrand Lanvin was a little younger than Tony, clean-shaven except for a pencil moustache, and had a very prominent Gallic nose. He seemed officious but amiable after a few minutes' conversation.

"Vous-etes le père du sous-lieutenant Jones?" he said, studying Tony's features with some puzzlement. "Êtes-vous sûr?"

"Absolument," Tony said, somewhat amused at the captain's astonishment. He pulled out his wallet and produced a photo of himself, Jackie, and Trey at his graduation from l'École Militaire.

Capitaine Lanvin studied the photo, then looked at Tony with a big smile on his face. "Bon. C'est une jolie famille."

"Merci. Pouvez-vous me dire où je peux le trouver?"

"Il est en reconnaissance."

"Quand reviendra-t-il?"

The captain shrugged his shoulders, then looked at his watch. "Vers... quinze heures."

Three o'clock. Tony thanked the captain and said he'd wait for him. The captain helpfully pointed out that there was a cantine next door where he could get a cup of coffee and perhaps a croissant. Tony availed himself of both, returned to the ready room and took a seat near a window where he could watch the planes taking off and landing.

The sky was gray and with only a few breaks in the cloud cover. There had been a great deal of rain over the past couple of months, a condition that had contributed to a stalemate between the two armies. Tony wondered how effective these airplanes could be in such weather and it worried him that it might make it difficult for the pilots to locate the airfield on their return. But he saw plane after plane make a safe landing.

By four o'clock it seemed that nearly all of the planes had returned. Several had bullet holes in the wings or the fuselage. The pilots came into the ready room, their goggles pushed up onto their leather caps, laughing and joking as if they had been enjoying a game of soccer. Their hands were in constant motion, describing the maneuvers of their machines during combat.

After scrutinizing the aviators–their helmets and goggles made it difficult to tell one from another–and seeing no sign of Trey, he went up to Capitaine Lanvin's desk and asked whether all of the pilots had returned.

The captain looked up from his logbook at Tony. "Tous? Non, pas encore." He looked down again and ran his forefinger down the list of pilots and their machines. "Il nous en manque six."

Six to come. Tony thanked him and sat down again next to the window. A light rain began to fall.

Over the next hour he counted four more planes landing, one of which lost a wheel as it touched down and crashed into a hedge at the end of the runway. Pilots and ground crewmen alike rushed to assist the pilot and pulled him out of the cockpit before the plane burst into flames. The pilot was unhurt, the fire quickly extinguished, and he and his fellow pilots returned to the ready room laughing and joking as the others had before. It struck Tony that this was an elite group of daredevils, something like a troupe of circus performers who reveled in taking risks.

There were still two planes missing. Tony looked at his watch. Five o'clock. It was beginning to get dark. The rain continued but abated somewhat and was now a light mist. Finally, another plane appeared about a half a mile from the runway. Its wings were dipping to one side, then the other, as if the pilot were having trouble controlling the aircraft. Capitaine Lanvin noticed this, as did the others, and they all rushed out of the hut and onto the field. Tony followed them.

The plane touched down with its left wheel first, bounced back up into the air, touched again with the other wheel, and somehow managed to settle onto the runway. The engine was popping and sputtering. Finally, it came to a stop and everyone rushed over to the plane and greeted the pilot with much laughter and backslapping as they had with the previous near disaster.

But this was not Trey.

Tony, forlorn and on edge, hesitated to apply to the captain again, so he went back to his seat at the window and continued to peer out at the increasing darkness.

The pilots were beginning to drink beer now, but the initial rowdiness had died down as they realized that one of their comrades was still missing.

Finally, the last pilot to land safely walked over to the window, a mug of beer in his hand, and looked out.

"Merde," he said. "Où est-il?"

It was clear as to whom he was referring. Tony stood and looked out as well. It was too dark for a safe landing now. And it was too dangerous for groundsmen to set out fire pots that the Germans could use for targeting.

"Vous l'avez vu?" Tony said.

"Oui," the pilot said. "Il a reçu un coup. La fumée sortait de son moteur."

"Smoke?" Tony said. "Did you see his plane go down?"

The pilot turned to him, surprised to suddenly be addressed in English. "Eh? You are English?"

"I'm Trey's father."

Like the captain earlier, the pilot found this hard to believe and looked him up and down. "You are sure?"

"Certainly I am sure. What happened?"

The pilot explained that he and Trey had been flying reconnaissance to determine the position of the German guns when a squadron of Fokkers descended upon them. They put up a fight, but there were too many of them. Both planes were hit, but the pilot was so preoccupied with keeping his own craft in the air that he lost sight of Trey.

"Did you see him go down?"

"Non, Monsieur. Perhaps he was able to land in a field. The Fokkers assumed it was a kill and came after me. They fired a few bursts, then when I dropped below a ridge they gave up and flew away."

"Did you hear an explosion?"

"Non. I am sorry, Monsieur Jones. But who knows? He may still be alive."

This was cold comfort for Tony, who drove back to Arras in the dark— headlights off, the road illuminated by occasional flashes of lightning–as it again began to rain.

What was he going to tell Jackie?

CHAPTER 90

Two days later Tony drove back to Paris with Philippe and three seriously wounded soldiers. One of the soldiers died along the way despite Philippe's efforts to revive him.

When they arrived at l'Hôtel Dieu, the dead soldier was taken to the morgue while the other two were taken up to the first-floor ward, which was now overflowing. In the noise and confusion, Tony managed at last to spot Jackie, who was attending a soldier on a cot in the corridor. Her hair was falling down in her face as she bent over to reassure the soldier that his leg wouldn't be amputated, and she kept pushing it back over her shoulder. When the boy finally seemed to calm down and close his eyes, she looked up at Tony.

"Why don't you just cut it?" Tony said.

"I guess I'll have to. There seems to be a shortage of pins, like everything else. Did you get a chance to see Trey?"

Tony still had not figured out how to break the news to her, though he had been rehearsing various stratagems all the way from Arras. "I met his squadron commander. They had a difficult day."

"Difficult? What does that mean?"

Tony gave her a kiss on the cheek and guided her along the corridor towards the cantine. "Why don't we have a cup of coffee and I'll tell you all about it?"

Jackie looked dubious but walked alongside him. "Speaking of haircuts, you could use a trim."

"There's a shortage of barbers at the front, too."

Once they were settled in their chairs at one of the trestle tables in the cantine, Tony took a sip of his coffee and looked at her. Still beautiful, he thought, even with the stress of her job and the emerging crow's feet at the corners of her eyes.

"Well?" she said.

"Well...I'm afraid there's bad news."

Jackie gasped and put her hand to her mouth as if to prevent her from screaming.

"But there's good news as well," he said.

"What...what's the bad news? Is he—"

"He was shot down east of Ypres."

Jackie stared wildly.

"But there's reason to believe he's still alive."

"Oh, Tony! 'Reason to believe'? What do you mean, 'reason to believe'?"

"His partner that day says he may have landed safely in a farmer's field. He saw him go down but there was no explosion, no fire." Tony was embellishing this image somewhat, having no idea whether there had been a fire or not, nor even whether Trey had had a soft landing in a farmer's field. But he wanted to allay Jackie's fears as much as possible.

"Then was he...captured?"

"There's no way of telling. He's simply listed as missing. But I would wager that he's sitting in some farmhouse right now having a warm cup of coffee just as we are."

"Oh, Tony—don't try to sugar-coat it for my benefit. What farm? The farms have all been obliterated. And coffee? Where would he get coffee?"

"All right. If you insist on the unvarnished truth, he's probably in a POW camp by now. But even the Germans are human. And there seems to be a kind of brotherhood among pilots that transcends national boundaries. If he's been captured, he'll probably be well-treated."

Jackie stared at him skeptically for a moment, then looked away at nothing in particular. Then she started crying.

"Jackie—"

"Oh, I can't be seen crying." She wiped the tears away with her apron. "There's so much pain and misery all around us. It's almost obscene to cry over Trey when he's probably safe while amputated limbs are being stacked up in the basement and boys are screaming for morphine."

Tony looked down at his coffee and suddenly felt guilty for drinking it. "We'll make it through. We'll all make it through. Captain Lanvin tells me that the Germans have been pushed back fifty kilometers. That's significant in this war. And the American army will be in on the fray and push them back even farther. It'll all be over in a matter of months."

"I hope you're right."

Tony left the hospital feeling encouraged by his own soothing words to Jackie. Of course he had no idea of when the war would end, and neither did anyone else. But optimism was contagious and besides, what other course could they take? Optimism, hope—whatever you wanted to call it—was necessary to prevail.

As he returned to the ambulance, he expected to find Philippe waiting for him, but he wasn't there. After waiting himself for a few minutes he became impatient and decided that if Philippe had dallied, perhaps visiting with one of the nurses, he might as well go for a walk. He still had a lot of pent-up energy, nervous energy, really; it would require some exercise to settle down.

As he walked along the Seine, watching the constant movement of bateaux, now laden with munitions and lorries rather than coal, he realized that he hadn't seen Inspector Rochard for a while. The Préfecture was just opposite the Parvis de Notre-Dame. He decided to pay the inspector a visit.

When he arrived at the Préfecture, however, he was told that the inspector had been promoted to Commandant de Police and was now at the Police Judiciaire around the corner on the Quai des Orfèvres. So Tony descended to the street again and managed to locate the entrance.

The desk sergeant directed him to an elevator, which took him to the third floor, where, at the end of a long corridor he encountered another reception desk, this one 'manned' by a woman. She was an attractive brunette and wore a uniform with chevrons on either sleeve. Tony wondered at this phenomenon and surmised that there must be a shortage of male recruits due to the war. After asking his name and business ("Je suis un ancien ami") she rose from her desk and knocked on a door just behind her.

"Entrez."

She pushed the door open and Inspecteur, now Commandant, Rochard looked up. "Monsieur Jones! You have come to help me with my English. And quite overdue, if I may say so." He rose from his desk. "Come in, come in."

The receptionist withdrew and Tony entered the office. "I think your English is as sharp as ever, Monsieur le Commandant. And I see you are moving up in the world."

"It depends on what you mean by 'up.' Yes, I have a larger office and a better view of the Seine, as you can see." He indicated the expansive view of the river and the Left Bank. "But I am overwhelmed by paperwork. I miss the, how do you say, *travail de terrain*."

"Fieldwork," Tony suggested.

"Ah. Bon," the commandant said. "Please have a seat, Monsieur Jones. We have much to talk about. In fact, I've been meaning to contact you about one item in particular."

Tony took his seat. "And what is that?"

The commandant, having just sat down, popped up again. He seemed to have lost no energy or enthusiasm for the job over the years. He went over to a filing cabinet and extracted a newspaper clipping. "Voilà! I don't know if you have seen this–it appeared on the back pages of *Le Figaro* only last week." He handed Tony the clipping.

"I haven't had much time to read newspapers, Monsieur le Commandant." Tony unfolded the article and read the header:

Détenu psychopathe déjoué par son propre système d'alarme

The article went on to say that the vicomte had improvised an alarm system composed of tin cans tied to a cord in order to warn him of the approach of a trio of escaped prisoners on Devil's Island. The system failed, however, or at least failed to defend him from his assailants, who entered his secluded cabin and strangled him with the cord. The intruders apparently thought that the vicomte, being the wealthiest prisoner on the island, had hidden some cash or jewels in his hut. They intended to then escape the island via a small raft they had constructed of fallen logs but were apprehended by the prison authorities before they could do so. The warden said that a posse in the area heard the rattling of the cans and rushed to the sound where they discovered the vicomte's lifeless body.

Tony looked up to see the commandant sitting at his desk with a Chesire cat's grin on his face.

"Better than the guillotine, no?"

Tony folded the clipping up and handed it back to him. "I suppose there's some kind of poetic justice in it."

"Justice–yes. A long time in coming and via a very circu-circu-"

"Circuitous."

"Yes–circu-*y*-tous. An excellent word. A circu-*y*-tous route. But justice nevertheless."

Tony wasn't sure that he could share the commandant's glee in the violent demise of the vicomte. But he had to admit that it was something of a relief to know that this unrepentant, deranged creature who delighted in the suffering of others and had always been protected by his wealth and aristocratic status was now forever silenced.

At that moment, there was a knock on the door and *la belle caporale* entered carrying a thick packet. She handed it to the commandant and said: "Le budget annuel, Monsieur le Commandant." Then she left.

Rochard picked up the budget, thumbed through a few pages and sighed. "You see what comes of a life's work in the préfecture, Monsieur Jones–paperwork. paperwork, and more paperwork. C'est très ennuyeux."

Tony rose from his chair. "You have my condolences, Monsieur le Commandant. I've enjoyed our little chat, but I must be going now."

Rochard stood and extended his hand. "Ah, yes, to the front, I'm sure." He seemed to notice Tony's white tunic with the Croix-Rouge armband on the sleeve for the first time. "I envy you, Monsieur Jones. The action, the excitement, saving the lives of our brave soldiers. Bonne chance!"

"Merci beaucoup, Monsieur le Commandant. À la prochaine."

Tony nodded to the receptionist-corporal, who smiled back, then retraced his steps down the long corridor, down the ancient steps rather than taking the elevator, and finally, with some relief, found himself on the quay where the sun was just breaking through the clouds.

When he arrived at the ambulance, he found Philippe with his foot propped up on the running board, elbow on his knee, talking to a pretty girl.

CHAPTER 91

Things did not look good for the Allies in January of 1918. Despite the inclement weather, the Germans mounted a bombing campaign against Paris that continued into March. Parisians took shelter in the new metro stations. And in that same month, a new threat manifested itself in the form of long-range shelling from somewhere outside of Paris. At first everyone thought these were bombs being dropped from high-altitude Zeppelins since no airplanes could be seen. But examination of the fragments revealed that they were artillery shells, which led to speculation that somehow the Germans had set up their canons in the forests just outside of the city. When this was proven not to be true, the only conclusion to be reached was that the Germans had devised some kind of 'Super Gun' that had a range far beyond anything possessed by the Allies. This notion in turn, spread fear among the population that they were at the mercy of an enemy with superior technology.

The long-belated entry of the American Expeditionary Force into the war finally began about this time, but only with a token force under General Pershing. However, this also marked the first time that American aero squadrons joined the fight to clear the skies of German bombers.

With more and more Americans in the war, the new American Hospital in Neuilly-sur-Seine was put into service and Tony found himself delivering wounded to this institution nearly as often as the Hôtel Dieu.

There was still no news of Trey. The French High Command sent Tony and Jackie a letter officially notifying them that their son was missing in action without further explanation. To make things worse, Jackie had come down with a particularly virulent strain of the flu. It seemed that this disease was spreading throughout the city, especially among health workers. Thus, on Tony's most recent visit to the Hôtel Dieu, he was directed to a special ward where Jackie was quarantined. He sat in a chair by her bedside and watched her as she slept. She was pale and the hollowness of her cheeks reminded him of the way Mme G looked when he saw her for the first time since she returned from California. He also noticed that she had cut her hair very short, just below her ears.

"Jackie?" he said, as she turned her head towards him and her eyelids fluttered open.

"Tony? Oh, darling, don't get too close."

"No, I won't. How do you feel?"

"Better. I think the worst is over."

Tony wanted to reach out and kiss her, but he restrained himself. A nurse stood at the door of the ward like a sentinel, guarding against any infraction of the rules.

"Have you heard anymore about Trey?" she said.

"Nothing. Well, there is something. One of Trey's compatriots said that he flew over a German airfield at Valenciennes and dropped a couple of bombs on it. Of course it was foolhardy and he drew a barrage of small arms fire, but somehow he escaped and noticed a camp with barbed wire around it. Flying low, he could see that the POWs were Allied pilots by their jackets. He thinks that Trey might be one of them."

"Well...that's something. But how would he know that?"

"He doesn't. Just a hunch."

Jackie sighed and closed her eyes again.

"When can you go home?" Tony said.

She opened them again. "I don't know. The doctor says maybe in a few days. Maybe sooner. I'm taking up space. But when I'm completely well, I'll have to come back."

"You don't have to do anything. You're a volunteer, remember?"

"Like you. Like everyone else. Are you going to quit?"

"No, of course not."

"Well, then."

Tony's respect for his wife grew with each day of the war. He didn't know where she got this resolve. Her mother, he supposed. Speaking of Lucinda, how was she faring in London? The Germans, he had heard, were sending Zeppelins over the city almost daily.

As if Jackie were reading his mind, she said, "Mama had a bomb land in her garden."

"What? How do you know? What happened?"

"I got a telegram from her. The lines are still open. She says a Zeppelin dropped the bomb but it didn't explode. A crew came out and defused it."

"What luck! What else did she say?"

"That she's still putting on plays in the city. But they have to do it by candlelight. And when the bombing's really bad, they go underground."

Tony smiled. "That's Lucinda, all right. The woman is invincible."

Jackie managed a laugh, then closed her eyes again and fell asleep.

Tony looked up at the nurse in the doorway, who nodded her head as if to say, 'Time's up!' He kissed the tips of his fingers and pressed them against Jackie's forehead.

As he left the hospital, he heard the usual explosions, though these seemed closer and more frequent. He had heard the Church at St-Gervais had been destroyed by a shell a few days earlier and that nearly a hundred people had been killed. He had no desire to go and gape at the ruins as others were doing, even though it was only just across the Pont Arcole. Besides, he needed to go by the apartment and see if everything was all right there. Camille had gone to live with her sister and the other servants at the baron's chateau at la Ferrières. There was no one to look after the place now that Jackie was in the hospital.

When he arrived at the apartment he looked up at the façade and what he could see of the roof. It looked intact. He started to enter the building when it occurred to him that he ought to check out Nat's building as well. Replacing the key in his pocket, he rounded the corner at Rue de Fleurus and saw piles of rubble in the street with firemen doing their best to clear it away. As he approached Nat's building, he looked up and saw a gaping hole where the atelier had been. The floors immediately beneath it had collapsed and the windows were gone except for the ones on the ground floor, though the glass had been blown out of those.

As he approached the front door, one of the firemen stopped him.

"Attention! Il y a un danger d'effondrement!"

Tony backed off but continued to stare at the hole. Were Carlotta and her friends in the atelier when the shell hit? He turned to the fireman. "Y a-t-il eu des blessés?"

"Oui. Ils ont été envoyés à l'hôpital."

"Personne n'a été tué?"

"Je ne sais pas."

Tony returned to the apartment wondering what had happened to Carlotta and her gypsy friends. Were they buried in the rubble? Did they survive and thus among those sent to the hospital? He would have to check at the Hôtel Dieu tomorrow to see. Maybe they weren't even home when the shell hit. And of course he'd have to send a telegram to Nat.

Nat's paintings–surely they were all destroyed. Ten years or more of work wiped out in seconds!

Tony admonished himself for being relieved at getting the last of his own paintings out before the shelling. How lucky could he get!

He went back to the apartment and found that there were some cracks in the wall adjacent to Nat's building. A couple of framed paintings–one of them a gift from Nat–that had hung in the hallway between the bedrooms had crashed to the floor. It occurred to him that this painting of Nat's was perhaps the only one of his that had survived the blast. It was quite a good painting, actually, of the gyspsy camp in the Bois de Boulogne in a Fauvist style. He leaned the paintings against the wall and went into his studio. Here he found no damage. Even a canvas he had left on the easel had not been disturbed. He sat on a stool and stared at it for a while.

He hadn't painted anything since he and Jackie joined la Croix-Rouge. Why not? Well, of course they were both busy with the war effort. But he had visited the apartment almost weekly since then and hadn't thought of picking up a brush.

What would be the point? It seemed like a frivolous use of one's time when there was so much death and destruction everywhere one turned. On the other hand, wasn't it his duty as an artist to record the anguish, the suffering, even the respites and solace in the midst of a war? Journalists did it, novelists did it, photographers did it. Why shouldn't artists contribute their perspective in their own unique medium? And as an ambulance driver at the front day in and day out, didn't he have something of value to say?

After staring at the blank canvas for nearly a half hour, he picked up a charcoal pencil and began sketching.

CHAPTER 92

At the Battle of Amiens in August, the German defenses broke down and the Allies rushed into the gaps through the Hindenburg Line. Gradually, the fighting shifted southeast to the Argonne Forest along the river Meuse. By September more than a million American troops had been thrown into the battle and Tony found himself evacuating wounded soldiers from the States, some of whom were even younger than Trey.

Jackie recovered from the influenza that was now spreading throughout Paris and threatening to overwhelm the Hôtel Dieu. It seemed that she had developed an immunity that enabled her to attend to victims of the disease without fear of a relapse. But many were not so lucky as she was and died despite her and the doctors' best efforts. The soldiers were the most vulnerable since they lived in the trenches where rats, fleas, and raw sewage combined to form a lethal cocktail.

Unfortunately, Tony was not immune and after repeated forays into the trenches of the Argonne, he contracted the disease. At first a fever, then vomiting. He was treated briefly in the field with sodium bicarbonate, then dismissing it as a bad cold, made a final run into Paris and promptly collapsed on the steps of the Hôtel Dieu. Philippe helped get him inside where he was properly diagnosed, rehydrated and treated with quinine. As the hospital was an incubator of the disease, and few beds were available anyway, he was sent home to the apartment where he was quarantined and looked after in the evenings by Jackie.

"You're becoming a first-rate nurse," Tony said between coughs as he sat in bed with his head propped up against a pillow.

Jackie was sitting next to the bed ladling out some chicken soup. "I just do what the doctors tell me to do. Open wide."

Tony obliged and swallowed the soup. "I think I'll do some painting. This is getting to be extremely boring."

"Not yet. You're barely hydrated to a normal level and you're weak as a kitten. Maybe tomorrow."

"I don't think I have a fever anymore."

"That's your opinion. The thermometer says otherwise."

Tony almost laughed but felt a pain in his chest and suppressed it. After finishing off the soup he closed his eyes and promptly fell asleep.

Jackie went back to the kitchen and cleaned up. Afterwards she made some tea for herself and sat on the balcony overlooking the Gardens. A couple of trees had been knocked down by a shell, their trunks shattered and sticking out of the ground like matchsticks. She wondered at their luck at being spared while the shells fell on either side of them, destroying Nat's building and wreaking havoc in the Gardens. Of course it wasn't over, but she hadn't heard any explosions for the last couple of days.

She picked up a copy of a newspaper that Tony had brought back from the front. This was one of the 'trench newspapers' that were written and published by ordinary soldiers at the front who were skeptical of the news about the war from traditional papers like *Le Figaro* and *Le Matin*. *Le Canard Enchâiné* was one of the most popular, often irreverent and sardonic and sometimes in questionable taste. But it also published news that the traditional papers either missed or ignored.

Jackie thumbed through this periodical, laughing at some of the cartoons and skimming over some of the more extreme political opinions. But one article on a back page grabbed her attention:

Liste des prisonniers de guerre à Montmédy

It seemed that a POW had escaped from a German-controlled hospital near Montmédy, just north of Verdun, that contained a number of French prisoners wounded in action. This escapee provided his commanders with a list of the POWs, both in the camp and the hospital. Among them was one 'Antonio Jones III, sous-lieutenant et pilote.'

Jackie nearly jumped out of her skin. Her teacup rattled around in its saucer and finally fell to the floor and broke into a hundred pieces, but she hardly noticed. She ran into the bedroom and found Tony sketching on a pad with a pencil.

"Tony!"

Startled, Tony looked up. "What is it?"

She slapped the folded newspaper and opened it for him to read.

"Trey! He's alive!"

Tony read the article carefully. "It appears so. I didn't have time to read it when I was at Verdun. Is there anything else?" He turned the page and found nothing more. "We don't know what condition he's in. Only that he's in a hospital."

"But the miracle is that he's alive!" She sat down beside him and took the newspaper in her hands. "There must be something here to indicate how he got there, what injuries he has. Oh, Tony! What if he's badly burned?"

"The pilot who saw him go down said he didn't hear an explosion or see any fire. He may just have a broken arm or leg."

"Oh, I hope you're right. Not that I want him to have any broken bones, but—"

"He'll be one of the luckiest casualties of the war if that's all he has." Tony started coughing.

"Do you want some more soup?"

"No. How about a glass of wine?"

"Alcohol isn't good for you."

"Shouldn't we celebrate? Is there any champagne in the house?"

Jackie smiled and kissed him on the cheek. "Maybe we can make an exception just this once. Oh, Tony—I'm so happy!"

"Well, remember—the war's not over. The bombing's not over. He could still get killed by our own troops."

"Oh, don't say that. How can you want to celebrate one minute and be so pessimistic the next? And I think the war will be over soon. All the newspapers say so."

"Let's hope they're right. On second thought, I think I'd prefer some red wine. The bubbles could upset my stomach."

"Red wine it is. I'll get it."

After their little celebration, Tony felt better and decided to get out of bed. He put on a robe and went into the studio, where he studied the canvas he had left unfinished for the past month. The charcoal drawing was only a preliminary sketch. Soldiers, some with bandages wrapped around their heads, sat in a trench smoking cigarettes with their backs against a wall of sandbags. Two Red Cross volunteers carried a seriously wounded young man on a stretcher past them, as they stared vacantly at his wounds. Shells burst overhead. The soldiers hardly notice. What are they thinking?

Tony mixed some paint on his palette and picked up his brush. What color was the sky? The trenches? The soldiers' faces? This was the challenge.

He worked until dinner time without a break.

Jackie came into the room and looked at the painting.

"It's so sad," she said. "Sad—but beautiful, in a way."

"'I think the shells bursting overhead is too much. What do you think?"

Jackie continued to stare at the painting for a few moments. "I think you're right. It almost looks like a Fourth of July celebration. The soldiers seem inured to it all."

Tony considered this. "Death is present *without* the shells bursting, isn't it?"

"Yes."

Tony took a damp cloth and wiped the bright red and yellow of the bursts away. Or rather spread them among the gray clouds. Now it looked as if there were a faint glow struggling to emerge from the darkened sky.

"I think that's it," she said. "Humanity triumphs over Death."

Tony wasn't convinced. "'Triumph' may be too strong a word. Perhaps 'Unvanquished' will do. You're more optimistic than I am."

Jackie smiled. "That's because I'm a woman and a mother."

CHAPTER 93

The Armistice was signed at 5:45 a.m. on November 11, 1918.

At eleven o'clock a canon was fired from the Eiffel Tower to signal the war was over. Church bells rang all over Paris and the inhabitants poured into the streets to celebrate.

Jackie and Tony, however, remained in their apartment until Tony went downstairs and purchased a copy of *Le Matin*, which announced that all Allied prisoners of war were to be released immediately. This news caused a rush to the train stations, though it could be days before the POWs arrived in Paris.

"How will we know when Trey arrives?" Jackie said, after reading the news.

"I'll have to go to the Gare de l'Est and camp out, I suppose." Tony had recovered from his bout with the flu and made his last run to the front two days earlier. He had asked every soldier he met if he knew anything about Trey. None did.

They could hear gunfire outside.

"Celebratory gunfire," Tony said. "As much as we'd like to celebrate, it's not safe. Let's wait till this afternoon and see if it calms down a bit."

"Then what?" Jackie said.

"Then I'll take a cab to the station. The first POWs should be arriving by then."

"Is there a separate train for them?"

"I don't know. We'll just have to try our luck."

They remained in the apartment until four o'clock, at which time Tony put on his jacket–he was now wearing his civilian clothes–and went downstairs to hail a cab. This was not as easy as it sounds, since many of the taxi drivers had parked their vehicles in the middle of the street and were sitting on the running boards or even the roofs celebrating with champagne and kissing as many women as would allow it. Tony finally found a driver on Rue Vaugirard who was reasonably sober and in need of a fare.

At the Gare de l'Est, Tony waited on the platform and watched as the trains arrived and soldiers, themselves in various states of inebriation, poured out of the carriages. Scanning the mass of blue and red and khaki, he saw no sign of Trey, and asked anyone who would listen whether they knew of him. Of course there were hundreds of other parents, wives, and girlfriends doing the same thing. Tony's heart sank as each soldier seemed to be met with their loved ones and the crowd thinned out with still no sign of Trey.

He remained as other trains arrived and went through the same process over and over. Finally, at eleven o'clock, there were no more trains and he reluctantly left the station.

When he arrived at the apartment Jackie met him at the door, wringing her hands. "Has he come?"

"Not yet. I'll go back tomorrow."

But the next day was the same.

On the third day, they sat at the dining room table lingering over a meal that contained fresh meat and vegetables for the first time in several months. But they took little pleasure in it.

"How could he have been left behind?" Jackie said, idly pushing peas around her plate with a fork. "There're no more trains, are there?"

"Oh, there'll be more," Tony said. "It's a long process. The military is more efficient at attacking the enemy than they are at demobilizing. I've heard there're still troops on both sides shooting at each other."

This was little comfort to Jackie, who continued to push her peas around. But just as she was about to rise to clear the table, they heard a knock at the door.

They looked at each other, doubtfully. It was now nine o'clock at night.

"Who could that be?" Jackie said.

"Maybe it's Carlotta returned to claim her things. I'll have bad news for her–her 'things' have been pulverized." Tony wiped his mouth with his napkin and went to the door, which was not visible from the dining room.

Jackie scooped up the plates and started for the kitchen.

"How did you get here?" she heard Tony say.

She stepped into the hallway and saw that it was Trey. She dropped the dishes, which clattered on the runner without breaking, and rushed to the door.

"Maman," Trey said. "Comment vas-tu?"

"Oh, Trey! My baby boy!"

She embraced him, ignoring the fact that he was on crutches and showered him with kisses.

"Speak English–I've suddenly forgotten all my French!"

Trey laughed. "Sorry, Mama–I've been speaking nothing but French for the last six months. But I've picked up a little German."

Jackie seemed to take notice that he was on crutches for the first time.

"What happened to your legs?"

"Broke both of them. Took longer to heal than I would have thought. But I'm okay. Any champagne in the house?"

"Of course," she said, putting her arm around him to support him even though the crutches were sufficient. "You know your father always keeps plenty of wine in the house–even during this horrible war."

"It's called hoarding," Tony said, with a laugh. "Come on into the dining room, son. Have you eaten?"

"We had some pastries on the train that some women at Reims passed through the windows. But I'm starving."

Tony took Trey's duffel bag, which was slung over his shoulder, while he and Jackie passed through the parlor where Trey stopped to look out the window.

"It's been a non-stop party," he said. "Torches in the Gardens, people dancing. What happened to those trees?"

"Shelling," Tony said, following behind him. "The Paris guns."

"The Paris guns? Our guns?"

"No–that's what the Germans call their long-range cannons. One of the shells destroyed Nat's atelier."

"I guess we were lucky, huh?"

"Very. Have a seat. Your mother will get you some Boeuf Bourguignon and I'll break out the champagne."

They sat down and toasted the end of the war, after which Trey devoured a bowl of the Boeuf Bourguignon and asked for seconds. When he was finished he leaned back in the chair and exhaled.

"Whew! That's the best meal I've had in a year," he said. "I'd forgotten what French cooking was like."

"I've had plenty of practice since you've been gone," Jackie said. "It's a wonder what you can do when you have less."

"But Trey–" Tony said, pouring some wine into everyone's glass, "you must tell us what happened. How did you manage to get shot down?"

Trey rolled his eyes. "Stupidity. We were flying low, trying to locate the German artillery. They had camouflage nets, you know. Then all of a sudden, these Fokkers came down out of the cloud cover–I don't know how they saw us–and attacked."

"What did you do?"

"Well, I didn't have much experience with dog fighting at that point. Fired a few bursts at a Junkers once with no effect, but that was all. These Fokker pilots knew what they were doing. One got on my tail, so I did a rather clumsy Immelmann like I'd been taught in flight school in an effort to get behind him. He outfoxed me with a maneuver of his own that put me in his sights again. My engine was hit along with the oil pan. Lots of smoke but no fire. I think the Fokker pilot thought I was done for, especially since I was so low to start with, and returned to his comrades. I saw a farmer's field and crashed into one of his haystacks. I thought it'd be a soft landing, but it wasn't. It felt like I'd hit a brick wall. Both legs broken."

"And did the farmer come out and help you?" Tony said.

"No. The farm was abandoned. I managed to drag myself out of the cockpit and waited for an explosion, but it never happened. I think I lost consciousness for a while and the next thing I knew I was looking up at a guy in a German uniform grinning at me. He wasn't a bad sort, really, and soon some others appeared and took me to the hospital in Montmédy. There was a separate section for pilots and officers."

"Lucky for you," Tony said. "Did they treat you well?"

"Ok. One officer–a captain–came around and asked me a lot of questions about my Nieuport 17. Power, rate of climb, and all that."

"Did you tell him?"

"Not at first, but then I realized he knew more about the plane than I did. I guess he was just trying to verify what he already knew. Besides, they had the plane and were tearing it apart."

"Did they feed you?" Jackie said.

"Sure. But they were short on fresh food just like everybody else. One night, though, they brought in some rabbit stew. God knows how rabbits survived in that scorched wilderness. Is there anymore wine?"

But before Tony could pour more wine, Trey fell asleep in his chair.

Tony and Jackie looked at each other as if uncertain of what to do. Then Tony rose from the table and collected the crutches, which he had leaned against the wall. As he did this, Jackie rose and went to Trey and kissed him on the forehead. He woke up again.

"What? Oh–I must have nodded off. Where's Camille?"

"She's with the baron," Tony said. "Come, old man–it's time for you to get a good night's sleep."

"Ah, oui? J'aimerais bien un autre verre de champagne."

"Plus de vin ce soir. Au lit."

Tony helped him up from the chair and slipped the crutches under his arms. Trey steadied himself and Tony escorted him to his old bedroom where he quickly fell asleep.

Tony emerged from the bedroom and gave Jackie a hug and a kiss.

"We're a family again," he said.

"Yes," Jackie said. "Our boy's home."

CHAPTER 94

When Tony brought his painting 'La Vie dans les Tranchées' to M. Dantec, the wily art dealer looked at it briefly and said that the public was not ready for it. However, he took it on anyway due to their long relationship and the painting hung in his gallery, mostly ignored, until November of the following year, when M. Dantec suggested that Tony enter it into the Salon d'Automne, which had been revived after a four-year hiatus.

"Les juges n'aiment plus tellement les scènes saignantes," he said. He seemed to have lost interest in speaking English once the war began.

"Saignantes?" Tony said. It didn't seem all that bloody to him, but maybe it was because he had seen so much of it in the trenches and the hospitals these past four years. "I've seen far more horrific paintings than this lately."

"*Cependant,*" M. Dantec said, "the judges are far less *sensibles* than the public. It may have a chance."

As it turned out, M. Dantec was right. 'La Vie dans les tranchées' won first prize in the 'Scènes de guerre' category, which was relegated to one of the galleries in the basement of the Petit Palais.

Nevertheless, it gained Tony some attention that he had not had since the outbreak of the war. And the painting had another unintended consequence: it brought out Mme de Rothstein.

Tony happened to be in the gallery at the same time and saw her unmistakable figure before the painting with her back to him.

"Do you think it's too gruesome?" he said.

As if expecting him, she turned around and smiled. "Tony—it's so good to see you.'" She kissed him on both cheeks, then leaned on her parasol, just as she had the first time he saw her some twenty years earlier in M. Dantec's gallery. "No, I don't think it's so gruesome—it's simply, as your title suggests, 'Life in the Trenches.' I think it reflects the humanity of these soldiers, showing their concern for their comrades, but also their weariness. Were you ever wounded yourself?"

"No, fortunately. My only injury was the flu. Nothing serious."

"Well, I'm afraid it's more serious for some than for others. The baron has been laid up with it for the past two weeks. I'm afraid he won't make it through."

"I'm sorry to hear that. Has it affected anyone else in your household?"

"J-P has it, and so does Sabine. However, they're young and I think they'll pull through. But the baron's very old, you know."

"And you?"

She smiled that seductively warm smile of hers that seemed almost out of place under the circumstances. "I must have some immunity. I don't know why. How is Jacqueline?"

"She's fine. She had it, but I suppose we're both immune to it now."

"Yes, it seems to work that way. And Trey?"

"He was shot down behind German lines."

"Oh, no!"

"But he's all right now. A couple of broken bones, but he's quite recovered since the armistice."

"Oh, good. I would so much like to see him."

"And Alex? How is he?"

"Doing well, though he has a limp that the doctors say will be permanent. And guess what? He's taken up painting."

"I'd like to see some of his work."

"And he'd like to see you as well. You're one of his heroes, you know."

"Am I? Well, when can I—"

"We're back in town now. Come see us anytime."

Tony took the metro home, thankful to get out of the cold, which was becoming more bitter as Christmas was just a few weeks away. He wondered at the fact that Mme G, as he still thought of her, continued to exude a sensuality that one would think would have abandoned her years ago. And she had regained most of the weight she had lost in the aftermath of the San Francisco earthquake. Not fat, simply filled out to her former proportions.

And of course there was the question of Alex—who was his father? His swarthy complexion somehow did not coincide or complement either his own or the baron's, though the baron always had a somewhat sunburnt look. Was it simply a matter of some wayward Mendelian gene that took its own serendipitous course? He supposed that was the answer—after all, Trey looked nothing like him, yet there was no question that Trey was his own son. Was there? There was always the possibility that Forbes-Robertson was—but no. Jackie was incapable of telling a lie, much less sustaining it over a period of twenty years. Mme G, on the other hand, was not above a certain amount of deception if it suited her purposes. Years of dueling with her abusive first husband must have made that trait almost a necessity.

When he entered the apartment he was surprised to see his old friend Nat having a cup of tea with Jackie.

"Tony, old man!" Nat rose to greet him and slapped him on both shoulders simultaneously. He seemed to size him up like a long-lost favorite pair of trousers. "Egad! You never seem to age!" He turned around and pointed to the back of his scalp. "Look at this–a bald spot! And getting worse every day. Before long Vivien will be trundling me off to the old folks' home."

"How is Vivien?" Tony said.

"Oh, fabulous! She's slipped into the Boston social scene as if it were a velvet glove. They're crazy about her! Can you believe it? Those old Boston biddies fawn over her like she's an African princess. Which she is, by the way."

"Really? A princess?"

"Well, once or twice removed. We traced her ancestry back to this Ibo tribe in southeastern Nigeria. Seems that her second cousin's mother was the queen. That means she's fourth or fifth in line–something like that."

Tony chuckled. "Then maybe you should move to Nigeria and prepare for the coronation."

"Don't make light of it, old man. Do you know that the king wears a headdress studded with diamonds the size of your fist? We met him. He owns several diamond mines spread out over 10,000 acres of rolling hills. We may very well move there."

"I hate to bring up a touchy subject," Tony said, "but what about Carlotta?"

A sudden gloom settled upon Nat's brow. "The bitch–" he glanced at Jackie. "Excuse my language, Jackie, but that woman has been a thorn in my side ever since I met her." Then to Tony, "She survived the blast that annihilated the atelier and now she's filed suit with the Cour de Grande Instance, but I don't think she has a chance. It'll be damned expensive, though."

"How did she and her friends escape the shelling?"

"They weren't there. They camped out in the Bois de Vincennes for the duration. God knows how they avoided arrest by the gendarmerie. Anyway, that's my problem."

"Where are you staying?" Tony said. "Of course you can stay with us." This elicited a shake of the head from Jackie, who was now standing behind Nat.

"Oh, thanks for the offer, old man, but we're staying at the Crillon. Good service, you know."

"Then Vivien's with you?"

"She is. Loves Paris, as I do. In fact, we've purchased the property at Rue de Fleurus and are rebuilding it. I suppose we'll divide our time henceforth between here and Boston."

After Nat left, Tony turned to Jackie. "Where's Trey?"

"He went for a job interview."

"A job interview? Where?"

"Suresne. An aircraft company."

"He's not going to be flying any time soon."

"No, but he says they need managers and engineers. It's a commercial company. Blériot, I think is the name."

"Blériot? The aviator who flew across the Channel before the war?"

"I think so."

Tony shrugged his shoulders. "Well, at least he's determined to support himself. But I wouldn't mind having him around for a while."

Jackie smiled and gave him a kiss. "I wouldn't mind having both of you around for a while."

CHAPTER 95

The baron's annual Christmas party was canceled due to his illness. Three weeks later he was dead. An announcement was published in *Le Figaro* that the funeral would be a private affair for family members only. And as the baron had quite a large family, members came in from England, Switzerland, and Italy and were accommodated at the chateau at la Ferrières, where the funeral was to be held.

This excluded Tony who, in any case, was not anxious to be one of the mourners. As for Mme Rothstein's invitation to come and visit at the townhouse in Paris, Tony decided that it would be best not to follow up on it. However, barely three weeks after the funeral he received a note, sent by a messenger, asking that he do just that. The appointed time was ten o'clock on a Saturday morning.

Tony did not wish to be deceptive where Jackie was concerned, but he saw no purpose in informing her of this appointment. So when the day arrived, he told her that he was going to visit M. Dantec, which was true–only after his appointment with Mme G.

Though the mansion on Rue St-Florentin was barely half the size of the chateau, it was still an impressive edifice. Tony stood before it for a few minutes trying not only to estimate the value of the mansion, but how much Mme G had inherited of the Rothstein fortune. Of course the baron had several children and several brothers and sisters. But even a fraction of the total estate would be an immense sum.

Mme G received him, as the baron had before, in the library. She was impeccably dressed as always and apparently did not feel compelled to wear widow's weeds. Her only concession to French custom was a black veil that did nothing to conceal her features.

"Is Alex at home?" Tony said.

"He is," Mme G said. Her face seemed to light up at the mere mention of his name. "Should I call for him?"

"Yes, of course."

Mme G went to a desk and pressed a button. "Michel–veuillez faire venir Alex." Then to Tony– "These electrical devices are marvelous, aren't they?

Saves so much time searching the hallways and shouting for someone."

"We haven't gotten so up to date at our place," Tony said.

"No? You're still in that tiny apartment on Rue du Luxembourg?"

"It's large enough for our purposes. Of course, now that Trey's home–"

Just then Alex appeared. It had only been a year or so since Tony had seen him, but he looked much older. Perhaps it was the cane that he used for support, or perhaps the distinguished-looking suit he wore, pinstriped with a high collar and black bow tie.

Tony rose to greet him and extended his hand. "You're looking fine, Alex. It's good to see you."

Alex shook his hand. "And good to see you, Monsieur Jones."

"Please–call me Tony."

"Well...all right."

"Sit down, Alex," Mme G said. "I think I'll leave the two of you to get acquainted a little better. After all, the last time you met, Alex was on his back drugged with morphine."

"Oh, hardly drugged, Mama," Alex said. "I remember everything Monsieur, uh, Tony did for me. And I greatly appreciate it."

"Well," she said. "I'll leave you–I have some business to attend to."

Tony felt a little awkward at this situation, as did Alex. Though he had spent a couple of days with him when he was wounded, Alex was in fact heavily sedated much of the time and there had been little conversation of substance.

They now sat opposite each other in a pair of comfortable leather armchairs.

"Well," Tony said, "your mother tells me that you have taken up painting."

"That's right. I went to art school for a while in Le Havre before the war came along."

"Well...what sort of painting do you do?"

"I like the Fauvists. And I greatly admire your work, too. Mama has taken me to the Salon and to M. Dantec's gallery. You're quite famous, you know."

"'Quite famous,' may be an exaggeration. I'm somewhat on the fringes. Everyone seems to be interested in the Fauvists, as you say, and the Cubists. Matisse, Braque, Picasso. I'm just trying to keep my head above water."

"You're too modest, Tony. I'd like to see more of your work. Maybe I could–"

"Certainly. Come see me at Rue du Luxembourg anytime. No need for advance notice. I'm home most of the time."

"That would be...swell. Maybe...tomorrow?"

"Sure. As I said–anytime."

There was a tense silence between them as each seemed anxious to broach a certain subject but neither knew how.

"Tony..." Alex said after an excruciating minute.

"Yes?"

"Are you my father?"

Tony remained silent for a moment as if collecting his thoughts. "When you were a child, Alex, barely old enough to walk, I saw a great deal of you. Even if today were the first time that I had seen you since then, I think I'd recognize your mannerisms, your facial expressions, the timbre of your voice. I was living with you and your mother at the time."

"Yes. I know. That's why–"

"You think we were lovers?"

"Yes."

"Well, you're right. We were lovers. And I've wondered about it ever since. But your mother insists that she doesn't know. She was seeing the baron at the same time."

"But the baron and I looked nothing alike. That leaves only you and..."

"And who else?"

"J-P."

Tony recoiled. "J-P? You must be joking."

"Well, it's possible. We have the same complexion. And he looks at me sometimes...well, like we share a secret."

"Highly unlikely, Alex. I think you can put that out of your mind. What it boils down to is me and the baron. And since he adopted you, you're one of his heirs. I think it's better for both of us if we just leave it at that."

"But the skin color..."

"Who knows how many swarthy, even black, ancestors the baron had? Pushkin was a black man, but hardly anyone in Russia seemed to know it."

Alex seemed to consider this for a moment. "Do you think the baron was related to Pushkin?"

Tony laughed. "I haven't the faintest idea. I just suggested it by way of illustration. At any rate, I hope you'll put this whole issue aside. Certainly we can be friends. I hope we will."

Alex seemed uneasy and unwilling to 'put it aside' as Tony said. He sat looking downcast for a full minute when there was a knock at the door.

"May I come in?"

"Of course, Amelia," Tony said. "We've had a very nice chat."

"Oh, good." She glided into the room and drew the curtains back. Tony noticed that she was no longer wearing her veil.

"Now, Alex," she said, "it's my turn. Would you mind leaving Tony and me for a few minutes? I'll see you downstairs for luncheon."

"All right, Mama." Alex rose and left the room.

Mme G came and sat down in the chair that Alex had just vacated. Tony stood when she entered, and seeing her comfortably settled, sat down as well.

"I won't inquire as to what you and Alex discussed, but I can guess."

"We're the ones always guessing. You're his mother. You should know the answer to Alex's question. Why keep it a secret?"

"It's not so easy as that. Even doctors cannot determine the precise moment of conception."

"But you must have an opinion based on—"

"Stop it, Tony. It serves no purpose. Alex is legally the baron's son. That's all he or anyone needs to know."

This did not satisfy Tony. They sat in silence for several moments, staring at each other as if they were an estranged couple competing for custody of their only child.

"You say that it serves no purpose," Tony finally said. "But Alex has a right to know who his father is. Are you willing to have him go through life plagued by doubts as to who he is?"

Mme G said nothing, though tears began to well up in the corners of her eyes. "I want the best for Alex. And I want him to be happy."

Tony continued to stare into her eyes as if to penetrate her soul. "Then you'll tell him. Is it me? Or the Baron? Or...J-P?"

The tears began to flow freely now and she tried vainly to wipe them away with a handkerchief. "You make me feel like a whore."

Tony started to laugh but checked himself. "I remember you defending the whores of Pigalle. But you're not a whore, Amelia. Just because you indulged your appetite in those days the way men have always done doesn't mean you're a whore. If that's the definition, then you're in good company with the likes of Madame de Staël, Catherine the Great, and half of the most prominent women of history. Is that all you're afraid of? Being accused of being called a whore? Well, Alex won't care as long as he can say, 'I am the son of so-and-so. He was my father.'"

She suddenly burst out with a violence that made Tony recoil. "All right! *You* are Alex's father!"

Tony sat in a sort of daze for nearly a minute. Of course he had always suspected the truth, but the uncertainty and mystery that surrounded the question made it somehow seem remote, not a responsibility of his. He looked down at the carpet. The stylistic representation of a Hellenic temple seemed a timeless reminder that this was a story as old as human history. But it didn't make his situation any the less difficult. He looked up. "Then what are we to do?"

Mme G wiped the last tears from her face and seemed to regain her composure. "I've always loved you, Tony—and no one else. When I first saw you at Monsieur Dantec's gallery, you seemed like a god that had descended from a cloud. A black man, a beautiful black man, possessed of an extraordinary talent. And an intellectual as well, with whom I could discuss any subject on an equal footing. Even the baron, who was highly intelligent and infinitely kind, nevertheless thought of nothing but amassing wealth and power. He was kind because he was emotionally detached from the people around him. But you, in addition to everything else, had a soul. That's why I was willing to share you with Jacqueline. You were too great, too expansive in your passion to embrace the whole world to belong to one woman. And now I offer you the same proposal that I did then. Come and live with me—and Alex. Be his father, every day. And bring Jacqueline if she will come. There's plenty of room for all of us."

Tony was stunned at this little speech even though he knew it was in keeping with Mme G's personality, her way of thinking. In a way, she had not changed over the years. "How do you know, Amelia? You said that—"

"I never slept with the baron. Nor J-P. Only you."

This was somehow even more stunning than the confirmation of his paternity. Now it was certain. And all these years Tony had thought Mme G was a free spirit! A woman who thumbed her nose at bourgeois morality! But now...now a great weight seemed to descend upon his shoulders.

"I can't come and live with you, Amelia," he said. "It's impossible. Even if Jacqueline were to agree. Which she won't. I'm sorry, but—"

"Do you love me?"

She had never asked this question before. It had always seemed unnecessary for either of them to demand love from the other. But now she was demanding—no, pleading for it. He couldn't disappoint her.

"Yes, Amelia. I do love you."

The tears began to flow again as she stood.

He rose as well and embraced her. Their kiss was tender, warmly felt, but brief.

"Tell Alex I will always be available to him," he said.

"Why don't you stay for lunch and tell him yourself?"

Now the burden had shifted, but it seemed lighter. "All right—I'll stay."

EPILOGUE

Antonio Jones III, known to his friends and family as 'Trey,' although strangers often said 'Très quoi?' when hearing his name, went on to a career as an airline executive, married an American girl he met in Paris at an air show, and settled in Rueil-Malmaison. He painted in his spare time but refused to let his father see his work.

Sebastian Alexandre Goldman-Rothstein pursued a painting career in earnest, but after years of toil without much success joined the banking firm of Rothstein et Frères where he rose to the position of Chief Financial Officer. He never married.

Jackie resumed her acting career after the war and was cast in several films, including *Les Enfants du paradis*, a hugely successful one directed by Marcel Carné and starring Arletty, the most popular actress of her day. As she was nearly eighty in 1945, Jackie was cast as an elderly flower woman who sells Arletty a bouquet of *garance* roses, emblematic of her character's name.

'Madame G,' as Tony always remembered her, died before the Second World War of breast cancer. One of her houses in Vienna was ransacked and burned by Hitler's Gestapo shortly after the *Anschluss* in 1938.

As for Tony, he and Jackie continued to live in the apartment on Rue du Luxembourg until the Second World War broke out, when they moved first to Rueil-Malmaison to live with Trey and his family, then to Nantes, where Tony was asked to serve as director of an art school.

It was about this time that he was awarded the Légion d'honneur by the president of France. He died shortly thereafter of a cerebral hemorrhage.

www.ingramcontent.com/pod-product-compliance
Lightning Source LLC
Chambersburg PA
CBHW070154120726
47909CB00001B/116